Chronicles of Osota
Warrior

by

Michelle Magly

Desert Palm Press

Chronicles of Osota - Warrior

by Michelle Magly

© 2014 Michelle Magly

ISBN-13: 9781500652272
ISBN-10: 150065227X

This is a work of fiction - names, characters, places, and incidents are the product of the author's imagination or are used fictitiously. Any resemblance to actual person living or dead, business, events or locales is entirely coincidental. All rights reserved.

No part of this publication may be reproduced, distributed, or transmitted in any form or by any means, including photocopying, recording, or other electronic or mechanical methods, without the prior written permission of the publisher, except in the case of brief quotations embodied in critical reviews and certain other noncommercial uses permitted by copyright law.

For permission requests, write to the publisher, addressed "Attention: Permissions Coordinator," at the address below.

Desert Palm Press
1961 Main Street, Suite 220
Watsonville, California 95076
www.desertpalmpress.com

Editor: Kellie Doherty
(http://editreviseperfect.weebly.com)
Cover Design: Michael King

Printed in the United States of America
First Edition July 2014

DEDICATION

For my partner, for my friends, and for my grandfather. He did not live to see this book published. I like to think he would have been proud, despite his distaste for fantasy novels.

Chronicles of Osota
Warrior

Chapter One

ALINA ALWAYS KNEW THEY would come to collect her. She saw the soldiers marching along the western cliffs, small black dots against the snowy landscape. The wind blew so hard that she feared one of the stragglers might be gusted off the mountainside.

The wind no longer bit into Alina like it did when she first arrived. The years had thickened her blood to withstand most of nature's lashes. She closed her eyes and inhaled, embracing the cold. The approaching soldiers posed no threat. No one had attempted to assassinate her in the eleven turns she had spent on the mountain, and everyone agreed no assassin would come in another eleven. She looked back at the stone keep, her home since she had been nine turns of age. It stood tall and crumbling, more worn down than when they brought her here as a girl.

She watched the men approach the fortress. She had imagined the scene so many times as a child, but now they were here. She turned and went back to the keep without a word. The wind pushed harder, sending snow biting into her skin. She blinked against it, her breath catching in surprise.

The guard on duty saw her approaching and ran to her assistance. "My lady," he called. He draped what he could of his dark blue cloak over her. Alina pulled the cloak around her and they walked up the keep steps. "You should not be out in this weather," the guard yelled over the wind. They reached the doorstep and together forced open the large oak door. They ran inside before the winds forced it shut again.

"I was on my way to the stables," she said, running a hand

through her windswept hair. The brown strands clung to her eyelashes. "I wanted to see if my horse was up for a ride, but these winds are too strong. Send someone to finish preparing my horse," she ordered. "I want to go out after the winds die down."

"Going for a ride this afternoon, my lady?" the guard asked. She nodded, more caught up with her task at hand. The soldiers were here and that meant she would be leaving. She walked to her room and searched for essentials. Small and unremarkable, her lodgings were like the possessions she had been provided. She had hardly anything worth packing. As she rummaged through her things, the keep's steward knocked on her open door. Alina turned and smiled at the old woman. "There you are, Greta. You can help me pack," she said.

Greta walked inside and stared at her with wide eyes. "By the Almighty, my lady, you are far too old to pretend someone has come to fetch you. We have received no news of a caravan coming, no word from Osota."

"A detachment of soldiers are approaching right now," Alina said. "You should receive notice any minute."

True to her word, a guard's voice rang through the keep, shouting, "Steward, Councilor Velora has arrived!" Greta's eyes widened and she hurried off to receive their guest rather than assist like Alina asked.

"It's not like he'll come inside or anything," she muttered. Alina had very little to pack in the way of possessions. The room held her clothes and a few personal items she had initially brought to the keep. The dresses she had here wouldn't be acceptable, and she could acquire better attire later. She dug out a travel pack to store her most valuable items in. Alina grabbed a thick book by her nightstand and eased it into the main compartment. She then opened a drawer in her desk and shoved documents and charts in to rest against the book. Buckling the flap, she opened a drawstring pouch attached to the side. She filled it with coin and a sack of runes and pulled the string tightly shut. Her jewelry came next. She tucked the rings and necklaces into the concealed pocket within her dress. Alina picked the second-to-last item out of her jewelry box, a decorative signet ring, and slid it onto the middle finger of her right hand before she pulled on her travel gloves.

The last item in the box lay in a hidden pocket. A thin silver bracelet made of strands intertwining with one another, creating a never-ending spiral—her mother's bracelet. *You can't take it,* she thought. She trapped the bracelet between her thumb and forefinger and rubbed the flexible threads together. This was the one thing she had allowed herself over the years. The one risk. If she returned home, though, she had to leave it behind. People would recognize it eventually, or a nosey politician would go digging through her things. The capital was much less forgiving than Eastwatch Keep.

She had prepared for this. Alina took the bracelet to the roaring fireplace in her room. It was not nearly as hot as a forge would be, but the delicate chain would warp beyond all recognition. She had no other choice. Tossing it into the fire, she turned away. Her chest tightened. She ignored it and crossed the room to put on the rest of her travel clothes. She had to fight not to look back at the flames.

As she tied her cloak at the neckline, a guard came to room and cleared his throat. She turned. He laid a hand over his heart and nodded in salute.

"My lady, the steward has requested you come outside to accompany her and formally greet Councilor Velora."

Alina rolled her eyes and grabbed her pack. "Very well," she said. The guard moved to her side and took her bag from her.

"You are going somewhere, my lady?" he asked.

Alina walked into the hall. "A Councilor is here. Why else would he have come?"

The guard carried the bag as she met Greta by the keep door. They stepped outside into the freezing winds. Every guardsman stood at attention, forming two parallel lines that framed the women as they walked through the courtyard to where the Councilor sat on his horse. The man and horse wore matching blue uniforms, the horse's saddle intricately decorated with deep blue ribbons and threads of gold with the Councilor's cloak dyed the same color. It signified him as someone important, though he did not need the cloak for that. With a frown, he peered down at Greta for the first time. His dark beard was well groomed, his face full and healthy, tinged red against the biting cold.

Greta curtseyed. "Welcome to Eastwatch Keep, Councilor Velora. Please, allow us to stable your horse and bring you inside out of the cold."

The Councilor nodded but did not dismount. "I do not have the time for such pleasantries today. I have urgent business with her Majesty."

"I beg your pardon, Councilor, but I must inquire as to why you humble us with your presence when her Majesty, Queen Alaina rests in the heartland?"

The Councilor's gaze flicked from Greta to Alina. She stared back, despite the wind whipping her dark hair about. He looked back to Greta and gripped his mare's reins tighter. "I regret to inform you of the queen and king's passing. Their souls rest with the Almighty."

Greta gasped, her hands flying to her mouth. "We had no idea. How long since their passing?"

"Three days' time. We set out for Eastwatch immediately following their deaths," he said.

"And so you departed," said Greta. She looked at Alina. "To retrieve—"

"Her Majesty Alina Alexandria Mura of Osota must return to the heartland." He eyed Alina. "I have been elected Regent to your rule, your Majesty."

Alina nodded to the guard who carried her bag. "I am ready to depart as soon as needed." The guard carried it off to a stable where he could tie it to her horse.

Regent Velora raised his eyebrows. "You are prepared already?"

"There is little to pack after living so…humbly for eleven years." Alina kept her tone neutral. She wanted the Regent to ponder if it was meant as a challenge.

He inclined his head. "It's for the better. We need to travel swiftly." The guard returned with Alina's horse, a small but powerful mare, mostly white with gray spots smattered across her coat. The leather bag was securely attached to the horse's saddle. She patted the beast's neck before pulling herself atop and settling into the worn leather.

Alina looked down at the guards assembled along with Greta. "I'll remember your kindness in the days to come, Greta"

Greta curtseyed. "That's a pleasant thought, your Highness. I know you never thought life up here so extravagant, but I would not be surprised if you catch yourself thinking back to these days years from now. Until that day comes, I expect you will be too caught up to look back on us." Greta smiled sadly and backed away. Alina nodded a final time before turning back to the Regent.

"Shall we take our leave?" he asked.

"Yes, Regent," Alina said. They flicked their reins and spurred the horses on to trot away from the crumbling old tower. Alina allowed herself only one glance back before she looked forward.

***

Senri sat in the middle of a forest clearing, picking at blades of grass while she waited. She sat before an old woman, the oldest woman in their village and their only seer. The seer took deep, shuddering breaths as she withdrew from her trance. The seer's webbed marks pulsated with the rhythm. One more deep breath and her trance broke. She looked down at Senri. Her eyes returned to their natural, amber color, and the thin, dark lines on her skin marking her seer's blood faded.

"Well?" Senri leaned forward.

"There is no mistake, child," Seer Mala said. "My sight shows that you must go to the heartland."

Senri frowned and leaned back into the dirt, uncrossing her legs and tucking her knees under her chin. "But I've never been to the kingdom, are you sure?"

Seer Mala nodded. "Every time the sight comes I see you wandering the streets of the capital dressed as one of the chosen Warriors, Senri. You stand there, as life-like and as clear as you sit before me now in this grove." She gestured to the surrounding trees. Senri's village rested nearby in the forest, closer to the base of the mountain. She had made special arrangements to ride out to the seer that day, and she had received the one answer she did not want.

"You must travel to the heartland." Senri hugged her legs closer to her chest and stared at the ground. Her father told her the seer would not be persuaded, but she had ignored his warning and rode out anyways. After all, this nurturing woman had to feel some sympathy. "My answer upsets you?"

Senri looked up and hesitated. "I…I'm not ready."

The seer sighed and leaned back, assuming her contemplative pose once again. "I know, I know. So young, only eighteen turns around the sun, yet you are not ill-prepared."

"I've never been there," she repeated.

The seer shook her head and sighed deeply. "It does not matter.

You are the most gifted of your age, more master of your technique than anyone here. You are meant to serve a greater purpose. What good does it do to stand around in a forest all day?" Seer Mala stared and lifted an eyebrow as if to challenge her.

"You seem happy to do it," Senri muttered, turning away from her gaze.

The seer laughed. "Oh child, you do have a point. But mine is the way of someone burdened with the sight." She smiled and jabbed a bony old finger at Senri. "You are a protector, a Warrior, touched by the Almighty. The trees do not need a defender. This forest is older than our entire village. It knows how to survive."

"I know, but I thought my skills might be better suited here, training other people and guarding the village. Isn't that a noble cause?"

Seer Mala frowned. "Yes, Senri, but it is not your cause. It is important that you travel to the heartland. If you stray from this path, the consequences are dire, and not only for you." She stared at Senri with such seriousness, Senri wanted to disappear into the dirt.

"But why am I so important?" she asked. Her throat tightened, and she had to swallow down a rising lump.

Mala's hard stare softened and her frown eased. "My dear child, what frightens you so much that you cling to this village?"

Senri took a deep breath and forced herself to regain composure. The last thing she wanted was to discuss her problems with the village seer. "I..." She flung her thoughts to the far reaches of her mind in search of an excuse. "I would miss my home too much." *Not a total lie.* Mala still seemed puzzled. *She doesn't believe me.* But she did not press the matter. Instead she settled back onto her rock and looked past Senri, out into the trees.

"Whatever bothers you Senri, make peace before this time tomorrow. For that is when the Warriors will come to claim their new protectors and you will no longer belong to this village."

Senri gulped and bowed deeply. "Yes, Seer." Her eyes prickled with unshed tears. She took another composing breath before rising and wiping her eyes. "Thank you for your counsel. I must return to the village. We have much to prepare for my departure."

The seer nodded, but before Senri could leave she said, "Do not be afraid of your potential, Senri." Senri froze, afraid of what the seer might say to her next. "The Almighty has blessed you with an immense destiny. Move with it rather than away."

Instead of responding to the seer, Senri turned and retreated through the forest. She found her horse, Stomps, exactly where she left him, lingering under a massive tree and casually eating his way through all nearby grass. The horse looked up as she approached and snorted, flicking his ears. "Well at least this outing was productive for you," she said, untying his reins. He nudged her with his snout and she patted him gently. "Ready to go?" Senri mounted him and dug her heels into his flanks. They took off through the trees, navigating the familiar path with ease.

They made it back to the village before sundown and Senri corralled Stomps in a large, fenced in field with the other horses. As she approached the main road, the market bustled with people weaving between the small houses, herding animals or carrying supplies. The village consisted of fifteen homes and the household businesses. The major road snaked past, between the heartland and the southern mountains, the latter holding the last few border lands before it gave way to dragon territory. The village would have grown into a major hub if the Kingdom of Osota had not banned all contact with the dragons. Senri preferred it this way. She liked the smallness of her village. She liked the scattered trees between houses and pathways. It was quiet, save for the inn on a good business day.

She walked by the blacksmith's first on her way home. Gustav had told her he had a gift for her. A weapon. Gustav hammered at a molten strip of metal while his young apprentice dangled from the bellows pulley. The boy yanked and tugged at it with no impact. Senri stepped in and helped him pull the heavy cord down, compressing the bellows with a whoosh. She pulled the cord taut, the rope chafing against her calloused palms.

The boy let go and looked up at Senri. "I could have done it myself!" He was Malcor, the local farmer's youngest son. At thirteen, his limbs had all bone and no muscle.

Senri smiled and released the cord. "You were putting up a good fight there, but the bellows was winning."

Gustav frowned. "Well if I had more help around here maybe I wouldn't have to make the kid dangle from the pulley all day." He still hammered at the strip of metal. "Maybe you should convince one of your brothers to help out here. The oldest one has got at least fifty pounds on you." He gestured at Senri with a hot pair of tongs.

"Hey, I'm not so little." She was naturally tall and powerful, but her training assured her strength.

Gustav laughed and picked up the hot metal with his tongs and lowered it into a trough of water. "Easy girl. I know you could lay me flat on my backside if you wanted." Steam rose up around his arms and he withdrew the glossy dark blade, letting it clatter down on a wooden table. "There we go," he said with a sigh. Gustav put the tongs aside and wiped his brow. Soot and sweat had mingled to form dark streaks. "Now, why are you bothering me?"

"You said you had something for me this morning," Senri said. She tugged at her cotton shirt. Even with her light clothes, the forge grew too hot.

"I did indeed." Gustav walked over to a cabinet where he kept special works. "It's not finished yet. I still have to attach the grip and pommel to the tang."

"Can I still see it?" Senri asked.

"What do you think I'm getting?" Gustav opened the cabinet and pulled out an incomplete blade. Senri walked over to get a closer look at the metal. Even unpolished, it still gleamed. "Solid steel," he said proudly. Senri nodded, knowing how great an honor he bestowed with the kingdom's iron reserves running lower every day. Malcor ran over to get a look at the new weapon as well. "Of course, the grip and the fittings will have to be steel as well. Did you have any design requests?"

"Put a dragon on it," Malcor yelled.

Gustav glared down at the boy. "Hush! We've no need to incite trouble with blasphemous decorations."

Senri rolled her eyes. "Surprise me, Gustav."

Malcor stood on tiptoe to whisper in her ear, "A dragon would look amazing."

Senri smiled and nodded at him. His idea held charm and irony, but it would upset too many people. Senri remembered the last dragon attack, and though the creature had not harmed any villagers, it had raided half of their livestock before the Scaled Vanguard had chased it off..

"That's enough peeking for you," said Gustav. He tucked the blade back in the cupboard and closed the doors. "You can see the completed work tomorrow when the Warriors arrive."

"Fine, fine," said Senri. "I'll see you tomorrow, Gustav."

"Bye Senri," Malcor shouted.

She waved at the boy and exited the forged and continued down the main road, taking the long way home in hopes of lingering at the inn. She slowed as the large, raucous house came into view. Even from a distance, music drifted over, the dancing and the banging feet stomping in rhythm. She waited for the right moment.

Soon after, the side door to the inn opened and a young woman stepped outside, swinging a bucket about and twirling her skirt to the music. The girl—Vella—took the bucket to the nearby chicken coop and spread feed out for the hungry animals. One of the few people Senri's age around the small village, she had long, shining locks of light hair that rustled over her back as she tipped the bucket over the fence and scattered the last of the animal feed. Senri sighed and ran a hand through her own choppy, fair hair, always so messy from training for hours on end. She took a deep breath and walked in Vella's direction. As she tried to appear nonchalant, Vella turned. Senri smiled and waved and the inn maiden waved back.

"How are you?" Vella called out.

Senri shrugged, reaching Vella. She was smaller, with well-proportioned limbs unlike Senri's long and awkward arms and legs. "I'm alright," Senri said. "I just got back from visiting the seer."

Vella nodded. "I heard you were going out there today."

Senri scuffed her foot against the dirt. Her stomach felt like it had dropped, or twisted itself into a knot, or disappeared. "Yeah," she said, looking down. She didn't want to look into Vella's eyes. Instead, she watched Vella play with the handle of the bucket, her hands tightening.

"So, what was the visit for?"

Senri looked up again, heat creeping over her cheeks. "I, uh…was trying to persuade her to…let me stay."

Vella laughed. "You're so odd. Why would you want to stay in this dull place?"

Her heart beat a little faster. She considered telling Vella it was to remain with her, but then her throat constricted shut. "I…I don't think I'll like the city life. It's too big there."

Vella shook her head. "You should be more grateful, Senri. I would love to travel to the heartland."

"So come with me." Senri's own boldness shocked her, but Vella just laughed it off.

"Oh, I can't do that, not with you and the other Warriors. How would I making a living?"

Senri took a deep breath, trying to summon courage. She found none. "Yeah, silly thought. Forget I asked." Vella nodded and looked like she would head into the inn when Senri asked, "Will you come see me tomorrow before I leave?"

Vella paused and turned to Senri. She smiled. "Of course I will. What kind of friend would I be if I didn't say goodbye?" Vella turned and entered the inn once more, leaving Senri outside with a feeble smile on her face and fading hopes in her heart. *A friend. Is that all?*

"You're pathetic, you know that?" The deep masculine voice startled her, and a weight pressed on Senri's shoulder as someone casually leaned on her.

"Shut up, Nat," she said, pushing the young man off her.

He chuckled and looped his arm through hers, clutching fiercely. Nat was only slightly older than her, but training had filled him out much better than her. He had been one of the two selected for the Warriors that year. She had the second honor. He stroked the dark ends of his sparse beard and watched the inn. "You could at least tell her you'd like to stroll her fields, given the chance," he winked and dodged a fist Senri aimed at his shoulder. "Just do what I do."

Senri looked Nat over. His shirt and trousers were dusty from field work, and his loose black curls gave him a roguish look. She rolled her eyes. "Well, not all of us can promise a woman the world then leave her the next day."

Nat held a hand up to his heart. "You wound me! You dare accuse an inductee into the Warriors of being less than honorable toward a woman?"

Senri shook her head, adopting her best posh accent. "I'm sure your honor shines brightly from one sunrise to the next, but with the dawning of every day so does your love dawn with a different woman in sight." She resumed walking back to her home, the sun nearly set below the horizon. Nat followed after.

"You're a Warrior, not a poet, Senri. Where did those clever words come from?"

Senri waved a hand at him. "I can be clever, though not in front of Vella."

Nat clapped her on the shoulder. "She's not even that remarkable. Just a country maid with her head in the clouds."

"And what do you know of fine women, Nat?" Senri stopped and turned, staring him down.

His grin faded as he walked up to Senri, no longer jovial in his step. "Look, anyone who doesn't notice what an amazing person you are is a fool and not worth your time."

He frowned. Senri squirmed, her emotions felt on display and she did not like the analysis. She shrugged. "Well... who else is there, Nat?"

Nat sighed and rolled his head back. "A lot of people. More than you can count. Now let's go." He nudged her toward her house. "You need to get home and get rest if the both of us are to depart tomorrow in a timely manner. And the first thing I'm going to do when we get to the city is take you to a tavern where you can flirt with all the inebriated beauties to your heart's content."

Senri shook her head and walked on with her friend. "Somehow I think that's more of what you want to do, Nat."

As the two strode back to her parent's farmhouse, Senri allowed herself a glance back at the village. She thought of Vella dancing in her flowing skirt and of all the travelers probably asking for her hand. *A stupid dream, falling for her.* Senri could not compete with the travelers of the world. *But tomorrow, I will be a traveler.* Perhaps some months away with the Warriors would make her more appealing to the young inn maiden. Senri smiled. Her mind filled with visions of her returning home a seasoned fighter, a legend, and letting the beautiful Vella swoon in her arms.

Michelle Magly

Chapter Two

THE NEW ARMOR PLATING glinted as Senri struggled into it. Next to her, Nat fought with his own new uniform. "If only the other Warriors could see us," he said, trying to tighten a leather buckle on his leg into place. The two of them stood out in an orchard behind the blacksmith's. They were supposed to report to the center of town as soon as they donned their new uniforms. The other Warriors would arrive soon.

Senri laughed as she pulled against her buckles. "I'm sure they had the same problem starting out. The leather isn't worn in yet, that's all."

Nat grunted. "Oh sure. Come over here and help me get this chest plate into place."

Senri sighed and helped him, yanking the leather straps on his back taut. With enough force, the two of them managed to fully outfit themselves in the official armor. The gold-leaf falcon on the front of their breastplates shone. The rest of it had been made from standard steel: chest, pauldrons, gauntlets, greaves, even boots.

The armor filled out her form a bit so she looked slightly less gangly. She almost felt more powerful just by wearing it. "You ready?" she asked.

"I'm more tightly packed than a stuffed turkey," said Nat. She punched his arm, and the steel plates clanged. "Ha! Just try to bruise my delicate skin now."

Senri groaned. "Whatever. Let's get out there. I'm sure that our horses are even waiting for us by now."

The two of them strode to the center of town, a large dirt clearing surrounded by market stalls and the entrance to the inn. A crowd of people waited for them. Three Warriors stood at the head of the crowd, two men and a woman. Covered in hack marks and dents, their armor showed signs of their service. Besides the Warriors, half the town was present. Senri's parents and three younger brothers stood off to the side. Senri's mother, blonde hair and all, waved at her as she approached. Senri smiled back, but noticed with a twinge her mother's tear-stained cheeks. Vella also stood with the well-wishers, though her gaze wandered.

Senri and Nat knelt down on one knee before the Warriors, bowing their heads. She remembered snorting with laughter when practicing with Nat.

"Apprentices Senri and Nathaniel," spoke a deep voice. Senri wanted to look up, but settled for studying the armor-clad feet approaching her. "You have been born with the gifts passed down from our ancestors. The day has come where you shall be accepted into our ranks as Warriors of Osota. Rise." They stood. The oldest Warrior looked at them with a creased face, his hair graying from his wispy top down to the scraggly ends of his short beard. His brow furrowed as he studied the two of them. "I am Valk, leader of the Warriors. Today, you will join us in our noble cause. But first, you shall prove your worth with a demonstration of power." Valk reached into his pockets and pulled out two smooth, fist-sized stones. He presented one each to Senri and Nat. She stared down at the object. "We have embedded an idol within each of these stones. According to your abilities, both of you should be able to retrieve them."

Senri took the stone in her hand and turned it over. It was new rock, not even completely cool. The heat radiated against her palm, invisible to anyone without her ability, her gift, the thing that had marked her for the Warriors since birth. She looked over to Nat, who gripped the stone in both his hands and took a deep breath. As he exhaled, the stone cracked and crumbled, breaking away in smaller bits until sand sifted through his fingers. He opened his eyes and plucked a small, glittering gem from within the remaining sand.

"It's a mountain," he said, holding the gem to the light. The cone-shaped and jagged cut white jewel, clear as water, sparkled in the light and casted beams of color in every direction.

Senri turned her attention back to her own stone. She breathed in, concentrating on the hot pulse. Her hands warmed, and then the stone warmed becoming soft and pliable. The heat rushed through her fingers. Insufferable, yet comforting. She pulled the rock apart like clay and dropped the smoldering fragments to the ground until she reached the yellow gem inside. She pulled it from the mess and dropped the rest. When her hands cooled and the pulsing stopped, the shape of a yellow sun sparkled at her. "How fitting," she muttered.

"The new protectors have proven their worth. One touched by the stone." He gestured to Nat. "And one by the sun." He nodded at Senri. "May their strength be our strength. May their enemies fall at our swords." The two other Warriors walked forward, each carrying a newly crafted sword and sheath. "May their hardships be shared so that each Warrior of Osota may stand united." The two Warriors knelt, holding the swords up. "Take your weapons, and may they forever serve the kingdom."

Senri reached for the glittering steel hilt. Her other hand grabbed the blue-dyed leather sheath.

"The Warriors of Osota welcome you," said Valk. "You are ready to join us in the heartland as we fight to defend our kingdom."

Senri and Nat both bowed. "Thank you," they both said. When Senri looked back up, the townspeople stared with smiles, as expected. She still could not get Vella to meet her gaze. Was she not impressive enough standing in shining armor?

"Your horses have been prepared for the journey ahead," said Valk. "You are allowed to say your goodbyes, and then we shall depart."

Senri nodded. "Thank you, sir." As she walked over to her parents she buckled the sword sheath to her belt, securing it comfortably against her leg. Her parents jumped on her, her father scooping her into his arms for a tight hug. He squeezed the air from her lungs. "Dad!" she wheezed.

"Be careful out there," he whispered.

The grip lessened and Senri gasped for breath. Her mother pried him away to give her a gentler hug. "He's just sad to see you leave," she said, her mouth near Senri's ear.

"It was not my idea to leave," Senri said, returning the hug.

Her mother withdrew and held Senri at arm's length. Her eyes watered, her thin blonde hair swept up into a loose bun. "You're just too young."

"I know. I'll be back though. I won't always be on assignments."

She felt someone leap onto her back and she nearly buckled under the weight. A pair of arms looped around her shoulders and two other people latched to her arms. Her brothers had found her.

"Be careful out there, Senri!" Garth, the one on her back, cried.

"Yeah, and bring us back something from the heartland," said Ean. As the next oldest, Ean's voice had just started to change. Still, Garth, Mattus, and Ean all looked alike with dark hair and freckles. Her mother shooed the boys off her.

"Thanks." She shook her shoulders to prevent cramping. "I, uh, I'm going to say goodbye to the others really quick." She looked around for Vella, but the girl had vanished from the group of villagers. Instead, she had latched onto the arm of one of the Warriors, well, nearly. Vella stood close to a woman with short, dark hair. They smiled and talked with one another. Senri held back a growl.

"Wrong arm?" said Nat. His breath warmed her ear as he swooped in behind her, moving through her parents.

Senri smacked the steel plate on his arm. "Shut it." She did not need her parents hearing of her unrequited love.

"You know, if you hurry maybe you both can partake in a...farewell ritual." His tone lifted in a suggestive manner.

"Nat!"

"What's going on, you two?" asked her father. He rubbed an end of his dark moustache as he watched them.

"Just some good natured ribbing," said Nat. He stared at her parents with wide, innocent eyes.

"Good," her father replied. "It would be a shame to start out a journey on an argument." He looked past the two of them and shook his head. "Here come your horses. Let me make sure the stable boys got everything." Her father went down the dirt road where two men led the horses.

"Senri." Her mother touched Senri's cheek. She looked back towards her.

"Yes?"

"You and Nat go say goodbye to the rest of your friends. I need to make sure your father doesn't harass those boys."

Senri nodded. "All right." As her mother walked away she turned to Nat. "Can we please interrupt them?"

Nat grinned. "Anything to go talk to that fine woman in armor."

The two strode over to Vella and the Warrior, who conversed closely to one another, closing off everyone else. Nat made short work of the barriers. "My lady, it is such an honor to be serving alongside you!" He slung his arms around the Warrior in a tight hug. The woman's eyes went wide and she backed up, trying to pull Nat off her. Too bad she did not know him like Senri did.

While the two grappled, she moved in. "Vella!" She tried and failed to sound shocked at seeing her there. Vella smiled. The grin seemed small…irritated. "Did you see the ceremony?"

"Yes, it was lovely," Vella replied, her voice short. She kept glancing over to Nat and the Warrior as they laughed with one another.

"We're, uh, leaving at any moment. I won't be back for a while."

Vella nodded. "I know. It will be quiet without you and Nat around."

"You think so?"

"Yes. Who else will I have to talk to in the evenings?"

Senri smiled and her heart fluttered. "Well, I'll come back and visit as soon as I can. I'm sure they'll let me return after I save the kingdom a few times."

Vella chuckled. "I'm sure you will be great, Senri. It looks like your party is gathering though." She nodded in the direction of the other Warriors mounting their horses.

"Oh, I guess I should be going then," Senri said. Vella nodded. The two stood there. Senri looked down into Vella's eyes with a plea. She wanted to do something brave, like hug her, or tell her how she felt. Instead, she said, "Goodbye," and walked over to Stomps and patted his mane.

Nat must have noticed her fallen expression. "No luck?"

"None," Senri replied. She thought back on the conversation. "Though maybe a glimmer of hope."

Nat groaned, clutching the reins to his horse. "Just give up on her." Senri shook her head. "Whatever. I'll have plenty of time to change your mind when we reach the city." He hoisted himself atop his horse and Senri pulled herself onto Stomps. Her horse shook his head, chasing away a fly.

"You two ready back there?" Valk turned in his saddle, craning his neck to look at them.

"Just about," said Senri. The villagers surged up around them for a final parting. Her parents each took turns squeezing her hand and telling her to hurry home. Her brothers shouted suggestions for gifts, most of them impossible to retrieve. Most people just gave her a nod, though she did feel a small hand tug on her pant leg from the left side of her horse. Senri turned and saw Malcor standing beside her.

"Slay something in my name." He grinned up at her.

Senri laughed. "Of course I will. I'll bring you back the head of the biggest monster I happen to kill on my journeys."

"I can't wait."

The Warriors started moving and Senri said her last goodbyes. She lightly dug her heels into the flanks of her own horse, urging him to follow the others. As they trotted away from the village, she turned back and watched for as long as her neck would allow. She watched until the forest swallowed her home from view. The trees she had never traveled beyond now flooded her vision.

***

The crowded city streets startled Alina. She clung to her horse's reins so hard her knuckles turned white. As they rode on, her grip relaxed and she adjusted to the chaotic surroundings. It had been so long since she had walked streets of the heartland's capital. Her removal from court at a young age had all but erased her memories. Now she was immersed in it once more.

Her eyes darted over the scenery, the subdued colors of the market stands and the faded look of the stone buildings. Worn down with crumbling bricks and broken-down walls, the houses and stores had fallen into the same state of disrepair as her tower. Blue banners displaying the symbol of Osota hung everywhere, a falcon stitched in gold, and even though people packed the streets, an eerie sadness fell over the place. Pamphlets advertising an old memorial service for the King and Queen littered the cobblestone streets.

"How did their majesties come to pass?" Alina asked Velora. He rode by her quietly.

He glanced at the pamphlets. "Illness. They both succumbed to the same disease along with some of the royal staff. We burned so much to prevent plague, and we hosted purifications in every room of the palace."

Sighing, Alina turned away to watch the streets again. Her gaze wandered over the civilians. Many dressed plainly, and few engaged in conversation. Everyone kept their eyes averted from Alina and her escort of soldiers. Too many beggars lined the streets. Even those who did not wail for coins looked shabby. Stalls holding luxurious silks and oddities remained untouched by the shoppers and barterers.

Finally, a pair of eyes caught hers. The dark green irises belonged to a young woman with an angular face. Her messy blonde hair had been ruffled from a breeze, and she stood in Warrior's armor, the plated steel glinting with the symbol of the Warriors, the same falcon on the royal banners. The woman watched her ride past, a hand secured around the pommel of a sheathed sword. Alina swallowed. The young Warrior made Alina shudder when she drew in a breath. The woman's gaze pierced her. She looked away to see if there were any other Warriors, and when she looked back, the woman had vanished. She blinked. Her breathing slowed and returned to normal.

"Regent," she said.

"Yes, your Highness?" The Regent stared at one of the market stalls selling cloaks as they rode by. He had not noticed a thing. None of her escort had.

"Have you assigned any Warriors to watch our caravan today?"

The Regent finally turned to look at her. "No, Highness. But Warriors are always present in the market. Why do you ask?"

"One held my gaze just now," she said, searching for the woman once more.

"Well, you probably saw the one on patrol then. They are very busy people sadly. I wish I had been able to obtain some as your guards."

Alina's grip on the reins tightened. She looked back to the Regent, eyes wide. "I'm to be assigned a guard?"

The Regent nodded. "Oh yes, for all hours of the day. We cannot have any harm befall you now, especially when we are in such a delicate political state of affairs."

Her stomach clenched and she recognized the foolishness of her expectations. *Of course they are going to watch you constantly. You're important now!* She chided herself as she took a calming breath, releasing the tension from her body. She could not be concerned about it now. For all she knew, the soldiers would be easy to push about and get rid of when she needed. "Am I to have no privacy then?" she asked coldly.

The Regent laughed and shook his head. "Your Highness, do not concern yourself with such things. We have not even assigned your guard."

Alina sighed and looked up to the bright noon sky. "I suppose you're right." Their caravan left the crowded markets and traveled to the upper courtyards. The palace as it grew larger and larger before her. It was grand, to say the least, towering high with marble columns and stone walls. Gargoyles hung from parapets and soldiers stood at attention on keep walls and every entrance.

"Are you all right, Highness?" the Regent asked.

"I had forgotten how big it was," she replied.

They rode through the main gardens first, a place lavish with rose bushes and other native flowers. She marveled at the multicolored blossoms and remembered how the garden staff could keep the blooms in place even through winter. Once they arrived at the palace steps, the soldiers dismounted and handed their horses off to stable boys before lining up on either side of the walkway.

A soldier offered to help her down and she accepted the assistance, her legs aching as they left the saddle. They had ridden nearly non-stop, only calling a halt out of necessity. As it was, Alina looked windswept and travel worn, something royalty should never look like. The Regent obviously picked up on it, for as he marched next to her he bent down and whispered, "Would you care for a guard to accompany you to a private chamber where you may change your gown? Riding skirts are hardly appropriate for court."

Alina nodded. "Thank you, Regent." Although prudish and short-tempered, the man had a good sense of decency and tact when it suited him. She walked up the castle steps with the Regent at her side. The doors seemed larger than she remembered as the guards held them aside for her. *Eleven years.* The doors had the same intricate carvings though, and the hall beyond still loomed. As they walked through the palace, Alina found herself staring and studying the once ghostly images of her past.

The Regent led her to one of the noble wings, to a room where her bag already sat. He excused himself and left her in the care of a chamber maid to help her wash and dress. The room held standard furnishings. A large bed, with dark red curtains falling over it, rested in the corner. An adjoining room held the bath, already filled with water. The chamber maid, a young plain woman, helped her undress and supplied soaps of different colors and fragrances. After the maid left, Alina removed her jewelry and set it aside on a shelf. She kept the signet ring, holding out her hand to examine it. The bright gold and gems shone despite her lack of hygiene. She had taken special care not to let anything happen to it. She finally lowered herself into the bath. The water, barely warm in the deep ivory tub, still felt wonderful on her cold, grime-covered skin.

After she scrubbed all the dirt away, she dried herself off with one of the soft towels supplied. It felt better on her skin than she could have remembered. She could not recall such an extravagant bath. Even the perfumes dazzled her senses. Someone must want her in the best possible mood for the coming Council meeting. The lace-embroidered garments with a matching green dress confirmed her suspicions. The Council did not offer such gifts for no reason. Her father had often raged about the Council pandering to his favor with similar offerings.

Alina slipped the garments on and studied herself in a large, bronze mirror. She tugged at the green dress, trying to smooth out any wrinkles. Finer than anything she owned, the color made her brown eyes light up like amber crystals. The dress was a close fit too, not exact, but close. Not many noblewomen sought out physical exercise like she did, something that would be much more difficult now. The deep green silk felt soft and smooth. The color seemed familiar somehow. She stared less and less at her reflection and more at the color itself. The green was piercing, cool, dazzling, almost like emeralds, like emerald eyes. *The Warrior in the market.* The thought chilled her, freezing her wandering hands. No, the dress was not really the same color as those woman's eyes. Alina breathed and smoothed out the dress once more. She shook her head, trying to clear the image of the mysterious woman from her eyes.

Alina was supposed to let the maid help her put the dress on, but after years of refusing Greta's help, she did it out of habit, though the laces in the back still needed to be tied. She fetched her jewelry, placing some of the items in a provided box and deciding to wear an old pendant her father had given her. She did not bother with silk gloves. The signet should be visible. The same maid returned to her room and helped her finish dressing and combed her hair. Alina sat dutifully at a low-backed chair and let the maid work through the knots gathered over the journey. As the woman smoothed out Alina's hair, she said, "Welcome back to the palace, your Highness."

Alina tried not to show a response to the comment. She suspected all the palace servants had spent days gossiping about her already. "What have you heard of my return?"

The brush faltered. "I beg your pardon, Highness. I did not mean any offense." The brush resumed.

"But you did not answer my question," said Alina.

"I have heard you were away for your own safety, your Highness, and the nobles have decided that you are safer here," the maid replied.

"And the truth?"

The maid kept brushing. She cleared her throat and pulled the brush through her hair once more. "There has been talk of a power struggle."

Alina frowned at her reflection. She had imagined the Council would not give over control of the kingdom so easily, but if the maids already whispered about it, her task might be more difficult. "That's enough for now." The woman stopped. Alina rose and looked the maid over. She wore a plain grey uniform and kept her plain brown hair wound up in a tight bun. Her blue eyes had a spark in them that matched the slight turn in the corner of her mouth. She had to be more shrewd than she seemed. "What is your name?"

The maid bowed. "Nin, your Majesty."

"Nin?" Alina had never heard the name.

"Short for Ninian, your Majesty."

"You seem to be an honest woman."

Someone knocked on the door. "Your Highness?" a man called out. "The Council of Osota is prepared to see you."

"See him in," Alina said. Nin moved to the door and opened it, revealing a young guard standing at attention.

"Highness, I am here to escort you to the Council chambers."

Alina nodded and stood. "Very well."

The guard led Alina to a large, open chamber somewhere in the center of the palace. Pillars stretched up to support a high ceiling and a faint breeze blew in from the open windows. The guard brought her up to another guard standing at attention in front of a set of large double doors.

"I have brought her Highness as the Council requested," he said. The other guard nodded and helped him open the large door to the chamber. A herald announced her arrival and stood aside to allow her entry. Alina had to resist the urge to squint when she stepped into the darker room. Large, heavy drapes covered most of the windows, letting a few rays of light in, but nothing more. The Council sat in a semicircle of raised daises. They stared down at her. Composed of one delegate from each of the eleven territories within the kingdom, it seemed everyone had arrived for this meeting.

"Lady Alina Alexandria Mura of Osota," said Councilor Gosman. She remembered him vaguely from her childhood. He overlooked a large province of the heartland. "You have been summoned before us due to the recent tragedies that have befallen Osota."

"The deaths of our monarchs, King Veston and Queen Alaina have left the people in grief," said another Councilor. Alina did not recognize the woman. "Furthermore, it has left us in peril, disorganized and disjointed."

Gosman spoke again, "My Lady, were you aware the monarchs left no heir?"

Alina nodded. She had to remain composed, and most importantly, harmless in their eyes. She was little more than a foreign entity to some of these people. Having been away since her childhood, she recognized few of the Councilors before her. They would regard her with suspicion, just as she would them. "I was led to believe I had no cousins."

Gosman nodded. "Correct. You are the only surviving member of the royal bloodline, albeit the connection is thin."

"Councilor Gosman," barked another man. Alina recognized him as Orwall, the ambassador of the eastern corner of the heartland and the capital city. Alina had seen much of him when she was young. "Your remark goes too far. Her father was brother to Queen Alaina, hardly what I would call a thin connection and closer than Demek's claim."

"Council members, we will not discuss the immediate claim to rule any further," ordered the woman who had spoken before. "This is not the purpose of today's assembly."

"Who else has claim to rule?" Alina asked.

The Councilors paused, as if waiting for someone else to speak up. Finally, an unknown man answered her. "My Lady—"

"Your Highness," she corrected.

"Highness," said the man. "While your right to rule by blood is strong, and no one questions it." He looked at Orwall. "You must realize you are young and have been removed from the political world for some time now—"

"Which is why I had the best tutors in all subjects possible while living in isolation."

Gosman narrowed his eyes. "What Councilor Tarish is trying to say is that we thought to have Lord Demek, the previous advisor to the king, assist with your position while the Council and Regent Velora help you prepare for this new role." Alina had never heard of a Lord Demek.

Councilor Orwall cleared his throat. "Normally, you would have been kept close at hand in the capital and trained, should this happen, but with the assassination of your parents, it seemed wisest to remove you from court and hope their majesties would produce a royal heir."

"But that is not the case, and I am here, fully capable and willing to learn what wisdom you have to offer and accept my duty. Who is to say this Lord Demek can lead our people better than I?"

"Sorez Demek was advisor to the late king and is a lord over one of the largest provinces in the heartland," said Gosman.

"Which happens to be your province," Orwall interrupted.

"Council members," said the same delegating woman from before. "It is clear this meeting is going beyond its use. Her Highness has agreed to the tutelage from the Regent and ourselves. I suggest we save this...discussion for another time." Alina studied the older woman. She suspected the wrinkles in the woman's forehead were from stress more than anything else. The Councilor looked intelligent and seemed fair. The woman turned to address her. "Your Highness, we shall resume the discussion of leadership after we have had more opportunity to assess your skill and the political situation."

Alina nodded. "Of course, Councilor," she said in her best balanced tone. "I understand that we must do what is best for the Osota Kingdom." She knew few of them believed her sincerity, but that was all right. She did not want their approval, just the means to keep Osota safe.

Chapter Three

THE WARRIORS STOPPED AND made camp late in the evening on their third day of travel. Valk said the capital was close, so they rode on for a few extra hours. Instead of pitching tents with the last hours of sunlight, they worked after dusk, Senri's fingers fumbling with various pins and ropes.

One of the Warriors successfully kindled a small fire. The man swore as the embers sputtered. She could feel the faint throb of the heat as it started to give up. She dropped her supplies and turned to the pile of wood. She stuck her hand into the center, where the fragile life form flickered. Senri breathed in, and as her heart beat, the embers glowed hot, searing the wood. As she exhaled the surrounding logs caught flame. She slowly withdrew her hand from the embers, letting the flames spread and anchor themselves. The fire blazed and expelled the shadows from their campsite. Senri smiled at the young man, his name was Yahn, and turned back to her tent.

"I'm an idiot," Yahn said.

Senri laughed and looked back at him. "And why is that?"

"I have battled with this fire every night while you're a walking flint-and-tinder." He rubbed his forehead with an ungloved hand before running his fingers through his shaggy hair. Yahn could manipulate earth like Nat. He was older though, a big, burly man with a growing collection of scars on his arms and legs. Senri saw it as a testament to the danger of her new line of work. Fear panged through her and she looked away. She knew it was ridiculous to be afraid. She was more gifted with the sword than Nat and more in tune with her abilities.

"You need help?" Yahn's words interrupted her dark thoughts.

She blinked and glanced back over at him. She shook her head.

"No, sorry. I was lost in thought. That's all."

Yahn nodded. "It weighs heavy on the mind...the first few days, that is." Senri focused on her tent supplies instead of answering. She did not want to discuss this with Yahn. She grabbed a rock and used it to drive one of the tent poles securely into the ground. He continued, "It's not nearly as terrifying as you would think though, at least not right away. You'll be spending most of your time training with the other initiates."

"How big are the Warrior's forces?" Senri asked. She wanted to change the topic.

"Oh, there's a fair amount of us." Senri heard him shifting around on the grass, moving away from the blazing fire. She moved to hammer in the opposite tent pole. "We take recruits from all sorts of places. Valk will have to ride out again soon to pick up some more recruits after we get back. We gained seven new initiates this year total. That's a lot."

Senri looked over at her new leader. Valk busied himself with finding an area to tie the horses so they could graze. He seemed to be having troubles since they were camping in an open plain. The tall grass surrounded them wherever their boots had failed to stomp it down. The sheer openness made her feel exposed. The wind blew too easily. The sky pressed down on her.

"You don't like the plains, do you?" asked Yahn.

"You have food to cook," Senri said. It irked her how, like Nat, he was able to read her emotions so easily.

Yahn sighed and tossed his hands up. "Well, if I had meat to cook, I would be doing so." He looked around the campsite as he stood and gazed around the field. "Nathaniel and Lanan were supposed to be back by now. Senri, why don't you go track them? They were supposed to be in that wooded area." He pointed to a small cluster of trees a way off. "Their footprints should be easy enough to follow."

"Fine," said Senri. She picked up a stick from the pile of spare wood and lowered it into the fire. The head caught and she pulled it out.

"I can get you an actual torch," said Yahn. Senri gestured to herself. "Oh, right. You control fire."

"Heat."

"Hm?" Yahn poked a stick into the center of the flames, pushing around the logs.

"I control heat," she clarified.

Yahn only shrugged and Senri took off, locating the footprints of Nat and Lanan, the short-haired woman. They should have been back with something or a report of nothing at all. Senri took comfort in the gentle heat coming off the torch. The entity chewed through the wood slowly to preserve itself. As she walked, the chirping of nearby insects and the faint clicking of animals followed her. She looked around, expecting to see a creature staring at her through the tall blades of grass.

The wind gusted and she stopped. Her fire flickered. The grass rustled. She stared in vain into the dark depths beyond her curtain of light. The moon, only a sliver that night, provided no help. *Stupid plains*. She moved her free hand to grip the hilt of her sword and continued moving to the cluster of trees.

She paused at the edge of the tree-line. Irrational fear gripped her muscles. It was too small to be a forest, but still large enough to hide a predatory beast. "I am too young for this." She held the fire in front of her. The flames crackled, but did little to expel the shadows from between the trees. She gulped. "Am I not a Warrior of Osota?" The footprints clearly went into the woods and no tracks exited.

Senri stepped into the woods. Twigs cracked underneath her feet no matter where she stepped, and each break grew louder as she walked deeper into the woods. She breathed a little easier when she realized the hushed sound of a forest had returned. She followed the footsteps until a twig she had not stepped on snapped.

Ahead of her, too far away to see what did it, Senri paused and listened, torch held out before her like a shield. After several tense seconds, someone giggled.

"Hello?" she called out. "Is that you, Nat?" The laughter gave way to shouts meant to scare her. Senri moved forward, searching in the dark for whoever made the noise. "Nat? If that's you and Lanan, please tell me you caught something for Yahn to cook back at camp."

"Is that why he sent you? He's an impatient one, isn't he?" She heard Nat's voice coming from the right. She turned and moved toward it. The clanking of armor floated her direction. Her fire casted light on the distinct forms of Nat and Lanan, both standing intimately close with half their clothing gone. Senri's jaw dropped.

"Really, Nat?" she asked, her voice rising. "You two were

keeping us from dinner just to..." Words failed her. She gestured with her free hand at the strewn clothes across the forest floor. "This?"

"Relax, kid," said Lanan. The young woman walked forward, tugging her shirt down over a well-proportioned chest.

"That seems a little difficult, considering the circumstances," Senri growled. Lanan pouted and ran a hand through her hair.

"Hey!" Nat pulled at a buckle to his armor. "Lanan simply knows a fine specimen of flesh when she sees one." He stroked a hand over his torso suggestively.

Senri pinched her brow and Lanan laughed. "Or I'm not too particular about my company."

Nat held a hand over his heart in mock hurt. "So this is the thanks I get for giving you a romantic evening."

Lanan shrugged.

Senri waved the fire at them in warning. "Did you at least get food? Or were you too busy eating each other?"

Nat held up a few rabbits. "Would I ever let you starve?"

"For a pretty girl? Yes."

"I have to agree with your friend," said Lanan. "You are too eager for love." Nat pushed his way between the two and they walked back to the camp. The grasslands did not seem so eerie with company.

"Both of you are so hateful," Nat mocked. "And you should be more grateful, Senri. After all, I pulled Lanan off of Vella for you."

Senri cringed. She knew whatever came next would be embarrassing.

"Oh," said Lanan, exaggerating the sigh with a long breath. "That's why Nat jumped on me, is it?" She stepped a little closer to Senri. Despite Senri's own impressive height, Lanan was still taller than her. She could feel the Warrior gazing down at her in amusement. She grinned and said, "You know, you could do much better."

Senri pushed Lanan aside. The flames on the torch danced high and burned quickly until a dying piece of wood cracked, reminding her to control the flames again. "What do you care anyways? You're too old for her." She glared at Lanan, trying to will her eyes to shoot fireballs at the smug grin. Sadly, nothing happened.

Lanan stood still. Her smile relaxed, amused. It annoyed Senri she did not equal a threat to this woman. "Just how old do you think

I am?" Lanan asked.

"I know you're too old to be going after village girls." Senri felt this answer would be good enough, that it would somehow shame Lanan. The woman laughed and Senri's anger burned hotter.

"Senri," Nat yelled.

She blinked and realized the stick she held was engulfed in flame. "Oh no!" she said. She tried to will the fire away. Lanan laughed harder. Nat attempted to find some cloth to smother it with. Finally, Senri lost control and extinguished the fire, leaving a smoldering, ruined stump of wood in her grasp. She stared at it, blinking through the thick darkness. Smoke curled off the ashy tip. It would not light again. Nothing would sustain it. She turned and threw the useless chunk as hard as she could. The grass swished and cracked as it landed somewhere around them. She looked into the utter darkness of the field and sighed.

"Great," she said. She turned and looked around. Nat stood by, fixing his shirt that he had almost torn off to smother the fire with. Her eyes eventually caught the distant glimmer of a fire, the one she had started. "There's camp," she said, pointing to the light. She walked toward it without waiting for the others.

Nat and Lanan moved through the grass behind her. She tried to ignore them. "You know, I am only twenty turns," Lanan said. Senri kept walking.

They returned to the camp in silence. Yahn stood from his spot by the fire as soon as he heard them approaching. "Well, you better have felled a great beast for as long as that took." Nat tossed him the bundle of rabbits. Yahn caught it and held the meager prize up to inspect it. "That's all?"

"They would have found more if they had not been so preoccupied," said Senri.

Lanan chuckled and Nat blushed. The sight of his embarrassment made her heart soften a little. She was not used to seeing him uncomfortable in a social situation. Still, she wouldn't forgive him yet and instead made her way over to her unfinished tent. With the light of the fire, she finished assembling it much quicker and hauled her supplies into its confines. She tied the thin cloth flap shut, an illusion of privacy. She pushed and stomped at the grass inside her tent in hopes of making it into a mattress, then grabbed her rucksack and tugged her blanket out. The cloth was heavy, hand-stitched by her mother for this journey. It flattened the grass out as she smoothed it over the ground.

Senri lay down on it and sighed. It was much more comfortable out here than it had been on the forest dirt. She closed her eyes and breathed deeply. She felt tired. Then again, she had good reason to be. The day had stretched on too long and she had lost control of that flame in a way she had never done before. The way the heat had surged over the wood upset her. The flame had eaten away everything, but it still burned. It thrived on the very air around them, growing, consuming. Senri knew she could have expanded the flame into an enveloping explosion of heat if she had wanted. The depths of her power scared her.

"Hey Senri," Nat's voice sounded from right outside her tent flap. "Did your mother pack any spices for you? This rabbit is going to taste awful otherwise."

"Hold on," Senri said. If he had approached with any other need, she might have turned him away out of spite. "I'm sure there is some in my bag." She grabbed her sack and stuck her hand in.

"Hello," said Nat, poking his head inside the tent. She pulled one wrong item out of the sack before losing patience and tipping it over onto her blanket, the contents scattering everywhere. "Find it yet?"

Senri looked down into the pile of her things and grabbed a small, sealed jar. "Here are the mixed spices. Are we roasting them or making stew?"

"Stew," said Nat. She made a face. "I know, but there's not enough meat to go around."

"And whose fault is that?" Senri grinned.

"I don't know what you mean." Nat exited the tent and Senri followed, her stomach grumbling. Nat handed the spice jar off to Yahn and Senri settled down by the fire. She stared into the center of the flames, letting the heat wash over her body.

"Mind if I sit beside you?"

Senri looked up to see Lanan standing next to her, a hopeful look on her face. "Go ahead." Lanan smiled and sat down beside her. Senri automatically tensed in her presence. She found Lanan threatening, but forced herself to relax. Lanan was supposed to be her ally, and seemed to want peace between them.

"I didn't mean to upset you back in the village," Lanan said.

Senri stared at the fire. "But it's odd that you lay claim to that girl when she obviously doesn't return the affection." She probably meant for the words to sound harmless, but Senri winced.

"I'll wait for her," she said.

Lanan laughed. "You see, I don't understand that about you. There is so much more out there and you are transfixed on one simple village girl."

"There was no one else in the village. Vella and Nat are the only two people close to my age. It's hard to imagine who else could be out there." Senri pulled her knees up to her chest and hugged them close.

"There are a lot of people. Trust me," said Lanan.

Instead of fetching the iron support rods, Yahn and Nat scooped their hands into the earth and pulled up columns of slowly solidifying rock, four surrounding the fire. They then worked to create a vented top to rest on the columns. They pulled their creation from the earth, loose dirt falling away from it, and set it down over the fire. They then rested the cauldron on top of it.

"Now that is a stove," said Nat, eyeing their handiwork.

"What did you two do?" asked Valk. His gruff voice pierced the calm that had fallen over them. He eyed the earthen stovetop, shook his head, and sat down by the fire, muttering something about proper ways of practice.

"The stew is cooking, right?" said Yahn. Senri could already smell the spices mixing with the vegetables and rabbit.

"Just wait until I get you back to the training grounds," said Valk. "You'll wish all you had to make were fancy stovetops." He turned to look at Nat. The young man gulped. "You should learn when it is appropriate to use your talent. Our abilities are a gift, and it is to be treated as such, not a tool to bend to your whim."

While Valk lecture the two men, Lanan leaned over and whispered in Senri's ear, "He's a little old-fashioned." Senri nodded.

"Did your mentors even teach you the origin of your powers?" asked Valk. He looked between both Senri and Nat.

"Of course," said Senri. "Our abilities are a gift from the Almighty." Though her instruction had been vague at best, Senri wanted to defend what training she had.

"Yes, the full story does start out with the Almighty blessing us with power. But it only gave them to a select few."

"Prepare yourself," whispered Lanan. "I won't begrudge you if you fall asleep on me."

Senri discreetly shoved her. "I'm sure it's interesting," she whispered back. With Valk sitting on the opposite side of the crackling fire, it was easier for them to get away with the small gestures and quiet conversation.

"The Almighty granted six abilities to six different humans. To the first one, it granted the knowledge of the earth so that this human might build a foundation for their civilization." Nat and Yahn gestured at their creation. Valk shook his head. "To the second, the Almighty gave dominion over water so that the humans could thrive on the newly shaped land."

"That's me," Lanan whispered. Senri stared at her and raised an eyebrow. "The siren of the seas." Senri struggled not to laugh.

"The third was granted dominion over all plant-life so that the Almighty's creations could sustain themselves with the land." He looked over at Senri. "The fourth was blessed with the heartbeat of the earth, fire, and the heat burning within all living things so that humans would always know the connection they shared with the world. The fifth human was blessed with the winds so that natural forces never eradicated the Almighty's work." He paused, looking at each of his students in turn. "And the last human was granted control over illness and health to guard against the spread of plague."

Senri had never heard of this ability. Shaman healers wandered through the village occasionally, but she never thought their power stemmed from the same source.

"These six were the original source, our ancestors. Over time, they sired children and spread their power through to the next generation, for centuries and centuries until now, where the power has manifested itself in us." Valk finished with a grin. He reached for a bowl and ladle and Senri removed the hot lid from the cauldron, the burning iron pleasant to her touch.

"But the original earth guy was supposed to build foundations for society," said Nat, grabbing his own bowl. "Wouldn't you say this creation is a return to my ancestor's roots?"

Valk shook his head. "Pups. You have no understanding for the nuances of our traditions. The select few given your training are an honored kind. The Warriors are the greatest defense of Osota."

"Not everyone gets as worked up as him," Lanan whispered.

Senri grabbed their bowls and poured out stew for each of them. She handed Lanan her bowl and took her own. The stew smelled good. It tasted good. That opinion could be aided by the lack of other food to eat though. They ate in silence for a long while.

Valk stood and brushed the grass from his trousers when he finished. "I'm turning in," he said. "The rest of you should do the same. We will ride with the morning's light." Senri could feel the tension ease between the rest of them as he walked over to his far away tent and disappeared inside it.

"Get used to the lectures," said Yahn. "He's fond of giving them."

"He is very...intense," said Nat.

"He's an excellent fighter, one of the fiercest I've seen," said Yahn. "He is stuck in the old ways though." He adopted a mimic of Valk's voice, "'Warriors fight, civilians produce.' He told me that when I made clay bowls on a field assignment one time. I told him he could eat dinner off the ground."

Senri laughed with the others. She shook her head and looked up at the stars. They shone brightly over the open plain, each one winking in and out of focus as her gaze travelled across them. The whole sky seemed to open up over her, like it would swallow her whole at any moment. "It's too big out here," she muttered.

"Then you'll be relieved when we reach the tight confines of the city," said Nat.

"We should be there any day now," said Lanan. She studied the stars as well. "We need to get some rest."

Senri nodded. She knew the tendrils of sleep lingered close in her mind, waiting to pull her under as soon as she lay down. "Sleep sounds good. Anyone else need the fire?" Senri asked.

Everyone shook their heads. She leaned forward and tried to extinguish the flame like she had done with the torch out in the field. It resisted her and she frowned. She had not played with extinguishing heat before, but she had imagined it would be a simple process to duplicate. All she managed to do was make the flames rise higher. Nat noticed her struggling and nodded to her. She withdrew her hands and he smothered the flames in earth. It took her a minute to adjust her eyes to the darkness. Now only the stars cast their light on them. Senri crawled off to her tent, muttering goodnight.

***

Alina paced up and down her room, hands clenched at her side and brow furrowed. "They cannot keep treating me like this."

"Treat you how, your Highness?" asked Nin. She sat altering one of Alina's new dresses in the corner.

"Like I am an incompetent child," she growled. "It's better if they believe me harmless, but this behavior? You would think they fear me starting a war!" She stopped her pacing and turned to glare at Nin. "Do they think I am that misinformed?"

"Perhaps they believe you are too well informed, Highness," said Nin, pulling a green thread through the emerald dress. "Perhaps they wish to bar you from negotiations in an attempt to keep you out of power." This was the third time in two days Alina had been sent away from a discussion concerning trade and alliances with other kingdoms. It seemed the Council always discussed a 'sensitive issue' too complex for her.

Alina shook her head and began to lap her room again. "No, that gives them too much credit. It would be better if they feared me for my competency, but not by much. And why do they fear me making a mess of things when they have done a fine job of letting the heartland slip into decline on its own?" This was a particularly enraging point for Alina. "I don't understand why they trust this Lord Demek so much. Everywhere I look, poor people are clinging to the skirts of the wealthy, begging for bread. If that were not embarrassing enough, the city of Osota itself is falling apart."

Nin looked like she might say something but Alina forged on. "It's not only this city though. They haven't been providing upkeep on any of the military outposts or towers. Did you know there was a perfectly good fortress that we rode past along the eastern border that is sitting empty?" She stopped and looked over at her young servant. "And what rumors have you been sifting through?" She had quickly discovered Nin was in tune with every bit of gossip in the palace.

Nin shrugged as she worked the needle carefully into the cloth. "The scullery maids have heard from the kitchen boys who heard from the cooks who heard from the dining servants that the Council is bartering an alliance with a western kingdom."

"And why should I not be allowed to witness that?" Alina ran a hand through her hair, taming the loose strands. "That sounds like an important thing for me to be part of."

Nin paused in her sewing. She looked up. "There's something not right about these people." Alina stopped her fussing and listened to the maid. "They come from across the sea. They walk like us, sound like us when they talk, but something is out of place. The whole palace is talking about it. Nobody wants to serve on them. Even the Councilors avoid contact with them. Everyone say it's…" She paused and seemed to be in search of the proper word. "unsettling to be around them."

"How so?" Alina asked.

Nin shook her head and closed her eyes. "There's something rotten inside them. They're so different from any other nation across the western sea. The citizens of Noshon trade with us, and they're the most pleasant people in court. I talked with one of the dignitaries from there the other day. He did not have kind things to say about this visiting kingdom."

"And…" Alina prompted.

Nin only shook her head again. "That's all I know right now. It's just…a bad feeling. Regent Velora is outraged that they were brought in for negotiations so soon after the death of the monarchs. They arranged everything while he was out fetching you."

Alina sighed and rubbed her temple. "If they are so…terrifying, then why are we forging an alliance with them? Resources?"

Nin shook her head once more and tucked a stray lock of hair behind her ear. "That is only a small part. I heard some soldiers talking. I think the only other alternative is war."

"So they swooped in to take us over in the midst of our own power struggle and we buckled?" The whole situation reeked of poor politics.

"We are still a sovereign nation, though, or we will be when negotiations conclude," Nin said.

"This is ridiculous," said Alina. Her jaw felt tight. "I need something to throw."

Nin looked up from the dress with a small smile. "Would you like me to send a boy to fetch some vases from the market, Highness?"

Alina considered the option for several moments. "No," she finally said. "I don't want them to think I am stupid and crazy."

Someone knocked on the chamber door and Nin rose to answer. She opened the door. "What?" The pale doorman shrunk under her maid's harsh gaze. Nin had gotten protective of her, to say the least. She scared the other servants into giving them complete privacy when they needed to talk. She understood the devastating effects of unchecked gossip.

"Pardon me, ma'am, but more gifts have arrived for her Highness," he said. Nin nodded and opened the door. Several maids walked in with boxes stacked high in their arms.

"More bribery!" Alina declared as they dropped the gifts on her bed. She looked over at her maid who attempted to conceal her laughter. "Nin, send that boy to the market, but have the vases delivered to the archery range. I have a better idea in mind."

The maid nodded and curtseyed. "Yes, your Highness."

Alina shooed Nin and other servants away and shut the door. She dug through her things in the chest at the foot of her bed and pulled out the book that she had brought and the small drawstring pouch. Alina opened the pouch and tipped the contents into her hand. The runes clacked against one another in her palm. Powerful little stones, their surfaces had been worn smooth over time. These were one of the few physical items she inherited from her mother.

She shook the leather pouch until a small white cloth fell out. She smoothed it out over the desk. She formed her thought carefully as she held the stones. Though she could rune cast, she was not nearly powerful enough to perform as many as she wanted with equal success. She finally tossed them, confident she had the right wording. The stones tumbled over the surface of the cloth and stopped, resting in a small cluster. She looked at the various symbols and flipped open her old book, skimming the pages. Finally, she closed the book, her reading less satisfying than she had hoped.

Alina had consulted the runes once already hoping to learn more of the mysterious Council meetings, but the results had been vague. This casting, however, proved to have a more definitive answer. Alina sighed and scooped the runes and cloth back into her pouch. The first suggestions from the runes told her to trust in her archery skills. If the runes wanted her to shoot arrows at sand-filled pots, so be it. As Alina put things away, she wondered if she had wasted the question by muddling together too many thoughts. She had wanted to know what to trust in, and the runes had given her one very clear answer to that. *Nin is loyal.*

"Your Highness." Nin's familiar voice sounded from the other side of the door. A knock followed. Alina crossed the room and opened it, seeing Nin smiling. "The boy is fetching the clay right now. Shall we prepare you an escort?"

***

The Warriors moved through the crowded streets of the kingdom capital with ease, even with their horses in tow. "Senri, what do you think of a real city?" Lanan asked.

"It's loud."

Lanan laughed, adding to the cacophonous clatter of the market streets. People bowed their heads in respect when they walked by, or would mutter something about getting out of their way. Senri felt the weight of the falcon on her armor a little more each time a person glanced at her.

"I take it we're important?" asked Senri, watching as a small child stopped and openly stared at them as they walked past.

Yahn rested a supportive hand on her shoulder. "I know we are not a large presence in the southern end of the kingdom, but to the people here we are heroes. The Warriors lead the soldiers into battle and collaborate on the most dangerous assignments. We even fill in where the city guard falls short. We cover patrols through here all the time."

Senri nodded. The market stands surrounding her were bright and flashy. Everything from clothing and cooking supplies to enchanted jewelry sat on display proudly in the afternoon sun. She noticed a distinct lack of iron-made goods. "So, where are we going?"

Lanan, whose gaze had trailed after some gypsies, looked over at Senri with unfocused eyes. "What? Did you say something?"

"I asked where we were going." Senri looked back at the gypsies to make sure she did not miss anything about them and noticed the low cut shirts on the men and women.

"Well, first Valk is going to take us to the barracks so we can put our possessions away. Then he will instruct Yahn and I to give you two a tour of the training grounds and the palace so you know where to stay out of." She winked when she said the last bit.

"Sounds informative," Senri replied.

"And the best part is you get to experience all of it with me and not some uptight soldier," Lanan teased.

Senri smiled and with as much religious fervor as she could muster, "Bless the Almighty!". Lanan laughed again. As they walked along Senri felt the end of her reins go taut and she turned to see Stomps stopped by a fruit stand. Her horse stared at the apples with pitiful eyes.

"Come on Stomps," she said, tugging at the reins. Her horse took this as a cue to lean forward and sniff the apples, his nostrils flaring with every breath. "Stomps!" she said, running over to the horse. She pushed his head to the side and apologized to the amused shopkeeper. "You know better," she told her horse. Senri glanced at the apples and then their price tag. She had no coins that would fit the purchase amount. A pamphlet nailed to the side of the stand caught her attention. The words, 'In honor of the late King and Queen,' caught her eye and she read on. Her heart skipped. *The monarchs had died?* "Excuse me, is this right?" Senri asked the apple vendor. She pointed at the pinned up parchment.

The man nodded. "I am afraid so. Their Majesties passed on a little over a week ago. Have you been travelling?"

Senri nodded. She read the pamphlet again, trying to decide what she should tell the others.

"What's holding you up?" asked Lanan. She was at her side, having walked through the crowd to get to her.

Senri pointed at the paper. "Does Valk need to know about this?"

Lanan's eyes widened as she read the pamphlet over. "Yes, he does." She grabbed the paper, tearing it from the stand and moved through the market streets after Valk. Senri tugged on her horse's reins and followed. Lanan pushed and shoved through civilians, muttering, "Official business, excuse me." Senri followed in her wake, easing Stomps through the small openings left behind. When she caught up to the others she saw Lanan had given Valk the pamphlet and he was busy reading it with Nat and Yahn crowding by his shoulder to get a look.

Valk's brows knitted together and his fingers slowly clenched the paper into a crinkled, ruined ball before he threw it onto the ground. "By the Almighty," he growled. "Yahn, Lanan. You two lead them back to the barracks. Get them settled and ready for training. I have business in the palace." Before they could affirm his orders he turned and forced his way through anyone in his path. He disappeared in the fold of people, leaving the four of them standing together in silence.

Yahn stooped and picked up the crumpled paper. He smoothed it out on his pant leg and read the crinkled writing. "Well, that's not good."

"I take it this is very recent news?" asked Nat, looking over the pamphlet. The four of them stood in the middle of the street. Senri rubbed the back of her neck. Lanan stood with her hands on her hips, head bowed, and Yahn stowed the paper into his trouser pocket.

"I suppose we need to get your horses to the stables then," said Yahn. "We wouldn't want to pay for all the apples in the market." The four of them laughed, but it was hollow. Senri patted her horse and they resumed walking, Yahn leading the way.

"What happens now?" asked Nat. He made sure to keep pace with the two older Warriors. Senri trailed just behind them.

"Well, the four of us will spend the day with a lack of proper instruction, which is nice," said Lanan. "But as far as the Warriors as a whole go, we will have to see what the new monarch decides to do with us." They moved beyond the markets and to the palace gates. The guard let them in. He looked frightened. Senri assumed that Valk had given him strict orders to let them through with elaborate consequences should he fail.

"But who is the new ruler?" Yahn asked. "They didn't have any children." They turned down a walkway that ran along the palace walls.

"They had a niece," said Lanan. "I'll bet she's around here somewhere."

"Why, where else would she be?" asked Yahn.

"I think they had her in hiding," said Lanan. "Don't you remember the big uproar about that assassination some turns ago?"

Yahn grunted in response. They reached the open courtyard of the barracks. Warriors and palace guards walked in between stone buildings. The thatch roofs were not as appealing as the stone-tiled roof of the palace, but the structures seemed well-built enough.

"You know who I feel sorry for?" asked Lanan suddenly. No one responded. "The Council. Valk is going to rage at them." They loitered in the middle of the courtyard.

"Valk scares me, you know?" said Nat.

Yahn shrugged. "It's because you're new. Once you get into some training with him and he sees that you are competent he'll start acting friendly."

"And if I'm incompetent?" asked Nat.

"You die," said Lanan. She nodded toward the stables located on the far wall of the barracks. "We have a task though. Get your horses moving."

Senri and Nat followed. "That's it?" Nat asked. "We just...die?"

"Well, killed in a mission is more like it," said Yahn. "There's an easy way to avoid that though."

"How?" asked Nat.

"Train hard and don't be a fool," said Yahn. They stabled their horses in a pen that opened up to a grassy plain beyond the palace walls. The stone barrier extended around the plain and wrapped back to enclose them. "Our barracks rest on the outer wall next to the stables." He pointed to their right. "The other two belong to the regular soldiers. I'll show you the men's quarters," he said to Nat.

"And I'll show you ours," said Lanan, looping and arm through Senri's and pulling her close. The contact made Senri feel strange. Lanan's blunt and sarcastic nature confused her, and she did not know what to make of their somewhat delicate acquaintance with each other. "And then we can see the sparring chambers and the archery range."

Senri wondered if the quickness in Lanan's voice held excitement or suppression of the uncertainty of the day's events.

***

The release of the arrow and faint *twang* followed by the humming vibrations of her bowstring did little to calm Alina's nerves. The shattering crack and tumbling of the broken vase was, however, extremely satisfying. She watched the sand run through the newly made crevices of the shattered pottery. She had briefly considered setting up the Council's gifts on the distant targets, but that may have been a step too far.

"Excellent shot, Highness," said her guard. Despite Velora's promise, all of her escorts had been composed of palace guards, not Warriors or soldiers. Alina stared down the field at the few remaining targets and stuck out her hand. Nin drew an arrow from the quiver and handed it to her. Alina settled the fletched end against her bowstring and drew back.

"Pardon me, Highness," said her guard. Her grip faltered for a second before she relaxed the tension, easing the bowstring forward and pointing her arrow down.

"Yes?" she asked.

"It appears we have visitors," said Nin, nodding toward the end of the field.

"I ordered the scheduled training closed," said Alina. She squinted at the four approaching soldiers.

"Shall I order them off the field, Highness?" asked her guard.

"They appear to be Warriors. What if they have urgent news?" asked Nin. The four walked down to the targets rather than straight for them. "Or perhaps they're simply ignoring orders," Nin sighed. Alina covered her eyes from the sun. The metal plates glinted. They certainly looked like warriors. She considered ignoring them until she saw one of them was blonde.

"Hold," she said as her guard took a step forward. "Let them approach."

The Warriors were too far away for her to pick out eye color, but the blonde one looked female. Something about her felt familiar to Alina. The way she moved, the gait, the grip of her hand on the pommel of a sword, all known, and as the woman moved closer Alina recognized the general shape, the facial features. Alina's breath catch as the woman caught her stare, just like in the markets.

"You there! Warriors!" she called out. The rest looked over. They had stopped by one of the unused targets and seemed to be discussing something. "Come here!" she ordered. The four of them leaned in and whispered to one another before walking over to Alina and her party.

Once they were in speaking distance Alina could plainly see that the blonde woman was indeed the one she had seen in the markets the other day. Her eyes were the same shade of green. She was young, close in age to Alina, and had a sharp jaw and trimmed body. *Definitely a Warrior.*

"Is there anything we can assist you with, my Lady?" asked one of the other Warriors.

"You will address her as Highness or Majesty or not at all," ordered her guard.

The four of them seemed genuinely shocked at this and one man whispered to the other, "Guess that's her."

In other circumstances, Alina might have been amused. But the stare of that young woman still burned in her mind, much more intense the first time compared to now. Right now the eyes seemed soft, confused. "You there," she said, nodding to the blonde woman. The girl straightened her posture. "Did I not see you in the market the other day?"

The girl still stared back. "I'm sorry, your Highness, but it was not me you saw."

"Are you sure?" Alina asked, disappointed. "You were not in the markets at all the last few days?"

The woman shook her head. "I apologize. I arrived at the market today. We were on the road before that." Alina watched the woman's gaze pass over her once before meeting her eyes again. "Are you alright, your Highness?"

The earth seemed to tilt beneath her feet, but no one else showed signs of instability. "No, I'm fine, just fine. The four of you, return to whatever you were doing." The Warriors all shared glances, but then bowed with hands over their hearts and walked away, whispering to one another.

"Your Highness, you do not seem well," said the guard.

"I'm fine," she repeated. She shook her head and blinked, but her eyes snapped back to the blonde woman walking down the field. "I was mistaken, that's all." *A lie. She's the woman from the market.* She had suspected a vision had happened; she had hoped she was wrong. *Damn those runes.*

"Shall I escort you to your chambers?" the guard asked.

Alina watched the Warriors move off the field. She meant to answer her guard, but stood silently instead.

"Your Highness?" he prompted.

Alina blinked and looked back to him. The bow seemed heavier in her hand. Her anger had dissipated. Now her heart hammered and her legs ached with the weight of her body. She rarely felt this off, only when severe attacks approached. "I think I should..." *I need to run.* "I think I shall retire to my chambers."

Nin retrieved the bow from her and took her arm in support. "Come, your Highness," she said, patting Alina's arm. "I'll have the servants draw up a hot bath for you."

Alina allowed Nin to pull her off the field. Her guard trailed behind. Once she was a fair distance away from the archery range she felt her strength return. Her legs held her weight better and warmth crept back into her fingers and cheeks. She pulled her arm out of Nin's supportive grasp and refused all help to climb the steps to the palace. The guards at the entrance exchanged looks when they saw Alina approach with the archer's brace still on her arm and the bow still carried by Nin but she did not care. She pushed past them and continued into the entrance hall.

Alina intended to go up to her room and sort through the mishap on the field, but fate did not wish to be kind that day. As she passed the main walkway to the meeting chambers, a clamorous and hurried voice shouted, "Lord Demek!" Alina froze and turned in the direction the shout had come from. In her days at the palace she had yet to meet the ex-advisor to the late king, and she considered herself overdue for an introduction.

"Your Highness," her guard called after her. Nin gently tugged at her arm as if to remind her of their original course, but she brushed the hand off her and kept walking. Two men stood ahead of her, one of them being Councilor Gosman, pale and hunched over, his hands tugging at the sleeves of his blue robes. The other man stood tall in crisp white pants and a white jacket embroidered in gold. Medals decorated his left side just above his heart and a royal blue cape spilled off his shoulders, flowing around him.

Alina's footsteps rang through the open chamber and he looked up from the whispering Councilor. A handsome man, his features could have been chiseled from marble. His dark hair was swept back into a ponytail with gray hairs frosting his sideburns. He smiled warmly at Alina, but the warmth did not reach up to his amber eyes.

Gosman looked up as well, halting in his sputtering. "Your Highness!" His words rang through the room. "What are you doing at the chambers? You know we are discussing sensitive matters—"

"Were discussing," said Lord Demek. He placed a gloved hand on the Councilor's chest and pushed him aside as Alina drew closer. "It is a pleasure to finally meet you, your Highness." The man swept into a deep bow, pulling his cape around with him. He glanced up at Alina. She stared down at him with her best apathetic look. "It is a shame you don't say the same about me." He winked and turned back to the Councilor, who looked as frightened as Alina shocked. "Do you not have that tax regulation to attend to?" Demek asked.

The Councilor swallowed and nodded. He still fiddled with the sleeves of his robe.

"But Lord Demek, you asked me to..." His voice trailed off when Demek frowned at him. Both looked confused. "I...my mistake. Pardon me, your Highness. I must excuse myself for the time being." He bowed, perhaps in the most respectful manner since she had arrived, and left, walking down the hall and away from the chambers. Alina watched him disappear around a corner. She noticed Nin and the guard standing nearby. They seemed tense, unsure.

"I apologize for that," said Demek. His voice was gentle and, had anyone else possessed it, soothing. But when Demek spoke it caused wariness.

"No need for an apology," said Alina, finding her voice once more. She tried to stand tall, to look authoritative like she usually did. "I find his company rather tiresome as well."

Demek smiled again with that false warmth and laughed. "They did not speak of your wit, Majesty."

Alina wanted to think he flattered her, but something in the man's voice sounded sincere. She had to refrain from looking away. Her fingers burned to touch the signet ring laying heavily on her right hand, the only reminder left that she should rule.

"But where are my manners?" he asked, breaking the silence. "I am Lord Sorez Demek of Osota." He reached for her hand with the signet ring and held it in his gloved hand. He bent his head and leaned down to kiss her signet, his lips touching the stone briefly before Nin walked forward and pulled Alina away. Lord Demek froze, hand still outstretched and head still tilted forward. His eyes darted up to Nin. "Did I offend you, madam?" He straightened his posture and smoothed out the front of his jacket.

"You are too presumptuous, my Lord," said Nin, with a curtsey. "Her Highness has recently taken ill and must be escorted back to her chambers."

Demek raised his eyebrows and frowned. "How terrible! No wonder you stand so silent and pale. Your Majesty, I must insist on accompanying you the rest of the way to your chambers, if not for your sake, then to allow me to atone for my audacious behavior." Demek extended his arm, gesturing down the hall as he waited for her to make a move.

Alina was cornered. Even if she refused his help, Demek would insist on accompanying her. Slowly, she curtseyed and bowed her head. "It would be an honor, Lord Demek." He smiled and they walked down the hall together, his right arm linked with Alina's left. Even with Nin urging her along as discretely as she could, Alina decided that she needed to use her predicament to her greatest advantage. "Lord Demek," she said.

The man glanced at her with a smile. "Yes, your Majesty?" he said. He seemed pleased, as if her willingness to speak with him was all he wanted.

"It has come to my attention that the Council is meeting with foreign dignitaries."

"And what concerns you about this, your Majesty?" Lord Demek asked. They walked at a leisurely pace down the hall to the noble quarters.

Alina wondered if he had moved into the royal suite. "I was only curious," she said. "The Council barred me from observing all meetings with them, saying it was too sensitive an issue for me to witness." Lord Demek frowned. His puzzlement seemed genuine. "And I thought it would be beneficial for me to observe these negotiations, considering I shall rule one day."

He rubbed his chin slowly with a gloved hand. "You are right. You should be actively involved in these political matters if you are ever expected to rule the kingdom in confidence. I must warn you though, these negotiations are...troubling on the mind." He paused. "But, you are twenty and able to make your decisions. I shall make sure you are free to attend the discussion next week."

Alina knew he played off an angle, but she did not care. He was the fool if he thought she would buckle under pressure. "Thank you, Lord. You are much more agreeable than your counterparts in the Council." They turned down the hall that led to her quarters. "Now, where are these diplomats from?" *I have yet to get a name from Nin.*

"They hail from the kingdom of Shedol. Have you heard of it before?"

"No, the name slips my..." The draining sensation of fatigue was coming over her like it had on the field. Her steps faltered and Nin's arm wrapped around her waist, holding her upright. Her arm slipped from Demek's grasp as she took another stumbling step forward. Her vision blurred and her ears pounded. *Not again, not now.* Her heart pulsed in her chest. Everything went dark for a moment. With a few deep breaths, her eyesight cleared and the room appeared before her again. It took several more breaths for the ringing in her ears to stop.

"...don't care what you say, she needs the attention of a healer." The voice sounded harsh. Lord Demek, no doubt.

"It is not your place to call one, my Lord." Nin spoke just as harshly, tugging on Alina's arm. "I will escort her to her chambers and then send for one." Alina blinked and tugged her arm out of Nin's grasp.

"Yes, I believe that is a fine idea." She spoke, surprising her attendants and Demek. "Lord, I am faint from the excitement of the day. My quarters are close by, we can manage from here. I give you leave to return to your duties."

"Your Highness, please, I want to help." He stepped forward and she backed up. Something had changed in his eyes. He looked genuinely concerned, more aware of the actual danger Alina faced in that moment. Usurpers should not seem concerned.

"Thank you, Lord Demek, but I do not require assistance. Farewell." She turned away and walked as quickly as grace and manners allowed her.

"Good day, your Majesty," he called after her.

Alina could imagine him bowing despite the lack of an audience. The feeling hit her once more, threatening to suck her under; her pulse quickened. She reached for her door and pushed it open, ignoring her servants. "Everyone leave me." The room darkened. Her balance pitched. "Leave, I need to rest." Alina stumbled farther into her room and Nin yelled at the lingering onlookers to get out. Everything kept coming in and out of focus.

"Your Highness, please lay down." Nin walked toward her.

The room pitched again. "Stay away from me!" Alina stumbled toward the washroom door. *How long has it been? Days? They'll all think I have gone mad.* "I'm ill." Alina felt the handle of the washroom door and pulled. "I need to be alone." Darkness danced in front of her eyes. "I don't want to make a mess on you."

"Your Highness, please trust me," Nin said.

Alina had already stepped beyond the threshold and pulled the door shut. She locked it, the tumblers closing with a satisfying click.

Nin's words echoed in her mind, clashing with what the runes had told her: *Nin is loyal.* "I can't do that," Alina whispered. She sank to her knees and leaned against the cool wall. She breathed deeply, every intake bringing her a little bit farther away from reality.

It crashed down on Alina with tidal-like force, sweeping her from her chambers and flinging her into the unknown. The palace dissolved under her touch, unraveling like thread. Her body hovered in nothingness for a moment and all she knew was the deep, rhythmic breaths she took. Then, like brushstrokes, the world reappeared around her in slow, measured sweeps. She sat on warm sands that sifted underneath her grasp. The cityscape of a foreign land spilled out before her. Rough looking men walked the streets. Thin, hungry, unpolished. Their sallow, sickly skin spoke of a difficult life. Screams drew her gaze to a cart full of even scrawnier human beings, malnourished. They sat bound in shackles.

The world shifted again and she stared at Lord Demek. He sat beside a man as the guest of honor at a feast. The people around him cheered, none of them her countrymen, all of them waited upon by slaves; emaciated people, once proud and now so thin and starved. Alina's breath caught and the images fell away, breaking like grains of sand scattered by a wind. Time flew past her. Fear, betrayal, hurt. She breathed in the emptiness.

And then she breathed in the stale air of her own washroom and everything fell back into place: the floor beneath her, the wall at her back. She heard Nin in the next room knocking against the door and pleading with her. She stood, swaying only a little as she walked over to her mirror. Alina gripped the rim of her countertop as she stared at her own blood-drained face and crystalline eyes. The brown color would return to her irises; it always did. The dark, scattering seer lines fading on her skin worried her most. Usually the marks were confined to her chest. Now they crept up over the low neck-line of her dress. That would not do.

"Your Highness?" Nin's voice pierced her thoughts. Alina shook her head and rubbed her eyelids. *How am I supposed to hide the lines if they had grown? Nin is loyal.* "Please open the door. I do not want to drag the locksmith into this." She could not imagine facing the council or anyone else not with the seer marks. *Nin is loyal.* "Your Highness, I will break this door down to assure your safety." She had to do something before her maid caused a scene. "You have three counts—"

"All right, Nin!" Alina called out. "I'll let you in. But please, promise me you will stay calm." Her heart hammered as she opened the door and stood aside, allowing Nin to walk in before shutting the door again.

"Your Highness, I don't see the need for these theatrics," Nin started. She looked around the room first, observing that there was no vomit or evidence of illness. She then turned to Alina. "I only want to hel—" Her words died in her throat as she caught sight of the seer's marks on Alina's chest.

Alina rushed forward and clapped a hand over Nin's mouth in case the maid screamed. She pushed Nin back into the wall, her grip tight. The girl's eyes widened. "Not a word," she said. "Nin, it is very important that you do not tell anyone what happened just now. It is also important that you never repeat what I am about to tell you." Nin stared at her, breathing heavily through flared nostrils as she nodded. Alina squeezed the woman's face a little. "You will swear it upon your name, Ninian. You will swear it upon the Almighty." When Nin nodded again, Alina lowered her hand, though she still kept the woman pinned.

"I swear on the Almighty," her maid whispered. "I will never betray her Majesty's secrets."

With the words spoken Alina backed away, though she still blocked the only exit for her maid. Nin was shrewd. "Good." Alina nodded and smoothed her hands over her dress in an attempt to compose herself. Her heart raced. She had never done this before. "Nin...". The maid stayed exactly where Alina had pinned her, staring at her wide-eyed. "Nin, I...I am a seer." The words sounded strange passing her lips, coming from her voice. A terrifying secret she had sworn to never reveal now hung between her and Nin, voiced, meaningless.

Nin looked at the faded lines on Alina's chest; she followed the pattern of the vein-like web as it disappeared under her clothes. She finally pushed off the wall and took a step towards her. "How?" she asked.

Alina shook her head. "Nin, you know how seers come into being—"

"I beg your pardon, Majesty," she said. "I meant how have you avoided detection for so long?"

In truth, Alina counted herself extremely lucky for alluding detection for so long. Her evasion had only carried her so far in the isolated tower, and now, in the heartland, she had failed.

"I got lucky." Alina shook her head and thought back to the first time a vision seized her. "I came into my powers when I was eight. I was fortunate enough to be in my room in the middle of the night when it happened." Alina did not mention that her mother had come to her, answering her child's hysterical shrieks when the visions had withdrawn. "I did research, learned what had happened and how to conceal it," she lied. Her mother, a seer as well, had taught her what to do and had warned her that if anyone discovered her gift she would be taken away. Seers of royal blood were not permitted to rule. Though she did not care how Nin chose to perceive her now, she did not want her mother's memory dug up simply because she was a seer in the Royal Court.

"It must have been hard," said Nin. She seemed to be in a daze, only half paying attention to Alina's words. It made the lies come easier.

"It was hard." This was true. "Though living in that keep made things easier." Alina remembered running from servants when a vision drew near. They left her alone for the most part, so they never took offense at her. She also played up being stubborn, royal, and alone. She threw tantrums when servants tried to help her dress. They learned quickly that she wanted nothing to do with them, and they were content to let her be. A spoiled girl with no parents and no future. They did not need to worry about her. Nin stared. Alina drew in a breath. "The visions were almost never a problem when I was little." She paused. "Every time I felt a bad one coming, similar to something like this, I'd run and hide. The attendants did not bother keeping a close eye on me when I was older."

Nin nodded. "How fortunate." The maid seemed upset. Alina worried that she might run and grab a guard. People told terrifying stories about rogue seers.

"Nin, you have to understand I'm not a danger to anyone. The stories about seers needing control and isolation are a lie."

"Of course I know that," said Nin. She took another step closer. "Your Highness, you need to trust me." Nin looked her in the eye and Alina swallowed. Intensity burned in her maid. It made her think she was little more than an asset to Nin, but to what purposes?

"And why is that?" Alina stepped back, suddenly wary of the plain woman. That deep look, the feeling of a trap looming around every corner, Alina knew this look, and Nin bore it. "Who do you answer to?"

Nin sighed and the intense look vanishing. She stopped and sat back on the counter. Alina relaxed a little with the girl a safe distance away, but she remained ready to move. Nin buried her face in her hands a moment before looking back up. "Shall we exchange secrets then?" Nin asked. "As a show of good faith."

What harm is there? Alina nodded. "Very well." She settled down on the edge of the wash bin. "Talk."

Nin rested her chin on her hand and seemed to think over her explanation. "You see the future, correct?"

Alina nodded. "Hence the name seer."

"But there are others gifted with powers, the energy readers, touched by the Almighty so humanity could shape their world. Each has their counterpart." Nin paused and looked down at her feet. "What do you think is your counterpart?"

She opened her mouth to speak, and then paused. Alina did not think seers had a counterpart. "I..."

Nin smiled and laughed. A small laugh, but better than her previous moodiness. "After the Almighty bestowed power over matter to some," she said. It sounded like a recitation. "The Almighty turned to two people. The first one blinked, and when they saw again it was only into the future so that humanity may control their destiny."

"I've heard this," Alina said, recognizing the story her mother had told her.

"You haven't heard the next part. Most people haven't." Alina tilted her head to the side and studied her maid. Nin looked nervous. "The second person put a hand to their heart and felt the warmth there. After, they could stare into the souls of others so that no one would fall prey to a corrupted spirit, and so I see intention."

Alina had to quirk an eyebrow at this claim. Old fables spoke of spirits who would look into a person's heart and punish them for wrong-doing, but she figured the tales were purely fictional to scare children into obedience. "How so?"

Nin picked at the hem of her plain skirt. The fabric frayed at the edges. "It's hard to explain. I suppose it's like how a seer experiences so many different types of visions." Alina remembered seeing the Warrior standing in the markets, how she had not even realized she looked at a phantom, compared to the sickening experience her most recent vision had been. "I look at people and I see different things inside them," Nin said. "I saw the souls of those Warriors today bleed out like ink on a page. One read heat, two earth, and one water. All were well-intentioned individuals."

Alina nodded, staring past the stone floor. "They were...intriguing." Thinking of the woman with the emerald eyes made her face flush.

"It's more than that, though," said Nin. "Their souls pulsed and radiated with such greatness. They are important to you, your Highness, whoever these Warriors are."

"You see greatness in people's souls?" Alina stood from the wash tub and strode around the room.

"I see a person's capacity for good or evil," said Nin. "It usually shines brightest when surrounded by others important in implementing that good or evil."

Alina stopped by the countertop and thrummed her fingers on the surface. "I guess that makes sense." In reality, it sounded insane, but she could not argue, not after experiencing a vision of all things. She thought back to earlier that day, when Demek had kissed her hand. "Why did you pull me away from Lord Demek? Does it have to do with his intentions?"

Nin stared at the opposite wall. Alina knew the woman was deep in thought. When Nin spoke, her voice sounded far away, "It does, I think. His inner intentions are smothered, but it's not like a criminal's soul, or a person's soul that has malicious intent. It's more like a void." Nin closed her eyes. Her head dropped. "It's like something has been removed, most of the time, anyways. Sometimes I see a flicker of what most people should look like, but I don't know what to make of it."

"Is it like he's dead?" Alina asked.

"No, corrupted," said Nin. "Empty and...rotten. It moves through him and tries to latch onto others. For this reason, I do not think you should spend time with him. You should know how temperamental fate can be."

"Have you seen this sort of thing before? I mean, a void where a person's intentions should be doesn't sound common."

"Only once," Nin said. She stood from the counter and smoothed out her skirts. "I saw the same emptiness in one of the visiting delegates from the western kingdom. But it is still not quite the same as Lord Demek. They don't...flicker like he does. He is different for some reason. But when I look at you, your soul speaks of nothing but good intentions. It shines brighter than any of the feeble politicians in that Council." Nin smiled sadly. "This is why you must trust me, your Highness. My service to you is in service to all of the people of Osota."

The words weighed heavy on Alina. The maid's admission only troubled her more. Alina closed her eyes and saw flashes of her recent vision, a warning perhaps? "I need you to get me all the information you can on these people and their kingdom." She opened her eyes and looked at Nin. The maid stared back for a long time before saying anything.

"What aren't you telling me?" Nin asked.

Alina smiled and opened the washroom door. "I will tell you more once I'm sure what fears are logical and which are ungrounded. We can plot a course of action from there."

Nin curtseyed before exiting the washroom. "Yes, your Highness," she said, adopting her simple manner once more. Alina followed after and shut the door. She felt odd about the exchange. She had bartered her information carefully, like a trader of secrets. Apparently, she had learned a few nasty habits from the Council. She groaned and lay down on her bed. The day stretched far too long behind her already.

Chapter Four

SENRI DID NOT LIKE her first night in the barracks. Whenever she tried to sleep, she found herself missing the distinct noises from her village. Instead of crickets and the bleating of cattle, the rustling of others surrounded her, shifting, sneezing, coughing. And when Senri did manage to tune out those sounds, her mind kept her awake with images of the young woman from the fields, the supposed heir to the throne as Yahn had guessed.

The woman had stared at Senri with eyes so wide and confused, as if Senri were an apparition. After the woman left, Nat had nudged Senri and said, "Stunned her with your good looks, eh?"

In the morning, Lanan tugged the sheets off Senri to wake her. She kept her eyes closed until Lanan shook her and sang songs of lusty women in a loud, piercing voice: *"I once knew Lady Madrigal, who invited me to peek under her shawl, so I went for a glance, and she took off my pants—"*

Senri winced and sat up. "I'm awake, alright? Now stop before I have it stuck in my head!"

Lanan laughed and stepped back. "Then get ready. We have barely enough time to eat before you're dragged away for training."

Senri's body ached when she stood, her legs heavy. She squinted against the early morning light creeping through the windows, then groaned and slumped over to her chest of clothes. The lid felt too heavy against her fingers. Lanan opened it for her. Senri pulled out a fresh shirt and trousers.

"Will I need my armor?" she asked.

Lanan nodded. She already piled her own leather and plates on a bed. Senri collected her uniform and they dressed in silence. Lanan hummed to herself as she prepared. Senri rubbed her eyes and pulled the fresh shirt over her head. She walked over to the basin tucked in the corner of their room and splashed cold water on her face. The shock helped a little, though her eyelids still felt heavy and her fingers slipped over the buckles of her armor.

Lanan arched an eyebrow. "Are you okay?"

Senri nodded around a yawn.

"You don't look like you slept."

"I didn't," said Senri. She finished pulling on the rest of her armor and took one last look through her trunk of possessions. She found the small sun gem and held it up to the light, smiling at the way it sparkled before returning it to her chest.

"Why? You have nothing to be nervous about," said Lanan.

Senri ignored the question. The other Warrior finished pulling on her own armor. Senri buckled on her sword. "I suppose I'm not used to the noise."

They left the room, taking a corridor to a large hall where the meals were served. The other soldiers and Warriors crowded the room. The noise of people talking and eating created a steady din. Senri followed Lanan to a table piled with food. She reached for a loaf of bread and tore off a chunk for herself. Lanan reached for an apple. The two ate quietly until Nat sat down across from them with a large thud.

"Good morning!" he said. Senri grunted. He looked thrilled to be there in his shining new armor.

"Morning," said Lanan.

"What's wrong?" Nat asked. He grabbed a pile of grapes.

"She didn't sleep," said Lanan.

"Oh," he said. Senri looked up and Nat winked at her. "Getting into trouble with the locals already?" Senri looked away. Nat laughed.

"Wait, I thought you said it was the noise," said Lanan. Senri stared down at her food with intense concentration. Lanan nudged her. "Could it be there's someone on your mind?"

"Oh, let me guess who it is!" Nat stood up and bumped the table, causing some grapes to roll away from his pile. Senri crossed her arms and buried her face in them. Nat always teased her about being infatuated with someone—well, Vella mostly—whenever presented with the chance. "It is probably that girl who served you dinner last night. Am I right?" Nat asked.

"Who says I was up all night thinking about someone?" Senri

mumbled.

"Senri." Nat slammed his palms on the table. "I've known you forever. You cannot exist without pining after someone."

"Well, I must have been pining after home, then." Senri lifted her head and grabbed some of the stray fruit.

"That's normal enough," said Yahn. He sat down and pulled Nat back into his seat. "It takes a bit to adjust for most people."

"Speak for yourself," said Nat. He corralled his loose food back onto his plate.

Yahn smiled. "You might miss home more after training. If you thought your village trainer had you on a tight schedule, you won't be too pleased with your new one."

Nat popped a grape into his mouth. "Who said I was complaining about the schedule? No, it was excellent there. Lots of space, time to do as I please. But there's only so much one can tolerate of the same fifty people for the duration of your existence." He took a bite out of a peach and chewed. "I like to think of this as a change in scenery, a positive one despite the cost to my freedom."

Senri saw an opening to shift the topic and took it. "By the way, how do we know our schedule?"

Yahn waved the question away. "We've been given orders. Lanan will escort you to your mentor. I'll take city-boy. They'll construct a training regimen from there."

Senri sipped some water. "Easy enough."

"When you work with your mentor, make sure to give it your all the first time," said Lanan. "You won't get a lighter workload if they think you're incompetent."

"Why would I even hold back in the first place?" asked Senri. The two senior Warriors shrugged.

"Newcomers get these strange ideas sometimes," said Lanan. "It never ends well. And besides, we've grown fond of you." She reached out and ruffled Senri's hair. Senri jerked away and smoothed down her locks carefully.

"Watch what you do there," said Nat. "You wouldn't want to ruin her looks in front of all the other recruits." He grinned even as Senri chucked an empty bowl at him.

Yahn shook his head and gulped down some water. "The two of you will be too busy to get involved with anyone."

"He's not serious," said Senri. "He only acts like sex is the only thing on his mind—"

"Which most of the time it is," Nat added.

Senri ignored him. "He gets like this when he is nervous or excited."

"How charming," said Lanan. "Coping with crude humor."

Nat shrugged and finished off the fruit. "There are worse ways." He brushed unruly dark curls away from his forehead.

The four of them finished eating and exited the hall. Outside, the sun barely moved over the horizon, casting the grounds in a dim pallor. Yahn and Nat said their goodbyes and departed. Lanan took Senri over to a gate that led out to an open field, walled off from the other areas. The grass had bald patches in certain areas. Some parts of the ground even looked singed. "So is this where all the heat readers train?"

"They start out here," Lanan replied. They walked toward a small group of Warriors standing near the middle of the field. They mingled with one another in loose formation. Senri hoped this meant she had arrived on time.

"War Master Graus!" called Lanan. She waved at an older man standing separated from the pack. He nodded at her. Lanan placed a hand on Senri's back and nudged her forward. "I have the latest new recruit for you, Senri."

She gave a firmer nudge and Senri stumbled forward. She regained her footing and immediately bowed, afraid to look in the eye someone addressed as War Master. "It is an honor, sir," she said, her weight pressing into one knee as she kneeled.

Her new instructor circled her. The other recruits shuffled around, waiting. A couple whispered. Finally, he said "Rise, Senri."

She did. Her new master stood in front of her, his face sagged and wrinkled, yet somehow still displaying a strong, healthy look. A fire burned in his eyes and his limbs looked taut even when draped in armor. He calculated his every move. No energy wasted. He held her gaze, challenging her with faded ones. Finally, he nodded. "You seem to have a good head on your shoulders. Let's hope the rest of you is in line with your manners." He turned to Lanan and nodded. "You may go now." Senri faced forward as her friend left, trying to remember the small amount of Warrior etiquette she had been taught in her village. It had been a minimal learning experience.

"Rank up," ordered Graus. The fellow Warriors shuffled into

lines, but Senri stayed where she stood. The master studied the lines, then her. "Pelman, move back a row. Senri, take his position for now. If you prove to have a good arm, I might move you to the front. We will be learning unit tactics first, then individual skills."

Senri glanced behind and a space opened at the end of the second line. She fell into rank next to the others, readjusting the sword at her side partly to remind herself it still rested there. Her hands, sweaty, slipped over the pommel. Their village instructor had also glossed over the group tactics. They had not seen a use of it with so few soldiers and such a small space to defend.

"We shall start with unit movement," said Graus. "If you all can move without tripping over one another, we might try something a bit more complex. I know some of you might be tired of this drill." He looked to the older recruits. Senri glanced at the men on either side of her—boys really. They looked unsettled as well. Perhaps she was not so far behind on her training then. "I want you to advance ten steps forward and keep the same formation. This box shape is mostly useless to standard combat, but it will lay the foundation to more complex, necessary formations. March!"

At his order, Senri stepped in line with the boys next to her, trying to measure her distance and keep rhythm. Someone bumped into her from behind. She ended up taking an extra step. At the end, everyone had to jostle themselves into the original place.

Graus smiled at them. "Not completely terrible. But you would be scattered in seconds in a real-life combat situation. Shall we try again?"

Everyone mumbled assent and moved back into position. It would be a long, long day.

***

"Your Highness."

Alina glanced up from the history text. Nin had reentered her chambers after eluding her all morning. "Yes?" she asked, marking the page in her book and setting it aside.

"I come bearing you a gift," Nin said.

"What kind of gift?" Alina furrowed her brow. "If it's another dress, I will throw you over the balcony like I did to the flowers I received this morning." Alina had spent most of the day keeping away worried dignitaries no doubt spurred on by Lord Demek gossiping about her 'illness.' She could barely mask her fury at their empty sympathy. The gifts had almost sent her over the edge.

"No, Highness," said Nin. "Actually, I did spend most of the morning abating fears and preventing the Council from sending a healer to examine you. But that is not my gift."

Alina settled back into her plush armchair. She had never seen Nin so pleased. "Go on," she said.

"Remember when you requested information on the Shedol nation yesterday?".

"Did you find some dusty old text Demek forgot to burn when plotting his evil scheme?"

Nin laughed. "Oh, no, Highness. Wouldn't that be convenient? Actually, I simply went down to the foreign dignitary wing and contacted the diplomat whose nation neighbors Shedol."

"You crafty girl," said Alina. She rose from the armchair. "Did you bring them with? I wish to speak to this person immediately."

"No, Highness," said Nin. "You must not be seen directly receiving dignitaries. You will have much more freedom if the Council perceives your behavior as passive."

"Oh." She looked at her history text to hide her disappointed frown. "Then when do I see them?"

"I've arranged a day of horseback riding for you, Highness," Nin said. "And Lady Vorica from the kingdom Noshon has graciously volunteered to give you lessons."

Alina smiled. "Then we shall begin preparations for a day of riding." Nin pulled out Alina's new riding skirts and helped her get ready. Alina mused over the sheer tact her maid possessed, too much to be a simple servant, as yesterday's confession had revealed. The clothes hugged Alina's body well. At least she had not gotten rid of all her gifts, this one from Orwall. She remembered liking him as a child, and suspected his gifts might come from some deeper well of concern. The alterations to her clothes seemed perfect, but as soon as Nin pulled the new shirt over Alina's head she knew they had a problem. Alina checked her appearance in the mirror and noticed the faded veins peeking over the rim of the collar.

"Someone will see this," she said, pulling the collar down.

Nin looked up from pulling at stray threads and furrowed her brow. "Oh yes, I almost forgot." She set aside the clothes and went to Alina's dresser. Opening a drawer, she tossed a few objects aside until she found something. She lifted a small jar. "This should do it."

"What should do it?" Alina asked as Nin removed the cap. A skin-tone ointment lay inside.

Nin scooped some onto her fingers. "Noblewomen use this to hide blemishes." She approached Alina and pulled down the collar to her shirt more. "Hold still." Carefully, Nin rubbed the ointment into Alina's skin. It felt cold and slick, but dried quickly once Nin rubbed it in. She finished quickly and added a layer of powder to finish the disguise. "This should work," she said, pulling the collar into place. "Just avoid sudden movements until it dries."

Alina put a hand on Nin's. "Thank you. Honestly, I don't know what I would do without you."

Nin paused as she replaced the cap on the jar. "Not all want to see you fail."

They took a less crowded route to the stables. Nin must have sent word ahead, because their horses were ready when they arrived. "Your Highness," said the guard on duty. He covered his heart and nodded.

"Good day," she replied.

"Regent Velora has requested you confine your outing to areas within the palace's reach. The Warrior training fields are open enough for a ride."

Alina sighed and tapped her foot against the ground. She looked to Nin, who showed no sign of concern. "Very well," she said. Nin waited for her to mount her steed before getting on her own horse. "Shall we ride out?" Alina asked. Nin nodded and they both urged their steeds forward. Alina let her mare fall behind Nin's. She did not want to appear overly competent at riding.

They rode out beyond the stables and through a gate into the training fields. Scattered pockets of troops trained. Nin led them in a wide arc away from the majority of them, out towards the tall grass where no one worked. "Lady Vorica has agreed to meet us over here. We shall go through a riding lesson and then be invited to join her for refreshments at her private estate."

Alina nodded. "Smart." Their route adjusted. Alina scanned the field, a group of Warriors marched in block formation, back and forth, over and over. Alina caught the glint of blonde hair and stared. The Warrior from the archery field had beads of sweat covering her face, her eyes narrowed in concentration. Alina looked away.

"Nin," she called, pulling her horse up alongside her maid.

The young maid glanced at her. "Yes, your Highness?"

"Do you know that girl we ran into the other day? The blonde Warrior?"

Nin eyed the training Warriors. "I'm afraid I don't, your Highness. She appeared to be new, though. This is the time of year new recruits arrive." Alina remained silent. They rode on further, stopping at a small, overgrown patch of the field where the only remaining tree stood. It grew tall, its limbs touching the top of the wall, leaves brushing against the stone. Nin cleared her throat. "I can arrange an introduction, if you like."

Alina glanced over at the Warriors again. "No. Not yet. I want to see how things unfold naturally."

"So you two do meet?" Nin asked.

Alina paused. She was not used to people asking her about her visions. "That is…unclear. When the time comes, we will know. You said she is important to me."

"Yes, but I do not see the when," Nin replied. "Sometimes, with the right intelligence, I can orchestrate certain events by making the right people meet."

"Exactly how many people are aware of your kind's existence?" Alina scanned the field for approaching horses.

"We are a well-kept secret." Nin looked away, covering her eyes against the sun. "Look." She pointed at an approaching figure. "Your instructor comes."

The figure moved closer, a woman in flowing clothes on a dark horse. The newcomer urged the steed on at a trot until she pulled alongside Alina and Nin. She slowed the horse to a stop, patting its mane and making cooing sounds in its ear. The woman looked up and smiled at them. Her skin was naturally dark, much like many of the folk living in the grassy fields of the heartland. Her eyes mirrored the tone of rich amber and her dark hair fell in a braid ending at her hip. Her clothes flowed with the wind, cream-colored silks hanging off her body. She looked strikingly different from the handful of westerners Alina had seen. She had expected someone more…elderly.

"Your Highness," she said with a thick accent. "It is an honor."

"It is an honor to meet you, Lady Vorica."

The woman smiled and shook her head. "You may call me

Ashali, if you wish. In my tongue it means 'elder.'"

"But you are so young," Alina said, confused.

The woman laughed. It resonated fullness. "You flatter like a true politician. Now come, show me how heartland royalty rides."

Though Alina thought herself an accomplished rider, she soon learned the many flaws in her own self-taught technique. There had been no riding master in the tower. She remembered stubbornly mounting a horse and demanding a guard take her out. Even if the lesson Nin had arranged served as a cover, it proved useful. They filled two hours, and by then, sweat clung to Alina's forehead. "My, this is challenging."

Lady Vorica seemed to take the hint. "I would be honored if your Highness would join me for refreshments." She bowed slightly.

"Yes, I would like that very much," said Alina. "Nin, prepare my escort. I fear the sun may roast me before we reach her Lady's quarters."

"Yes, Highness." Nin rode her horse ahead while Alina and Vorica rode side by side at a slower gait.

"Your lady-in-waiting is a sharp one," said Vorica.

"She is," Alina replied. She scanned the field, but the Warriors had moved somewhere else.

"She speaks of you with high regard."

"Does she?" asked Alina.

The diplomat nodded. "She says you seek knowledge, to know of my people and their strife."

"How am I to rule without knowledge of my surrounding allies?" Alina asked.

The diplomat laughed again. She bent in her saddle and shook her head. "You have a talent for tact and care. You might outlast the politicians yet."

"Might?" Alina furrowed her brow.

"You have been raised with these political animals. You move as they move."

"I'm different. I care."

"Time will show that," said Vorica.

They reached the end of the field and continued riding out to the stables. Nin waited there with a mounted escort of two guards who led them into the city. Alina dreaded her visits out of the palace. The citizens suffered in the streets, and she felt moved to do something silly, like toss her jewels at the beggars. That would only make them a target for robbery or exploitation, though. No, she had to find much more discreet ways to help her people. She would not let them transform into the emaciated ghosts from her vision.

This ride through the city, however, remained uneventful, since they stayed in the upper echelons where dignitaries and high-ranking nobles lived. Lady Vorica's home laid on a sprawling piece of land complete with a stable and attendants who received their horses. Unlike many of the dignitary homes, this one felt welcoming rather than opulent.

"This way, your Highness," said Vorica, once Alina had dismounted. She directed them along a garden path up to a side entrance of her home.

Alina left her guards at the door, instructing them to keep watch for followers. With only the three of them and Vorica's attendants around, Alina breathed easier. The home comforted her too, smaller than the sprawling castle, warmer, with thick, cozy rugs covering the tiled floor.

"Shall we take tea in my private study?" asked the diplomat.

"Yes, please," said Alina. She glanced around at the oddities decorating the home. Porcelain objects sat on the shelves, miniature sculptures of creatures she had never seen. Tapestries hung on display, the whirling, warm patterns so different from the jagged edges of the palace's art. "Your home is lovely."

"Thank you," said Vorica. "Have a seat anywhere you prefer," she said, gesturing openly. She grabbed a tray of tea and carried it over to their table before seating herself from across Alina and Nin. She kneeled into a cushion and took up the steaming teapot, tipping its contents into the three cups. When all were full, she placed the pot down again and lifted a cup in both hands to pass to Alina. "When I was a girl, my mother taught me that there is nothing more valuable in negotiations than being able to serve tea well."

Alina took the cup from her and smelled the hot liquid. She almost hummed when she detected cinnamon and other spices mixed together. Sipping the contents, she found it tasted strong, but good. "This is excellent," she said. Nin took a sip from her cup and nodded.

"Thank you," said Vorica. "It is not often I entertain such pleasant company." The diplomat lifted her own cup and took a sip.

"Now." She set it back down on the plate. "You are here for more than tea."

"The people from across the sea, the ones in negotiations with the Council right now... the ones from Shedol." Vorica nodded for Alina to continue. "What can you tell me about them?"

The diplomat looked down at her folded hands then back at Alina. "They are a troubled people," she said. "Their land holds very little resources, which caused them to live in clans, very splintered, primitive." Alina remembered the dark, barren surroundings from her vision. The rough-cut table, the dryness, a total absence of life. "But they managed, trading what they could with whom they could. We do not prefer to do business with them. They are slavers." The admission made Alina's stomach clench with worry.

"Who do they enslave?" Nin asked. "Not their own."

Vorica shook her head. "Sometimes their own. Mostly they trade ores they mine out of the barrens for slave labor. Though I doubt your country is trading its people," said Vorica. Alina's face must have paled because her skin grew cold. The nightmarish vision troubled her. "I suspect they are bartering ores for foodstuffs. However, you should advise your Council against business with them."

Alina considered this and took a sip of tea. Vorica seemed quite familiar with their customs, and the Council would never be stupid enough to enter into slave trade. "Your conviction is strong."

"And earned," said the diplomat. "They are raiders, vicious warriors. My country barely holds its bordering villages against them now. It used to be a few stray bands to chase off; now they attack with tactics and thousands of men. They have been united under someone."

Nin placed down her teacup. "Have you voiced these concerns to the Council?"

"Many times," said the woman. "But I am not from the heartland. My opinion only goes so far. Certain members have accused me of fearing a powerful alliance between my two neighboring countries."

"And do you?" Alina asked. She held Vorica's gaze despite the dizziness she felt. The vision threatened to overwhelm her once more. She inhaled slowly through her nose in an attempt to keep her focus.

"I fear the armies of Shedol," said the diplomat. "I fear power in the wrong hands. And I think we share those fears. Perhaps your Council shares them as well. Not all alliances and trade agreements are made willingly." She lifted up the teapot. "May I offer you more?"

Alina shook her head and placed down her cup. "No. Thank you for everything. We must return to the palace. We don't want the Council in an uproar over my disappearance."

Lady Vorica smirked. "The Council has been in an uproar ever since you were fetched."

Alina laughed and rose from her seat. She bowed her head like she had observed the servant do. "Thank you again."

The diplomat opened the door for them. "I hope you found everything you were looking for. One of my maids will show you to the stables."

As Alina and Nin were led away, the maid leaned into her and asked, "Was this acceptable, your Highness?"

Alina watched a stable boy run to fetch their horses. "It was. Nin, I need to tell you what I saw." Neither of them spoke further. Instead, Alina listened to the pounding of her own heart on the ride back to the palace.

Chapter Five

IN THE FIRST FEW days of training, Senri managed to keep pace with her instructor. By the fifth day, her arms felt far too heavy to lift on their own, let alone use a sword. Still, she put on her armor and went to the training field as instructed, the same field from the first day. She remembered seeing the princess ride by, or the queen-to-be, or whatever royalty she was. The woman had held Senri's gaze again. Senri had only been able to sneak glances, drinking in small sights of the flowing brown hair and the retreating frame balancing on a horse. She had stopped when her instructor had asked if they should practice their drills for the nobility.

Only Graus waited at the field for her. "Welcome, Senri," he called out, waving her over.

She approached the master. "Where are the other soldiers?"

"We start individual training today," Graus replied. "An assessment of combat skills. We would rather you fight the experienced than each other. Less casualties." He chuckled while Senri stood awkwardly in the grass until she remembered to keep the posture he had shown them. "Well, draw your weapon." He pulled his sword from the scabbard. "Show me what you can do."

Senri pulled her sword, trying not to show the fatigue wearing her down. They had yet to work with weapons. "When do we start?"

"Now!" He lunged forward, his stooped body suddenly powerful, filling out the armor with hidden muscle. Senri raised her sword and blocked, pushing the blade to the side rather than using force. She wished she had a shield, her empty left hand feeling useless at her side. Graus swung at her again and she once again deflected.

"Where's your offense?" he yelled.

Senri backed away, putting space between them. She felt the heat rushing to her palms, rushing through the sword. She would not have to be on the defensive if this strategy worked, but did not know how her mentor would handle losing a sword. She attacked, but he deflected it. She had to side-step the counter. She needed to keep him playing with her for just a bit longer. She pointed to his midsection for a thrust and circled under his sword arm and up, going for the exposed collarbone. He stepped back and blocked her sword, too quick for disengages, but what should she expect from an instructor? The metal in her sword had heated quickly, leaving sizable dents in the master's.

The next time he came at her she tried a press attack, blocking his blade and taking it with her pommel as she charged him down. He twisted his sword out of this and backed away. Senri's arm ached. "Do I meet expectations?"

Graus swatted at her with his blade. She blocked. "No talking in combat," he said.

Senri breathed deeply, working up a sweat. Fatigue would catch up to her soon. She had to end the fight somehow, make a stalemate. She concentrated on the burning in her fingertips, the hot metal of her sword. When she attacked Graus again, she feinted heavily into his left. She pulled back and cut down, knowing she would never reach him, aiming for his sword.

Her superheated blade cut through his, leaving a bent, ruined piece of metal curling over itself when she pulled her blade away. Graus looked down at the weapon and laughed, tossing it aside to lay smoking in the grass. "You figured that one out then?" Senri sheathed her own sword. "Very clever. Lucky for you I was not using a tempered blade. My combat sword also resists warping at higher temperatures." He kicked the ruined piece of gear. "This slag is hardly worth what it costs to forge."

"So why use it against me?" asked Senri.

"I wanted to see your party tricks." Graus rubbed his graying beard. "Tell me, can you read the heat within other beings?"

"Can I what?" asked Senri.

"What all can you do as a reader?"

"I push heat into other objects through touch." Senri looked out at her hands, the pulsing heat dissipating. "That's about it."

"We have some work to do then," Graus said. When Senri

frowned, he added, "Which is good, considering how quick you are in single combat. We need to work on something else with you."

Senri still frowned, but she felt better hearing him acknowledge her skills. Swordplay had been something her village praised her for. "What can I do as a heat reader then? Besides start fires."

"You can quell them, for one," Graus said. He kneeled down in the grass, pressing his hand into the earth. The crackling and smoke came before the flames biting into the field in front of him. "Draw the heat from it," he said, standing up and brushing himself off.

"I don't know how," said Senri. She stared at the fire, watching it grow bigger and remembering her failed attempt on the journey to the capital.

"Of course you do," said Graus. "You were able to withdraw the heat from your hand and thus from your sword."

"Yes, but that's different," said Senri.

"How so?" His thick eyebrows set themselves low, making him look irritated.

"It's…it's metal. It conducts heat. This is an actual fire." Senri gestured at the growing flames.

"So conduct the heat out of it," said Graus.

"It's not that simple."

"Are you disagreeing with me?"

The fire crackled. It spread through the grass, struggling against the hearty green blades.

"Fine," she muttered, kneeling down.

Senri pulled off the plating on her forearm and rolled up her sleeve. Unlike controlling the heat in one part of her body, she had no idea if she could contain a live fire to just her palm. With her forearm bare, she stuck her hand into the flames, the heat licking her cool skin. She drew in a breath, balancing out her hand's temperature with the flame to avoid damage. She concentrated on the fire, how it sucked in oxygen. She searched for the source of heat, where it burned hottest. Finding it growing from the center of the flames, she held her palm over it, willing the heat to come into her hand. It refused to budge and she pressed her hand down, smothering the flame instead.

"Well, now that is cheating." Graus chuckled.

Senri stood and brushed herself off, rolling her sleeve down and staring at the charred grass. "I couldn't do it. I don't know how."

Graus sighed and clapped her on the shoulder. "We will work on it. Tell me about it though, the sensation."

Senri related the feeling of the hottest part of the fire, its search for oxygen, knowing where it was hottest. "It wouldn't budge," she said.

Her mentor stroked his beard and nodded. "Well, at least you are on the right track." He looked up at the sky, shading his eyes with his hand. "We have more work to do, of course. Your swordplay needs refinement and I have some exercises to hone your skills as a heat reader." He looked once more to the ruined sword of his. "For now, go get me another blade. Your session is not yet over."

***

"We bring to order this session of the Council," declared the head Councilor. Alina sat off to the side rather than stand in the center of the room. It felt good to sit in the shadows behind Councilor Orwall. She only had to endure the occasional awkward glances from other Councilors rather than the full brunt of their stare. "Continuing from our last session, we shall conclude discussing preliminary trade agreements with the kingdom of Shedol. Is the dignitary present?"

A man seated on the other side of the Council stood. He wore flowing robes and a wrap that extended up over his head, making only his face visible. "As you requested, Councilor," he said with a small bow of his head. "I am here and ready to finalize our agreement."

Alina leaned forward in the seat. This man seemed much more refined than his other visiting westerners, his accent smoother. Still, something about his presence made her squirm. She tried to ignore the feeling.

The head Councilor unrolled a length of parchment, setting weights down on the edges. "The trade agreement reads as follows…" Alina rolled her eyes. The Council could make the most important of tasks seem tedious. "Whereas Osota shall exchange these grains for the following weapons…"

So it is the metal. She had heard rumors of the troubles miners faced. Many of the expeditions in search of new ore had yielded nothing. While the man droned on about exchange rates and specific clauses, Alina looked around the room. Many of the Councilors stared at the speaker, and those who did not watched the diplomat from Shedol.

Half-listening, she moved her seat back further into the shadows. No one paid attention. Orwall had the responsibility of watching her and he had decided she was too old to need watching. She looked around. Behind her, the floor curved up and away, behind the other Council seats. Alina stood from her chair and slowly lowered herself to behind the pedestals.

"I'm sorry, Councilor, but please hold a moment." Alina froze. Her heart hammered against her ribs. Nin had warned her against something like this, but she needed more information to act on. "I have to disagree on that last clause listed."

Chatter broke out amongst the Councilors and Alina exhaled a held breath. As the Councilors argued, she crept along the backside of the room, following the curve of the wall. She reached Gosman's riser and noticed a pile of papers laid by his chair. He attempted to yell over the other voices. She reached out and withdrew a few pieces of parchment from the stack before ducking underneath the riser. Out of sight, she knelt down and opened the document. As hard as she tried, her breathing sounded loud in her own ears. Every heartbeat resonated like a thunderous clap in her body. She decided she hated stealth.

Only the largest paper held promise, a map of the heartlands. Many of the familiar landmarks and locations were filled in on it, plus a few extra notes Gosman had made. Alina scanned them, finding nothing of interest until she reached the western edge of the map. There, written in small text, inked the words *territory camp*. She did not know the jargon. She had never seen someone notate this specific way on a map before. It had to be a personal invention of Gosman's. She stared at the spot on the map, trying to commit it to memory. If Gosman was involved in anything devious, that spot on the map would reveal it, and Alina suspected he might be more heavily involved with the visiting dignitaries than he let on. The marker lay just off the coast, bordering the scrubland and wheat fields. Once she felt she could relocate it on another map, she refolded all the papers and crawled out from under the riser. The Councilors still fought with one another, though the roar had come down to only a few voices. Alina tucked the papers back where she had found them and returned to her seat. Orwall still conversed with the other Councilors.

"I understand that we need basic items for defense," said Orwall. "However, I will not allow the trade for those items to rob us in the process."

"This percentage has been negotiated down significantly," said Gosman. "We will get nowhere if we continue to bicker over small margins."

"Councilors," the Shedol diplomat spoke. They quieted. "I can understand hesitation over the proposed agreement. If it will please Councilor Orwall, we are willing to consent to a small reduction in the amount of grain traded for swords."

No one protested. Alina folded her hands in her lap, watching them think it over.

"That is a generous compromise," said Councilor Tarish. "We will have to discuss the details once Lord Demek is present."

The head Councilor spoke again. "If there are no further complaints, we shall move along to the next order of business." He shuffled through his papers. Alina let her thoughts wander. If she paid attention, she would get angry at the injustice of their tactics and then she would make a scene. She looked across the room to the diplomat from Shedol. He watched the other Councilors, as if there was nothing more fascinating than discussing tax rates.

Alina leaned back in her chair and looked at the floor, frowning. She had not been born with a strong desire to lead. She hated listening to the politicians when she was little, still hated it. She'd rather be direct about a problem, while they always wanted to compromise and weave around sensitive issues. Her father taught her to care though, he had convinced her of the beauty of Osota.

She thought back to the long rides he would take her to the villages and how he would reach out to the commoners on behalf of the crown. Those trips remained precious in her memories. Her and her father would dance with the farmers and sit with them at the feasts rather than at a head table, isolated. He would always lean down to her and say, "These are your people, Alina. One day, you will need to care for them."

Alina shook her head, blinking away the thought. While the trips had been fun, she always felt an enormous sense of responsibility had been handed down to her. Her father had possessed the common touch. Even more, he had seen the struggles of Osota and had taken actions to remedy them. *I try to care for my people, but it is impossible when half the men in this room are so unfamiliar with the real Osota.* Alina ground her teeth. She wished Nin could sit with her in this stuffy, unbearable room. Nin would say something witty against the Councilors and the two of them would have a good laugh.

Finally, the session came to an end. Alina's jaw ached. Still, the meeting had been a success for her. Alina rose with everyone and took Orwall's offered arm. A kind man, she tolerated him much more than many of the Council members. "Did her Majesty enjoy the session?"

She smiled up at him. "Yes, it was enjoyable to witness diplomacy at work."

Orwall laughed as he escorted her out of the room. "You are far too kind. There are moments I wish to beat my brow upon a wall rather than argue with them any further." They paused in the large hallway. "You are lucky. I wish I possessed such patience." Alina nodded. Nin approached with another guard to escort her back to her chambers. Before he let go, Orwall dipped his head down to her ear and whispered, "Though you would do better to remain in your seat, next time."

Before she could say anything, he passed her along to Nin, bidding his farewell. Still stunned, she barely managed to turn and say, "Farewell, Councilor Orwall." Even then, her voice wavered. As they walked away, Nin raised a questioning eyebrow, but Alina shook her head and glanced over at the guard. Nin gave a slight nod.

Once they reached her quarters and excused the guard to the hallway, Nin spoke, "What did Orwall say to you?"

Alina sat down at her dresser, removing the jewelry she had put on for the session. "He informed me to stay seated next time," she said, trying to sound casual.

"You did not," Nin said, moving to the side of the dresser. "You were sneaking around in there after I told you to make no such attempt." Alina opened a drawer and pulled out her own folded and worn map. She shook it out and opened it on the top of the dresser. "Did anyone else see you?" Nin asked.

Alina pulled a quill and ink bottle over, then began scanning the western edge of the map. Her map was slightly larger than Gosman's, so she moved slightly inland, looking for the landmarks that had framed his own. "I doubt anyone saw," said Alina. "And even though

Orwall saw me, he did not see what I did. It was impossible for him to see me behind Gosman's riser."

"Did you take anything from Gosman?" Nin asked.

In the past few days, Alina had insisted Nin drop formalities when they were alone, but the incessant interrogation made her want to order the maid to start referring to her as 'your Highness.'

"Of course not," she said. "I am not a complete failure at espionage. I looked at one of his documents, a map." She gestured to the paper in front of her. "It only had one special marking on it…here." She circled the rough area where the *territory camp* had been. "After, I replaced the map and returned to my seat. I swear no one else saw me."

"It was still an unwise risk," said Nin, studying the spot on the map. "Territory camp. What is that?"

"It's what the map said." Alina put away the quill and ink.

"That…sounds vague and intriguing," said Nin. She peered over the paper. Alina had told her about the vision of Shedol taking Osotan slaves. While Nin said she had not heard any news of this in the agreements passed around, she had been open to further investigation on her own terms.

"Which is why we need to send someone to check it out," Alina said. She looked down at the map. "Gosman and the other Councilors are hiding something from me. Even Orwall, though he's much kinder about it than the others. Whatever it is they are hiding, it must be troublesome at least." She shifted in her chair to study Nin and clapped her hands together. "So, I want it to appear as though the camp was stumbled upon, and no large forces are to be sent. I think we will do better if a small group discovers it. That way there is no cause for confrontation."

"And if the group gets captured or overwhelmed?" Nin asked.

"You will have to make sure they have orders not to engage any unknowns," said Alina. "I fear what may happen if we send guards out there. I cannot think of an excuse that would not cause suspicion. But I do not know anyone else we could send."

Nin crossed her arms, her brows furrowed. "I do."

"Who?"

Nin shook her head. "I'd rather you not know. The less you are tied to this, the safer you remain."

With a sigh, Alina leaned back in her chair. "Very well. Go ahead and have your mystery and intrigue."

"I will," said Nin. She picked up the map and folded it into a neat square. "If there is nothing else you require, I have a scheme to set in motion."

"Off with you," Alina said, waving her hand.

Nin fetched her cloak and satchel, then tucked the map in a hidden pocket on the inside of her skirts and left. Alina remained at her dresser, staring at the plush carpet. Her heart raced. The plotting, the sneaking, she did it all so easy in the moment. But left alone with her thoughts, she had to wonder if it was acceptable. *I gamble with many lives and to what end?* The memory of the vision flashed before her: the slaves, ruin, and corruption. Nin had been horrified when she explained the vision. But something more formed a pit of fear inside Alina. Yes, she worked to stop this, but how did she expect to achieve such a goal when every vision she witnessed had come true?

Michelle Magly

Chapter Six

"WHAT DO YOU HAVE there?" Senri asked, sitting down at the table with Nat and the other Warriors.

Yahn eyed a thick sheaf of papers while he ate the midday meal. "Orders for a field exercise," he said.

"Involving who?" Senri grabbed some fruit, while Nat took a loaf of bread to eat. Basic training still filled their mornings, while individual practice or mentoring sessions took over their evenings. Senri had yet to make any improvement with Graus over the last few days. She feared Graus's frustration over her lack of progress.

"That's the strange thing," he said. "They've picked the four of us to do it."

Nat looked up from his plate. "Meaning you, me, and the girls?" He nodded towards Senri.

"Yes. I guess Valk must have liked the way we worked together. Figured if me and Lanan are watching you two, everyone will come back alive."

"From what?" asked Lanan. She sat down by Yahn, running a damp cloth through her soaked hair. She helped redirect a canal early that morning, much to Valk's displeasure. He tended to grumble whenever a Warrior did something non-combat related. She leaned over and read the paper. "A field exercise with those two? I thought they would assign a mentor for something like that."

Yahn shrugged. "They have been busier than usual, and we are fairly reliable."

Nat laughed around his food. "Sure you are. No offense, Yahn. It is more Lanan than you."

"I resent that statement," said Lanan. She threw her cloth at Nat, who caught it and slapped it back on the table. Nat lifted his cup to his lips. Lanan laughed. "Perhaps I will make your cup of water attack your throat on the next swallow."

Nat froze and put the cup down. "You can't do that."

Lanan raised a challenging eyebrow.

"Well, what's the field assignment?" Senri redirected the conversation, setting aside her breakfast for the moment.

"Routine patrol," said Yahn. "We aren't even approaching the border or the woods." He spread a map on the table indicating a western route looping a wide arc. "Perhaps a ten-day's journey to and back."

"That's awful long." Lanan scanned the route once more.

"It's a rather out of the way destination," said Yahn. "It will give us time to reflect and know the land."

"I can't wait," said Senri in relief. "I don't know how much longer I can stand Graus hanging his head in shame every time I fail to magic the fire away."

"It's not magic," said Nat, eyeing the cup of water and swallowing. "Someone was saying other masters of heat can do it."

"Am I a master?" asked Senri. "No. "

"Don't bother worrying about it," said Yahn. He picked up the map and tucked it back in with the other papers. "Graus expects the best out of everyone."

"I had no idea," Senri said, rolling her eyes. "When do we depart?"

"We have leave to do so immediately," said Yahn. "The supplies and mounts are already prepared for us."

"That was quick," said Nat. He finally drank some water. Lanan winked at him from across the table. He put the cup down once again. "I swear, I'll run dry from fear."

"Can we leave today then?" Senri asked.

Yahn looked over at Lanan. "Would that work for you?"

Lanan took the papers from him and glanced through them. "I suppose, this seems fairly standard. Sounds like a lovely rest."

"I'm going to pack my things, then." Senri rose from the table. "See you all at the stables."

In truth, Senri could not get away from the training grounds fast enough. She could barely take the pressure Graus put on her. She did not know why he expected so much of her. When she had asked another heat reader what Graus taught him, he had described some sword fighting techniques Graus had skimmed over with her. Senri had been too scared to ask any other readers of their progress.

In her room, she packed what remained of her mother's spices and extra clothes. Supplies had been set aside for them. She already wore her armor and sword, but before she left, she grabbed a hunting bow and arrows. They would need to replenish meat. She walked down the corridor, lost in thought, and nearly ran into Lanan.

The older woman grabbed her shoulder. "Woah, slow down."

"Sorry." Senri tried to move past, but Lanan kept her still.

"Why are you in such a rush to leave?"

Senri looked down. "I just need to get out, you know? Move around." She shrugged her shoulder in an attempt to dislodge Lanan's hand. She wanted to be left alone.

Lanan let go, but didn't go to her room. "I'm here, you know, if you want to talk or anything."

Senri's cheeks felt hot. She blinked, trying to will away the blush. "I'm going to get my horse ready." Did they all think she was some fragile child that needed watching? She retreated to the outer courtyard, walking down to the stables. The midday sun beat down on her.

Just as the note had said, four horses had been prepared for them at the stables. Senri found Stomps saddled, laden with supplies, and ready with the others. She smiled, grateful Valk had remembered her companion. The horse tossed his mane, and Senri patted his snout. "I've missed you," she said. Stomps flicked his ears. "Have they treated you well? Gotten enough to eat?" She had not been able to visit him since her training, much less ride him. But Stomps had been well-groomed and seemed to be the same weight as she had left him. The horse snorted hot air into her hand. She laughed.

"I never had a horse of my own." Senri knew the voice. *Lanan.* Obviously she had done a rush job packing as well. "What did you say his name was? Pounce?"

"Stomps. I gave him the name when I was younger." Stomps leaned forward and rubbed against her forehead. She chuckled and pulled away. "He would always paw the ground when I came out for a ride, like he was excited. He could have been nervous too, I guess. He was very young at the time."

"He seems sweet," said Lanan. She selected a brown mare and

tied her travel bag to its saddle.

"He's...interesting," said Senri. "He has his quirks, but yes, I suppose sweet is in there as well." She loaded her own supplies onto his back. "Are Yahn and Nat on their way?"

"They'll be a few more minutes," said Lanan. "They wanted to finish eating first."

"Boys," Senri muttered.

Lanan smiled. "I would have stayed too, if you had not left in such a rush."

Senri's fingers froze with the knot they tied. She turned to the other Warrior. "Did Nat say anything?"

Lanan shook her head. "He's clueless. I, on the other hand, possess proper empathy."

"You're an interesting woman, you know that?" Senri resumed securing her supplies, hunting for a spot for her arrows on the already packed saddle.

"Are you coming on to me?" Lanan ran a hand through her short black hair. "If so, you're terrible at it."

Heat snaked up Senri's cheeks. Lanan teased her, she knew. Still, something about the thought of them being romantically involved felt extremely...awkward to her. She shook the thought from her mind. No, Lanan seemed far too like herself. Senri cleared her throat. "I'm not really trying with you. Maybe if you grew your hair out."

Lanan laughed. "Is that what I've been doing wrong? I see how it is. You like the girly ones with the dresses and the long hair flowing in the wind."

"At least I know what I like." Senri slipped the bow onto the horn of the saddle.

"I'm simply not as choosy as you," Lanan replied. "And not that it matters, but I am currently spoken for." The two shared a smile, and though Senri shook her head, she could not help feeling better. Lanan leaned on her horse. "Anyway, what has you so eager to leave?"

Senri groaned and rested her head against the saddle. *Curse Lanan and all her persistence.* "If I explain, will you leave it be?"

"I swear on my honor as a Warrior."

"All right." Senri patted Stomps's side, looking for a distraction. "I...I don't know if I measure up to the other recruits."

After a long pause, Lanan asked, "You mean in regards to

progress in your training?"

Senri nodded. "It sounds ridiculous, but I'm afraid that if I never improve they will send me home."

"They won't do that," said Lanan. The speed of her answer caught Senri off guard. She turned to the older woman and raised an eyebrow. Lanan shifted a bag on her mare's saddle. "I mean, they might not let you fight if you are not fit for combat, but they find a use for you. We readers are far too few to be wasted. You are a valuable member of the Warriors as long as you still draw breath."

Senri frowned. "So what will they send me to do if I cannot fulfill my master's training requirements? As I recall, Valk seemed irked at the thought of a Warrior being anything but."

"You could work in a forge, I suppose," said Lanan. "Most of the heat readers here are also our blacksmiths. And don't listen to Valk. His views on our use are too impractical to carry any weight with the other masters."

Senri wanted to probe further, but Yahn and Nat joined them, making a very loud entrance into the stables.

Nat grinned. "Here we are again, ready for a grand adventure."

"Yes, as grand as patrolling the grassland can be," said Yahn, throwing his pack onto a horse's saddle. "One would think we would be sent to take care of bandits." He swung up into his saddle. Senri mounted Stomps as well. "Are we all ready?" asked Yahn, turning in his saddle.

Nat finally settled himself on his horse. He picked up his reins. "Yes."

"Let's not waste any more time then." Yahn flicked his reins and the four of them steered their horses out of the stables and beyond the Warrior's encampment. Once out on the road, Yahn directed them to a path heading west. "We'll follow this for a day or so, then break off as the route requires. There should be enough land marks to make our way through and back without much trouble."

The riding helped Senri. The knot of fear within her slowly untangled itself as they moved along the wide dirt road. The dry land billowed dust up around them as they rode. A hot wind blew at their backs. Senri found herself swallowing and reaching for a water skin. The route followed a small stream. They stopped beside it that the evening to water their horses.

"I have never been in such dry heat," said Senri, dismounting her horse. Stomps dipped his head into the water and drank.

"Hand me your water skin," said Lanan. Her face glistened with sweat and grit. Senri tossed the near-empty sack over and Lanan lowered its mouth to the water. Lanan skimmed her fingertips across the surface and a small section of the current flowed backwards. "This method helps remove impurities," said Lanan. "I'd rather not wait for a kettle to boil. We have a bit of a ride ahead of us."

"The dust has gotten worse," said Yahn. He walked over to Lanan and handed her his and Nat's water skins. She tossed the full one back to Senri and started on the others.

"It was better, I take it?" Senri patted Stomps's shaking flank.

"This is farmland." Yahn wiped his brow. "They are supposed to get some rain. Enough to keep the soil healthy." After filling the water and splashing their faces clean, Yahn instructed them to mount up again. "There's a residence a few hours away that will lodge us for the night."

They rode at a slower pace, the horses heaving under the burdening heat. The air stilled. The fields of yellow grass turn into organized rows of yellowing crops. Workers moved between the rows, creating irrigation canals. Water readers like Lanan pulled gentle waves over the soil, into the heart of the field before releasing the water once more. Senri had realized Osota was not as well off as a kingdom since she came to the heartland. They faced many struggles, some of which Senri did not know if they would overcome or not. She could not vanquish drought with a sword.

The sun dipped below the horizon, but Yahn continued on, until the twilight hour had almost faded. They turned off the main road and to a small farmhouse. Yahn dismounted and turned to them. "Wait here." He walked up to the porch and knocked on the door. Firelight flickered through a window. She squinted against the glare of the last of the sun rays, trying to see if anyone moved around within. A woman came to the door. After Yahn muttered something she embraced him. She waved at the other Warriors.

"Come inside," she called. As they dismounted, a man exited the house. He clapped Yahn on the shoulder and walked over to the rest of them.

"I'll stable your horses if you want to head inside," he said, gesturing at the doorway. They followed Yahn into the cottage, but stopped in the mud room to kick off their boots. Voices chattered in the next room and Senri followed Lanan through the doorway. Yahn stood with the same woman and two children. The kids grabbed at his armor and sword, hanging from his arms. The woman scolded them while she chopped vegetables at a counter, but Yahn laughed.

"Let them play," he said.

The woman smiled and caught sight of them standing at the doorway. "Oh, come in," she said. "Sit by the fire." Senri cautiously selected a chair. Lanan and Nat sat beside her. Senri inhaled and caught the scent of soup. A dark cauldron sat in the flames of the fireplace. She could only guess it held soup. "And you were saying you rode out today?" the woman asked Yahn. He nodded. "Such a large party for a patrol." She gathered the vegetables and dumped them into the cauldron..

"They're new recruits," Yahn replied.

Senri looked around the farmhouse. It was small and warm. Dried herbs hung from the ceiling along with fresh vegetables. The woman gathered bowls and ladled soup into them. She placed a bowl and spoon in front of Senri. She looked down at the broth filled with vegetables and meat. "Thank you..."

"Mara, I'm Mara," she said, handing soup to the others. She moved to the opposite end of the kitchen, grabbing cups and a pitcher of water from the many cabinets.

Senri tried the soup. It was warm, and very good. She bit into a potato, savoring the soft, crumbly texture. She tasted rabbit mixed in as well. "This is amazing," she said, taking a sip of the broth. Better than any rabbit stew they had forced down on the ride into the capital.

Yahn refused a bowl that Mara offered. He still let the children hang from his arms. "I'm alright for now. Is Onera around?"

The children began singing, *'Onera, Onera, my one and only true! I tell thee my heart beats only for you!"*

Chuckling, Yahn shook the little ones from his arms. "You too are far too energetic for so late at night." He placed his hands on his hips. "I'll just tell your father to work you both harder."

"Both of you, off to bed before I get your father to think up night chores," Mara scolded. The threat sent them running down the hall, their feet thudding like hooves. Mara smiled and pulled her wispy dark hair back. "Such energy," she sighed. She turned to Yahn. "Onera will be in soon. You might as well sit while you wait."

Boots thudded on the porch outside and the door opened. "Horses are stabled," said the man from earlier. "And they've plenty of hay for the night."

Mara gestured to the crowded table. "Thank you, Jathan. Meet our houseguests."

Jathan nodded rubbing his thin beard. He eyed the cauldron. "Is there anything left for me?" he asked, eying the cauldron.

Mara set a bowl down in front of Yahn, shoving a spoon into his hand. "There's plenty left." She handed him a bowl. Her husband kissed her on the cheek.

"I'm going to turn in," he said, taking the bowl with him into the back of the house.

Mara put a loaf of bread on the table and Nat reached for it, eyes wide, but Yahn stopped him. "You give too much," he said, picking the loaf up and handing it to Mara. "We have our own supplies." Yahn let the bread stay on the table, though he shook his head ever so slightly when Nat went to take half the loaf. Nat caught the glare and shortened his taking to a reasonable portion of the heel. Yahn had yet to touch his own serving. Senri reached the bottom of her bowl too quickly and used a hunk of bread to soak up the remaining broth. Even though she knew seconds were available, she did not want to face Yahn's disapproving stare.

While they finished their meal, someone else entered from the rear of the house. "Mara?" called out a woman's voice. "I'm in from the field. The soup smells lovely by the way." The voice drew closer and Yahn rose in his seat.

"We have visitors, Onera," warned Mara. She had grabbed another bowl, scrubbed it clean, and filled it with the last of the stew.

"Oh? Anyone I know?"

A young tanned woman with golden-brown hair stepped out from the shadowed hallway, her flaxen skirt brushing over her legs. Mara shoved a bowl into her hands, but the young woman's eyes widened when she saw Yahn standing in wait for her. She stopped mid-gait.

"Yahn and the new recruits are on a field assignment," said Mara, disappearing into the kitchen.

"Hello, Onera." Yahn shifted from one foot to the other. Senri smiled, she could not remember ever seeing him nervous.

"You're here," she said. The woman's face showed no response.

"Has something happened?"

"No," said Yahn. He smiled, but did not take a step forward. "We are lodging for the night while on a patrol." He gestured toward the worn bench. "Won't you sit with us?"

Onera finally smiled, one to match Yahn's and shook her head. "Of course." She came to the table and placed her bowl down. She embraced Yahn. His cheeks turned red before he returned the hug. "I've missed you," she said, pulling away. As they both sat down, Lanan shot Senri a confused look across the table.

"Onera," said Lanan.

The woman looked up from her soup. "Yes?"

"I've met you before." Lanan, rested her chin in her hand.

"I'm a Warrior. You may have seen me in training."

"But why are you in farmer's garb then?" Nat had finally stopped eating enough to join in on the conversation, though Senri knew he would still be hungry.

"I read plant life, energy," Onera said. She swung a leg over one side of the bench. "Watch."

Senri leaned over to the side as Onera press a dirt-smeared hand into one of the crevices in the floor. At first, nothing happened, but a faint hint of green grew out of the earth. The tendril wrapped itself around one of Onera's fingers, clinging tightly even as she sat up again. Finally, the tendril snapped and withered as she shook her hand free. "Almost all Warriors with this skill have traded in blades for farm work these days, considering the drought and all." She dusted off her hands and picked up her spoon. "It's the only way most crops have made it this season. And we need all the grain we can get for trade."

Senri stared at her empty bowl. She had eaten some of the bread. Guilt clenched her stomach. "It sounds like noble work." *More important than practicing patrol.*

Senri, Lanan, and Nat had all finished their meals. Yahn and Onera seemed to be content eating next to each other in silence. Lanan made kissy faces to Senri from across the table and Senri had to suppress a laugh.

Nat stood, shoving his bowl to the middle of the table. "Where are we sleeping?"

"The barn," said Yahn. "There should be clean hay to throw your blanket over."

As Nat left, Lanan stood as well. "Let's make sure he doesn't eat the rest of our provisions, Senri." She threw a sideways glance at Yahn and Onera.

Senri's eyes widened. "Oh yeah, good plan." She stacked her bowl in with Nat's and stood. "Let's go."

In the barn, Senri fetched her things and found a good spot of hay. Nat already lay not too far from her position, a blanket pulled up around his torso and a half-eaten apple in his hand. He snored. Senri laughed and spread out her own blanket before pulling off her sections of armor. Lanan winked as she set up her own blanket a few haystacks away. "Don't wait for Yahn."

"No, I'm sure he has too much planning to take care of," teased Senri. The two laughed before settling down.

Senri pulled her blanket up to her chest, then crossed her arms and closed her eyes. She found herself wishing she had someone next to her, someone to hold like Yahn. But when she tried to conjure thoughts of Vella, she found her memory dimmed. Instead of the golden hair, she kept seeing brown.

Yahn woke them early the next morning, and they set out to ride as soon as their supplies were packed. They did not say farewell to their hosts. The next couple days of travel almost blended together for Senri. They did not stay over anywhere else, but made camp along the roadside. On the third day of riding they departed from the road and traveled through grassland instead of farms. It looked nearly identical to Senri, only less fences. On the fourth day, scattered pockets of trees broke the grasslands and an expanse of woods appeared on the horizon to the south. It had been so long since she looked at a map she hardly had her bearings anymore. She asked Nat, "Do you think our village lies in that direction?"

"And to the east a little," he said. He pointed a ways back from where they had been riding.

"How are you sure?"

Nat grinned. "The stone never lies." He looked over at Yahn, who led them along their pathless trail. "How do you think he knows where to go?"

Senri raised an eyebrow. "How would he know that from stone?"

"It's a reader thing," he replied. "There's just a...sense whenever I touch the earth. A feeling, you know? It's easier for more experienced readers. Some can even give you the exact distance to a place, but it's extremely difficult."

"So, Yahn can sense the exact place we are heading?"

"I doubt exact," said Nat. "More like a general direction."

Senri shook her head. "To sense something so far beyond yourself."

They rode well into the night and stopped in a field clear of trees. "It's a little open," said Lanan, looking around as they dismounted.

"We'll see anything coming at us. Set up a fire."

They ate and relaxed. Senri mulled over the exercises Graus had instructed her to go through every night. She crossed her arms and stared into the fire instead. The actions seemed meaningless to her. Breathing while staring into the heart of a flame, trying to cup the fire and pull it into herself. All of it ended in frustration. That night, Nat and Lanan sat with her while she concentrated on extinguishing the campfire. She squinted at it, though that never helped, and took a deep breath. The flame flickered and her friends yelled, pointing at the dimming light. Senri shook her head. "That wasn't me."

While the others talked, Senri lay down on her blanket and stared at the stars. She fell asleep with Graus's voice filling her mind.

Yahn roused her before dawn. "Get up," he said. She felt his boot nudging her shoulder.

Rubbing her eyes, she sat up and stared into the darkness. Their fire was gone but the warmth remained. Yahn must have smothered it. "Something wrong?" Senri asked.

"There's an encampment not far from here. I don't have a good feeling about it."

Nat yawned and scratched his head. "So what are we going to do about it?"

"We need to get in close and take whatever information we get back to the palace," said Yahn. He helped Lanan to her feet. "There's too many to make contact. We leave the horses here and stay hidden."

Senri's fingers slipped as she grabbed her sword and attempted to buckle it to her belt. As she pulled the last notch into place, Yahn urged them on, walking slowly through the tall grass. They did not have to travel far. Even though the encampment had settled in a cluster of trees, the flicker of firelight still glowed. Yahn led them down to the south end where patches of forest trickled into the grassland. They moved from pale patches of grass to dark trees. Senri's heart beat harder as they moved closer to the encampment. Figures shifted within the trees. One walked close to the camp perimeter, a man in studded dark armor. His sword hung in a sheath from his hip, though he kept a hand close to it.

"He seems jumpy," muttered Senri. The man continued on and they moved a bit closer, stepping into the bushes. The shrubs were thin with few leaves. They made ideal concealment. The four Warriors moved close enough to observe the camp movements. Yahn made them stop and crouch down.

"Here is good enough," he said. They lay a good stretch from the camp. "If we are sighted, we run for the horses." Yahn looked at each of them in turn before looking over at the encampment.

"They look like bandits," whispered Lanan.

"But their armor matches," said Senri, spying a similar outfit on another patrolman. "Mercenaries?"

"If they were, it would be for someone off the western shore," said Yahn. "We are too far from any other kingdoms or cities."

"What if they're our own?" asked Lanan.

Nat craned his neck and shifted his position. "There's something over there." He pointed to the far entrance of the camp. Senri followed his gaze.

A large, hulking object rolled through the grass. The details got obscured in darkness, but it seemed boxy, and definitely not alive. The object halted at the entrance. Two men who had pulled it stepped away and talked to the guard.

"It's a cart," said Senri.

"Holding what?" asked Lanan.

"Does it matter?" Yahn turned from the encampment. "It could be supplies, weapons, blasting powder. They obviously do not belong out here so close to the western shore, no matter who owns them, if anyone owns them. We leave and report this at once."

"Wait," said Senri. The cart shifted once more, toward the firelight of the camp. The cart crawled into the light. Senri squinted as she tried to see beyond the shadows. Something felt wrong about it. It felt warm, as if it had a belly full of life. The warmth did not feel like livestock did, however. Senri furrowed her brow, confused. As quickly as the feeling came, it vanished, leaving her blinking against shadows once more.

The cart rolled completely into the light. Bars rose up around its edges similar to one that might hold a wild animal. Instead of paws scratching at the encasing iron, hands did.

"Slaves," said Yahn.

Senri's stomach clenched with unease.

"Or prisoners," said Nat.

"You have to be at war first." Yahn shook his head. "We're leaving."

The hands captivated Senri, the large ones, the small ones. Children's hands. Tiny heartbeats fluttered in terror. The heat ebbed. She had never felt life like this. It startled her. "We can't. We need to save them." She rose and took a step forward. Yahn grabbed her and yanked her down into the shrub.

"How many of them are there? Thirty?" Yahn snarled. "And you think you can take on all of them?"

Senri backed away from Yahn, throwing his hand off her. "We have to do something."

"We get reinforcements. We outman them," said Yahn. "We do it the smart way or we die."

The sensation of those trapped people struck her again. She breathed. *Is it getting hotter?* Senri felt a pulse beating within the camp. *People hundreds of them.* "They have more. More than just that. Those people might be dead or gone in ten days."

"What choice do we have?" Yahn stood and closed a fist around her arm. "You think I want that to happen?"

Lanan stood as well. "He's right, Senri. They outmatch us."

Senri looked between the two. She felt dizzy, overwhelmed by the feeling of heat snapping in and out of her senses. It surrounded her. She rubbed her eyes. Her hands burned. "Alright," she said. "We should—"

Mercenaries leapt at them. Senri drew her sword, but the heat overcame her once more. A club met her stomach and she wheezed, but could not draw enough air to satisfy her lungs. She panicked, breathing in short gasps before her vision faded. She plummeted into oblivion.

Michelle Magly

Chapter Seven

"TELL ME AGAIN." ALINA tapped a finger against the desk. She had turned quiet study time into a debriefing from Nin. The two had barely received a moment alone in days between her lessons and meetings with officials. Not to mention, Regent Velora insisted on her accompanying him in his duties. "Who did you send?"

"Four Warriors," said Nin, just like she had told her the first time. "You need not know anymore."

"Nin, how many Warriors do I know? I doubt knowing their names or talents will put me at any risk, and knowing you, they are most likely arranged to discover this encampment in the most accidental way possible."

Nin grinned and looked away. "They might run across it in the middle of a routine patrol. But do not concern yourself with any further details, Highness."

"Nin, did you send the blonde?"

"Which blonde? The new recruit?" Nin asked. Alina sensed she had the truth at hand, though Nin refused to say it outright. "Why would that matter?"

Alina sighed and shook her head. She turned to a pile of papers she was supposed to be reading through. They were new tax regulations and the Regent wanted to discuss them with her. Instead of concentrating on the documents, the vision of the woman came to mind. No matter how often she dismissed it, she could not erase the image from her mind. Something about the stare held her attention. Under different circumstances, she might have considered it attractive.

"Your Highness?" asked Nin. "Why would it matter if the

blonde one went?"

She pushed aside the papers and rubbed her forehead, a terrible habit she had been scolded for doing as a child. "It's nothing, Nin, I envisioned the woman standing in the market."

"Another vision?" Nin stepped in closer, lowering her voice. "And you did not tell me?"

"It happened before we met." Alina waved a hand at Nin. "On the ride into the city. It was minor, nothing like the spectacle you witnessed."

"Spectacle or no, you had a vision of this woman in the city." Nin paced back and forth. "What if she dies? What if I just rewrote the course of time?"

"You sent her?" Alina asked. She rose from her chair. Nin stopped pacing.

"Well, I did not know of your vision beforehand," Nin yelled. When Alina's eyes widened Nin quieted her voice. "Highness, you must be open with me from now on about anything and everything. Otherwise I cannot guarantee your safety. The girl with the Warriors has something significant to do with you. That is why I sent her. She may be the only one capable of obtaining whatever information there is; but if you and her are supposed to be here in the capital together then I may have just ruined any chances we had." The maid turned away from Alina and crossed her arms.

Alina frowned. "And so what if I saw her in the markets. It might happen after her return. Why not let me worry about my visions and you concentrate on the state of people's souls."

Nin turned, her eyes flashing. Her voice came out low, threatening. "Don't you dare make a joke of this. You have no idea what hangs in the balance of what we do."

Alina stilled. The people trapped in chains, her people, all suffering surfaced in her mind. The sight sucked her into a shallow vision, one giving her brief glimpses of faraway lands.

"Forgive me, Nin," she said, withdrawing from the sight with a blink. "I did not mean to make light of the situation. But I do realize what we are risking. I saw it, and I have yet to experience a vision that failed to come to fruition. We are fighting against the grain of time and so much more. Yes, Nin, I know what hangs in the balance."

Nin took a deep breath, as if she might say more. Instead, she curtseyed and said, "I apologize. I have matters to look after." She left without another glance at Alina.

Alina stared at the floor and crossed her arms. Nin's claims unsettled her. The thought that the Warrior may die made Alina's stomach pitch. She shook her head. Ridiculous, she knew, having only conversed with the Warrior once and for a limited time. She had no reason to feel worry for one person over all the others who risked themselves for her. Yet the blonde haired Warrior seemed important somehow. Even though her vision had been a whisper in the markets, it still whispered strongly the same thing Nin worried about: that this woman should not fall to harm.

***

Senri opened her eyes to a blindfolded darkness and breathed in a damp heat that stuck in her lungs. She sat upright, her bottom sore from sitting on the hard ground. When she tried to shift, her hands were tied behind her back to a pole and her feet tied at the ankle. The back of her head ached.

"Hello?" When she spoke, her voice cracked in a hoarse whisper, her throat dry and lips split. She had been unconscious for a while.

"Senri," whispered someone next to her.

"Nat?" She turned in the direction of the voice. Her neck protested.

"Keep your voice down. They already beat Yahn for talking too much."

"Is he here?" Senri whispered.

"Sleeping, or trying to. Don't know how he fell asleep in that position."

Senri cursed the blindfold over her eyes. Not even firelight filtered in from under the seam. "You don't have a blindfold?"

"They chained our wrists to the tent top after we used the stone to escape," he replied. "That's when they took the blindfolds. I don't think they understand how reading works though. We can still feasibly escape. We only needed you to be conscious."

"Right, when do we—"

"Guard's coming. Act asleep."

Senri shut her mouth and sagged her head and shoulders.

Footsteps crunched against the dirt as someone walked into the tent. She tried to breath normally, but her heart pumped far too quickly to draw the even breaths of someone at peace. She hoped the person did not notice.

"Quiet now, are you?" a man asked in a thick accent. No one answered him. "Good, maybe next time I talk about the other girl." The guard chuckled and exited the tent. She waited a few more seconds before talking to Nat.

"Where's Lanan?" she asked.

Nat remained silent. Blood pounded in Senri's ears.

"They took her," Nat finally replied. "She tried something with the water and they hauled her away. Think they need her for purification. Not much but stagnant puddles around here."

"She won't help them," said Senri.

"She will if she thinks it helps us."

Senri swallowed, thinking of Lanan working with the camp water, making it drinkable for their captors, chained, beaten, maybe worse. "We need to leave."

"Well, now that we have one less body to tote away, that's a possibility again," said Nat. "Yahn," he whispered a little louder. "Wake up. We're leaving."

Someone on Senri's other side groaned. "She done with her nap finally?"

"I'm good as long as I can work heat into my hands," said Senri. Even as she spoke, she willed the fire into her fingertips. She felt her fingers heat up against the rope binding her wrists. "Should we leave now?"

"It's the middle of the night. I don't think we will have a more favorable time," said Nat.

Yahn coughed. "We break our bonds on my count. Then we find Lanan and go."

"Weapons and armor?" Senri asked. Gustav had made her such a beautiful sword. Guilt twisted through her.

"Secondary," said Yahn. "You two do what I say, when I say it, and we might not need them. We make our move in three, two, one."

The countdown happened too fast, but Senri seared through her rope all the same. She reached out with shaking hands to burn through the rope around her ankles. She had never faced a foe like this, outnumbered, weakened. They might die. The bonds snapped off and she stood on trembling legs. Rock shifted and chains cracked as Yahn and Nat broke free of their restraints. She pulled the blindfold off and blinked into the darkness.

Yahn moved to the front, leading them toward the exit. He tackled the outside guard to the ground and the earth sucked him under, his screams silenced. Senri's eyes widened. Nat extinguished the torch and Yahn walked into the shadows, avoiding the well-lit areas of the camp. Senri had no idea how he knew where to find Lanan. Perhaps he felt her tread on the ground from years of working with her. Perhaps he searched blindly.

They moved along the perimeter of the camp, ducking behind the dark tents. Senri's instincts yelled at her to run, to break free of the stifling, overwhelming heat of the camp. Death filled this place. But she ignored the instinct, knowing she could never abandon Lanan and live with herself. Yahn pulled up the sides of tents and peeking under. He finally stopped at one and ducked under. Nat and Senri followed.

Huddled in a corner lay Lanan. She had been stripped of her armor and clothed in rags. Her face had been bruised and smudged with grime. Her hands and feet were covered in muck and bound. She slept on the dirt, her body twitching against the night air. *How can she be cold when I'm sweating?* Senri stooped and severed the bonds quickly. Lanan woke with a jump, pulling away. Yahn bent down and covered her mouth in case she screamed.

"It's us," he whispered. "You're okay. We're leaving."

It took a moment, but the horror faded from Lanan's eyes. They watered and Yahn scooped her into his arms, holding her close. Senri could not remember seeing her ever looking so frail. Lanan sobbed into his shoulder. Red marks marred her wrists. She had struggled against something. Senri wanted to help, kneel down and take her friend's hand, but she did not. Senri's heart beat wildly and the impulse to run coursed strong in her veins.

"They'll find us if we stay," she whispered.

Lanan pulled herself from Yahn. Streaks of tears broke through the dirt on her face, but determination had set in her eyes. She stood up with Yahn's help. "I can walk," she said, but did not brush his hand from her arm. The four of them left out the back of the tent. Instead of walking away, Yahn led them around toward the front entrance.

"I heard one say they found our horses," he whispered. "We need transportation to make it back."

Something about this plan seemed terrible to Senri. *Why not run to the forest?* They could easily dodge them in the trees. But without the swift transportation or any weapons they would quickly succumb to hunger or be recaptured. *Am I not a Warrior? Find your courage.*

Much of the camp lay sleeping and the guards had spread thin, assured that their captives had the fight beaten out of them. Yahn found the armory and pulled them inside. This time, Nat took care of the guard inside, scooping up rock from the earth and smashing the man's skull with it. He fell down, blood trickling from the wound. Nat laughed, most likely out of shock. "I think I killed him." His face took on a greenish hue.

"And he deserved it," growled Yahn. "Get a weapon."

Senri glanced around. The armor and weapons matched with a symbol of a seven-pointed sun setting over an ocean engraved on every piece. Senri pulled on a breastplate and greaves. If they were going to escape, they might find time with a disguise. She belted some of the daggers from the weapons rack, but stopped when a familiar glint caught her eye. The engraved steel grip of her sword rested on a table with the other confiscated weapons. They had even left the sheath and tie for her belt. Senri secured it around her waist.

"Hey," she called quietly. "Our weapons are here."

The other three approached the table and armed themselves. Nat had already donned as much armor as possible and even wore a full helmet. Senri took one of the half-plate helms instead. As long as no one got too close, she would be fine.

Lanan's arms trembled, bruises traveling up her shoulders and neck. Senri approached her friend. Lanan frowned at the armor. "I know I should dress."

Senri took up a breastplate. "I'll help."

Lanan slipped on the breastplate and Senri helped her with the gauntlets and greaves. Her shaking stilled some when Senri bucked the sword to place. "Thanks," Lanan muttered, her hand drifting to the weapon.

"Still might want to avoid fighting," said Senri. She held Lanan's shoulders, trying to catch the woman's gaze if only for a second, but Lanan's eyes wandered. She kept glancing at the tent entrance. Senri shook her head and looked over at Yahn and Nat. "Are you two ready?"

"Just about," said Nat. They buckled the last pieces of armor into place.

Yahn nodded. "We head out the back. I saw the make of the camp when they took me out to be whipped. The stables are just ahead of us."

"Should we try for a distraction?" Senri asked, remembering pieces of her training.

Yahn shook his head. "A fire or an earthquake would not work. They know we have powers. They're not idiots, sadly." He paused and took a deep breath. "So, we stick to the shadows and leave without drawing any attention. On my lead."

The three of them followed Yahn to the back of the tent. After he ducked under the flap, Nat and Senri helped Lanan through. She shook worse than the rest of them. They remained by her side, each holding an arm as they led her through the black shadows, always keeping Yahn in sight. They paused at one of the gaps.

Yahn had led them to the open corral where some horses had been left out for the night. Even in the dark, faded tones of moonlight Senri recognized Stomps standing with a few other horses, including the others from their party. Their saddles and supplies had been stripped. Damn.

"I'll pull some fence posts free. Then we leave," Yahn said. He walked over to the corral fence and tugged at the posts. The horses shook their manes. Some whinnied and stepped back. The ones familiar with him moved closer.

A voice cried out in the dark. "Hey!" The rest came out garbled, a tongue unfamiliar to Senri. The man walked forward, still yelling, his tone changing to a threat when Yahn refused to answer him. Torches and lamps flared to life across the corral as guards came out. Yahn swore and tossed another uprooted post aside.

"Come on!" he said. The guards ran now, Yahn's language ruining whatever his disguise had granted. Senri wanted to listen, but Lanan stood by her, paralyzed, and she and Nat struggled to move her from their cover.

"I'm not going back," she muttered. "They can't get me."

"Move and they won't," yelled Nat.

Lanan finally stepped toward the horses. Senri kept looking from the horses to the approaching men. It would be close but they still had time. The stifling heat of the camp threatened to suffocate Senri no matter how deeply she breathed. The haze seemed to block her vision. Her heart pounded, her sight wavering as the temperature rose.

Another yell sounded out. Senri felt the heat draw closer. She turned and saw another man approaching them, running, arms outstretched with a sword waving in his grasp. She felt as though her fever had broke. She let go of Lanan, pushed her and Nat away, shouting, "Run!" as she charged toward the attacker. He raised the sword to strike. She deflected it with her left gauntlet then reached forward and seized his face. Heat poured from her hand, burning his skin. He screamed into her palm. The heat of his body washed over her. She pushed all she had back into him. She breathed in, no longer hot. When she blinked again light flooded her eyes. It dazzled her, her hand burning white hot while the man's life ebbed underneath.

"I see it," she said, her voice a wisp of steam and smoke in the night. "I see it!"

His heat wavered. His muscles gave out and he dropped from her grip. Senri raised her hand in front of her face. It still glowed. She shook her head and stared, the world swathed in shadows save for the reddened blips of life backing away from her. She staggered forward and reached for another, grabbing hold of the man's throat. His cries gurgled. The flow of heat came easier this time. She smiled.

"Senri!"

She blinked and the world returned to normal, the temperature sinking in her body. She released the mangled man. The other men stared at her with wide eyes. Some approached with swords. Senri's panic took over and she ran for Stomps, the only familiar sight in the renewed midnight. She leapt for him, grabbing around the steed's neck and pulling herself astride. He took off, chasing the other Warriors as they fled.

They raced into the forest, the pathless route losing them in the dark. The cold night air whipped her hair and branches lashed at her sides. Senri tried to bring back the overwhelming heat, but nothing could call the flames. So she rode, cold and blind until dawn's first light. Yahn let their horses halt. Senri collapsed to the forest floor.

Chapter Eight

THE SUN ROSE, WARMING Senri's skin. It hit her fingertips first, crawling slowly over the forest floor until it reached her face. The light made her see red. Her eyes fluttered open, and she saw a tree's canopy rather than darkness. That was an improvement. She groaned, pushing her stiff hands against the forest floor as she tried to rise.

"By the Almighty," she muttered, feeling the ache from riding her horse without a saddle. Thinking back on it, she could not fathom how she stayed astride Stomps for the duration of their ride.

Stomps had stayed near her. A stream rushed by, perhaps the only reason the horses had not left them. Senri sat up and rubbed her face. Bits of grass and rock fell off. Around her, the other three Warriors lay huddled in sleep. She glanced past them, looking every direction possible. Trees surrounded them. *But the capital is east, and the forest is south, so if we head northeast*—A groan interrupted her thoughts. Much like her own waking, Yahn pushed himself up from the forest floor in a slow arc. His hair stuck up on one end and dirt covered his entire left side. The smudging did little to hide the bruises.

"So, we're still alive?"

"I think so," said Senri.

Yahn shook himself and pulled his legs up into a sitting position. "We're doing better than I hoped then," he said. He looked for the rising sun. "We'll be setting off that way." He pointed just north of its beginning trajectory.

Senri nodded. She pulled her legs up to her chest and crossed her arms over them. "How long were we prisoners?"

"A day or two, maybe," Yahn said. "I'm not entirely sure. They hit my head very hard."

"I'm sure," said Senri. She glanced around the forest floor. Her stomached ached for food, and drink. Without adrenaline coursing through her, she was weak. "I need food." Senri crawled toward the noise of water.

"Where are you going?" he asked.

"To find it, hopefully." Senri found the creek bank easily enough and dug up the roots of some familiar water plants. She had picked and eaten them for lunch all the time as a child. She turned and held up a fistful of watery roots.

Yahn leaned forward, squinting against the morning sun. "What is it?"

Senri shrugged. "We called it river root in my village." The spindly threads had to be washed carefully in the flowing water. Hard scrubbing made the pieces break away. She finished washing as big a handful she could carry and brought it back to Yahn, settling down beside him. "Do you like yours cooked?"

Yahn smiled and picked up one of the stringy clumps. "I don't know how I like it."

A groan came from the two other Warriors, and Nat attempted to roll off his side.

"Good morning," she said. Without bothering to heat it, Senri popped the root into her mouth, chewing the watery, somewhat tasteless meal. Next to her, Yahn ate his own helping.

"What did we do last night?" Nat whispered, trying and failing to sit up.

"Nearly died," said Yahn. "Want breakfast?"

"Is it my favorite?"

"If your favorite is waterlogged roots," Yahn said as he took another bite.

Nat sat up and blinked several times. "River root? Can I have some?"

"There's plenty in the banks," said Senri. She pointed in the direction of the stream. "Go get it."

Nat groaned and stumbled off, but he returned with a full armload of the roots. He sat next to Senri "Will you cook?"

She took a clump of roots from the top of his pile and clenched it in her fist like she had done as a child. She willed the heat from her core into her hand again, but this time it came slower, cautious almost. She furrowed her brow but did not push herself any harder.

When the root became hot enough, she opened her palm and broke concentration. "Here," she said, handing it back to Nat. He took it from her and ate. Senri shook her head and went back to her own food.

"Senri."

She looked over at Yahn, who studied her with a strange gaze. "Yes?"

"What happened when you burned those men?"

Senri looked down at her hands, remembering the wavering red dots of people, her own energy, the overwhelming sensation of power, rage. "I'd rather not talk about it."

"But you will tell Graus?" Yahn asked.

Senri nodded, biting into another clump of roots. "I will. I don't think your worry should be directed at me, however." She nodded over at Lanan's sleeping form.

Yahn frowned. "We should wake her. I'd hate for us to linger any longer than necessary." Yahn got up and walked over to Lanan. He knelt over her and pressed a hand on her shoulder. Her eyes flew open. She gasped, rolling away until she saw Yahn. Her expression softened, but something still clung to her, an unshakable fear.

"We need to go," he said.

After the four of them ate their fill of the roots and drank from the stream, they mounted their horses. Senri winced, her body bruised from riding all night without a saddle. Stomps shook his shoulders and whinnied. Yahn led them out of the woods and onto the prairie. Senri suspected he led them to the nearest farmhouse. They needed essentials. She had no idea what awaited them back in the city, or if they would reach it if the mercenaries still trailed them.

***

Nin did not return with news of the Warriors for several days. Alina would throw her a glance and the maid would shake her head and return to cleaning or folding clothes. One evening, Nin approached Alina while she prepared for bed. She froze in her task of pulling on her nightgown. A vision troubled her again, another small one that flashed scenes before her eyes, obscure ones with soldiers battling, an overgrown tree, a flash of emerald eyes, a mountain top. She blinked it away.

"Your Highness," Nin said, opening the door and shutting it behind herself. Alina fumbled to pull her nightgown over her head. "My apologies," she said, locking the door behind her.

"What is it?" Alina asked, smoothing the white material down.

"I have news of the Warriors." Nin's hair tangled about her face and her cheeks reddened from running. Her breathing, however, remained even.

"Have they arrived?"

"No," said Nin. "But the dispatched scouting party found them moving toward the capital. We just received the messenger they sent ahead. The party has to move slower due to injuries."

Alina's throat tightened. "Are they hurt?"

"Nothing too serious. Though one of them seems to be suffering trauma. They were taken captive and escaped." Nin clenched her hands together. Alina stared out the window. "Your Highness, they have succeeded beyond a doubt in proving whatever is on that map endangers the kingdom and that Gosman withheld the information from us."

The moon had begun its rise over the horizon. Alina watched the sphere slowly creep into view. "They could have died. They could have died for me and not even realized it."

"Many people will die before this is through, your Highness. No matter the outcome, there will be deaths."

Alina turned around and glared at the maid. "I'd rather avoid as many as possible."

"That is a little idealistic."

"Sometimes I wonder whose side you are on," Alina spat.

"Yours, Highness," Nin said, giving a mock curtsey. "But you must understand I have been a player in this game longer than you. Pieces have been lost, and more will fall to win."

Instead of offering another insult, Alina changed the subject. "When can I speak to the Warriors? I want them to brief me first. At least, directly after their commanding officer. No one gets their hands on them before me. I refuse to let them get further entrenched in this by becoming a tool for someone else."

"They are a three days ride away. Officially, you will receive them to award medals of bravery." Nin paused, picking at the sleeve of her cloth. "The Councilors hardly approve of you speaking with common soldiers." She smirked.

"Well, at least you are good at scheming," Alina said. Some of her previous frustration with the maid left.

"It is one of my specialties, Highness," said Nin, adopting her playful manner again. When Alina did not respond, she excused herself from the room.

***

Riding in the company of other Warriors and on proper saddles raised Senri's spirits. They offered her something to eat other than scavenged roots and her heart soared. The ride passed easy enough. The senior officers spent the first night questioning Yahn over what happened. If they had not been familiar with him, the group might have had problems claiming they were Warriors and not mercenaries.

After the first night, the other Warriors barely spoke to them. They did not say much until reaching the outskirts of the city, when Lanan pulled up on her horse next to Senri. "Well, isn't that a sight," she muttered as the palace appeared on the horizon. Senri tried to offer her a supportive grin. Lanan had been quiet for the majority of their ride..

A courier met them at the market's edge and told them to report to Valk. The Warriors cut through the markets and moved into the outer circle of the palace. While they led their horses to the stables, a group of foreign dignitaries walked past them. A man wearing thick robes caught sight of them, and then craned his neck back to stare longer. Senri's eyes met his and he looked away.

"Huh," she said.

"What was that?" asked Nat. He had been busy loosening the straps on his borrowed armor.

"I caught someone staring at us," Senri said. She glanced back at the retreating men. "He looked like a diplomat or something."

"I'm sure we look ridiculous," said Nat. "Do me a favor and jump in front of me if any beautiful women cross our paths. They should not suffer looking upon me in this state."

"They should not suffer looking upon you at all." Lanan's humor surprised Senri, though her upbeat tone had yet to return.

The group barely had time to hand off their horses before Valk approached them. A lower ranked Warrior accompanied him, speaking fast and trying to keep up with the leader's lengthy steps. A deep scowl cut across Valk's lips.

"What happened?" he asked, stopping in front of Yahn. "Who took you?"

Yahn detached the borrowed gauntlet he wore and gave it to Valk. "We were taken prisoner by whoever wears this into battle. They had a whole armory in their encampment."

Valk studied the gauntlet before swearing and tossing it into the dirt. "It figures an entire army would unload onto our shores while the politicians squabble over who should lead." For a moment it looked as if a vein in Valk's neck might burst, but he took a deep breath and paced the ground instead. "Where were they?"

"Near the end of our route, sir," said Yahn.

"Of course they were." Valk pinched his brow. "Do you have anything else to report?"

"They were unfamiliar with the ways reading works," said Yahn. "That was the only anomaly."

Valk grunted, crossing his arms across his chest. "Well, the four of you should go clean up. You are expected to recount your tale in front of her Highness tomorrow. She wants to award you medals." Just as they began walking away, Valk grabbed Yahn's forearm. "I expect a full written report before nightfall. Every detail counts."

Yahn nodded and they walked back to the barracks. Lanan and Yahn went to the infirmary to be treated. Senri got dismissed, so she went to the kitchen to find a meal. Orders soon arrived for her to report to Graus, Yahn's doing most likely. She wadded up the paper the orders had arrived on and chucked it. The last thing she wanted to do was report to Graus. She swallowed her stubbornness and walked out to the nearby training field where Graus held all his meetings.

The old Warrior stood still amidst the calf-high grass rustling with the wind. He did not turn to greet her. He never did for any of his students, but waited for them to greet him.

"Good afternoon, Master Graus," she said, uncomfortable standing in her own borrowed armor.

He still did not turn. He stood with arms crossed over his glinting steel armor. "I see you lost your uniform."

"It was not by choice."

Graus glanced over at her. "No, I commend your efforts. You did everything you were supposed to. You made it back alive."

"Is there something you wanted, Sir?" Senri ached all over. She wanted to go relax, not receive a lecture.

"I have been told something happened while you and the others escaped." Graus turned to her with an eyebrow raised. "It has me puzzled."

"Puzzled, sir?"

Graus stepped forward and waved a hand as if to dismiss his own words. "Describe the experience. Tell me how it felt when you attacked the men with your bare hands. Yahn tells me you looked entranced."

The wind gusted and Senri ran a hand through her dirty hair. The blinding heat had been so much and so alien. She had dwelled on it some after first experiencing it, but she preferred to not think of it with the memory of burning flesh under her fingers.

"Everything just got...so hot. My hand was molten. I..." She paused and shook her head. "I overwhelmed the soldiers with the heat."

She did not say any more, but Graus seemed satisfied with the information. He rubbed his grizzled cheek, staring past Senri. "Such a feat is difficult. Much harder than the current techniques I'm showing you." He gave a short laugh. "I guess all you needed was a little adrenaline."

Senri looked to her feet. Her face grew hot. She had yet to achieve anything Graus had requested of her. "The practice isn't helping. I can't control this power like the others."

Graus laughed again.

"What's so funny?" Senri asked, looking up.

"You're further ahead than most the Warriors several years your senior," he said.

Senri looked at the grass. What Graus said sounded like a joke, but it had to be true. "Why do you push me so much then?"

Graus sighed. He shuffled around, crunching the grass. "You're strong. I want to see that strength flourish. We don't have enough accomplished heat readers. I'm the only master as of now. Unchecked power gets you in trouble when you do not know how to wield it."

"You think I'll hurt someone?" Senri asked. The wind picked up, cooling her skin.

Graus rubbed his beard. "Or fail to save someone. You've got a good head. I'd like to use you in more difficult missions if you were better trained." Something about his tone suggested a wistful note, perhaps something Graus had been waiting for ever since they made him a trainer. Or maybe Senri exaggerated her own importance. "You might even be good enough to pass along to the Scaled Vanguard. Of course, that's after the Warriors have their fill. You've been through enough for one day though. We can resume training after your audience with her Highness tomorrow. You are dismissed."

Usually, Senri would leap at a chance to get off the field, but this time she hesitated. "Sir?" she asked. Graus nodded for her to continue. "Do we really have to retell the whole story of our capture?"

Graus smiled. "The princess is not a frail girl. She asked for an audience not because she wants to be dazzled with tales of heroism. She wants to take part in the defense of her land. Do not let the politicians fool you. I knew her father. He was razor sharp and taught her everything. He'd be on the throne right now if he had not been assassinated."

The princess made Senri feel strange. She thought of the confused woman in the field half the time and of a fictitious spoiled little girl the other. She had no experience to ground her perceptions in other than that first meeting. "I suppose I'll see for myself tomorrow."

"That you will," said Graus.

Senri took this as her cue to leave the field. She wandered back toward the barracks to find new armor. Then she would eat. If luck stayed with her, she would get to sleep in her bunk that night.

Chapter Nine

REGENT VELORA FROWNED. "THIS is foolishness, Highness."

"And you would know foolish acts so well, Regent, having let an opposing army land ashore under your watch." A muscle in Alina's jaw twitched. The two of them stood on a balcony overlooking the gardens. A faint breeze blew, chilling her. Alina knew he wanted to say something just as vicious back. She wished he would. That would prove he saw her as an equal at the very least.

Regent Velora's face reddened. "Lord Demek and I have been doing our best," he said, looking away. "It is difficult to keep order when a kingdom's leaders have been assassinated. Too many countries would take advantage of us. It is impossible to track everything."

He spoke the truth. Despite his cold demeanor, Regent Velora did everything he could for the kingdom. He could not see how the alliances he struggled for led to a far worse path, however. Alina would have professed her vision long ago if she thought it would not leave her exiled and everything would be lost. Instead, she played this diplomatic game. "I apologize, Regent. I am aware the trials of this nation are monumental. What is one person to make a difference?"

The Regent cleared his throat and squinted up at the sky. "You'd be surprised, Highness. That is why I wish you would reconsider this meeting with the Warriors. It makes you too vulnerable."

Alina scoffed. "I highly doubt these Warriors plot against me."

"Yes, but you have ordered away your personal guard for the meeting."

"They will be stationed in the next room within shouting distance," said Alina. "Nin will remain by my side. There is nothing to worry about."

Regent Velora shook his head. "You scheme like you can play this political game. I desperately hope I underestimate your abilities."

Alina stood still, refusing to rise to the bait. She looked out across the gardens. Four figures approached from the far end. "My guests are coming. You may leave us."

"I will see you for your evening lessons, then." The Regent turned around sharply and walked away. The door snapped shut a little louder than it should have. She had irked him. Nin and another guard entered the drawing room a moment later.

"I have finished all preparations," Nin said.

Alina leaned over the balcony's edge, her fingers playing with the signet ring on her right hand. She had decided that morning she should wear it at all times, no matter the company. Spotting the blonde girl, Alina's stomach knotted. A silly infatuation. The well-defined woman had sharp features and an obviously taut body even with armor covering it. So what if Alina got goose bumps looking at her? The Warrior's plate armor gleamed, most likely polished for the occasion. She sighed and turned back to Nin.

"Good," she said. "Make sure our guests arrive unhindered."

***

Senri gripped her sword pommel to keep her hand from shaking. Something about approaching the palace to speak with the princess felt less like an honor and more like a challenge. What did she know of proper etiquette? At best, she would offend her Highness with poor manners. At worst, she would cause a political incident on behalf of the Warriors. She took a deep breath when they ascended the steps to the palace. They were stopped by guards at the top.

"State your business," said one.

"We have been requested by her Highness," said Yahn. He passed the guard on his right the document proving it.

While the guard opened and read through it, the other guard addressed them, "You will need to leave all weapons here. None outside of her Highness's guard are allowed to be armed."

Senri almost unbuckled her sheath, but a man in a formal uniform approached them from within the palace. "Wait," he said.

The guard reading the paper turned. "Regent Velora, how may

we assist you?"

He walked down the hallway and stopped in between the guards. "Are these the Warriors her Highness requested to see?"

The guard handed Regent Velora the order. "It appears so."

Regent Velora snatched up the order and read through it. "Very well, carry on." While the four of them disarmed, the Regent walked out the palace and down the stairs, but as he passed Senri he whispered. "Her Highness is in danger. Be wary."

She turned and almost called out to him, but the man walked so purposefully she had nothing more to do but hand her sword over. *Why did he have to give the cryptic message to me? Why not Yahn?* The older Warrior stood too close to the guards. With Senri lingering in the back, she had been the only one the Regent could whisper to unnoticed. Politics be damned.

"An escort will arrive shortly," said one of the guards. "You may wait in the main entrance." Both gestured with their spears, and with a nod, Yahn led them inside and midway down the hall.

Yahn stopped by some benches. "So far, so good. This has to be one of my best visits to the palace yet."

Nat shifted his stance. "Is it usually more uptight? Because I think they could have made us strip to be doubly cautious."

Lanan scoffed. "They will search us before we are allowed into the same chamber as her Highness."

"Then what will they think of the scrap of metal?" Senri asked Yahn. He had taken a piece from one of the enemy gauntlets to show to her Highness. They did not recognize the symbols on it, but the princess might.

"I dulled the edges. It looks like nothing more than a religious pendant."

Nat rolled his eyes. "Good to know the kingdom's own Warriors are trusted so deeply."

Yahn hushed him. "We don't need to give them a reason to lock us up."

"They might not need one," said Senri, remembering the Regent's words.

The other three turned towards her. "Really?" asked Yahn, an eyebrow raised.

"That man who passed me, the Regent, said her Highness was in danger."

"Excellent," said Nat, clapping his hands. "I am rather fond of cryptic warnings."

Again, Yahn hushed him. "Someone's coming."

Senri looked down the hall. A palace maid walked towards them. She stopped in front of Lanan, smiled, and curtseyed. "Welcome. My name is Ninian, maid-in-waiting to her Majesty Alina. If you will follow me, I shall escort you to her."

The four of them followed along. Senri found herself having to check her arms at her sides, because her fingers constantly wanted to trail out and touch the beautiful tapestries, all a deep blue with the same falcon painted on her armor, stitched in gold. Other halls held paintings, statues, suits of armor. Senri had never seen so many fineries crammed into one area. The only artwork close to this grandiose display she had seen hanging off the back of a trader's wagon.

"I don't suppose I have to inform you of proper decorum with her Highness," said the maid. She glanced over her shoulder and smiled at them all in turn.

"We were lectured on it this morning," replied Lanan.

Senri looked over at the other Warrior, surprised to hear her speak up so quickly to a stranger when she had done nothing but shy from them ever since their rescue.

"We apologize for that," said the maid. "It is rare that royalty entertains anyone lower in rank than a general. The Council wanted to maintain some semblance of formality."

"Sorry if we stepped on any toes," said Nat. Yahn shot him a look.

But Ninian laughed. "On the contrary, her Highness enjoys this break in tradition."

They came to a large antechamber guarded by three men. "You will now be searched before being presented to her Highness," said Ninian. "A formality we could not do away with."

The search was far less invasive than Senri had imagined. The guards prodded their armor in a few places and made them remove the chest plates, a relief for Senri considering how hot the largest section of her armor became. Ever since the Regent had spoken to her it seemed to stifle her. After the guards checked their sleeves for concealed weapons and patted down their ribcage, the Warriors were allowed to dress. One of them found the scrap metal Yahn had brought with. He stared at it, feeling over the smooth edges, then handed it back to the Warrior.

"Nice pendant," he muttered.

Once they looked acceptable again, Ninian placed a hand on the door. "I will now present you to her Highness."

When the maid opened the door another guard stepped out and joined the others in rank. Ninian pulled the door wide open, revealing a large room filled with couches and bookshelves, not the princess's quarters. Yet there her Highness stood. She carried herself tall, though Senri stood half a head taller at least. Her hands lay folded before her back and her face held a look of serenity. Her soft features made her seem fragile, though her eyes had no softness. Her brown hair had been braided back in an elegant manner.

"Presenting to her royal Highness Alina Alexandria Mura: Yahn, Nathaniel, Lanan, and Senri, Warriors of Osota," said Ninian.

The four of them stepped inside. Senri's heartbeat mimicked the night of their escape from capture. She barely managed to keep her breathing controlled and watched Yahn carefully, copying his every move. When he kneeled, she did so as well and bowed her head, trying to tame her rampant nerves. *She's the princess, not a dragon.*

"Welcome, Warriors," said Alina. "It is a privilege for me to honor you for your heroism. Your efforts uncovered a great threat to this kingdom." The door closed behind them. She felt a cord drape over her neck, the medal everyone had alluded to. She glanced to the side. The maid draped one over Nat's head. "For your bravery, we bestow upon you medals that recognize your act of heroism. You may rise." The four of them stood. Senri reached for her missing sword, needing something to hold onto.

"Your Highness." Yahn fumbled with something in his pocket. Senri recognized the metal torn from the armor. "We found this in the encampment." He handed it to Nin, who handed it to Alina. She looked it over. "All their weapons and armor bore this symbol. They were very organized."

"This metal is different from ours," she said, turning the piece over in her palm and tracing the points of the sun.

"It's tougher," said Yahn. "It did not cut easily from the gauntlet."

Alina sighed and handed the scrap back to Nin. "What else can you tell me? All details are important."

While the others listed details of the encampment, Senri thought back to the night of their escape. She wanted to put the memories from her mind. They usually caused nightmares if she dwelled on them too long, one memory in particular.

"They had prisoners," Senri said, interrupting Nat's account of the stable conditions. Cages filled with bodies. "Farm hands. They caged them like slaves."

"They what?" asked Alina.

"They brought them in by the cartload," said Senri. "I'm a heat reader. I could feel them." Her heart thudded and the air felt thick in her lungs. Her head swam with the memories.

"How did this happen?" Alina asked, shaking her head. No one had a response for her. The encampment had been on the border of their kingdom, backed up almost to the western sea, but no reports had reached them of bandit raids. Senri had thought the news of constant raiding of villages and farms, the taking of prisoners, would make it back to the capital. Apparently the invaders had left no one to report the catastrophes.

"There is one more thing," said Yahn. "Senri, fought them. Grabbed one by the face and burned him. They had us surrounded, but as soon as she did that, they backed away. They feared her more than any of us."

Senri did not remember any of this. She only remembered the pulsing, searing fire of her hand as she clutched the man. Their faint red life had fluttered in their bodies. She swallowed.

"You grabbed one?" asked the maid.

Senri nodded. "I did. What of it?"

The maid glanced at Alina, but remained silent.

"I suppose we have the most important information sorted out," said Alina. "Please, enjoy your reward." She gestured at the medals. They stood awkwardly in silence. Senri did not know what conversation was suitable for a princess. No one else seemed to either. Alina frowned. "Thank you for your honesty. Nin can show you out of the palace." They turned to be led from the room. As Senri moved to join them, Alina called out, "Wait."

They stopped.

"You, Senri," she said. "Could you stay a moment longer?"

Senri looked to Yahn, who shrugged his shoulders. Nat looked back and forth from the princess to Senri. She could only imagine what thoughts ran through his head. "I suppose I could," she said, trying to keep her voice even.

"Very well," she said. "Nin?" The maid escorted the others from the room. After the door closed, Alina turned to her. "You must think I'm very strange." She avoided looking directly at Senri.

"I'm sure you have your motives," said Senri.

"True. Though I have to admit it's refreshing to be around you and your comrades. I cannot remember the last time someone forgot to address me without a 'highness' attached."

Senri did not know what to do, so she stepped toward the balcony. She needed the fresh air. "I apologize if we offended, your Highness."

Alina sighed and approached her. She stood in front of the balcony entrance. "You don't have to do that. You and the other Warriors fight and die for this kingdom. I do not require you to behave like unruly Council members."

"I am not familiar in the way of politics, Highness," said Senri. The air seemed thick in her lungs. She was not supposed to give details to the princess. *Will I be executed for it?* The Regent's own warning echoed in her head.

The princess shook her head. "They are not as familiar as they should be, either, but I would rather not talk about the Council members any more than I can help."

"Is there something I can do for you, Highness?" Senri should probably mention something about what the Regent said now that they were alone.

"Did I not just say you didn't have to...never mind." Alina shook her head. "You attacked and killed one of your assailants."

"I burned two." Senri avoided looking down at Alina. She stared out at the balcony instead, basking in sunlight. The stones shimmered with heat. She blinked. The heat still shimmered.

"What happened when you did so?" Alina asked. The princess adjusted her stance and stood a little taller.

"I think I saw their core," said Senri. The stone balcony almost glowed with heat. She breathed in but could only catch Alina's perfume-heavy scent. She shook her head to clear her mind. "The world dissolved. Or I thought it did. I saw shadows and red. Everything is brighter here." The words traveled on without her. She found it increasingly difficult to focus on the hard lines of the stone railing. "Your Highness."

"Yes?" Alina sounded like she spoke from under water. Or maybe Senri was under water?

"The Regent said something." Her thoughts drifted. She looked up and the edges of the world blurred. A faint red pulse crawled along the ceiling. No, above the ceiling.

"The Regent said what?" Someone scaled down the roof from outside. The person dropped down, armed with a knife.

"Move!" yelled Senri.

She pushed Alina aside, sending her flying into the adjacent wall. Senri reached out. Missed. The assassin pulsed a dull red from under the dark clothes. She grabbed the arm with the knife. She clutched hard, the overwhelming sensation crashing back down on her. This time, she understood it. Her free hand grabbed the man's neck. Heat flowed from his body into her. The man howled.

"Who sent you?" she yelled.

The man said nothing. She breathed in, letting his life flow from his body into hers. The light dimmed, flickered, would have gone out if the door had not crashed open and the guards had pulled her away. She let go, snapping out of the reader's trance. The princess screamed and the guards gasped. The man's nearly frozen form slumped to the floor, his lips blue. Senri blinked and stared at her hands. She had done it. She had taken the heat out of a fire.

***

Alina had never once considered herself to be in danger. She suspected an assassin might come for her, but needed to lure out whoever it was. Even without weapons, a Warrior of Osota would never be truly disarmed. Regent Velora had played his part beautifully, everyone had. Only when Senri had pushed her aside and acted with deadly precision did she realize how lethal a fully trained Warrior could be. But she was not fully trained. Alina had expected this young Warrior to kill for her. And the Warrior almost had. Alina sunk into a nearby chair.

"Are you hurt, your Highness?" a guard addressed her. Two others dealt with the half-frozen assassin, binding his hands behind his back. The fourth one had pulled Senri aside, out onto the balcony. "Your Highness?"

"I—" She breathed. Her chest hurt from where Senri had pushed her. "I'm fine." She tried to rise, but her legs shook too much. "Take that man to the dungeons." *Put the urgency elsewhere.* She did not need people fussing over her. She wanted to go to the young Warrior, see if she was well. If only her damn legs stopped shaking.

"We will, your Highness. Everything is under control." The two guards dragged the assassin out of her room. Shortly after, another guard escorted Senri out. The remaining guard stayed by her side until both Nin and Regent Velora crashed through the door and ran to her.

"Your Highness!" said the Regent. "Thanks the Almighty you are uninjured." He paced in front of her while Nin sat by her side, taking hold of her hand. Alina stared at the doorway, her stomach in knots. The Regent shook his head. "This was a terrible plan." He looked over at the guard then pointed at the door. The man nodded and exited the room, pulling the door closed behind him. "Did you find out anything useful?"

The Regent's expectant gaze brought Alina out of her trance. She pried her hand out of Nin's grasp and pulled the metal scrap from her dress pocket. "They gave me this, and informed me they are taking slaves."

Regent Velora blanched before he took up the piece and turned it over in his hands, staring at it closely.

"Do you recognize it?" Alina asked.

"Yes," he said, rubbing his neatly trimmed beard. "It's troubling, to say the least. I've read the reports, and seeing this only confirms the worst." He handed the metal back to Alina.

"And what is the worst?" Alina asked.

"The weapons and armor come from a foreign army, not a mercenary band," said Velora.

"So a kingdom has landed hostile troops on our shores and is taking our people as slaves, possibly worse. What are we doing to counteract this?" Alina tried to stand again, but Nin held her down.

The Regent sighed and let his hands drop at his sides and paced again. "We are doing many things, Highness. Valk has dispatched the best of his Warriors to clean up the immediate mess. The Councilors have been in discussion nearly nonstop with visiting dignitaries."

"And what are we doing in preparation for war?" asked Alina.

The Regent halted and stared down at Alina. "I beg your

pardon?"

"This is an inexcusable act of aggression," she said, nudging Nin aside and standing up. "We have no other option. To let another kingdom take our resources and people without retaliation invites further abuse."

"Your Highness," said Velora, his expression wearisome. "The situation is more complex than that."

"Really? Because the way it was explained to me, it sounded fairly simple."

"We cannot simply spring into war whenever a problem arises—"

"What would be an appropriate problem, then? The assassination of a monarch?" Velora avoided making eye contact with her. Her voice rose. "People are being taken against their will and killed!" The Regent froze. Alina released a breath she had been holding. It felt good to finally yell. "I will not stand aside and let Osota be trampled into the ground. You and the rest of the council may believe me to be a defenseless, stupid girl, but I see what is happening. I just thwarted an attempt on my own life."

"Your Highness, I—"

She cut the Regent off again. "I am not helpless!" She paused. Her throat hurt from holding back tears and frustration. "Neither is this country, and if you do not bring this evidence to the Council and demand their action, I will."

Velora turned red in the face. He looked down. Alina noticed his hands clenching tightly into fists. "I will present this to the Council and demand...stronger action," he said. "But you must have the Warriors testify, especially the one that saved your life just now. The Councilors are scared, your Highness. This kingdom is not ready for full-scale war, especially with anyone capable of producing these weapons. At the moment, we negotiate or perish."

Alina shook her head. "A kingdom enslaved by its own hand is no better than enslavement by an enemy's. I will speak to the Council when you are ready. The young Warriors will be there."

Velora held her gaze for a moment. He nodded. "Very well, I will inform you of the Council session details when it draws nearer." He looked down at Nin. "Keep her out of trouble." He ordered a guard to stay within arm's reach of Alina and walked out the door.

With Velora gone, Alina sat down beside Nin and buried her

head in her hands. "That was dreadful."

"He thought you were going to die."

Alina shook her head. "No, I was never in danger. If you...if you saw what that Warrior did, how quickly she acted. Oh, by the Almighty, I don't know why I thought I would be fine with this."

"Are you hurt? Did she do anything to you?" Nin asked, lightly touching Alina's arm.

She shook off her maid's attempts to coddle her. "No, no. I'm the one at fault. That woman, I used her to an end..." She glanced over at the guard who stood by her room entrance. "I need to think through this. See what you can do about getting the guard out of here."

Nin nodded. "It may be beyond my abilities at the moment. But I will try." She rose and exited the room.

Alina ignored the guard, the only person remaining. She settled deeper into the armchair. Soon, the Councilors and lords and ambassadors would be flooding her with concern and incessant questioning, none of which would be in an effort to help Osota. She sighed and shook her head. The Warrior, Senri, had barely looked eighteen turns. *What if I had underestimated her ability? What if the assassin had killed Senri?* This thought, not that of her own mortality, haunted Alina far more than anything else that had come to pass that day.

Michelle Magly

Chapter Ten

"YOU DID WHAT?" ASKED Graus. Senri shrank back from her mentor, though nowhere in the field offered her any protection. She had put off the meeting as long as possible, aided by the paranoia of the palace guard. She had successfully gone two days without confronting him about what happened in her Highness's quarters. Finally, the summons came for her to meet him and she could think of no readily available excuse.

"I pulled the energy from the assassin's body," Senri said. Graus only stared at her. "I didn't have time to think. I just did!"

"Of course, you're just fortunate you were able to do something." Graus paced the field. "Of all the things... why could you do it on a person and not an actual flame?"

"I can do that now, as well," Senri said. Somehow, she did not think this would help her case.

Graus stopped pacing and stooped to the grass. He grasped handfuls of it and ignited the dry strands. He straightened. "Do it."

Taking a deep breath, Senri stepped forward and lowered her hands into the flames. She blinked and saw the heat of the flame in its pure form. She took a deep breath, then another, and drew the heat of the flame in with her until it cooled to the point of vanishing. She blinked again and stared at the smoking remains of the grass. She stood and brushed off her hands. She expected a lecture from Graus. Instead, he laughed.

Have I singed my clothes or something? "Sir," said Senri. "Sir, if you don't mind me asking, why is this funny?"

Graus tried to stifle his chuckles. He managed to bring himself under control. "Looks like all you needed was someone to be courageous for."

Senri blushed and looked around, trying to see a possible route of escape rather than suffer her mentor's abuse. "I didn't find it funny at all. I could have killed him."

Graus took a few deep breaths and soon a grim expression set on his face once more, though a small smile tugged at the corner of one lip. "No, girl, I suppose it's not funny at all. I suppose I'm more overjoyed than anything."

"At an assassination attempt?"

"At you," he cried, gesturing at Senri. "You're a natural hero. Think on it, you couldn't do squat with your powers when asked to because you're too nervous. The second someone else is put in danger, your fears burn away, pardon the turn of phrase."

Senri stared at her mentor. What was so special about survival instincts?

"You're courageous, Senri," he said, smiling. "One of the most courageous recruits I've seen in a long time. Most of these imbeciles, you have to hammer it into them over years, but you pushed aside a woman you barely knew to take the full brunt of an attack without a second thought."

"I wasn't thinking," said Senri. She felt awkward from the sudden appraisal.

"That's what I mean. Your instinct is to protect. That is what makes you a good Warrior. No amount of skill with a blade or your powers comes close to good instincts."

"I...thank you, sir," she said. She glanced over to the barracks. It would be nice to get off the field and somewhere quiet.

Graus must have noticed where she looked. "Getting tired of an old man's rambling, eh?" Senri did not respond. Instead, she snapped back to attention. He smiled. "I suppose I can let you go early today. But we resume training at first light tomorrow."

"Thank you, sir," said Senri, giving Graus the slightest bow before turning and walking away.

Senri had initially thought of heading to the barracks, but the more she dwelled on returning, the more she realized she would be swamped by admirers once again. As secret as the meeting with her Highness had been, nothing could stop the rumors of Senri's heroic act. Someone had asked her if she fought off five men at once. So she had two choices, turn right and go to the barracks where she would punch Nat until he stopped singing the new ballad he had composed of their deeds, or turn left and leave the palace through the rear gates. She went left.

A lady lingered at the entrance to the field. She wore a cloak with the hood drawn up, nothing unusual for the weather. Senri nodded as she approached the woman and muttered, "my Lady."

"That was a rather short training session, Warrior," said the woman.

Senri stopped and turned around. She knew that voice. Her Highness Alina smiled at her from under the hood. She winked and raised a finger to her mouth. Senri panicked. "What are you doing out here, your High—"

Alina grabbed hold of her by the chest plate and swung her around to the other side of the wall, pushing her up against the stone surface and pressing into her. Senri's eyes widened, realizing how close Alina's face was to hers. *Could they chop off my head for this?* "Not a word about that, understand?" Alina said, her voice low.

Senri gulped. "But you're out here with no guards and clearly in danger and I—"

Alina pressed a finger against Senri's chest. To the Warrior's relief, she backed away, but only slightly. "I am Lady Cecile, the most recent noblewoman to gain the favor of the Warrior's newest celebrity."

"Who's that?" asked Senri. She found it very hard to think with her royal Highness pressed against her. Alina stepped back and released her from the wall. Senri exhaled.

"You, silly," she said.

"And why are you out here?" Senri asked, trying to corral her thoughts. She had to convince Alina to return to the safety of the castle.

"Because I needed to talk to you in private," Alina said. When Senri opened her mouth, the princess shot her a glare. "In secret."

"What happens when the guards find you missing?" Senri asked. Something would go horribly wrong at any second.

"They won't," said Alina. She stepped back, but still blocked Senri's path if she tried to run for the barracks. "They will find the real Lady Cecile enjoying the hospitality of my maid. Incidentally, she and I sound very similar when yelling."

Senri's head reeled. What she would give to be stationed

anywhere but the palace. "I suppose she looks like you?"

Alina smiled and gestured to the dress she wore. "We even traded clothes for the day. Though she does not know the true purpose behind it. Poor thing thinks I traded because I loved the shade of violet." She made a face and picked at the overly-floral pattern on the gown. "As it is, she thinks I'm at my studies."

Senri rubbed her forehead. The whole ordeal sounded like a mess.

"I'm not a fool, Senri," Alina said.

Senri looked up.

"I would never...I try to avoid putting others in danger for me." The apparent glee vanished from Alina's face. "I actually wanted to talk to you about that."

Senri might have run for it, but the princess looked so troubled that Senri nodded. "All right." She bowed for extra effort. "Where do we go, Lady Cecile?"

Alina looped an arm through hers. "Out the palace's rear exit and for a stroll in the fields. And please, try to be less formal around me."

"Won't a guard recognize you, though?" asked Senri. She walked where Alina pulled her, down the side of the palace to where the hedge garden lay.

"They won't if you act like I'm the flirtatious little noble you've absconded with."

Senri's stomach did a flip. Perhaps she should have run. She felt trapped now. If she tried to tell a guard she had the princess on her arm, she would be in just as much trouble. "And how do I do that?" Senri asked. They approached the garden. Palace staff would likely linger nearby, waiting for a chance to catch the rogue princess.

"Brag about yourself. Boast of your deeds and exaggerate your accomplishments."

Senri grinned. She still felt as though a guard would snatch her up at any second, but the tension began to wear off. "You sound quite familiar with this form of wooing," she said. If she was going to be prisoner of Alina for the day, she might as well enjoy it. Better than listening to Nat sing of how she fought off a chimera with only a bucket and rope.

Alina nudged her. "I've had to entertain a few suitors in my life, even in exile." They walked within the garden. Senri could not believe the leisurely pace Alina kept. Senri would be more comfortable making a run for the gates, but she supposed that looked too suspicious. The second time she tugged on Alina's arm the princess arched an eyebrow. "So eager to have me all to yourself, Warrior?"

Senri almost tripped over her own feet. "No, never! I mean yes, but it's not like that and—" Alina's laughter cut her off. She took a few composing breaths, trying desperately to get into character. *What would Nat do?* "My lady," she began, trying to keep her voice formal, "are you familiar with the latest ballad regaling my deeds?" They walked past a fountain and Alina turned towards the gate.

"Perhaps a little," she said. "But not nearly enough. Tell me what it sings of." Alina sounded so serious and interested, how did she act so well?

The guards and gate waited in the distance. Senri readjusted the arm Alina clung to and tried to maintain the easy-going demeanor Nat would have. "Well, one verse claims that I fought off a bristlebear single-handed at age ten."

"Quite the feat," said Alina, nodding her head.

"But that's wrong," said Senri. "I was actually nine, and there were four of them."

"Oh I don't doubt it," said Alina. "A Warrior as strong as you must have been on hundreds of adventures. It all sounds so..." Senri felt Alina's hand squeeze her forearm. "Daring." The two of them stopped at the gate. Senri tried to smile in a lofty way.

"Hello," she greeted the guards. They nodded at her.

"What's your business beyond the gates?" asked the one closest to Alina.

"I'm just taking Lady Cecile on a stroll," said Senri. Alina did not help matters by leaning into her. The warmth of her presence sent Senri's heart racing.

"Hey, you look familiar," said the guard next to Senri. At first, she thought he referred to Alina, but his gaze focused on Senri instead.

"I do?" she asked. She prayed her voice did not crack.

The guard smiled and his posture relaxed. "Yeah. You're the Warrior everyone's been singing about."

"Oh, really?" Senri asked. She would strangle Nat later that night.

"It was the best tavern song I'd heard in a long time," he said.

"Her golden locks shone in the sun. Another battle finally won."

Senri could not place this line. It must be new. She nodded like it sounded familiar. "Good, good singing voice."

"You think so?" asked the guard. He looked over to his comrade. "Come on, let's get the gate open." Before he turned to begin his work, he leaned in towards Alina. "And don't worry Lady Cecile, you're in good hands." He winked and helped pull the heavy wooden doors aside. Senri nodded at them as she and Alina crossed the threshold. She thought she would feel safer once they left the palace grounds, but sentries watched the field from atop the wall. She had to will herself to not look back.

As they walked, Alina sang softly, *"A glorious beauty that's never been beat, she stands ten feet tall in her stocking'd feet."*

"Where did you hear that?" asked Senri. She led Alina through the tall grass over to a wooded area where they might be better concealed.

"One of my guards sang it this morning," she said. "Quietly, of course. Have you heard the refrain?"

Senri shook her head.

"None out-brave her, she's our savior. Senri, the savior of the Queen!"

"That is horridly inaccurate," said Senri.

"I agree," said Alina. "You're nowhere near ten feet tall."

"And you're not a queen," said Senri. They had almost reached the forest edge. They would not delve deep into it, just linger by the fields.

"I will be," said Alina. She pulled her arm from Senri's as soon as they reached the tree line and noted the absence of contact. Senri had almost forgotten it was an act. "For the time being, it serves to give the people hope and enrage certain Councilors."

Senri stopped and examined the trunk of a tree, finding this easier than staring at Alina. Now that they were alone, Senri found the whole idea terrible, not because the princess could be in danger, but because it tormented her to be so near Alina. She did not want to acknowledge that she thought the princess was beautiful. In the aftermath of the assassination attempt, Senri had thought for a long time as to why she had reacted so quickly to save Alina. The princess, a decent person, had shown concern for her people, especially when Senri had mentioned the army taking slaves. Alina's expression had been one of horror. Even if she wrapped herself in a web of political deceit, every action she made spoke of something more, something desperate, like she raced against time.

"Besides, you really did save me," said Alina.

Senri turned away from the tree. Alina stood close to her once more. Senri shook her head. "I was doing my duty."

"And you performed it admirably," said Alina. "That is why, I'm afraid, I must call upon you again. We will present the evidence you and your comrades found soon. The Council will not want to listen, so we need as many people to testify as possible."

Senri glanced around the woods. She feared the Councilors waited to leap upon them and accuse the two of sedition. "Why not send a letter to Valk and ask him—"

"There are those that would do all they can to bar you and the others from the meeting," Alina said. "No one beyond you four can know of this."

"But how will we even—"

"My maid will provide further details and will escort you and the others to the Council chambers when the time arrives." Alina paused and smiled up at Senri. "Is this all suitable?"

Senri ran a hand through her hair. "I'm not one for politics. I wouldn't know what to do, what to say."

"Just be honest. That is all I ask of you."

The plan sounded solid. Senri looked around like a way out might appear. She dreaded the idea of speaking before the Council. But Alina thought it would do some good. "What if they try to hurt us?" Senri asked. "I cannot risk the lives of my friends."

"You will have my protection," Alina said. "As well as that of the Regent. He asked for you personally."

That seemed to seal it. Senri thought of her friends, if one of them would object. She could not think why. "I'll talk to the others. We'll be ready to speak on your behalf."

"No, not on my behalf. You speak for Osota in this matter, and for all those wronged by that army."

The princess said this with such certainty it empowered Senri. She nodded. "Thank you, your Highness."

Alina smiled and shook her head. "I am Lady Cecile. Or have you forgotten which woman you lured out into the forest?"

Senri laughed, taking Alina's arm within her own. "Forgive me, Lady, I only wished to imply your beauty and grace make you as worthy as a queen." She meant it as a joke, but then again, perhaps the sentiment rang true.

"At least you know how to flatter a lady." Alina patted Senri on the arm. "I think I've had enough of our wild tryst in the woods."

"Allow me to escort you home then, my Lady."

Alina leaned into her once more as they walked from the woods. The palace walls were a fair distance away. Senri wished she did not have to return to them quite yet. But Alina had not dragged her out to the forest because she was fond of her.

"How old are you?" Alina asked.

The question shocked Senri. *Where does my age fit into the political game?* Senri could not decide how to answer. Eighteen turns sounded so young. And not fair, considering her birthday was less than a month away. "I am almost nineteen turns, my Lady."

Alina laughed softly. "So, eighteen?"

Senri nodded. "So, what about you?"

Alina sighed. They walked a little slower. "Twenty turns."

"You will make a young ruler," said Senri, trying to pick up a conversation.

"Yes, the Council would be inclined to agree."

"But a good one."

Alina glanced up at her. "You believe that?"

Senri held her gaze. "Well, you did kidnap me in an attempt to save your people." She smiled at Alina, a gentle smile, unforced. Her voice had found a softness she usually reserved for one person, and that woman resided in a village hundreds of miles away.

"I feared you would find all these secrets distasteful," said Alina. She looked relaxed. Her shoulders had finally dropped their tension and she smiled softly as she talked with Senri. "I hate playing this game with the Council. When I rule, I'll never do it again. I'll have an open, honest policy." Alina's hand crept down the metal arm guard. Senri hardly noticed. "The last thing I want is to put you in danger again, Senri."

Her voice held the same softness as Senri's. "Again?" Senri asked. She meant to make a joke about how the assassin hardly counted as danger, but something shifted in Alina's eyes, stalling her. She looked down and Senri could not get her to meet her gaze again.

Alina opened her mouth to speak, but as she did her hand came in contact with the bare skin of Senri's wrist. Senri gasped, feeling the cool touch, then blinked. Alina had a bright core, nothing like the smothered life forms in the encampment. Nothing like the assassin. She looked around, blinded by the energy seeping from the world. She blinked, forcing her powers closed as she guided Alina's hand away from her skin.

Alina looked at her, frowning. "Senri? Can you hear me?"

Senri shook her head in an effort to clear her thoughts. "They're different."

Alina blinked. "Who?"

"The assassin. The soldiers. They look different."

Alina shrugged. "All people do."

"No, no, not like this," said Senri. The princess still looked confused. Senri stopped walking. She did not want to get within hearing range of the gates. "When you touched my wrist just now it triggered my powers." Alina loosened her grip around Senri's arm. "Not like that." Still, she let Alina pull her arm free and turn to face her. "Anyway, I looked at you. I saw your...your center of heat. It was different."

Alina took a step back, raising a hand to her chest. "Different how?"

"Normal, I think," said Senri. "The guards look like that, too. We all have a brighter source of heat inside us. The others, they are dimmed, like someone has tampered with it. Somehow, they are not functioning like the rest of us."

"Odd," Alina muttered. She gazed past Senri.

Senri gripped her by the shoulders. "My Lady?"

Alina seemed to snap out of a trance. She looked up at Senri with wide eyes. "Yes?"

Senri raised an eyebrow. Alina had been so alert all day. "We should get you inside."

The princess nodded. "Yes, that would be best."

They resumed their walk with little chatter. When they approached the gate they put on a show for the guards, flirting as they opened the doors. Senri heard one mutter as they walked away, "Those Warriors have someone different on their arm every day." She rolled her eyes, but did not turn and challenge the man. Besides, she had a bigger problem standing right next to her.

"How are we getting you back into the palace?" Senri asked. She looked at the high stone walls and wondered how Alina had gotten out in the first place.

"Leave that to me," she said. She seemed to have returned to her normal self. She even offered Senri a wink. "I'll show you the way."

Alina lead her to a secret tunnel open out next to the palace's sewage drain pipe. Concealed behind the large iron bars blocking the sewage pipe, Senri thought Alina had gone mad until the princess pressed a hidden seam within the stone surface and pried open a small door.

"Thank you for your time," Alina said, standing by the entrance. Senri remained on the other side of the bars. She smiled at Alina.

"Anytime, my Lady." She bowed once more and Alina laughed.

"I might take you up on that offer." Alina slipped past the entrance and slid the stone door back into place and disappeared into the darkness beyond.

Senri sighed, a slight ache pained her chest. She looked at the sky. The sun would soon set. She shook her head and began her walk back to the barracks. It had been nice to speak with Alina alone, without the interruption of a guard or assassin. But the time spent had also been torture. Alina had been charming and likeable. Enchanting, even. She held so much kindness within her, so much concern for her people. When it came to politics, she acted ruthlessly and without hesitation, but in a way that made her more attractive. She was not afraid to defend her people.

Senri groaned and buried her face in her hands. Just for a moment, she wished the world could dissolve and leave her out of its complexities. If she knew what the extent of greatness had meant when the seer told her she was destined for it, she might have run away. She would trade all the greatness promised her to be a simple country girl once more, and perhaps for Alina to be a peasant alongside her. The ache in her chest radiated. As long as Alina held ambitions to rule, Senri could forget about being anything more than a subject to her, despite how much the princess flirted.

***

The latest development in Senri's powers troubled Alina. She did not know what to think of the difference in the soldiers and assassin. A priest would say that they looked different because of their unholy practices, but religion held little sway over Alina. As much as Alina attended the ceremonies and listened to the traditional accounts of their roots, she did not put stock in the Almighty's power to intervene. Whatever power had put the land into being left behind the readers and seers to protect it. Divine intervention seemed a foolish notion, as far gone as a children's fable. No, the difference in the people of Shedol was likely their own doing.

Lady Cecile seemed delighted to dine with Alina for the evening and trade back gowns. Alina said all the necessary, courtly things a woman like Cecile would expect, and even arranged for a guard to escort her back to her manor.

Alina spent the rest of the night discussing with Nin. Some arrangements had to be made before the meeting with the Council. The interrogation with the assassin had turned up nothing. No other sources remained to be tapped. They had little left to do besides set a time.

"There is something though, not for the meeting, but for my own curiosity." She retrieved the scrap of metal from her jewelry box and handed it to Nin. "Take this to the palace blacksmith. I want to know what it is made of, and how, if possible."

"No, keep that," Nin said. "I can bring him a whole suit of armor, instead."

Alina wanted to ask her maid how she had leverage over such things, but knew it was better not to know. She dismissed Nin for the night and prepared for bed. For the first day following the assassination, everyone had insisted she have a guard by her side at every second. Alina refused to allow one in her sleeping chambers, but she consented to extra sentries, including men who scrambled onto the roof over her window. She slipped under the covers, the shadow of her window guard playing on the other wall. No one would send a second assassin, especially after the failure of the first one. She had made her point. She was young, yes, but not stupid or vulnerable. It would be more likely that someone would attempt to poison her food. After carelessly expressing this sentiment to the Regent, he had ordered a taster for every one of Alina's meals.

This bothered Alina most of all. At least the guards had been trained for combat. A taster could do nothing against poison, only hope someone had the correct antidote on hand. The worry that someone would die protecting her plagued her thoughts. She scolded herself. As a leader it was expected that people would die for her.

That only strengthened her sense of guilt. Alina tried to shift her thoughts to a less troubling subject as she tossed and turned in bed. They latched onto Senri.

Senri, the tall, strong, beautiful Warrior had saved her life without a second thought. Alina had never been so infatuated in her life. She could not get the woman out of her head. When she closed her eyes, all that came to mind was the memory of Senri linking arms with her as they walked. The woman's company had been refreshing that day. In a way, she felt selfish for dragging Senri out to the fields with her. It had been unnecessary and dangerous. But she wanted time alone with her. She had hoped to find Senri dull and careless. Instead they enjoyed a lovely walk together.

If Senri were male the situation would be less complex. The Council would have still raged about the class difference, but she could cross that boundary easier than gender. The whole kingdom could care less who soldiers and farmers fell into bed with, but Alina needed heirs, and her political situation prevented overcoming that fact. With a sigh, she set aside her thoughts about the Council and their disapproval. She let herself wander in the memories of her and Senri, nothing else. She yawned and pulled the blankets around her before falling into a light sleep.

Some time during the night, a thud awoke her. Alina sat up in bed, pulling a knife from under her pillow. She stared at the shadows of her room, too scared to shout for help. The window remained latched. Moonlight flooded through it. Perhaps she had misheard. She lowered the dagger. Then someone stepped from the shadows.

"Who are you?" she whispered. The moonlight slid along their legs and up a lean torso as the person stepped into view. Alina nearly dropped her weapon as she recognized the firm jaw line and angular features. "Senri?" The woman took a silent step closer. It was impossible for Senri to be in her room at an odd hour of the night. "How did you get in?" Senri stepped closer. *She must have taken the tunnel I showed her.*

Alina knew she had to call for the guards, or at least get Nin from the adjoining room, but Senri stood before her without armor in a sparse tunic and pants. She reached a hand forward like she wanted to touch Alina. Alina set down the dagger and swallowed. Her mouth felt dry and the room too hot.

Slowly, Senri sat down on the bed. She looked over at Alina with the shy glance she had grown familiar with. Alina's breathing grew shallow and her head a flurry of thoughts. Senri leaned forward, her eyes promising every intention of what her actions implied. Alina's body acted for her. She leaned toward Senri as well, tilting her head to the side, her eyelids closing.

The kiss she wanted never came. Instead, her breathing hitched and her eyelids flew open. Her room lay empty and she lay in a tangle of her own sheets, sweat beading down her forehead and along her body. Alina tossed the sheets aside, unwinding them from around her legs and smoothing down her nightgown. She looked around the room with wide, disbelieving eyes. Her dagger lay next to her pillow. Checking, she found the sheath tucked in between the headboard and the mattress.

"It wasn't a dream. Couldn't be a dream," she whispered. She ached too much for it not to be. She rose from the bed and searched the room. She checked the shadows first, then she shook out the curtains, then her own sheets, then under the bed. Nin still slept peacefully in the next room.

The passage. Alina walked as quietly as she could to the secret panel in her bedroom wall. She examined the seam. It looked undisturbed to her, but she pried it back and fetched the key to the hidden door behind. She turned the lock with shaking hands. Surely Senri would be on the other side, or at least proof that she had been. The door swung wide to nothing on the other side. She fetched an oil lamp and lit it after dropping the flint and tinder a few times. She checked the tunnel and found it empty, only her own footprints from when she returned. Alina frowned, closing and locking the passage.

Her scattered thoughts settled with the help of the luminance. Alina took a deep, calming breath. It could have been a dream. Still, something felt off. She took the lamp into her washroom and set it down on the counter. Alina went to the mirror and stared at her reflection. She pulled the neck of the nightgown down to her collarbone. The seer's mark spread just a little higher than it had the other day. Or did it not? Alina could not tell. She moved the nightgown back into place and picked up the lamp once more. When she returned to bed, she turned the lamp down low, but did not completely extinguish it. If she was having rampant visions, she'd rather have a little light in the room.

Alina tossed and turned, but could not find comfort enough to fall asleep again. The dull throb between her legs made sure of that. She turned onto her stomach and bit into her pillow to keep from screaming as she lowered a hand between her legs. More than anything, she had wanted Senri to kiss her.

Chapter Eleven

NAT MERCILESSLY TEASED SENRI. She could only imagine what he would have done if she had truthfully retold the encounter with Alina rather than making up a watered-down story. Thankfully, the others agreed to testify without much persuasion. Lanan agreed to it first.

Senri pulled her aside later. "Are you sure you can do this?"

Lanan looked at her with a darkened glare. Her bruises had gone, but something still did not sit right within her. "We need to stop them. I'd do anything if it meant putting an end to it."

"I'm not doubting that we need to," Senri clarified. "I'm just..." She hesitated as she searched for the right words. "worried about you."

"Well don't be. I'll be all right." Some of the hardness left Lanan's glare. "I appreciate your concern, Senri. I am getting help, though, I promise."

Senri allowed Lanan to leave, but still felt concerned, despite Lanan's reassurance. She approached Yahn about it, he sighed and rubbed his cheek. "She's not going to go kill herself, if that's what scares you. I've been talking to her. She's just a little unnerved. Try talking to her without bringing up the subject. She's mostly normal if you do that."

Senri shook her head. "It's hard to see that when she's so serious. Before, she usually laughed off everything with a joke."

"You saw the army."

"Well, yes, but we have one too. Won't we just drive them off the land?"

Yahn shook his head. "Things are bad. Valk argues with the Councilors and the Councilors argue with the diplomats. The

Warriors sent a regiment to take care of the army and they found an abandoned campsite."

"Did they ship off shore?" asked Senri.

"No. They most likely retreated north along the coast. If we had reacted sooner, we could have stopped them. Now they are going to be entrenched in the mountains."

"That sounds bad." Senri had always assumed Osota possessed enough military prowess to take care of any threat. After growing up on tales of how their kingdom drove back the dragons during the Burning Times, she had thought the valley invincible.

"There are both advantages and disadvantages to being enclosed in mountains," said Yahn. "If we were more active in our defense, a bordering fortress could have dispatched troops to intercept them. As it stands, our best hope is that they starve once winter arrives. The bulk of our troops are already dispatched to eastern garrisons and outposts along the forest edges. Our forces and supplies are abysmally low. You should treat this matter seriously. It may lead to war."

The following days, Senri spent more time training than she previously had, much to Graus's approval. The extra training helped clear her head of all thoughts of Alina and of the conversation with Yahn. If she were too exhausted when she collapsed in bed at night, she could not spend hours thinking about her. She began to find equilibrium in her life once more. She even smiled at Nat when she sat down with him at breakfast.

Nat grinned. "It's so lovely to see you pulled that stick from your ass. You were beginning to get this really pained look on your face."

Senri flung a grape at him from her plate. "I've been thinking through some things is all."

"I hope it's not what next verse to add to your song, because Corson already did that." Nat took a bite from an apple.

"How many verses are there?" Senri had given up on stopping the song. Just as long as she did not hear it.

"Well, it started with twelve original quatrains," he said. "But with additions from the others, it might be close to over fifty."

Senri shook her head and ate her food.

"I was thinking of adding a line about you and the lovely princess," he said, nudging her arm. "A royal fling is just what that song needs."

"That's not even funny." Senri put down her fork and knife. "They could kill me for that."

"Not without evidence of a long term affair," said Nat. He took another bite from the apple and chewed. He arched an eyebrow. "Has the princess found a new royal plaything?"

She wanted to look away, but that would be too incriminating. She stood her ground. "I haven't touched her."

Nat laughed. "Well, that doesn't sound cryptic at all. Don't worry. The song is harmless. While it mentions you sleeping with scores of people, it never specifies which ones."

Senri smiled and patted her friend on the arm. "Thanks, Nat."

She had every intention of heading to the training yards after breakfast, but as Senri and Nat exited the barracks a young woman stopped them. "Warriors," she called out. The two stopped and looked at the cloaked woman. Nin.

"Hello!" said Nat. He grabbed Senri by the arm and dragged her over to Nin. "What brings you down from the palace?" The maid gave them a mirthless stare. Nat swallowed and straightened his posture. "How can we assist you, ma'am?"

"You shall accompany me to the council chambers," she said. "All other duties have been excused for the day."

"It's time, then?" Senri asked.

Nin nodded. "I've sent the other two ahead. They will meet us at the palace entrance." She glanced at their armor and then their faces. "I'm glad you have the sense to look presentable." She turned and walked through the crowds. "Come with me," she called over her shoulder.

The two Warriors glanced at each other before running after Nin. They caught up and slowed their step to match hers. A sense of dread overtook Senri as they left the Warrior's stronghold. She did not know whether she feared speaking to the Council more or seeing Alina again.

Yahn and Lanan waited by the palace steps for them. They fell into stride beside them as Nin led them into the palace and down a series of halls. Their path ended in a large, open room with tall standing marble pillars. Two guards stood on either side of large double doors.

"Are these the Warriors the Regent spoke of?" asked one.

"They are," Nin replied. "Is the Council ready to receive them?"

A guard shook his head. "Regent Velora will send his page to collect you."

They only had to wander the antechamber for a short while. Most of the discussion sounded like mumbled nonsense through the double doors.

Finally, a young man opened the door a crack. "Regent Velora is ready to receive you."

The four Warriors exchanged glances before letting the young man show them into the council chambers. Senri looked around at the men and women sitting in the high-raised seats. Some glared down at them. Some looked relieved at the sight.

"I present you the Warriors who discovered the enemy encampment while on routine patrol." Regent Velora spoke. Senri found him seated with the other Councilors. Alina sat next to him. She smiled weakly up at the princess. Alina gave her the barest hint of a grin. She looked like she would be sick. Senri took a deep breath and tried to prepare herself for the worst. After all, they faced worse on the battlefield.

***

Watching Senri walk into the Council chamber proved to be the hardest part of the day for Alina, not the yelling matches. The Warrior looked up at her with such hope, such assurance, and that smile; it hurt Alina to throw someone so genuine and trusting into the animal pit.

"What is the meaning of this absurdity?" Councilor Gosman demanded. He rose from his chair and pointed at the Warriors. "We never discussed bringing outside testimony into this debate."

"They are eye witnesses to the main event," said Councilor Orwall. "I, for one, would like to hear what they have to say."

"We are here to discuss privately—"

"Is that why the foreign dignitaries from Shedol have been allowed to attend?"

"Councilors!"

Alina leaned out of her seat, looking down the rows. Lord Demek stood. He looked between the bickering people, then at Alina.

"The Warriors of Osota are honorable and brave," he said, turning his gaze on them. "We would be glad to hear what they have to say of their ordeals." He sat down, straightening the collar on his jacket. It had received a few more decorations since Alina saw him last. A gold cord across his chest recognized his new rank as ruler alongside the Regent. "Please, speak." He gestured at the Warriors. They stepped forward.

The Councilors remained silent for the duration of the story. The eldest Warrior did most of the talking, again. He seemed to be the self-proclaimed leader of their group, the best-spoken out of all of them. Alina tried not to dwell on the disaster Senri might have caused when explaining the events. She spoke bluntly, something Alina enjoyed about her, but the Councilors would have torn her apart for it.

At the end of the tale, Councilor Tarish spoke first. "That is a fascinating account. But the fact remains that nothing ties this band of mercenaries to the Kingdom of Shedol."

Regent Velora rose from his chair. "Actually, I have with me a certain emblem." He pulled from his pocket the scrap of metal that bore the symbol of Shedol's army on it. "Ambassador." He addressed a cloaked man standing at the far side of the room. "Would you agree this is the symbol of your nation?" The man strode forward and examined the symbol. It looked exactly like the insignia on his robes, the seven-pointed sun lowering into the ocean.

"It is similar," he said. He turned and walked back to his position.

"It is an exact match!" said Orwall.

"Warriors," said Velora, ignoring the outcry. "Would you say the army's weapon and armor bore this symbol?"

All four of them nodded.

The ambassador huffed. "This is insulting! We speak honestly when we say no troops have been dispatched to your shore. How do you know these men are not just a group of deserters? I assure you we are as eager to investigate the matter and resolve it. But if you pursue aggressive actions against us, we will defend ourselves."

"No one has taken an aggressive action against you or your people, Ambassador," said an older woman. Calna, if Alina remembered Velora's lesson correctly. "We only wish to protect our people."

"By throwing around false accusations?" asked the ambassador. Alina had to admit he played a convincing part. "And what disturbs me most are these rumors your princess spreads of enslaving Osotan farmhands."

"Didn't you listen to anything he just said?"

The outcry had come from Senri. She stepped forward into the center of the room.

Senri glared up at the ambassador. "They had an armory. They took slaves, hundreds of them! Where is a band of rogue mercenaries taking hundreds of slaves to? If they were bandits, they would not be bothering."

"You dare accuse my people of illegal slave trade?" The ambassador took a step toward Senri before another pulled him back.

"There was an encampment of men moving slaves along the western shore," said Orwall. "Where else would they move them to?"

The meeting dissolved into a mess of shouts from there. Alina buried her face in her hands, trying to drown out the yelling. She had been foolish to think the Councilors would simply see the truth. And exposing Gosman's ties to the army seemed out at the moment. Clearly, some of them had decided an alliance with Shedol was better than any other alternative and worth any cost. No amount of proof would change that. She shook her head. She could think of only one thing to do.

She stood and cleared her throat. "I believe there is only one option at hand."

The Councilors nearest heard her and quieted. The rest of the room followed.

"We are divided." Alina looked at the Councilors one by one. "I am sure everyone here feels they are doing what is best for Osota." Her eyes locked with Demek's for a moment. "But we cannot allow ourselves to argue like this. We must stay united. Otherwise, this threat, regardless of who orchestrates it, will dismantle us. I propose a compromise."

Everyone stared at her. Alina felt both exhilarated and terrified. She had never spoken so openly before, or so loudly. Like a ruler.

"All right," said Lord Demek. "What is your compromise, Princess?"

Alina wanted to slap him. Of course Demek would rub her inferiority in her face. All she wanted was to end the fighting. "While the kingdom of Shedol conducts its investigation, I recommend a thorough reinforcement of Osota's borders. In my time away from the capital, I was able to observe the kingdom's defenses. Fortresses lay empty and patrol units are far too sparse. This lax in security can be expected when negotiating the line of succession." She paused. No one looked outraged. "However, we have witnessed the repercussions. We cannot do nothing, yet we cannot go to war."

She waited for someone to speak up, to give her a word of encouragement.

Lord Demek spoke first. "A sound plan of action, your Highness. However, our military means are stretched far too thin for a total reinforcement. We lack the reserves of iron and other metals to forge the necessary defenses. We cannot deploy troops to garrisons without armor." He looked over at the ambassadors. "The current trade negotiation with Shedol is to remedy that. This breach in our defenses is most troubling. There is no easy solution to it, Highness."

"Lord Demek." Velora spoke up. "You stated in a previous meeting that negotiations should hold until we have determined the candidness of our potential ally. Does this conflict not call for investigation?"

At first, Alina thought Velora had somehow outwitted Demek, or that he had struck a particularly sore point, because the life momentarily drained from Demek's face. His eyes unfocused and he blinked several times, looking around as if he had not seen the Council chambers before. "I said what?" he asked, brow furrowed. He sounded confused. Velora repeated himself and Demek nodded. "Yes, and while this normally would require a delay, summer is ending and with it the travel time needed to conduct a proper investigation. I suggest that we move forward with a limited, short-term agreement that can be reassessed later." He stared across the room at Velora the whole time he spoke. Alina glanced back and forth between the two, wondering what sort of unspoken threat lay between them. Demek had power, power that went beyond anyone else in that room.

Regent Velora proceeded to adjourn the meeting. Alina felt his hand on her shoulder, but she did not move. She needed to sit. She needed to block out the memory of her vision, the one of her people enslaved and of Demek drinking with the enemy. No matter how she struggled or schemed, she could not seem to outwit her gift from the Almighty. She saw the future. Who was she to think she could alter it?

***

Senri charged at the training dummy, roaring. She raised her sword high over her head and screamed as she swung down for the first blow. The blade bit deep into the wood. She tugged it free and hacked at the post once more. She hit it from every direction, knocking it a little looser every time. She did not stop until she had hacked halfway through the dummy's torso and splintered off most of its left flank. She yelled one last time and sank the sword into its head. Senri release the grip, letting it stay embedded in the skull. Her own rage startled her. Before arriving at the capital, she had thought little of Osota or its safety. She always assumed it would remain that way. Seeing those prisoners changed that. Watching the leaders of the kingdom fail to act solidified it.

"I think it looks better that way," said Lanan. The Warrior stood at the entrance to the training court and leaned against a rack of swords. She smiled, something Senri had not seen in a while.

"Why are you happy?" asked Senri. She walked over to the rack and fetched a spear. The weight seemed fairly balanced as she hefted the pole arm. Winding her arm back, Senri threw the deadly weapon at the target. The spearhead sank into the dummy's chest, knocking the post back even more.

"I'm not," said Lanan. "I'm as angry as you. I just don't show it by ruining training equipment."

Senri scoffed, pacing the length of the courtyard. "They'll make another. Or this whole place will burn to the ground when the Shedol armies march in."

"They won't destroy us, just make us a subjugated territory and drain us for our resources."

"If we fought back, they—"

"We're not fighting back though," said Lanan. Her tone darkened. Senri stopped pacing and looked at her. Lanan scowled. "You think I don't know what's happening? We don't have the resources to take on that army. They're going to take Osota and suck it dry. They're going to keep stealing poor farmers and enslaving them. They're going to cut more throats, like the children they threatened me with when I wouldn't help them." Lanan's eyes shone with tears. Senri tried to respond, but found nothing to say. "Everyone else wants to do nothing. I think we should change that."

"And how do we?" Senri glanced around the training ground to make sure they were alone.

"We can't. But her Highness can most likely stir up some trouble." Lanan looked more like her old self. The fire flared back to life in her eyes. She blinked away the tears. "I think she needs some encouragement though."

Senri walked to the training dummy and yanked out the spear. "From who?"

"You."

The spear almost slipped from her grasp as she twirled around. "Me? Why me?"

Lanan's smile broadened and she shrugged. "She seems to prefer talking to you. You tell me."

"I…we…it's nothing like you're implying." Senri placed the spear back on the rack and returned to the dummy for her sword. "Besides, what are four Warriors and a princess supposed to do?"

"That will be for her Highness to decide. She's quite the planner. I'm sure she's putting something into motion right now."

"You can't know that," said Senri. She sheathed her sword and made to leave the training grounds. Lanan blocked her way. "How am I even supposed to reach her?"

Lanan raised an eyebrow. "I think you know how."

Senri shook her head. "You're insane." Lanan did not move. Senri looked away and swore. "I'll be back, if the palace guards don't kill me."

As she passed, Lanan pressed something into her hand. "A lock pick. Nin might have said you'd need one."

The small copper wire looked as useful as a rock. Senri had never picked locks before. "I'll refrain from melting door handles."

She pocketed the wire and left the training ground. Twilight had fallen over the kingdom during her attack of the dummy. She had started by setting fire to the field then extinguishing it all with a breath. The exercise had been therapeutic and reckless, both things she needed after the Council released them. She had only switched to the training dummy when Graus came outside and ordered her to stop before she burned down the entire plains.

The sewer entrance lay unguarded, as usual. Did the palace staff even know of its existence? She heated the iron bars and bent them aside. She did not feel like picking the lock to them. Once through, she reheated them and put them back into place, carefully smoothing out the metal to not leave marks from her grip. The hidden door proved more obstinate, however. She ran her hand along the surface, looking for the invisible seam. It took her a quarter hour to locate the correct groove on the pockmarked surface. Once inside the tunnel, she found herself in complete darkness. She blinked rapidly.

At first, Senri tried moving along the tunnel without the help of sight. After clanging against the stone walls too many times, she removed her weapons and armor. The straps evaded her grasp as she tugged the plates free. She set her armor by the door and set off once more. Her hands reached in front of her, skimming the rough surface of the tunnel. Reaching stairs, she climbed onward, cursing Lanan and whoever else put the idea into her head. *Nin, that's who gave her the lock pick.*

Senri reached a dead end. She felt along the wooden wall until she found the small door handle. Nearly dropping the lock pick, she attempted to bypass the door. She almost gave up, but finally moved the copper wire up and out. She heard the tumblers fall into place and the handle lurched down under her grasp. Behind that, a false wall rested in place. Faint beams of light seeped in through the seams. She pushed it aside and winced from the sudden flood of light. She crawled forward through the opening and stood. Something clattered to the floor. Senri glanced toward the sound. Alina stood by her vanity in nothing but a thin, white shift. Senri's gaze moved to Alina's exposed collarbone, then up along the neck until she noticed Alina's completely shocked expression.

"Senri!" Alina said.

She gulped and realized she had been staring. She turned away, covering her eyes. "Your Highness, I'm sorry! The others made me do it. I'll just leave now." She stooped to retreat back into the dark tunnel once more, but the princess rushed forward and slammed the hidden door back into place.

"Oh, don't do that," Alina said, positioning herself in front of the doorway. Senri looked away once more. "By the Almighty, what is wrong?"

Senri's heart leapt. The whole plan seemed horribly flawed now that she stood in Alina's bedchambers. She kept her eyes fixed on the floor. "You're indecent, your Highness," she mumbled. *I'm going to get my head chopped off.*

"Am I really that terrible to look upon?"

Senri turned back to Alina. "No." But she still stood in nothing but a shift, so Senri turned away again. The room felt uncomfortably hot. "I mean, it's not proper for a Warrior, or anyone, to look upon a lady in a state of undress."

"Did your parents tell you that?" asked Alina. Senri heard the false wall panel move back into place and Alina's footsteps.

Just look at the floor.

"I'm putting on a robe," said Alina. "You can look now."

Senri looked up. Alina tied a blue silk robe around her waist. It covered most of her body sufficiently. "I'm sorry, your Highness. I shouldn't have come."

"Senri, it's fine," said Alina, placing a hand on her shoulder. "How did you get all the way up here anyways?"

Senri looked down at the hand. Her gaze followed the arm, up to the shoulder, then Alina, who studied her with a strange expression. Her face felt too hot. "Well, you did show me the entrance, I should go. The others said we should talk, but I'll come back later or…" She stooped to pry the panel off the wall once more, but Alina's hand on her arm stopped her.

"Don't." Alina caught her gaze. She pulled gently. "Please. Stay."

The touch of her hand caused warmth to pulse along Senri's arm. Alina's fingers tugged again and she stood up, but avoided looking directly at Alina. "All right."

Finally, Alina removed her hand. Senri crossed her arms and looked around the room, anywhere but at the princess. A large four-poster bed lay in the center, but that only caused heat to sear through her once more. She looked down at the carpet again. The carpet seemed safe. "Um," said Alina. Senri glanced back at her. Her eyes wandered the room as well. "Won't you have a seat?"

"Oh, yes," said Senri. "Where?"

"Over here." Alina walked to the far corner of the room and gestured to a couch and armchair. She piled all the excess pillows on the armchair and sat down on one side of the couch. Senri considered removing the pillows on the armchair, but feared hurting

Alina's feelings. She sat down on the far end of the couch and wedged herself safely into a corner. Alina smiled and crossed her legs. The robe shifted, revealing the creamy, smooth skin of Alina's shapely calves. Senri gulped and looked at the table.

Definitely getting my head chopped off.

"Can I get you anything?" asked Alina.

How could she sound so innocent? "No." Senri pushed her hands in between her knees. "No, that wouldn't be appropriate with you being a princess and all—"

"Senri."

"Yes?" *Don't look at her.*

"Please, don't enforce the concept that I require more respect than you. I already said I reserve that pomp for my Council members."

"Right." She forced herself to glance at the princess and smile. "I guess I'm just nervous. This whole time I've been convinced someone is going to walk in and execute me."

Alina laughed and leaned further back into the couch. The robe sunk over Alina's curves and accentuated the swell of her breasts. Silk left little to the imagination. Senri averted her gaze again. "No one else will enter this room tonight," Alina said.

"Really?" *Think of training. Think of anything else.*

Alina shook her head. "I was fairly...stern with my orders. As you can imagine, it's been a terrible day."

"It has been," Senri replied.

"It's why I asked you to stay," said Alina. When Senri glanced at her again, she no longer appeared so seductive. She had curled up in the corner of the couch rather than sprawl across it. A crease had formed in her brow as well. "It's difficult to be alone through this. I know I always have Nin and the guards close at hand, but they make poor company to spend time with."

Senri nodded. "You enjoy spending time with me?"

Alina smiled. "I do," she said, resting her chin on her hand. The smile faded. "But I doubt you risked decapitation to lounge in my room with me. Something about 'the others' put you up to it?"

"Oh." Senri looked down at her folded hands. Now that Alina mentioned it, she felt sorry for her being trapped behind the palace walls. "Yes. Well, Lanan told me I should come talk to you, let you know we aren't ready to give up. " She finally met Alina's gaze without blushing. "And that if you ever need us, the Warriors stand ready to aide you in any way."

The princess smiled once more and looked out the window. "Lanan says that? And what does Senri say?"

"I will fight for this kingdom with everything I have." She remembered the yelling in the Council meeting and shook her head. "I don't care what those Councilors think." She stood up. "Your Highness, we are not ready to lay down our weapons."

Alina glanced back and studied her. "Thank you, Senri, I promise to keep fighting." She stood from the couch and smoothed out her robe. "You should go now, before someone discovers us."

Michelle Magly

Chapter Twelve

IT HAD HURT TO send Senri away so abruptly the night before, but the Warrior's actions had reminded Alina of something. *I am the rightful queen. They see me as a leader.* No one befriended their leader. She had desperately hoped the friendly banter would stay, but as soon as the conversation shifted to a serious topic Senri got lost in formality. *And what did I expect? A heartfelt confession? She's terrified to be around me.* Alina wandered the aisles of the palace library. Guards remained stationed at all entrances and Nin was away on an errand. In contrast to the previous night, she needed time alone. The tall bookshelves allowed her to easily get lost in the expansive, quiet room. Windows along the south wall provided a gentle, indirect light to read by, and several tables lined the gaps between shelves for scholars to take a seat and study. No one else was in the library at that moment, however. Her guards had dismissed everyone.

The blacksmith had said some enlightening things about the enemy metals. According to Nin's report, the metal had been formed from a mix of iron and one other ore, cormenite, neither of which readily available in Osota's farmland. Most iron reserves had run dry in the eastern mountains, but flanked by mineral-rich terrain, the kingdom had to have scouting reports of the geology somewhere.

Alina ran her fingers across the dusty parchments. She settled for trade manifests documenting back to the formation of Osota. Osota had to get minerals from somewhere, or at least document who offered to trade it. She pulled down a box of scrolls, then sheets of paper. She dragged these over to a table and began with the oldest information first. The first handful of scrolls proved useless, outlining the border exchange agreements for the country. Then it progressed to food exchange. She skimmed through papers for hours before she found any hint of trading for ores, and then it only recorded trade for precious metals like silver.

By afternoon, Alina had waded through most of the documents dating up to the century before the Burning Times. She glanced around the library. The guards still remained at their posts and Nin did not hover nearby. *Good.* She needed more time to work. The documents even started to prove interesting, especially as the war with the dragons drew closer and closer on the timeline.

The trade manifests started showing small amounts of ore being received over the years: a little iron taken from one kingdom, a little copper from another. Even cormenite appeared on the list. Still, the totals at the bottom of the sheets always indicated a dwindling supply. The kingdom had not been able to sustain its needs with its current trade partners, much like present day. Finally, during the first year into the Burning Times, Alina discovered a trade proposal. The paper had been folded away into an envelope between the other manifests. She shook it open and smoothed it out on the desk. Her eyes widened. *Dragons?* She reread the paragraphs at least three times to make sure. Yes, it was a proposal for trade with the dragons. The idea was not completely outlandish. Alina had never met a dragon, possibly because they had been banished from Osota after the war, but she knew they possessed as much intelligence as any human. It was their infamous tempers she had grown to fear. An average dragon stood around eight feet tall. With the added capability to breath fire and tear flesh with their claws, making one upset usually resulted in the human dying first.

Alina scanned the contents and discovered one Osotan king had intended to trade cattle for large quantities of ore. The document remained unsigned. She folded up the proposal and slipped it back into its envelope. While she returned the other papers to the shelf, she left that one out. After checking the date again, Alina went to the history section and retrieved several texts written on the era, particularly ones detailing the escalation to war.

Her hands shook as she turned open the first page of an old tome. The useless texts blurred over the causes of war. They described increasing skirmishes with the dragons that spilled over to slaughters, but nothing said in plain terms why the Burning Times had begun at all. Frustrated, Alina shoved the books aside and returned to the trade proposal. She checked the ruler's name inscribed on it, His Majesty Marcus Regan Osota IV.

The name sounded vague. When she checked for a biography, she returned to the table with only one. It held barely one hundred pages and proved even more frustrating than military texts. The biography focused on his early years and ignored his downfall and death. She wanted to fling the book across the room, but settled for shoving it aside and letting it topple to the floor.

Alina sighed and reread the Burning Times. She flipped to the section containing maps and tactical reconnaissance reports. Several of the Osotan strategic camps had been positioned near iron deposits within the first ring of mountains. The lands were rich with ores, rich enough to supply two independent countries for ages. The dragons had ore, but they lacked fertile grasslands to keep large herds of animals such as cows. King Marcus had proposed a trade agreement. *How had it fallen through?* While she knew they possessed equal intelligence, she assumed the dragons were hungry, vicious beings only interested in flaying humans alive, but she had been raised on those stories. Obviously, one king had thought differently.

Alina cupped her chin in her hand, thinking. Much animosity existed toward dragons in Osota. Children heard tales of their cruelty and aggression during the Burning Times. The kingdom banned communication with them strictly for protection. No one wanted to mistakenly lure a dragon back to their village. Even representations of dragons had been banned. Any idols, paintings, or sculptures bearing a likeness to a dragon were destroyed. The Scaled Vanguard, dragon hunters, killed rogue dragons spotted flying over Osota. The message could not be clearer: dragons are bad.

"Reading about dragons?"

Alina blinked and looked up from the book. Lord Demek stood on the other side of the table, smiling down at her. She pulled the book closer to herself. "I found my latest lecture on the Burning Times lacking. Since it was the last war Osota engaged in, I felt it would be the most important to study."

Demek walked to the side of the table and picked up the book she had flung off. "Most wise of you, your Highness." He set the book down on the table. "And have you learned more?"

Alina kept reading the same line over and over. She did not want to acknowledge Lord Demek's presence or encourage him to linger. "A bit."

The chair opposite her scraped against the floor as Demek sat down. She clenched her jaw and kept reading.

"And of King Marcus?" His question met silence. Demek drew in a breath and pulled the biography over. "He was possibly one of the most important kings to our country... most disgraceful, to be sure. But also most important."

"I wouldn't know why, nothing is said of him." She glanced up from her text. Lord Demek studying the envelope holding the trade proposal.

"I think you have an idea," he said, his gaze flitting back to Alina. She met it instead of turning away. "You're a very bright woman, after all."

At this, Alina looked back to her book. She did not like the sincerity in Demek's tone. "I'd assume he died in battle, since the next king was crowned in the middle of the war."

"Close. The truth is a little more complicated, however." He paused, drumming his white-gloved fingers on the table. "Are you familiar with the reasons why seers are forbidden from rule?"

Alina froze. Demek's voice sounded so causal, so non-threatening. He had to know something. She decided to play along until he truly put her in danger. "They are far too dangerous and unstable to rule a nation wisely. A monarch's decisions should be guided by judgment, not by a desperate race against or toward certain visions." She remembered the lecture well from her youth.

Demek leaned forward in his chair. "Yes, but, did you know Marcus was a seer? Our first and only Seer King."

Alina shook her head. "It is not common knowledge."

"No, the history books do an excellent job of glazing over it. King Marcus witnessed a vision, or so he declared, of Osota united with the dragons in an invincible alliance. He set out to initiate trade with them, wrote up a generous offer of cattle to supplement their lean diets. The dragons turned away his messengers though, said a true monarch would come to them directly. Do you know what happened when he arrived in the dragon's country?"

Something terrible, I'm sure. Alina shook her head.

"The dragons called him false, decided that they were too great to ally with lowly humans. They consumed his heart." Demek touched his hand to his chest. "And flew his body back to the capital as an example. King Marcus died senselessly, so assured by his own visions he put himself in direct danger and sparked the bloodiest war of our time. His actions shaped this nation, your Highness, but they did not shape it for the better." He paused. Alina knew he was watching her. "I want you to be a person that shapes this kingdom for the better," he said, his tone softening.

Alina shrugged, still studying the book. "And why is that?"

Demek sighed and leaned back in his chair. "I knew your father, believe it or not. I knew him before you were born." Alina looked up and met his gaze. Something seemed different about him. "He was a good man. Though I barely had time to see him or your mother once you came into this world. I was sent away. Diplomatic matters, you see."

"Where were you sent?" Alina asked, though she could already guess.

"West," he replied. Demek held her gaze for a moment, as if challenging her to ask further, but Alina remained silent. "I only saw you once when you were a child. A few days after you were born, I believe." He stood from his chair and smiled down at her once more. A change had passed over him again. "I shall leave you to your studies, Highness." He gave a slight bow. "Good day."

Alina dared not move until Lord Demek walked out of sight and the echo of his footsteps faded. She exhaled and shut the book. He knew something, or at least guessed close enough to the truth. What did he mean to do by telling her that though? Alina saw only two possibilities: he wanted to scare her into abandoning any pursuit of the throne, or goad her into doing something so rash it got her killed.

She pulled the text forward that detailed the history before the war and smiled. Perhaps she would attempt something rash. That would at least get the Council's attention.

***

On the day of Senri's birthday, Nat pulled her aside as she walked to the mess hall and trapped her in a fierce hug.

"Nat!" She pushed against him, trying to free herself. Her friend held on a moment longer before letting her stagger away. "What the hell was that for?"

"You looked like you needed a good birthday strangling." He grinned and tried to slick back what remained of his curly hair. His instructor had recently shorn it.

"Thanks," said Senri. Her ribs felt a little bruised. "Any other surprises?"

Nat shrugged. "Lanan and I might be taking you out to a certain tavern tonight."

"Oh no," said Senri, pointing a threatening finger at him. "Please, Nat. I don't need to get out."

He grabbed her by the shoulders. "Senri, you don't take advantage of any of your free time. You just mope and train. People are being deployed left and right. You are going to have a night of revelry before we are sent off to some remote fortress."

"We're still only trainees, Nat," she said. "We have time."

"No, you're not talking yourself out of it. We're going out. That's final. Meet us back at the mess before sundown." Nat gave her one last smile and left.

As she ate breakfast, Senri tried not to dwell on the thought of the night's festivities. Training that day involved more complex unit movements followed by conditioning. The grueling runs had become less of a pain over time, but Senri still did not look forward to them. Before they began the first lap, however, a courier approached their drill instructor. The drill instructor bent her head and listened to him before looking over at Senri and beckoning her over. She broke rank and joined the two. The courier looked at her.

"Are you Senri of the Warriors?" he asked. She nodded. He passed her an envelope. "Message for you." He glanced over at the other Warrior. "She's also been exempted from the day's duties."

The drill instructor glared at the courier. He turned and walked off before she had a chance to speak her mind. Senri, on the other hand, remained captive.

"Well, open it," her drill instructor said.

Senri broke the wax seal and squinted at the neatly formed letters. It read, *meet my by way you came last, -A.* She folded the letter and placed it in her trouser pocket.

"Is it important?"

She nodded. "I think so, ma'am."

"Then get out of here before I change my mind."

Senri saluted and jogged off the training field. She turned away from the barracks and moved along the palace wall, walking as casually as she could to the sewer entrance. Senri had kept the lock pick on herself ever since Alina had sent her away those several nights ago. The irrational part of her had been hoping for something like this to come along. Alina had been so cold when she sent her away. At first she had worried she had been rude or too informal, but then realized that Alina had repeatedly asked her to be anything but formal with her. The princess had probably been irked by Senri panicking every other minute. It was hard to remain calm around Alina, especially when Senri had to force herself not to stare openly at her. She shook her head. As much as Alina wanted them to be friends, Senri was certain that anything further was strictly off limits for many, many reasons. She would just have to remain formal with Alina. Hopefully, it would put enough distance between them until she could control her feelings.

***

  Alina paced her room. She feared the message would go astray, or that Senri would not be able to make it or be too afraid to. In truth, she hoped Senri would show up for more than just the reasons of talking to her. She missed the Warrior and her awkward shyness. Alina walked past her vanity and turned around for another pass. She almost yelped when Senri appeared before her, standing in trousers and tunic and staring with that longing gaze.
  "Senri?" she asked.
  The young woman approached her with silent steps, keeping her emerald eyes locked with Alina's. Alina backed into her vanity, her legs bumping into the furniture. She breathed a little faster, trying to ignore the familiar sensations. This couldn't be happening. Senri still approached her, her eyes fluttering shut. Alina could not help closing her eyes and leaning in toward the Warrior.
  Her breath hitched and she opened her eyes. Senri had vanished. Alina stood alone in her room, her chest rising and falling in uneven gasps. She turned and studied herself in the vanity's mirror. As her amber shade returned, Alina groaned and shook her head. The vision had been growing more incessant. She looked at herself again to check for her seer's markings. The lines stayed hidden underneath the cream Nin had given her. A few moments later, a thump against the false wall panel startled her, and she turned to see Senri pushing it aside.

"Good, you're here." Alina went to Senri's side and helped her up before replacing the wall paneling. She tried to push the recent vision from her mind. "No one noticed you coming?"

The Warrior shook her head and dusted herself off. "You asked for me, your Highness?"

"I...yes." The formal manner caught her off guard. She missed the stumbling, misspeaking woman who had broken her way into the palace. "I thought you would be pleased to know I have a plan."

"You do?" Senri's face lit up.

Alina smiled. "I think I do. I need to work out some more details. Of course, I need you to agree with the whole thing first. It won't work without you and your comrades." Alina paused before continuing. "It...requires a certain amount of risk."

Senri shifted her weight and looked at the floor. "I'd do anything to keep you...the kingdom safe, your Highness."

Alina sighed and looked away. She walked over to the window and looked down on the palace grounds. Somehow, the idea of Senri giving her life for the throne did not sit well with her. "Don't say things like that."

"Like what, your Highness?"

Alina shook her head. "And stop calling me Highness, I'm asking everything of you. I think you've earned that right."

"Yes, your...yes." Senri kept her distance. She seemed to be thinking something over. She kept glancing around the room and then back to Alina. Finally, she said, "And what was your plan?"

Alina sighed. Close enough. "I want to make an alliance with the dragons."

"What?" Senri backed away.

Alina knew that talking others into going with it would be a feat in itself. "The dragons have the ore we need to fortify our troops and they need food we have."

"But that's heresy! They'll eat you alive."

"I don't think so," said Alina. "I did some research, and before the Burning Times, no laws existed against the dragons. Osota did not interact directly with them, but there was no great stigma against them either. They were neutral."

Senri folded her arms. "And what makes you think they'll stay neutral when we cross into their mountains uninvited? They've terrorized my village!"

"Really?" asked Alina. She placed her hands on her hips, challenging Senri's closed-off stance. "In your lifetime? Did they kill many?"

Senri paused at the prompt. She frowned and seemed to think it over. "No, I guess...the last one stole sheep."

"See?" asked Alina. She let her hands drop from her side. "They need food."

"How do you even propose we do this?" Senri began pacing the room. Alina found the behavior adorable. She had to stop herself from reaching out and grabbing Senri by the arm when she came within reach.

"A small team of Warriors takes me down to the Southern Pass and up to the nearest dragon city."

Senri stopped and turned to glare at Alina. "You are not travelling that distance."

"And why not? The last time an alliance was proposed, the dragons refused to speak with anyone other than the monarch."

"And what happened to him?"

"A...misunderstanding," Alina said. She felt somewhat guilty for leaving out the details, but she did not truly lie to Senri, only left out the lethal part. The knot forming in her gut tightened.

Senri looked at the carpet. "I don't like it." Alina liked how frankly Senri spoke with her. Perhaps she would steer their future conversations towards tactics and planning more often. Senri resumed her pacing. "But I don't like the armies of Shedol more. And how would we even get you out of the palace? The Council would be up in arms if you went missing."

Alina snorted. "I doubt they will care. Either way, they would not notice my absence if I were to extend a generous offer to Lady Cecile to come stay in the palace. You see, her parents just passed away and she is quite lonely in her estate."

"The Council is not blind."

"No, but it will give us time for me to leave the city and at least reach the kingdom borders without being noticed." Alina smiled as Senri seemed to think this over. "And any other concerns you might have, don't worry. I've thought of those too."

"Will you come back alive?"

"What?" The question threw her. Senri stared at her, and even though she wore no armor, her gaze had never looked closer to that first vision Alina had of her standing in the market. Alina blinked, trying to reassure herself she was anchored in reality.

"Will you come back alive, Highness? Did you make a plan for that? Can you guarantee your safety?"

Something about Senri's gaze looked pained. Alina wanted to know why, but the current situation was no time for selfish desires. Alina thought about her response instead. *Do I have a guarantee for Senri? The visions.* They had increased in regularity and vividness recently, so many different ones, always a slew of untranslatable events...except for, perhaps, the visions of Senri. It seemed unfair to rest all their lives on frequent visions, however, when Alina worked to prevent a particular one. What determined the course of time for them if she could not even master this gift? She glanced back at Senri. "I wouldn't ask if I did not think us capable of surviving." *Another half-truth.*

This seemed good enough for Senri because she crossed her arms and nodded. "Very well. I trust you."

Alina smiled and stepped forward, wanting to embrace Senri, then remembered her place and halted. She did not want to frighten her away. "Good, all that remains is to find a detachment of Warriors who we can trust."

"I can talk to Nat and Lanan tonight," said Senri. She glanced out the window. "Actually, I should go see them right now."

Alina turned and glanced out the window. The sun barely touched the horizon. "Oh, you don't need to leave so soon. I was actually hoping we could..."

Senri rubbed the back of her head. Her cheeks had picked up a faint blush. "I'd love to, your Highness, the problem is that Nat wants to take me to a tavern tonight seeing as it's my birthday."

"Oh." Alina's hopes fell even more. She looked away. "I understand, have fun." She tried to offer Senri a smile, but failed.

"I will." The Warrior slowly walked toward to the panel.

"And Senri, happy birthday," Alina said. This time, she managed to hold her smile.

Senri paused. She grinned. "Thank you, your Highness." She stooped down and pulled the false wall out of place. She went through the door left Alina alone once again in her bedchambers.

Alina frowned. For a moment, she had considered asking if she could come with to the celebration. Then the absurdity of the thought hit her. Alina could not sneak out to a tavern. What if someone recognized her? What if someone did not recognized her and threatened her? Accompanying Senri anywhere would probably ruin any enjoyment for the Warrior. Senri would be a nervous wreck, snapping at anyone who looked at Alina the wrong way.

Anger coursed through her. She hated being isolated like this. The last time she had gone on an outing with friends had to have been when her parents both lived, before the visions had struck her. After, her parents had monitored all playtime with others. When Alina had complained, her mother explained the alternative, a life far away from others without parents or friends. *Well, isn't that what I have anyways? A kingdom that does not even want me and a handful of pawns who would rather be elsewhere.*

Alina lay down on her bed, sighing. She closed her eyes and let herself get lost in the memories of her youth. She pictured her mother, her hair so similar to Alina's, braided down her back in a way Alina tried to imitate. She always wore long-sleeved and high-necked gowns, to hide the seer's blood in her veins. She remembered how her mother had pulled her aside one day after her music lessons. She looked worried, pale. "Alina, my dove," she said. "I have something to tell you." She brought her to one of the stone benches tucked away in the palace gardens. "Your Aunt Alaina had another miscarriage."

Alina had not understood what a miscarriage was or why her aunt had several of them over the course of trying to conceive, so she had never been as devastated as the adults around her. Now that she thought back on it, she remembered whispers throughout the palace of bad omens. Everyone had been spooked by the events. But Alina had stared up at her mother, confused, and asked, "Will I ever have a cousin, then?"

Her mother shook her head. "I don't know." But perhaps she had always known her aunt and uncle would never conceive, because she leaned down to Alina and said, "You must promise me something." Her mother glanced around to check for anyone nearby. Alina had been confused by it all. "Can you promise your father and me something and not tell anyone?"

Being nine at the time, Alina had been eager to prove she was just as mature as everyone else. She glanced around like her mother had and nodded.

"If anything should ever happen," her mother began. She remembered her small hands being clasped in between two larger ones. "If your aunt and uncle decide not to have a child, if your father and I should pass on as well—"

"You won't!" Alina had cried.

"If we should," her mother said, holding Alina's hands tighter. "Promise me that you will take care of Osota."

"I will." Alina had answered so quickly. She had been so blind to the struggles.

"Promise that you will do everything you can to make sure you rule this kingdom, and make sure that it prospers, my dove."

"I promise, mother. I do."

Alina had not had time to reflect on the implications on this promise. Her parents had died within the week and her resolve had strengthened even more. She had spent the funeral service thinking of travelling with her father to remote settlements, of the time they had spent together with the common folk. No, Osota would never suffer abuse. Her parents did not want that. The kingdom itself had become the last connection between her and her family. She would never forsake that.

Alina shook her head, trying to banish the memories. It was never wise to dwell on the past, but the present did not offer her much comfort. She squeezed her eyes shut, trying to block out images of Senri going down to the tavern, perhaps even linking arms with a stranger and finding comfort for the night with someone else.

***

Nat dragged Senri into a fairly busy tavern and pressed a full mug of beer into her hands the first chance he got. She stared down at the drink and arched an eyebrow. "You really aren't holding back, are you?"

Nat laughed and clapped her on the shoulder. "It's your birthday! I want you to enjoy yourself."

Senri stared at the drink. Her mind and heart ached from the recent encounter with the princess. Alina seemed to have that effect on her. Maybe she really did need a night away from the barracks. She took a sip.

"That's a good girl," Nat said. "Now what was it that kept you in the first place? You weren't on the training fields."

Senri took an even longer gulp from the beer, trying to stall for time. Nat raised an eyebrow. She looked around for Lanan, but the other Warrior had disappeared. "I was visiting with someone," she said. Even though she tried to relax her posture, the corner of Nat's mouth twitched. She squirmed. "Not like a friendly meeting or anything, business, actually."

This proved too much for Nat, and he snorted into his mug of beer, spittle escaping with the laughter. "Is that what they're calling it? Because there are several items of business I need to address tonight." Senri punched him in the shoulder. He winced and rubbed the spot on his arm. No armor to protect him that night. "Since when could you throw a punch?"

Senri shrugged. "That training has to do something."

"Yeah, I guess it does." Nat rubbed his arm a bit more. "So, this 'business' is actually serious then?"

"It is." Senri thought back to the princess's request. She could not bring up the subject in a crowded tavern, obviously, but she had to let Nat know something was going on. "There's an important mission we've been offered," she said. Nat nodded for her to continue. "She…uh…the master said there was a high factor of risk involved."

Nat frowned. "Tell me when you don't have to enjoy yourself. I want you to have fun for at least one night."

Before Senri could press the matter anymore, someone mounted a table. *Lanan.*

"Can I have everyone's attention?" Lanan yelled. The tavern quieted and turned to her. She looked a little nervous, but swallowed and continued, "We have a special guest here tonight. In fact, there's a song about her that I think we're all familiar with. A song about a certain hero, a savior. I think we could honor her by singing it tonight." Lanan winked at Senri, who bit back a groan and tried to escape, but Nat caught her and held her in place. A chorus of chuckles and shouts of approval rang through the audience. Lanan stepped down from the table. Someone pulled out a lute and strummed a chord, humming along with it.

"By the Almighty," groaned Senri. She rubbed her forehead and looked down at the floor, preferring not to be mocked for her blush. The lute-player sang the first few lines solo, but people joined in as soon as he hit the refrain. Tavern patrons clapped and stomped their feet in rhythm as it picked up pace to a suitable drinking song.

Lanan slipped between Senri and Nat and hung an arm over either shoulder. "Happy birthday," she said. Senri stared at her beer. "Care for a dance?"

Before she could protest, Lanan yanked her beer out of her hand and swept her onto a newly cleared area of the tavern. People whistled and howled while other couples joined them. Lanan would not let her go. She blushed as she let the other Warrior maneuver her into the proper position before bounding around the dance floor with her. As they moved to the intricate steps, Senri's shyness slipped away, and she laughed as one of the verses claimed she had slept with over twenty women and men.

"You like that one, hm?" asked Lanan.

Senri yelped as Lanan twirled her around. "It couldn't be more false."

"Oh, we know," said Lanan. "That's the point of the song though. It's serves to lighten people's spirits more than to inform."

"Happy to be of service then," said Senri. More and more people joined. They traded partners back and forth. The tune eventually ran out of verses declaring Senri's feats and jumped to another song.

When Lanan caught her arm again, she leaned in and asked, "So, have you seen enough young city-folk to be convinced there's more than that one girl in the whole village?"

At first, Senri did not know who Lanan referred to. Then, her eyebrows rose as she remembered one of their first conversations. "Oh, Vella," she said. Lanan laughed. They parted momentarily in a step of a different peasant dance and rejoined hands. "I suppose you're right."

"Are you still caught up on her?" Lanan asked. "Because more than one person has been watching you this night. We could orchestrate a collision."

Senri shook her head. "No, that's fine, thank you though."

Lanan sighed dramatically. "Very well then," she said. The weeks had lightened her spirits from the sorrow-ridden person who had been rescued. She spun Senri around one more time. "Though I think I should stop hogging you."

She stepped away only to be replaced by Nat, who pulled Senri boisterously onto the dance floor one more. "You know, it's good luck to dance with the birthday girl."

Senri rolled her eyes. "It's good luck no matter who you get a dance with."

"I'm wounded," declared Nat, adopting his familiar false bravado. Senri tried to punch his arm, but he caught the fist and forced her into a dip. Senri shrieked and he pulled her up again. "No trust," he sniffed. After a few minutes of hysterical attempts to dance, the two friends disentangled themselves. They stood on the sidelines, panting and leaning against a wall. "You know, I think that girl there has been eyeing you the whole night."

"Really?" asked Senri. Her voice held no hint of interest. She wasn't anyways.

"Yeah, right next to the bar. She's holding the two mugs."

Senri pretended to search. The young woman clearly studied Senri. She looked away. "I don't see her."

Nat grabbed her arm. "I'll just have to introduce you two."

Senri pulled her arm away and leaned against the wall once more. "No, I'd rather not."

"What?" asked Nat. He turned to Senri and frowned. "You're not still trying to stay noble and pure for Vella, are you?"

"Not really," said Senri.

"Then you should have no problem getting to know a new person." Senri still did not budge when Nat tugged on her. "Oh come on! What is your problem?"

She shrugged his hand off her arm. "I just don't feel like it tonight. You know, maybe I need to take a break."

Nat rolled his eyes. "To need a rest from an activity, you need to be engaged in it in the first place. I, for one, know you are not." Senri looked away and shoved her hands in her trouser pockets. She looked around for her beer mug. Her throat felt dry. "Or maybe you are," Nat said. He slinked back against the wall next to Senri. "Maybe you've got a certain woman on your mind after all. Brown hair, protective temperament, royal—"

"I don't." Senri turned to Nat with a glare. "I don't have any woman on my mind, okay?"

Nat took a step back and raised his hands. "All right, then I'm sure you'd have no problem dancing with that poor girl just to make her happy, hm?" He gazed down at her in challenge. Senri knew he waited for her to buckle or to confess to something. Well, she would not. Alina was off limits, non-existent in her realm of possibilities.

"Fine."

Nat raised an eyebrow. "Really?"

Senri nodded. "I'll do it."

"Right now?"

"Right now."

Nat grinned. "Excellent, I'll even help—"

Senri shook her head. "I'll do it myself, Nat."

Before her friend could add anything more to the conversation, she pushed off the wall and walked toward the woman who had been watching her. When she saw Senri approaching, she smiled, and then looked behind as if she expected Senri to walk by. "No, I'm looking at you," said Senri. *Act confident. Act casual.* "Uh, not that I was watching you or anything." *Well, there went that plan.*

The woman giggled and set down her mugs. "I don't know if I'd mind you watching."

"You don't?" asked Senri. Joy rushed through her. She had never had someone actively engage in flirting with her. It felt nice. "I mean, yes, you probably wouldn't." She ran a hand through her hair. "Not that I mean..."

The woman smiled even more. "Something tells me the verses embellished a little on your refined charm."

"Well, they did want it to be a good song." To her delight, the woman laughed again. Still, something felt off about it, hollow. She much preferred Alina's laugh. Senri shook her head and forced the feeling down. Nat had been right to mock her for her infatuation. "I was wondering if you'd like to dance, actually."

The woman eased off the bar countertop, extending her hand. "I think I'd like that."

Senri took the hand, but no warmth shot through her at the touch. She smiled anyways and pulled the girl onto the dance floor. Halfway through the first song, they kissed. Senri felt the warm lips against her own, but no passion coursed through her. She kissed back out of curiosity's sake, and when the woman pulled back she realized she did not even know her name.

Chapter Thirteen

SEVERAL WEEKS OF CAREFUL planning went into the set-up of Alina's departure. Senri and her friends agreed to accompany her and Nin finished the arrangements for Alina's double to stay at the castle. Alina had gone back and forth on deciding whether Nin should stay behind or accompany them. Someone would need to stay and extend the use of Lady Cecile beyond a few days. Nin seemed to be the perfect candidate, only Nin found the idea of being away from Alina unsettling.

"I was given the task to watch over you," Nin said. "It would be wrong to abandon you."

In the end, they both decided the success of Alina's plan hinged on Nin staying behind and leading the others astray. They even roped in Lady Vorica to assist in misdirecting. As the days passed, Alina still felt unsettled. She did not know if anything would work the way they intended, though Senri had assured her that all aspects of the plan were solid on their end. Finally, the day of their departure arrived.

It started with Senri knocking out the concealed panel and entering Alina's room. "Are you ready, your Highness?" She had managed the trip fully armored that time, having grown familiar with the passage.

"I…yes, I am ready," said Alina. She had dressed in borrowed slacks and a tunic that day, unfamiliar, yet necessary, clothes from her usual gowns. "Let us go."

Senri led her down the tunnel. They descended slowly in the dark confines. She rested her hand on Senri's shoulder in order to guide herself, trying to ignore the tingle in her hand even though she touched the cold armor. It might have had something to do with the concealed envelope lying underneath her tunic.

"Um, your armor is here, Highness." Senri came to a halt and Alina removed her hand.

"Where?"

"Hold on a moment."

A torch sparked to life in Senri's grasp. A full set of Warrior's leather armor lay by the entrance to the tunnel. Senri picked up the chest piece and handed it to her.

Alina slipped it on, fumbling over the straps. "If you could…"

"Oh, right." Senri placed the torch in an old, rusted holder that had been nailed into the tunnel wall years ago. She stepped behind Alina and tugged on the straps. The armor tightened around Alina's chest. Senri pulled harder and Alina felt something press awkwardly against her stomach.

"Wait a minute." She pulled the chest piece off and set it down. She retrieved the small envelope hidden in her tunic and handed it to Senri. "I know it was a while ago, but happy birthday."

Senri raised her eyebrows and took the envelope. "I…thank you, your Highness. You shouldn't have gotten—"

"I wanted to, please, just take it."

Senri pull the flap back to the envelope and reach a hand inside. She pulled out a thin, gold chain. A small pendant rested at the bottom it, circular with a faint inscription etched into the gold. "It's beautiful," she said, holding it up in the faint torchlight. She spotted the markings and pulled the pendant closer. "It says something."

"Savior of the Queen," Alina said. She blushed, remembering the scrutiny she had received when she ordered the jewelry crafted.

It could have been the torchlight, but Alina swore she saw Senri blush. "Thank you," Senri said. She raised the chain and pulled it over her head, letting the pendant slip down underneath her armor. "I'll wear it always." As touched as Senri sounded, she avoided meeting Alina's gaze and her voice caught.

"Is something the matter?"

Senri shook her head. "No, Highness. We should get the rest of your armor on." They dressed her in silence, pulling the armor on and tying her hair back in a suitable style for a young Warrior. Still, Alina would need to wear a helmet. Senri had brought along a concealing style. She slipped it over Alina's head. She stared at Senri through a small slot.

"Why would I be wearing this within the walls?"

"Training exercise," said Senri. "Some Warriors wear them for a few days to grow comfortable with the limited vision."

The two of them left through the sewer gate and walked down to the barracks. Alina had to step carefully since night had fallen. She barely saw past the torchlight through the helmet's visor. Instead of turning down to the Warrior's barracks, Senri and Alina continued onward to the other side of the palace, near the archery fields. They nodded at other Warriors as they passed. After they passed the exit to town, they moved with more caution. Alina nearly jumped when a Warrior turned down the same alley as them and approached. When Senri nodded at him, he stopped and looked them over. They came to a halt as well.

"Where are your orders?" asked the man.

Senri reached into her belt pouch and withdrew a folded slip of paper. She handed the forged orders over to the Warrior. This had probably been the most difficult piece to obtain. The Warrior named Lanan had produced an acceptable draft after several days of practice with watered down ink. Alina swallowed as she waited for the Warrior to finish reading over the assignment. It declared they were to patrol the archer's wall for the first night shift. It even bore the proper signatures. Or at least the Warrior would think they were proper.

He handed the paper back to Senri. "Carry on."

Senri led her down the archery targets and to the far corner. Instead of heading up to the walls for patrol, Senri let them into the dungeon. They descended the steps and took the first right corridor available, a secret exit in case of siege. The door on the end only worked from the inside so no one could infiltrate the palace grounds through it. They stopped at the very end of the tunnel.

Senri rested her hand on the hatch leading up to the surface. "Are you sure about this, your Highness?" She looked down at Alina.

"Yes, Senri." Alina's arms trembled under her armor, nervous enough without Senri second-guessing her. "I need to do this."

The Warrior nodded and pushed up against the hatch. The hinges moaned and earth crumbled as she burst forth into the night. She turned back to Alina and offered her a hand. Alina took it and let Senri help her up into the fresh night air. She took a deep breath and looked back at the wall. Senri set the hatch in place, invisible with the layer of field grass grown over it. The two set off for a nearby cluster of trees. Once they were in the small wood, Alina breathed a sigh of relief and removed her helmet.

"Who goes?" someone asked from behind the trees.

"The Savior," Senri replied dryly. From the tone of her voice, Alina guessed she had grudgingly agreed to the code word.

"Nice to see you two," said Nat, stepping from the trees. Lanan emerged as well.

"It's nice to see you got out safely," said Senri. "Are we all here, then?"

"Yahn and Onera are saying their goodbyes." Lanan grinned. "The horses are just beyond the trees. For palace mounts, they are fairly reliable."

"We train excellent horses, even if they are not intended for war." Alina stepped forward. "Thank you all for coming, but we should continue with the plan if all is well."

"Right, I'll fetch the lovebirds." Lanan disappeared farther into the trees and returned with Yahn and the woman named Onera. She was average height, but slender. Something about the way she walked suggested grace. She stepped barefoot through the grass and the plants almost stirred around her.

"It's time, then?" Yahn asked. Senri nodded.

Onera stepped forward, dressed in a simple tunic and skirt, and nodded to Alina. "Do not fear, your Highness. None will find your tracks by the time I finish here."

"I thank you," said Alina. "You do not know how much it means to me that all of you are so willing to help in such a dangerous task." The Warriors watched her with furrowed brows and unsmiling faces, a seriousness in their expressions Alina had not expected to find. They held more respect for her than any of the Councilors.

Lanan spoke, "None of us want to see Osota fall, Highness, you are doing more for this kingdom than anyone else."

Alina did not know how to respond. Yahn saved her from having to. "Well, the horses should be ready," he said, nodding over his shoulder. "We can saddle up and go."

As they moved out, Yahn lingered with Onera. Alina glanced behind and watched the two embrace in a tight hug before letting go. Onera stepped out onto the field and raised her hands. She moved forward, the grass rustling as she walked, erasing any trace of footprints they had ever left on the plains. She was a very talented reader, from what Alina could see. She would later erase as much of their horse tracks as she could.

Alina looked away and followed Senri to the horses laden with supplies. Yahn walked past her and swung into the saddle of his own steed. Alina walked over to the remaining horse and cautiously pulled herself upon it. She had never ridden in armor, or done anything in it, for that matter.

Without a word, the group brought their horses into line and set off through the forest, southward, moving slowly through the dense trees before breaking out onto a field an hour later. Alina looked over her shoulder and glanced at the far away capital one more time. She had not expected to leave it so soon. She shuddered. She might never see it again.

***

They rode through the night and well into midday. Once they reached a gathering of trees, Yahn called for them to stop. They would not be pursued so quickly, but all the same, Senri would rather not give reason to attract attention.

Senri dismounted, her sore legs complaining as soon as her feet hit the ground. The armor stifled her. Leading Stomps to a small creek with the other horses, she let him drink. As she unbuckled her breastplate, she remembered the pendant lying around her neck, the pendant Alina had given her. It made her somewhat guilty about the night spent with the girl from the tavern—Tala.

She pulled her tent supplies from her horse's pack and dropped them on the ground. It would be best to get a fire going first, something that would burn hot with very little smoke. Gathering kindling from the surrounding trees, Senri also grabbed dry branches she could break apart later. She enjoyed the quiet task. It gave her a chance to be away from Nat and Lanan's teasing. "Senri?" The sound of her name almost caused her to drop the branches. She turned and saw Alina standing close by.

"Did you need something, your Highness?"

Alina looked at the ground. Her brow furrowed and a blush spread over her cheeks. "I…well, it's a silly matter really, and if you are busy, I suppose it can wait but I—"

"The task, your Highness?"

Alina frowned and glanced back at her camp supplies. "I am having trouble assembling my tent correctly."

Senri almost laughed. "Is that all?" She tucked the kindling under one arm. "Here, I'll help."

Alina smiled. "Excellent. This way."

The tent looked like a heap of junk when they reached it. Alina had miss-tied several knots and placed the poles at the wrong corners of the cloth. Senri set down the kindling and crouched over the materials.

"What did you do to it?" she asked, trying to pull the pieces apart.

"I do not know. I don't usually set up tents."

Senri laughed. "You could have asked for help sooner."

"Well, I asked your friend Nat, but he said he was dreadful at it and that you would be much more suited."

"He what?" Senri glanced across the camp to where Nat worked. He gave her an innocent smile. *I'll kill him.*

"Is something wrong?"

Senri shook her head and picked up another piece of the tent. "No, I'd be happy to help, Highness." The rope took a good while to untangle, and Alina kept hovering and asking questions about the application of certain pieces. Finally, Senri managed to get the tent to cooperate and stand up correctly. She even shook one of the poles to test its durability. "I think it's safe, your Highness."

Alina knelt down beside her and pulled aside the tent flap. Senri looked at her, heat rising to her cheeks as her hands followed the movement of Alina's slender fingers. Despite trying to force the thoughts away, she could only think of the mistake in the tavern.

Alina leaned back from the tent, smiling. "Thank you, my savior."

Senri looked away. "Well, yes, I guess. Um…I'm going to set up the fire now."

"All right."

Senri picked up the kindling and turned to go. She stumbled and nearly fell, but regained her balance and took the armload to Yahn's fire pit. Alina's laugh followed her. *Don't look back. Just go build the fire.* Senri dumped the kindling into the pit and went to fetch sturdier logs to last through the night. The forest muted the sounds coming from the camp and allowed her to think as she walked around.

"You know, you sulk too much."

Senri turned and glared at Nat as he sauntered through the forest. "You could have helped her with the tent."

Nat walked over and gathered up dead branches. "But it was funnier to watch you do it. Besides, she likes you."

Senri jerked another branch out from the undergrowth. "She does not."

He raised an eyebrow and smiled. "Princess Alina, right? Brown hair, warm eyes, about this tall?" He raised a hand to Alina's estimated height. "Yes, her. She likes you quite a lot. What have you been doing in those secret meetings with her?"

"Nothing, and shut up." Senri pushed him away and stacked another fallen branch onto her pile. "It's not funny."

"I think it is quite adorable, actually," said Nat. "You two sort of play at flirting with one another, as if having feelings were against the rules."

"She's the princess," said Senri. She almost had enough firewood to head back to camp.

"And she's out on a suicide mission with us. Have a little fun." Nat thumped her on the back. "You can at least enjoy her company, if not pursue a real friendship with her. I'm not saying look up her royal skirts." He grabbed her shoulder when she tried to leave. "I'm not trying to be an ass. Just take my advice and have a little fun, will you? Stop treating her like a fragile thing. She kind of hates it when you do."

Senri glared at him, but her expression softened when he picked up some more branches and offered them to her. "I don't know if I will ever have you figured out, Nat."

"I'm a simple man, honest, and in good faith, I promise to behave through dinner."

Senri laughed and they walked back to camp, carrying the wood over to the fire pit.

Lanan joined them. "Finally, I'm ready to eat."

"You retrieve the firewood next time," said Senri.

She arranged the kindling the best way she could before igniting the branches. Nat and Yahn retrieved the cooking supplies, including a small, water-filled pot for the stew. The group set up quickly, throwing ingredients in without paying much attention to the combination. Inevitably, Alina walked over, fussing with her leather armor, as she looked into the pot.

"What is that?" she asked.

"Our meal," said Senri, glancing back toward the princess.

"Yes, but what are you cooking?" she asked.

Nat smiled. "Stew, your Highness, I'm afraid the roasted venison is all out."

Alina blushed. "I...I didn't mean..."

Nat laughed. "Relax. I like to tease. You'll have to get used to it." Senri shot him a scowl. "I mean, I could knock it off, I guess."

Alina grinned. "Oh, ignore her, I prefer that people treat me normally. The titles can be distancing sometimes."

"Well then, I am happy to serve." Nat bowed and offered her an empty bowl. Alina giggled. Senri noticed her eyes followed his hand, and then his tall form as he stood and walked over to the pack horse.

"He's a fool to everyone," said Senri. The statement shocked her as soon as she said it, not that she had declared the obvious about Nat, but the derisive manner in which she said it.

Alina raised an eyebrow at her. "It's a quality I admire. Everyone is on level ground with your friend."

Senri nodded and turned her attention back to the fire. She crouched and pretended to give it some thought. After a while, she reached a hand into the flame and readjusted a log. Alina's shout caused her to pause. She glanced back at her. "What?"

"Your hand." Alina's eyes widened.

Senri glanced back into the fire, her fingers engulfed in flame. "Oh, don't worry about that." She pulled her hand out and waved it at Alina to show her undamaged skin. "You don't have much experience with readers, I take it?"

"I hardly get the opportunity to see them perform such tasks. I mean, manipulating plant life...they do that in the gardens all the time. I just...you're not hurt, are you?" She extended a hand and looked at Senri expectantly. The Warrior looked around, hoping to find some form of misdirection, but Alina would not be persuaded. "I just want to look. It will take a moment."

Senri raised her hand and let Alina take hold of it. Small jolts traveled along her skin where Alina touched. The princess rubbed the back of Senri's hand, as if searching for blemishes. Alina turned

Senri's hand over, running her fingers over Senri's palm. Senri's whole hand felt like it had ignited. She pulled back. "See? No damage."

The answer seemed to satisfy Alina, or perhaps her brusqueness conveyed her uneasiness, because Alina maintained her distance with her the rest of the day. The group ate and spoke together, but as the sun began to set, the fatigue from the constant riding seemed to catch up with them. Yahn arranged shifts for the watch.

Senri had the third watch, so she crawled inside her tent and tried to sleep. As much as she wanted to drift off into a deep slumber though, she awoke every so often and glanced out the tent flap. Had they really made such a clean escape? It felt too easy, being out in the wilderness with Alina. Then again, escaping unnoticed had been the goal all along.

Senri closed her eyes and pulled her blanket higher. Her turn for the watch had to be close. She'd be the most useless protector ever if she fell asleep during it. *I'm a useless protector anyways, getting caught up in my own lovesick thoughts after barely a day with her.* She rubbed her palm, worry tightening her stomach. Her hand still throbbed from Alina's touch hours before.

Michelle Magly

Chapter Fourteen

TRAVEL WORE ON NORMALLY for the second day. Alina kept trying to angle her horse over next to Senri's so they could talk, but the Warrior kept finding excuses to stray. Yahn needed help with something. One of the pack horses had fallen too far behind. Senri thought she saw something off by the forest's edge. Senri avoided her.

For the last leg of their journey that day, Alina switched tactics and moved to ride next to Nat. "Greetings!" He waved as she approached. Alina nodded and fell into line next to him at an easy gait. "Enjoying the ride?" he asked.

Alina glanced over at him. With the sparse beard and curly hair, he looked roguish, almost handsomely so. In a few more years, he would grow into being quite the man. "I would enjoy it more if the company were more amiable." She glanced over at Senri, who currently rode at the head of the pack with Yahn.

Nat followed her gaze. "Ah. You've noticed her poor manners, then?"

"Is that really all it is?"

"No. I'm afraid you intimidate her," Nat replied.

"What?"

He pointed at her. "You in all your regal elegance and beauty are an intimidating woman. You are sure of yourself, headstrong, and you stand up for what you believe in. On top of that, you can outshoot any of us here with that thing." He nodded at the bow Alina had slung over her body. She had strapped a quiver of arrows to her horse for the ride as well. It completed her look as a fellow Warrior. Nat grinned. "You are nothing like any of the girls back in our village."

"You and her hail from the same place?"

"Grew up together. It's a small, quiet place. We are passing through there to get to the southern mountains. It's really insignificant compared to the capital."

"And there were no other girls like me there?" she asked. Nat shook his head. "Well, what about Lanan?"

"Not from the same place. Anyways, she's tall, taller than Senri, and she's a Warrior, so she has the occupation to match that intimidating demeanor. You are a princess, a damsel, but you don't quite fit Senri's perception of a damsel."

Alina huffed. "Does she expect me to sit idly by and let others do my work? I am not some delicate—"

"No, no." He held out a cautionary hand, motioning for her to be quiet. "She admires all that about you. She just doesn't know how to act around you, Highness. Senri was always a bit of a rule-follower, very old-fashioned minded."

"So how do I get her to drop the formalities?" Alina watched the way Senri's body shifted with the horse's gait. Even with armor on, she liked to imagine she could see the powerful form underneath flexing and bending with the motions. *Formalities are not quite what I intend for her to drop.* Alina looked down.

"You have to trick her into being chivalrous, like getting her to set up your tent," Nat replied. "Eventually, she will realize you are a human and ease up a little. I think she realizes already, honestly."

Alina let her gaze linger on Senri before glancing back at Nat. "And how do I know all your advice is sound? You speak for her so surely."

Nat smiled sadly. "You were not close to anyone your age growing up, were you?"

Before Alina could answer, Nat spurred his horse onward to the front of the pack. Alina stayed in the rear, letting her mount amble along, trusting the steed to keep up with the others. Nat's comment caused a small pang of jealousy in her. Alina had often imagined what it might be like to grow up as one of the children in the villages her and her father visited. It became another reason to love Osota. So many of its people seemed happy, much happier than her.

As they rode on, Alina remembered how drastically the landscape of the plains changed in the fall. The grass took on a yellowish hue, deepening as it dried. Whenever the wind swept over the rolling hills, the strands crackled against themselves. Trees reddened in the distance as well. The colors mingled on the horizon and contrasted against the blue sky.

"Princess!"

She blinked and looked away from the horizon. Senri rode toward her. She smiled. "Well, I see I am no longer to be ignored."

Senri looked at her, eyebrows raising. "You let yourself get so far away from the others." She nodded back at the pack. Everyone else stood a good distance away from them. They had stopped moving and sat turned in their saddles, waiting.

"I'm sorry," said Alina as she looked back to Senri. "I let myself get distracted."

Senri's hand went to the pommel of her sword. "Is there something wrong?"

Alina shook her head. "I was admiring the landscape." Senri still looked around as if bandits would spring from the ground.

"What about it?" Senri asked. Her brow had furrowed as she stared at a cluster of trees.

"It's a beautiful scenery," said Alina. "Relax."

Senri removed her hand from the grip of her sword. "Oh." She avoided Alina's gaze.

Alina sighed and shook her head. "How much farther is the ride today?"

"We will stop at the next river. A few hours, maybe."

"Will you ride the distance with me?" asked Alina. "I would love the company."

"If your Highness wishes it."

The stiff reply might have hurt Alina, but the nervous wobble in Senri's voice softened the blow. The Warrior's restricted manners made her want to scream. "Only if you wish it, Senri. If you bend at knee for all my whims, you may regret the position it puts you in."

Alina spurred her horse to ride on. She smirked as she imagined the confused look on Senri's face. When the Warrior caught up with her, she noticed a pink tinge on Senri's cheeks. She laughed. They caught up with the group and resumed their steady pace. Senri stayed with Alina rather than move ahead with the rest, possibly afraid of a public reiteration. After they traveled for nearly a half hour in uncomfortable silence, Senri spoke up, "I'm only trying to keep you safe, Highness."

"I know," Alina replied. "But you need to stop placing me on a pedestal. We are staking our lives on one another."

Senri did not respond, though the tension seemed to ease between them for the rest of the day's journey. Either way, Alina liked having Senri at her side. She rode with Alina until they stopped to make camp for the evening. Senri dismounted first and walked to the side of Alina's horse. She held out an expectant hand.

"And what is that for?" Alina asked.

"I thought you might need some help down," said Senri, smiling. Alina's grip tightened on her reins.

"I'm perfectly capable of getting myself down," she said, trying to sound neutral and unoffending.

Senri's smile faded and she lowered her hand. "I know, your Highness." She took a step back. "I was only trying to be polite."

Alina sighed and dismounted her horse. "I'm sorry, you have to understand that people waited on me night and day in the palace. It was a little wearisome."

They walked over to the pack animals and helped the others pull their supplies down. Senri tugged her tent kit free and walked away. Alina looked over the pack animal and tried to remember which bundle of items belonged to hers. She bit her lip and glanced around. She caught Senri's eye and saw the Warrior arch an eyebrow at her. *No, I have to keep looking.*

A bundle of supplies suddenly lurched forward off the horse and Alina jumped to catch it. Nat smiled at her from the other side of the mare's flanks. "Thought you might need that," he said, then grabbed his own supplies and walked over to join the others. Alina clutched the bundle of supplies close to her chest. *Curse the whole lot of Warriors.*

As she tried to set up her tent, Alina found the same problems reoccurring from the night before. She had sworn she did everything exactly as Senri did, but the damned tent refused to stay standing. She grabbed fistfuls of the cloth as it tumbled down for the fourth time and resisted the urge to rip it apart. A piece had to be missing.

Alina threw down the tent cloth and walked through the tall grass, searching for anything she might have dropped between herself and the pack horse. A light wind gusted over the plains and caused the grass to ripple. She soon gave up and returned to her unassembled tent. By then, everyone else had put theirs together. She sat down and picked up the pieces to hers once more. The evening sky seemed free of clouds, but that could change in a heartbeat.

"Is everything all right, Highness?"

Alina turned. Senri stood close by, looking down at her with a somewhat puzzled expression. She glanced down at her own tent supplies and swallowed. "I swear I made note of how you did it. But it refuses to cooperate."

Senri knelt down beside her. "You mean it's still giving you trouble?"

Alina nodded and handed over the supplies. Senri took the rope and stake from her hands, their fingers brushing together momentarily. The contact made her skin heat. Alina sat back and watched Senri work. Her eyes followed the deft movements of Senri's long fingers. She had taken her time studying them the previous night. Even so, she had not had her fill of the strong hands. The overwhelming urge to interlock her fingers with Senri's startled her from time to time.

The framework of the tent stood precariously in a matter of minutes. Senri's brow furrowed and she quickly searched the ground around herself. "There's a piece missing."

"I thought so." Some of the tension eased in Alina's stomach. "I was beginning to feel severely incompetent."

Senri looked over at her. "You should have asked someone for help. I know you aren't too keen on letting me, but there's a camp full of people willing to do so." A moment later she added, "your Highness."

"Senri!" Alina almost toppled the half-assembled tent as she tugged at the rope. "I refused your help earlier, because I was perfectly capable of getting off my own damn horse, not because I had anything against you. In fact, I was trying to make the point that I do not need special attention."

"But you let me do this." Senri gestured at the tent.

"Yes, and I am grateful for your assistance."

"So why get all upset over me wanting to help you off your horse?"

"How many other people were you rushing to help dismount? Ever since we left the palace you've been making an extra effort to make sure the dainty little princess is not disturbed by the wild and untamed plains."

"That's not why I wanted to help you off the horse."

Alina heard the hurt in her voice. She suddenly regretted her harsh words. She sighed and dropped the rope. "So, why did you?"

Senri glanced up at her. A faint blush crawled up her cheeks. "No reason," she muttered. She brushed her hands together and stood up. "I can fashion you a new piece for the tent, give me a moment."

The Warrior walked away to the center of the camp where the others had dragged most of the supplies. Alina blinked and shook her head, muttering curses to herself. *She finally decides to flirt a little and I brush it off as over-protective impulses.* Alina stood and straightened her leather armor. Royal courtship had always been so easy. Parents did everything for the prospective lovers, and then the two lovebirds did not even meet until the day of the wedding. Her own parents had discussed potential marriage candidates for her, even at such a young age. Maybe having the freedom to choose hindered her.

***

After many days of travel toward the village, Senri accepted Alina flirting with her. Every night, something seemed to go wrong with her tent, though Senri believed this to be Nat's intervention more than anything else. Either way, she helped Alina set it up every time. The previous attempt still burned fresh in her mind and made her whole body go flush. She had suggested Alina tie the knots for the posts, and when the princess could not get the rope to behave, Senri reached forward and wrapped her hands over Alina's, guiding them gently through the steps. Halfway through her instruction, Alina gazed at her with a deep blush on her cheeks. Senri had cleared her throat and continued on, determined not to call attention to it. The dreams following that night would have made Nat blush. Senri's own face reddened at the memory, her breath caught.

That morning, Lanan leaned down next to her while she prepared breakfast and whispered, "Try not to call her name out so much next time you go to sleep."

Senri's eyes widened and she almost spilled the oats she cooked over the morning fire. "What?"

Lanan winked and went back to securing her supplies.

As they rode the last stretch to the village, Senri kept glancing over at Alina, trying to gauge if she had overheard the sleep talk. Alina caught her glances. "See something interesting?" She slowed her horse down to ride next to Senri. The path through the forest left little room for the party to drift.

Senri swallowed and looked away. "Nothing in particular, no." Segments from the dream flickered through her mind, a body underneath her, like the night at the inn, only Alina smiled up at her, kissed her on the cheek and then her collarbone. She blinked the images away.

"Well, your mind appears to be elsewhere entirely. Is it a pleasant place?"

"Where?"

"Wherever your thoughts are escaping to."

"Oh." Senri tried to suppress the thoughts of the dream and stared at the horn of her saddle. "It's not so interesting." Although she tried to act casual, she knew Alina noted the way she shifted around too much.

"Are you nervous about returning to your village this evening?" Alina asked.

Honestly, Senri looked forward to seeing her family again, but she would not get anxious until Nat returned from scouting ahead. She took hold of the lifeline anyways. "Yes, I suppose."

"Do you have loved ones you will be visiting?"

"A family, yes." Senri smiled, remembering her little brothers and their endless energy. "My parents and three brothers. Though they might be disappointed I didn't bring back a trophy for them."

"They expected you to bring back spoils of war?" Alina raised an eyebrow.

"Oh no. That was a small joke between us. They'll be glad I'm returning in one piece." They both laughed. Senri glanced over at Alina and grinned. The princess looked down and tucked a strand of hair behind her ear.

"And...is there anyone else you look forward to seeing?" The question came forth hesitant. Senri tried to catch Alina's eye and determine what she meant by it, but Alina stared straight ahead.

"The other townsfolk, I suppose. They're good people."

Alina sighed. "No lovers, then?"

"Huh?" Senri's eyes widened. "Oh, no. No one like that in my life, currently."

A corner of Alina's mouth turned upward. "I see."

Senri looked away as her face grew hot, the lilt in Alina's tone much too obvious. Yahn cried out a greeting and waved a hand at Nat, who had returned from his scouting mission. He waved back and Senri pushed her horse closer to the front of the line. The party came to a halt as Nat rejoined them. His horse looked worn from the hard riding.

"News from the village, then?" asked Yahn.

Nat nodded and grinned at Senri. "They were asking about you, I think the whole town is coming out to welcome us."

"Well, that won't look conspicuous at all," said Lanan. Senri turned in her saddle and saw Lanan smile at her.

"They just know how to give a proper hero's welcome," said Nat.

"Let's not keep them waiting, then," said Yahn. "I would hate to deprive your adoring public."

Even though his tone was dry, the others chuckled. The group set out again in a matter of minutes. Senri patted Stomps's mane as they rode deeper into the forest. She recognized certain trees and hills from her short journeys beyond the village. Even though she had seen the leaves turn to fall colors many times, she had missed an entire season. Yellowed leaves already began to blanket the forest floor. Winter would settle in soon.

"And there you go again." Once more, Alina's voice pulled her from her thoughts.

Senri blinked and turned away from the forest floor. "I'm sorry, your Highness. I just find it odd to be returning home after so long."

Alina nodded and raised a hand to a branch she passed. She plucked a fiery leaf from its stem. "Try staying away for years." She released the leaf into the wind.

The sadness behind the words made Senri realize how petty her complaint sounded. "It must have been hard."

Alina's fingers tighten around the reins of her horse. "It is."

With everything Alina had been through, Senri marveled that the princess had not run away to a bordering kingdom. It would have been much easier. Somehow, Senri knew that Alina would balk at the idea of running off while Osota suffered. "We should be at the village soon," said Senri. "Less than an hour away, easily."

"You must be excited." Alina smiled, though it did not carry up to her eyes.

"You could call it that." Senri glanced around, trying to find another landmark. "Nat said we were in for a big welcome. I hope you don't mind."

This time, Alina smiled genuinely. "I look forward to it, I have not been to a village since my father passed on to the Almighty. I always enjoyed my time with him, away from politics and lessons."

The conversation ebbed from there. Senri found herself too distracted by the thought of returning home to engage in meaningful talk. As they moved closer to the village, an odd sound came from the village. She cocked her head to one side and listened. It sounded so familiar, like a song she had heard a long time ago…Senri's eyes widened. "Oh no."

Alina twisted in her saddle. "Hm? Is something wrong, Senri?"

As they drew closer, the noise formed the unmistakable hum. "Very, Nat is going to die."

Alina's brow furrowed. "Why? What happened? Are we in danger?" But Senri did not need to answer, because the chorus of "Savior of the Queen" finally rang out in full clarity from the village. Alina laughed. "I'm impressed it made it this far."

Senri frowned. "It's not funny. Nat!"

"Oh, shut up," he called back. "Can't you see I'm listening to some quality music?"

From the sound of it, every single villager had to be outside singing, and as soon as they broke through the forest, Senri saw the confirmation. Every household had emptied out to the front of the village to greet them. Her family waved. Her brothers jumped up and down. Ean looked impossibly tall, and Garth and Mattus had grown a bit as well. Nat's cluster of brothers and sisters stood at the forefront of the villagers. Every single person sang along at the top of their lungs. Senri hid her face in her hands.

Her family approached her before they reached the village. Her mother had tears in her eyes and her father helped her down out of her saddle. He hugged her tightly. "You didn't really kill all those bears as a child," he mumbled into her ear.

Senri laughed and hugged him back before being passed along to her mother for a breathtaking grip. The unintelligible wails almost formed words, but became lost in the sobs. Senri grimaced and rubbed her mother's back. She had hoped her mother would not take her absence so badly. By the time her mother finished with her, her brothers had barraged her with every question imaginable: "So are you on a secret quest? Did you really hold off a battalion of bandit-assassins single handed?"

To this, Nat hollered, "I helped!"

His own siblings hung off his arms and neck while his parents stood close by. Her brothers took off to get Nat's much more exciting version of their travels and Senri got passed from villager to villager, shaking hands with most of them. Malcor hugged her just as fiercely as her mother. He seemed to be several inches taller, though Senri knew she had not been away long enough for that to be the truth. Gustav stood beside him. He nodded at the sword hanging from her horse's saddle pack.

"Didn't lose it, I see?" he asked.

The same sort of greetings dragged on for what seemed like an eternity. Senri's parents informed her about the bonfire in celebration of their return, though her mother nearly burst into tears when she learned they would ride out in a few days again. Eventually, Yahn suggested everyone go about their business, and when the villagers showed resistance to this, he asked for help stabling the horses and preparing the feast. Everyone mobilized in an instant, leaving only a few stragglers standing at the town entrance.

Before he left for the corral, Yahn leaned in close to Senri and muttered, "I sent Lanan to check the perimeter. Do not leave Alina's side for a second."

Senri glanced over her shoulder at Alina, who stood quite alone after being helped off her horse. Some of the villagers glanced at her, but everyone else had gone off. She nodded and Yahn joined the others who led the horses away. Senri approached her.

Alina smiled, looking around at the village. "Such a lovely welcome."

"Yes, they get a little carried away some—"

"Senri!"

She looked back toward the inn. Vella descended the front door steps, only this time the young inn maid waved and smiled like Senri used to. Senri nodded. She had no time to devote to Vella's half-attentive looks. The village woman probably wanted to find Lanan anyways.

"Senri, you're back!" Vella walked over to her, blushing. Her breathing seemed a little heavy.

Vella's attention remained tightly fixed on Senri. Such intensity reminded her of every time she had stared at Vella and nearly willed her to look back like she did now.

"Hello, Vella. How have you been?" Senri could have sworn the princess scowled as she glanced back and forth between Senri and Vella.

Vella glanced down at her feet and played with a lock of blonde hair. "I've been all right. The village has felt so lonely since you left."

"Probably because Nat is not around to cause mischief." Senri looked around for Lanan. Where was she supposed to take Alina? She could just imagine Yahn yelling at her for letting the princess loiter outside.

"You've been all that travelers talk about." Vella took a step closer.

"It's not me. It's that silly song Nat composed." Senri glanced over at Alina, who smiled wickedly. "And don't you say a thing about it."

"Oh? And who is this?" asked Vella. Wrong move.

"Did you not hear?" asked Alina. They had all agreed to never inform someone of Alina's true identity until arriving in the dragon lands, though something about her composure screamed trouble. She looped an arm around one of Senri's. The Warrior practically jumped. "I thought the song detailed it quite well."

Vella's eyes widened and Senri heated almost to the point of combusting her clothes.

"Oh," Vella said, flipping her hair back. Somehow Vella made the move look threatening. "I see you brought some souvenirs back from the capital."

Oh Almighty, take me from this world now. She felt Alina lean on her even more.

"You never mentioned her," said Alina.

This remark did it. Vella frowned and took a step back. "I can see why you would prefer village life, Senri, if these are the manners they cultivate in the city." Vella turned on her heel and marched back to the inn.

Senri felt like she might be sick, though she felt Alina's body shaking with laughter. Alina waited until Vella had disappeared into the building before asking, "Have you been up her skirt?"

"What?" asked Senri. She pulled her arm from Alina and stepped away.

Alina smiled and pursued. "You heard me, have you had a look up her skirts?"

"I...never!" said Senri. "And why did you have to go and pretend to be my...well..."

"Your lover? Because I cannot exactly say who I really am, and it was absolutely hilarious to watch her reaction."

"But she's mad at me now!" Senri ran her hands through her hair, tugging at the ends.

Alina shrugged. "So, do you care?"

"No! I mean, I had things to do and she was pestering me—"

"I would too, if you had gone up my skirts and left."

"But I didn't!"

Alina grinned. She looked far too satisfied with herself. "Well, she certainly wishes you had." She walked farther into the village.

Senri followed. "She never showed any interest before. I swear, she's never been that persistent in talking to me. I think she might be ill."

Alina stopped and laughed. She turned back to Senri. "Do you realize what has happened?" Senri looked at her with a raised brow, so Alina continued, "She's enamored with you now, probably because of all the tales of your heroics—"

"Rumors," corrected Senri.

Alina raised a finger and pressed it against Senri's breastbone. "Not all of them." She removed the accusatory finger and walked onwards. "Though I daresay some of those stanzas are a little too licentious even for my imagination."

Senri chased after the princess. Her ears burned with blush. "And what does that mean?"

"Best you not know," she said. Senri caught up and Alina slowed to a more leisurely pace. She glanced up at Senri. "Would you like to show me the sights, then?"

She gulped. Perhaps letting her watch over Alina had been a mistake. If Vella let word spread that Senri had returned home sporting a new plaything, Yahn might throttle her.

Chapter Fifteen

PRETENDING TO BE SENRI'S lover might have been a step too far, but Alina enjoyed herself far too much to reconsider her choice. Senri led her around the town in the most discreet manner possible, sticking to the less-populated alleys and behind the shops and barns. By the time they had completed half the circuit, Alina stopped. Senri had been rambling on about the trees in that particular section of the forest and their bark properties according to the season, but soon came to a halt and turned back to Alina.

"I thought you wanted to see the village," she said.

"Yes, well, when I requested that, I assumed you would introduce me to the villagers rather than lead me down dark alleys," Alina replied. *And tell me about tree bark. I think that's the last thing I needed to know about.*

"I can't have you out in front of the town!" Senri massaged the side of her face and gestured at the buildings with her free hand. "People are not supposed to know you are here."

"Which is why I am here as an ordinary person, your lover, as Vella would think."

Senri folded her arms across her chest. "And would you have me introduce you as such to the whole village? Half of them probably think so thanks to Vella."

Alina smiled and glanced at the backs of the buildings. "Well, introducing me to everyone would certainly be less scandalous than running around with me in the shadows. Who knows what we could be doing back here?"

"Nothing," yelled Senri.

Alina arched an eyebrow. "And is that what the town will think?"

"I..." Senri's shoulders sagged. "Fine. Who shall I introduce you to, oh lover of mine? My parents?"

"Actually, I would love to meet them." Alina could have laughed at the look of frustration on Senri's face, but suddenly the panicked look vanished.

Senri raised her eyebrows and nodded. "You know, yes, that sounds like an excellent idea. I get to make up your name, though."

She led Alina down an alley and back into the center of the village. They took off on a dirt road towards the outskirts of town.

"You don't need to," said Alina. "You can tell them I was named after her Majesty Queen Alaina."

"Fine," said Senri. She walked rigidly, like a soldier off to battle.

She reached out and grabbed Senri's forearm. "Wait."

Senri halted and glared at Alina.

Yes, I have definitely pushed her too far. "I'm sorry, all right?" she said. "I'm sorry if I put you in an awkward position by implying that we are lovers. I just wanted to have some fun, but you have got to relax." Senri tried to protest, but Alina pushed on, "I know you want to protect me, but if you keep worrying over me so much, people will begin to suspect something is wrong. I figured spreading a rumor that we are lovers would help excuse some of your erratic behavior, but if you keep tailing me like a mother griffon, people will know we are hiding something." She paused and watched the realization seep into Senri's expression. The frown softened and her eyebrows unknitted. Alina gestured to the bow and quiver of arrows she wore "I'm supposed to be a fellow Warrior. I can take care of myself. Act like it."

Senri tried and failed to speak several times. "I...suppose it makes for good cover." She looked around the village as if suspecting eavesdroppers to descend from the tree tops. "We could have discussed it before, though."

Alina shrugged. "It was somewhat of an in-the-moment decision." She grinned and Senri rolled her eyes.

The two continued down the path. Senri kicked small piles of leaves as they walked. "My family has never had the pleasure of me bringing someone home. I don't know what they'll do. Interrogate you, most likely."

"They will be nothing compared to the Council."

Senri laughed. "You would think that."

The two walked farther away from the village, out toward farmland. The plots were small, not enough to account for an entire farm. The cleared land laid barren save for scattered fall leaves. Harvest had already gone by for these people.

"What does your family do out here?" asked Alina.

"We have an apple orchard," said Senri. She gestured at the cleared plots of land. "This serves as a grain supply. We only trade it with the villagers. The apples, though, are bartered with the merchants that come through."

"The daughter of an apple farmer," Alina mused. They walked past the farmland and back into the forest.

A cottage soon came into sight at the end of the path. Alina wanted to take hold of Senri's hand, to entwine their fingers together and feel Senri's palm against her own. She had the excuse to. If Senri made a fuss, she could insist it was for the better of their appearance, but then it felt as though she took advantage of Senri. She wanted Senri to want her. Senri's behavior had swung between so many extremes over the journey she had no idea what the Warrior desired.

"Here," said Senri.

Alina felt warm fingers snake between her own and Senri's hand squeezed hers. She looked down at their interlocked fingers, heat flooding the back of her neck.

"I thought we could at least play the part." Senri smiled down at her and Alina's face heated even more. Her heart beat frantically against her chest.

Alina took a deep breath. "Just play?" She glanced up at Senri and watched her face turn red. She smiled though, making Alina's breath catch. *Perhaps she does want me?*

Senri opened and closed her mouth a few times as if she searched for the words.

"Hey, Senri! Who's that?"

The shout made Alina jump. She almost expected to blink and find herself waking from a daydream, but everything remained as it was. Senri's hand stayed in her own. They still walked down a dirt road to Senri's house. One of her siblings ran forward, or she assumed he was as the little boy waved to them, his loose tunic hanging around his neck and trousers scuffed at the knee. He ran up to them and Senri withdrew her hand, sweeping the boy up in her arms.

"Hey!" She hefted the boy up over her shoulder like a sack of flour. He squealed and banged his fists against the backside of her armor.

"Put me down," he yelled, causing a clamorous clang with his fists.

"Senri!"

Two other boys stepped out of the house, the same ones who had greeted her. One looked close to Alina's age. Senri placed her smallest brother down so that her other two could hug her properly.

"Sorry we didn't stick around earlier," the tallest one said. "We figured mom wanted you to herself for a little."

"Yeah, and now she's going to cry into the food," said the middle child. "Couldn't you have waited to come over?"

"Mattus!" Both Senri and the eldest brother spoke at once. They even moved to punch him on the arm, but he side-stepped their blows.

"Senri, who's that?" The youngest one tugged on Senri's arm and pointed at Alina. Senri glanced back at her and winked.

"This is someone very important to me, Alina. She is a Warrior I have been training with."

"Is that what the city-folk call it?" asked the eldest one.

"Ean." Senri glared at the boy. Alina raised a hand to her mouth to cover the growing smile. "Go on then, introduce yourselves." Senri stood aside to allow them better access. The smallest boy ran up first and grabbed her hand.

"I'm Garth," he said, squeezing her fingers in a hard grip.

"Hi, Garth." He released her fingers and Alina flexed the stiffness out of them.

"Mattus," said the middle child. He took her hand and cordially kissed the top of it.

Alina laughed. The boy had not even hit puberty. "My pleasure."

The tallest boy nodded at her. "Ean."

The five of them stood in the middle of the path. The three boys glanced between Alina and Senri, as if they did not know who to devote their time to. They all looked different from Senri with their dark hair and freckled complexion, though something about their facial expressions and mannerisms seemed mirrored in one another.

Senri cleared her throat. "Um, shall we go inside, then?"

The cottage felt small to Alina. The entrance opened out to a kitchen and sitting room. Everyone squeezed in the doorway, elbowing one another as they kicked off boots. Senri's parents arrived soon after and Alina went through a whole new round of introductions. "This is Sonya and Markos," Senri said, gesturing to each of them. In turn, her parents smiled hesitantly at Alina. Senri's brothers taunted her mercilessly about bringing someone home, and her parents, while being completely welcoming, still treated Alina like she was an oddity. Senri's mother, upon examining their armor, ordered the two to go change into something more appropriate for dinner. Senri fought but soon lost and shyly led Alina away to one of the small bedrooms.

Alina shut the door behind them and examined the room. It had to be smaller than any of her living arrangements. She could not imagine how someone as tall as Senri moved around comfortably while sharing with a sibling.

Senri stooped over an old, wooden chest and pulled garments from it. She set some clothes aside on the floor. "These should fit you." Senri nodded at the pile. "I think they fit me a few years ago, before my last growth spurt."

Alina grabbed the clothes and looked around the room. "Where should I change?"

"I won't look." Senri pulled her own clothes from the chest and straightened up. She kept her back turned to Alina.

She looked down at the coarse-spun clothes. Senri had given her a skirt to wear. Before she could change, she heard the clanking of metal and looked up. Senri had unbuckled her armor and laid it down along with her chain shirt. The plain flaxen shirt underneath looked crumpled and stained from several days of use. Senri pull the hem up over her head, revealing the smooth, muscled expanse of her back. She tossed the shirt aside and Alina caught a glint of light off a delicate golden chain. Senri still wore the necklace she gave her.

Alina looked down. It was rude to stare. Instead, she changed into her own clothes. As she finished tying the skirt in place, Senri said, "Let me know when you're done."

She tied off the last knot and faced Senri. "All right."

The Warrior turned around. She wore a simple tunic and trousers. Somehow, away from the capital, the clothes seemed much more rural. The small pendant rested on the outside of her shirt. Senri's hand reached up and touched it, probably to make sure it stayed in place.

"You look—" Alina stopped herself. *Beautiful.* She had blindly lusted after this woman, practically thrown herself at her. Senri deserved more, though. Much more. "Senri, we don't have to pretend to be lovers. I don't want to make your life any harder than it is for my sake."

Senri stepped forward and looked Alina over. She straightened Alina's tunic and pulled the strings to the front slit tighter. Then, she tucked a strand of Alina's hair behind her ear. It was all Alina could do to keep from shaking with nerves. Senri's fingers lingered on her cheek. "Sometimes it's nice to pretend."

With that one statement, Senri sapped all of Alina's willpower. Her gaze drifted down to Senri's lips, then back up to her eyes. Those emerald eyes, just like she had first seen in the market, only this time Senri truly stood before her.

Senri's hand lowered. "Come on, we shouldn't keep them waiting."

***

Evening had approached quickly. Senri sat at the inn bar with Nat and Lanan while Alina and Yahn danced with the villagers outside. The bonfire had attracted everyone's attention and left the inn pleasantly quiet for the three friends. Senri twirled an empty mug on the countertop.

"And how did the dinner go, then?" asked Nat. "You two weren't feeling each other up under the table?"

"No." Senri shook her head. "Nothing like that. My parents were really polite. My brothers were, well, you know." She shrugged.

Lanan laughed and took a swig from her own mug. "Senri, you're the only person I know to get in such a fix."

"And what does that mean?" Senri leaned over the counter and glared at her friend.

"The girl you were hopelessly pining after is now plotting Alina's death, and the girl you are currently pining after wants you and you don't even grab the line she's thrown you."

Senri slumped back into her bar stool and stared at the

countertop. "She's happy here, I don't think I've seen Alina so happy."

Nat grinned. "She's had you to herself all day, why wouldn't she be?"

Senri nudged his arm. She lacked the conviction to punch it like usual. "It's more than that. She's happy about being normal. She likes being Alina, the sharpshooter in our company of Warriors. She likes being Alina, the simple village girl who met me during training one afternoon at the archery range."

"Not a complete lie," said Lanan.

"Yeah. It's not like she has a responsibility to the whole kingdom or anything." Senri snorted. She thought back on the dinner they had shared with her parents. Senri had almost been convinced of the guise herself. "Sometimes I think she forgets that she has to go back."

"Who could blame her? I'd run away from the palace first chance I got if they wanted to put me in charge." Nat tipped the last of his mug's contents into his mouth.

"Do you think she plans on returning at all?" asked Senri. The topic had puzzled her all afternoon. Both shrugged.

"Why not ask her?" said Lanan.

"Because that would be too practical," Nat replied. "We don't do practical."

Senri glanced down at her empty mug. Her mother had said something earlier that day about brewing cider. "No, I think practical might be a good thing this time." She pushed the mug aside and stood. She fetched her sword from the rack and retied the scabbard to her belt.

Her friends said their goodbyes and she took off out the back door of the inn. Senri's stomach felt like a pit, and the feeling only grew worse as she walked back to her parent's cottage. She thought over what she would do if Alina did decide to stay out in the villages. As much as Senri wanted to have Alina to herself, something about running off with her felt wrong. She wanted Alina the way she was, fully committed to the betterment of others and selfless in her duty. The heart of their problem showed clear. They could not attempt an honest relationship without being dishonest to themselves.

***

Alina loved dancing with the villagers. It did not matter that Senri sat with her friends in the inn. She was having too much fun. One of the village guards danced with her at first. Then, he passed her on to the blacksmith's apprentice. He babbled on about Senri, retelling stories from their childhood while they danced.

The dancing reminded her of being a child. Only this time, she let the small children hang from her arms and dance on her toes. Alina wanted the night to go on forever. Waking up the next morning meant returning to reality. A song finished and her latest dance partner, a young boy, thanked her and ran off. Alina smiled and hugged herself against the cold. Perhaps she would go drag Senri out for a few dances. But when she turned to leave, an old woman stopped her with a hand on her shoulder.

"I've been looking for you," said the crone.

Alina frowned and took a step back. "I'm sorry. You must have me confused with someone else."

The old woman shook her head and stepped closer. Alina swallowed a gasp as the firelight revealed the seer's marks etched onto her skin. "No, child, I have seen you many, many times before."

Aside from her mother, Alina had never encountered another seer before. She had only ever caught far-off glimpses of the temple seers or village hermits. They lived in seclusion. Speechless, she stared and waited for the woman to do something.

"Please, come with me," the old woman said. "It is time we spoke."

Alina thought about ignoring the old woman and heading to the inn, but something about her demeanor seemed trusting. She obviously knew who Alina was and had not reported her existence. It would only take a few seconds of searching to confirm Alina's seer markings. She glanced behind at the dancers to make sure none waited for her, and then took off with the old woman. She led Alina away from the bonfire and into the forest.

"Where are we going?" she asked. The village grew pitch-dark around her, the music slowly fading in the distance.

"To my grove." The old woman stayed close, a dark silhouette. "It will be safer to talk there."

They walked for a long while. The cold autumn air made her shake and she wished she had stayed by the bonfire. Finally, the trees fell away and revealed a clearing bathed in faint moonlight. The old woman stepped onto an outcropping of rocks and sat down. The way she so easily folded her legs and settled suggested this was a daily activity. The old woman gestured at the ground in front of her and Alina seated herself.

"You have come a long way."

Alina nodded. "I had to."

The old woman looked down at her. The seer's markings crisscrossing over her face melted into shadow. "You fight to save your people from slavery, but your actions may fling this kingdom into all-out war."

"A subjugated kingdom means everyone is enslaved, not just those taken as cattle." Alina remembered her father saying something to this effect long ago. She liked to think he would be proud to see her speak that way.

The seer nodded. "Yet you have not been completely honest with those helping you." She gazed past Alina, into the forest. "You said no one would be harmed. I think you know this conflict will cost lives."

"I…I've seen our safe return." Alina tried to recall the almost-kisses with Senri, the visions in her chambers. They had to mean something.

"I have seen strife. I have seen anger, mistrust, fear. These are caused by lies."

"But I have had visions!" Alina leaned forward. "Are you telling me that the visions are arbitrary and can change?"

The old woman blinked. "Fate is not fixed into place. Your suppositions are dangerous, however. Tell me, how much training have you received?"

Alina settled back down and thought back to the brief lessons her mother had given her. They focused on hiding her ability through sheer willpower. "I—"

"You suppress your gift and it lashes out unpredictably." The seer looked down at her. "It is hardly your fault, though. If I express any anger, it is toward those who made the decision."

"Did you take me here to insult me?" Alina stood. "I've done the right thing. Don't question that."

"You have." The woman nodded. "You have done the best you could. I have taken you here to assist you, and before we can begin, you need to understand what you have done wrong."

Alina rubbed her arms, forcing the chill away. "What would you have me do, then? Ignore my visions?"

"I would have you practice proper meditation and control your visions," said the seer. "As of now, you are a slave to them and your emotions. They show you fractured glimpses of the future and come and go at random. If you had been properly trained—"

"I would not be where I am now. I would be sentenced to life in a tower or village somewhere and Osota would fall under the heel of Shedol." Alina paced the grove. She wished she had Senri at her side.

The seer nodded. "I am not questioning where our paths have crossed. Osota is on the brink of war or enslavement. If the kingdom has any hope of surviving, you must be in control of yourself. I do not want you to throw someone's life away because of an incomplete vision or fantasy."

Alina's temper chilled. She turned back to the old woman and stepped forward. "What have you seen?" The old woman did not respond. "What happens? Does...does Senri..." Her voice died.

The seer looked at Alina. Her brow furrowed. "Your actions put her in considerable danger, more than if you were completely open with her, but Senri's life is ultimately in her own hands. And you might lose her sooner than you wish."

Not Senri. Not her. I'd rather die. "Name it. I will make it happen. I will order her to stay here, send her away to the capital. I—"

The old woman shook her head.

"I won't let her die," yelled Alina. "I can't."

"Why?"

"Because I care for her!" The answer seemed so obvious. How dare the old woman question such a thing? Alina's head ached.

"But why is she special? If there comes a time that the trading of Senri's life is worth a thousand, will you still value that one above all others?"

Alina threaded her fingers through her hair. The pain worsened. "I...no...I mean...I don't want to live without..."

She gasped. The trance swept over her before she could run or do anything. The world swept away and she stood in the palace once again. It lay in ruin. Tapestries hung in tatters and the walls crumbled around her. Soldiers fought: Shedol against Osota. A dragon roared in the distance. She breathed and it felt like fire. The world around her burned. It crumpled like ashes. She breathed again. The ashes fell away. She descended into that abyss of reality once more. She slowly opened her eyes and the seer stood over her. Sprawled on the forest floor, Alina groaned and tried to sit up.

The seer reached out a hand and pulled her into a sitting position. "Do you see how easily your emotions hold sway over you?"

Alina nodded. Her skin felt clammy. She crossed her arms and rubbed herself for warmth.

"I brought you here to teach you control and to help you pursue a mastery over your abilities. Without these teachings, you will forever be enslaved to your own visions, and that path will ruin you." The woman smiled and sat back down on her stone slab. "My name is Mala."

Alina nodded and took a deep breath, her thudding heart returning to its normal rhythm. "What will you teach me?"

She tried to calm down and focus on whatever Mala intended to tell her. But Alina's mind still reeled from the vision. The seer's warning stood out more prominently in her mind, chasing the others away. No matter what vision haunted her, Alina feared Senri's death most of all.

Michelle Magly

Chapter Sixteen

ALINA SAT ON THE worn wooden bench. Usually, a servant would stop her from dirtying herself so, but she could do as she wished out here. She might have taken fuller advantage of it if the evening's events did not weigh so heavily on her mind. Her borrowed flaxen skirt would be fine caked with a little earth. The lesson with Mala had lasted for perhaps an hour. When Alina returned to the village, Yahn had encouraged her to return to the inn, but she insisted on staying out for just a little longer.

At the moment, she stared into the heart of the bonfire. The heat of it flushed her cheeks; the smoke blew her way and she squinted against the ash. The fire calmed her, despite the intensity of the heat in her latest vision, the one she had experienced in the forest. She worried about the war she drove her kingdom toward. It seemed inevitable from the glimpses of her vision. Was it still worth it to ally with the dragons? Or was all time on a fixed point that she could not sway? Mala had instructed her on nightly meditations. They would encourage visions to come and give her a small amount of control over them. If she practiced enough, she would be able to actively seek out visions tailored to people's requests, like professional seers did, but the amount of training required would take up too much time and be too difficult to cover up. Someone sat down on the bench beside her, interrupting her thoughts.

"Mind if I join you?" Senri asked. Alina shook her head, studying the way the flames ate at the wood. When Senri cleared her throat, she looked over at the young woman and smiled. Senri grinned back, her face silhouetted by the light of the fire. "I brought you something." Senri lifted up a mug and gestured to her.

Alina took the offered drink with a nod. "Thank you. You did not need to…"

"I wanted to," said Senri. She held her own mug so tight her knuckles whitened.

Alina sniffed her contents. It was hot, whatever it was, and it smelled sweet. She took a sip.

"This is delicious." She took another small sip, savoring the bittersweet flavors on her tongue. "What is it?"

Senri picked at the rim of her cup. Her face looked flushed, but it could have been the fire. "It's a cider," she said. She looked up at Alina again with a shy glance. "Distilled from the apples in my mother's orchard. She made me this all the time on cold nights." Senri drank some of hers, staring over the rim at her. Alina met the gaze, but then Senri averted her eyes. Alina's heart ached. She looked down.

"That's very sweet of you," she muttered. She looked back to the fire. They sat like that for a while, drinking in silence. Alina liked the quiet, feeling naturally peaceful about sitting shoulder-to-shoulder with Senri by the bonfire. She sighed, knowing they might not have a moment like this again.

Senri tipped her mug up and emptied the last of the drink into her mouth. The young Warrior wiped away the foam from her lip. Alina smiled. *Who knows? We could have this moment again.* Senri set her mug down in the dirt and looked back up at Alina. "Can I ask you something, your Highness?"

Alina's smile shrank. She hated how Senri's demeanor could shift so rapidly. She turned on the bench, crossing her ankles. The shift to formalities probably meant she would not like whatever conversation approached. "Of course, Senri."

"I was just wondering." Senri looked up at the sky and then out at the village. "Why are you doing this?"

Alina looked at her hands resting in her lap. "What do you mean?"

"Why are you fighting so hard for Osota?" Alina glanced over at Senri. The Warrior studied her close. Senri took a deep breath. "I mean, it would be easy enough for you to let someone else take care of all this, or even leave the kingdom. But here you are, doing all you can."

A cinder popped in the fire and both women looked over. Alina watched the flames again. No one had ever asked her that question. Her reasons defined the way her life had shaped itself. Not to mention the fear the vision instilled in her. The thought of telling someone usually meant vulnerability. Emotion, true and raw, could be a loose end, a weapon in any person's hand.

Alina thought of the vision of war. Her people fought back. Everything had been in ruin. Was that a better future than enslavement? Alina shook her head. Usually, she would never discuss such feelings so openly. But that night, with the fire, the stars, and Senri at her side, sitting and watching, she altered her decision. She suddenly needed to talk to someone, to reassure herself she acted for the right reasons. "You love this village, Senri."

The Warrior nodded. "Of course, I—"

Alina shook her head. "It wasn't a question. It's obvious every time you look around. When you see these people together, talking, laughing, working, thriving." She paused and thought over her next sentence. "It fills you with something. It's greater than happiness." Alina looked beyond the bonfire flames, out to the forest she knew surrounded them. "That is what I feel for this kingdom," she said.

Senri nodded.

Alina knew the simple and truthful answer would satisfy Senri, but she deserved the whole answer. "Since I was a girl my mother told me I might one day have the chance to rule Osota." Senri raised an eyebrow and Alina laughed. "She did not plot or scheme, my mother was...she worried for my aunt and uncle. They had tried so hard for children, even back then." Alina had considered telling Senri her mother had *seen* it, but she did not feel ready to relinquish that secret, despite Mala's warning. Senri might move beyond reach if she told her, and she wanted to pretend they could be together just a bit longer. "She told me if I was ever offered the throne I had to take it."

"Is that all?" Senri asked. She sounded disappointed.

"No," Alina replied, thinking of the signet ring hanging from a chain around her neck. "My mother told me there were terrible people who would fight for the throne if I did not lay claim. She knew...I mean I think she knew there was an assassin after them. A few nights before my parents died she came to my room…" Alina's throat tightened, her eyes watering.

Senri reached over and rested a hand over Alina's, the contact warmer than the fire. Alina looked up. Senri leaned forward. "You don't have to talk about this if it hurts." Alina let herself stare selfishly into Senri's eyes, and for a while Senri stared back. Then the Warrior blinked, looked down to see her hand covering Alina's, and pulled away. "Forgive me."

Alina sighed. "You're so noble," she muttered.

"What?" asked Senri.

Alina smiled, eyes lingering on the dying flames of the shrinking bonfire. "It's nothing. That night, though…" She remembered her mother opening the latch on her door, shushing her and sitting down on the edge of Alina's bed. "she came to my room and gave me this."

Alina pulled the chain over her head and handed it to Senri. The Warrior held the signet ring as if it were a hot ember. Alina smiled and accepted it back from Senri's shaking grasp. She slipped the chain back over her head. "She told me to keep it safe, she told me that no matter what, I was to keep it, no one else. She then told me that if they…if anything happened, I needed to do everything to keep Osota free. These people, the Councilors willing to let Shedol into our kingdom, they do not offer my people freedom." She closed her eyes, remembering the cold, empty wasteland from her vision, and then opened them again. The bonfire seemed smaller.

"I suppose that's a good reason," said Senri quietly. Alina nodded and looked up at the stars. They shone brightly. Alina checked the positioning of the constellations and chuckled softly.

"What?" asked Senri.

"Is that really the position of the owl?" Alina asked, pointing to the constellation.

Senri looked to the sky. "Yes, that's the owl. Why do you ask?"

Alina sighed. "For starters, it is terribly late and I should head to the inn." Alina rose and brushed the dirt and grass from her clothes. Senri stood with her.

"What else does it mean?" Senri asked. The two walked away from the bonfire, searching for the small lamp hanging at the inn door.

Alina played with her skirt, twirling it lightly as she walked. They stopped in the middle of the street, the faint glow of the inn's oil lamp washing over them. Alina looked at the position of the constellation again. "It means I missed my birthday."

Senri looked up at the constellation then back down at her. "Oh, your Highness, you should have said something, I would have gotten you a gift."

Alina laughed again. Her eyes met Senri's. She suddenly realized they stood very close, close enough for her to feel Senri's body heat. "Call me Alina," she said, feeling bold.

"Excuse me, your Highn—"

She pushed a finger against the Warrior's stomach in warning. She could feel the firm muscles of Senri's body underneath the shirt. "I said call me Alina." She made sure to use her firmest tone. "That is what you can give me for my birthday," she added, her soft demeanor returning. She let her hand rest over her Warrior's abdomen. She felt the muscle rise as Senri breathed in.

Senri smiled down at her, flashing in a small grin. Her voice came out soft, for only Alina to hear. "I think I can do that, Alina."

It sounded so natural coming from Senri. It soothed Alina and made her giddy at the same time. She looked down at her hand still pressed against Senri and then up at the smiling woman. "Senri," she whispered back, almost an invocation.

Something clanged. A clatter came next, then the tumbling crash of metal falling over itself and the two sprang apart. Alina frowned, looking around for the sound while Senri moved in front of her, hand at the sheath of her sword. "Go inside, Highness." The softness had gone, Senri all soldier once more.

"Senri, I think it was only a—"

"Go," Senri said. She turned and looked back at her with such a hard stare Alina stepped back. Senri's face immediately softened. "I'm sorry. It's probably nothing, but I want you to be safe. Please, go get some rest."

Alina started to protest, but the pleading look in Senri's eyes stopped her. "Fine, but you need to get some rest too."

"I will," Senri replied. "I'll head back to my parent's farm as soon as I find out what that noise was."

Alina nodded. "All right then." She stepped back to the inn door, her fingers wrapping around the handle. "Goodnight, Senri." She pulled open the inn door.

"Goodnight," the Warrior said back. As Alina stepped inside and let the door close behind her, she heard Senri say quietly, "Alina." The inn door shut and Alina stood alone in the dark with nothing but the flicker of the hearth embers and her own hammering heart for company.

Michelle Magly

Chapter Seventeen

THEY LEFT THE VILLAGE first thing the next morning. Some of the villagers asked them to stay one more night, but Yahn insisted they depart. Senri knew he feared pursuers, and reasonably so. Anyone tracking them would have gotten a nice window of opportunity to catch them with the time spent loitering at the village. Ideally, they should have resupplied and moved on. Senri glanced up at the mountain path they followed. She would not blame anyone for the delay. She had dreaded this part of the journey most of all.

Senri had grown up on stories of the mountain's impassibility from wandering merchants. Dragons were dangerous, after all. But some attempted the climb. Occasionally, a weather-worn traveler would descend from the mountains, filled with stories of bloodthirsty bandits and the towering dragon cities resting on mountain peaks. The trail revealed just how troublesome the climb would become for horses. Most of the greenery faded a ways up. Scrubland took over past the timberline. The wind would be unbearable at the pass, but for the moment, they stayed low enough along the trail.

By the time they found an appropriate area to camp, the sun had set and twilight faded to gray. Storm clouds gathered overhead, and Senri hoped their menacing look masked a lighter shower. She somewhat dreaded setting up the camp that evening. The crash that had interrupted her and Alina the previous night had only turned out to be a nosey cat poking around in Gustav's forge. But now they were camped way off from the road, hidden by scrubland and trees in the mountain pass. With the way things had developed between them, Senri might not object to any of Alina's advances. Instead of dwelling on what might come, Senri dismounted Stomps and removed her pack to let him graze. She moved to a relatively clear area to set up her tent and got started. When Alina moved to set up her tent nearby, Senri smiled. Senri finished and walked over to help the others start a fire. Alina still struggled with her tent, though she seemed to be setting it up well enough. Usually, she would call Senri over to help by then.

"We're out of firewood," said Yahn. He worked on setting up a pit. The pitiful amount of kindling would barely last an hour. He took one of the last sturdy branches and wrapped the end in linen. "Go fetch some more." He passed Senri the branch.

Senri nodded and gripped the top of the torch. She breathed in and it ignited, illuminating the space around them. "I'll be back." She turned and walked toward the bordering trees.

Alina looked up from her completed tent and waved. "I did it!"

Senri stopped and examined the tent. "Good job."

"I suppose it is." Alina stood and glanced over at Senri. "And where are you off to?"

"Collecting firewood," Senri replied. She gestured over at the trees. "Want to help?" The suggestion surprised her. Did she really just ask a princess to help her gather wood? It was a nice excuse to spend more time with her, something Senri had avoided for the duration of their journey. She liked the way Alina's features softened every time they spoke, how her shoulders relaxed and her mouth eased into a smile. Senri found herself following the curve of that smile more and more, tracing the lips with her eyes.

"Senri?"

The question interrupted her musings. Alina looked at her. Senri blinked. "I'm sorry, did you say something?"

"I said I'd love to accompany you." Alina had grabbed her bow and quiver. She stepped forward and glanced to the woods. "Shall we?"

Senri grinned and gestured with her torch. "Right this way."

They walked away from the camp and into the trees. Senri looked over at Alina and caught her staring. She looked away again, heat rising on her cheeks. The torch sputtered and she had to concentrate to get it back under control.

"So, where should we look?" asked Alina.

They had gotten far enough into the tree line that plenty of felled branches lay close at hand. Suddenly, Senri wanted to stop looking for firewood and spend a moment alone with Alina, perhaps just talking. She shoved the feeling away.

"We should be fine here." Senri gestured at the downed tree limbs.

Alina plucked at her bowstring. "Right." She moved to pull the bow over her chest and free up her hands, but Alina paused. Her gaze shifted to the outer edge of the trees and Senri looked as well, but could not spot whatever Alina seemed to see. Alina's hand came out and pushed Senri. Alina gripped the fletched end of an arrow. She knocked it on the bowstring and shot. Something cried out and fell. Alina lowered her bow.

"What was that all about?" Senri glanced from the spot in the woods to Alina and her bow.

Alina shouldered the bow. "I thought we could use something fresh for dinner." She marched off toward whatever she had felled.

Senri followed. "But when did you learn to shoot a bow that well?"

They arrived at a downed rabbit. "I had a lot of practice at Eastwatch Keep," said Alina. She bent over and picked up the slain animal, the arrow neatly lodged in its head.

"A little bit more than that," said Senri. She had never seen someone nail a rabbit so precisely before. She almost suggested they should actually collect firewood when a flash of lightning lit up the sky and the boom of thunder echoed. Alina yelped and leapt closer to her. When the rumbles faded, Senri grinned. "Something you want to tell me?"

Alina glanced up at the sky. "No. Nothing. Let's get the firewood and get back to camp."

Senri smirked and followed Alina to some downed branches. The wind picked up. They gathered faster. Soon, rain fell, slowly at first, then in sheets as they walked back to camp. The thunder boomed once more and Alina dropped a piece firewood. "A little jumpy, aren't you?" Senri bent to pick it up, adding it to her own rather large armful. The wind blew even harder and the torch guttered.

"Thunder is startling," Alina said. They walked close together, hunched over against the sheets of rain and driving winds. The torch had gone out and Senri tucked the branch into the rest of the others she carried. When the campsite came into view, Senri frowned.

"You might want to pick up the pace," she said.

"Why?" Alina had to shout over the roar of the wind.

"Because your tent is blowing away."

"No!" Senri followed her as they pushed against the storm and back into camp. Alina's tent hung by one post, then the cloth tore and it tumbled away in a mess of fabric and rope. "No!" Alina ran toward the fleeing supplies, but Senri reached out and caught her by the arm.

"It won't do you any good. The storm is too much!"

They found Yahn and the others breaking down camp and corralling the horses. He looked up and waved them in closer, clothes sopping wet. "There's a natural overhang up ahead!" he yelled over the howl of the storm. "Nat and I can fortify it against the winds and it should provide enough shelter to sleep through the night. Gather what you can before the whole camp blows away."

They went over to Senri's tent and broke it down. Stomps followed them and allowed the two to sling items over his back without much complaint. Senri made sure to tie the bundle of firewood in place with her tent supplies.

"Is that it?" she asked Alina. The two glanced around, but Senri doubted they would find much of anything else. "Let's go. Yahn said he'd lead us out."

They rejoined with the rest of the group. Nat and Lanan stood beside one another, clothes dripping, having removed their armor in anticipation of settling in for the night. Nat leaned in close to Alina and asked, "I don't suppose you are a wind reader?" She glared.

Yahn led them along a ridge and around the side of a hill. Senri gripped at the reins of Stomps as if he might blow away while Alina guided her own horse nearby. By the time they made it around the hill and under the overhang, not a stitch of Senri's clothing remained dry, but at least they had shelter from the wind. Senri grabbed the firewood first and set out to make a campfire. She had the branches dried and lit in moments, providing them sufficient light. The rest of the group pulled tent supplies down.

"My tent is gone," said Lanan.

"Mine too." Alina rested her forehead against her horse's saddle.

Yahn and Nat worked on reinforcing the overhang against mudslides. They held their fingertips to the rock walls and felt for the areas of weakness. "Pair up," Yahn said.

"What?" Senri whipped around from her station at the fire.

"I call Lanan!" Nat shouted, glancing over at Senri. "Better cuddle up."

"I'll kill you," Senri growled. Her friend just laughed and continued his work. Senri turned back to the fire, but nothing remained for her to do. She pretended to fuss with it anyway.

"Senri." Alina sat down beside her, but she remained focused on the flames. "I...do you have the tent set up yet?"

She shook her head. "I think I'll sleep outside."

"Absolutely not, not in this weather."

Senri couldn't look at Alina.

"Is the thought really so repulsive?"

She broke away from the flames. "No! I didn't mean—" She stopped when she saw Alina grinning at her. She had to stop falling for that.

Alina winked at her. "I won't bite." Senri felt her face go flush and looked away. Alina laid a hand on her shoulder. "I'll be good. Just please don't sleep outside because you fear for my virtue as a lady."

A hint of a smile tugged at Senri's lips. "You mean there's a virtuous woman in there?"

Alina laughed. "There's that sense of humor. Help me set up now. I don't think I can do it right a second time." They both stood and brushed themselves off, bits of leaves and mud falling to the ground.

After setting up the tent, they returned to the campfire with the others to eat the evening meal. Alina's downed rabbit made for a good addition to the stew, and the warm broth helped abate the cold, though Senri had no problem keeping herself warm. She offered to help dry their clothing with some careful heat reading, though she found it difficult to keep from searing anyone's skin as she gently ran her hands over the sopping wet clothes. They sat and talked, arranging the first watch. Senri tried to take the first watch so that Alina would be asleep by the time she returned to the tent, but had somehow ended up with early morning.

As the others got up and left, Yahn looked over at her from across the fire. "Get some sleep."

Senri nodded and stood. Alina followed her back to the tent. Senri began undoing the straps on her own armor. Usually she would do this inside the tent, but she wanted to give Alina the chance for privacy, but the princess removed her armor outside, too. Alina peeled off the various pieces and crawled inside the tent. Senri shook out her tunic and rubbed her head. You can do this. The thunder boomed again and Alina yelped from inside the tent. Senri crouched down and crawled inside. Alina already lay huddled under a blanket.

Senri arched an eyebrow. "Are you all right?"

Alina nodded and lowered the blanket. She scooted to the side for Senri. "Thunder has always alarmed me." Senri moved closer but did not get under the covers. She turned and tied back a corner of the tent flap to allow firelight inside. "Aren't you going to sleep?"

"I don't need a blanket," Senri replied. "I won't get cold."

"Senri, for the love of the Almighty get under this blanket and sleep like you would on any other night, or so help me I will go sleep outside in the rain."

The glare Alina gave her showed no sign of bluffing. Senri nodded and pulled some of the blanket on top of herself, though she stayed as far from Alina as possible. She pulled the blanket taut and laid down. "Good night." She closed her eyes, knowing she had no hope of falling asleep.

"Would you stop being so juvenile?" Alina asked. She gripped Senri's arm and pulled, making her roll over and face Alina. She pulled Senri a little closer to her. She frowned as she felt Alina's skin icy. She had been a fool to think anyone would be comfortable in the middle of a rainstorm. No wonder she wanted Senri close.

As if reading her guilty expression, Alina said, "Not all of us are magically able to heat ourselves."

Senri blinked. Alina was close, extremely close. "I...I'm sorry." She could feel Alina's body heat, could smell her. It felt nothing like the night at the inn, nothing at all like the brief moment she had shared with that other woman. Alina reached a hand up between them and Senri flinched. "What are you doing?"

"You have something in your hair." Alina reached forward and plucked out a leaf. She showed it to Senri and smiled. They lay there in awkward silence for a moment. "I don't suppose you've shared your bed before?"

"What?" Senri frowned, stopping herself from scooting away.

"Keep it down," said Alina, grinning. "We don't need the whole camp hearing." With the wind howling so loud, Senri doubted the camp would hear them shout at one another if they so chose. "But if the question troubles you so much, you need not—"

"I have, once." Senri waited for Alina to react, for her to frown and push her away or to scold her, but she did none of those things. They stayed close, barely touching. "It's not something I'm proud of."

Alina's brow furrowed. "Why?"

Senri remembered the night. She remembered fumbling and being nervous. The act itself had been simple enough and they both found physical release in one another. Still, the ache in Senri never left. "I didn't want to sleep with her. I only did because I thought it would make me feel better."

"You had no feelings for her?"

Senri shook her head. Alina's eyes had drifted down. Neither of them bothered to make eye contact. Eventually, Senri sighed and shifted closer. Alina glanced her way.

"And what about you?" Senri asked. "Any bedfellows?"

Alina laughed softly and closed her eyes. "A few, during my last couple of years at Eastwatch Keep. I had essentially grown up with one of the maids. When we reached seventeen, we started…we did not do anything serious until perhaps a year later, then the others found out and had her sent away."

Senri had the urge to wrap and arm around Alina. Her hand shifted as she thought about it. "Did you miss her?"

Alina shook her head. "No. I knew it would happen. Anyone I got too close with afterward got sent away. Soon they wised up stopped allowing people close to my age to work there."

"Why didn't they just watch you more closely?" Senri tried to picture being locked away in a fortress. Try as she might, the images never came.

"They felt sorry for me," said Alina. Lightning flashed and she moved closer. The thunder sounded distant. "I was an orphan who had been locked away as Osota's last resort. I had tutors and horse riding lessons and archery, but none of it came close to being a system of family and friends, as much as they tried. I suppose it was the greatest kindness they could do to send away my lovers rather than execute them."

At these words, Senri shifted away slightly. She swallowed at a lump in her throat.

"Oh, they can't do anything like that now." Alina's fingers wrapped around her shoulder and held her in place. "I will rule my kingdom, Senri, no one else."

Senri tried to smile as Alina's hand rested on her face. The tips of her fingers traced down Senri's cheek and neck. They stopped at the necklace chain. Senri's heart beat as Alina's fingers stayed. The princess kept her gaze focused downward, so Senri stared pleadingly at her forehead. She tried to speak, but words stuck in her throat.

"Would you want this," Alina's voice hovered barely above a whisper. "If I were not sworn to the throne?"

The block cleared in her throat, more out of necessity as she gulped in air. "Alina." *Damn the formalities. She deserved honesty if nothing else.* "It is your dedication and love for the people of Osota I find admirable and worthy about you." The words tumbled from her lips so quickly. Only after they were said did Senri realize how long she had held back. Alina's fingers still touched her collarbone. She thought she saw her smile in the waning firelight.

"You said something about pretending the other night." Alina's hand lay flush against her chest, almost like it had before. "What if I did not want to pretend?" Alina looked up at her, brown eyes wavering.

"Alina." Saying the name intoxicated Senri. It felt incredible, even in a breathy whisper. They stared at one another. Senri's fingers rose to brush against Alina's shoulder. She wanted to pull Alina close to her so badly. "I know you want this, but we would only be fooling ourselves." She took a deep breath and waited for Alina to say something. When she remained silent, Senri continued, "I do not want to start anything and then have to stop because of your duties, and I know your duties will come before me. I won't let it be any other way."

Alina readjusted. She scooted up a little higher. "If I were queen, they'd have to listen to me. I'd be allowed any companion—"

Senri shook her head. "Any plaything."

"Stop. Don't you dare say that." For a moment, Senri thought Alina might smack her. Her face flushed. Then, Alina took a breath and composed herself once more. "I'd never let you be that."

Senri looked away. "You wouldn't, but the Council might."

She felt sick for making the argument. They were in bed together. She could not have ached for Alina more if she wanted to, and Senri was doing all she could to make it not happen. A small part of her knew she did not want to experience that kind of fulfillment with Alina without them having a fair chance. Politics would always stop that fair chance. Her temperature rose.

"Senri." Alina's hand moved to her cheek. "Senri, I won't let them control me. I will give Osota everything it needs, but the individual I choose to...to..." Alina removed her hand. "Your skin is hot."

Senri blinked and moved further back from Alina. She had let her temperature escalate too much. She closed her eyes and concentrated on lowering it. Her thoughts jumbled. "I'm sorry, I'm not used to having conversations like this."

Alina smiled weakly and touched Senri's arm. This time, her hand did not jump away. "It's all right. Neither am I." Their eyes stayed locked. Senri wanted to kiss Alina. Instead, she rolled on her back and wrapped an arm around her.

"Here," she said. "We should get some rest."

Alina rested her head against Senri's chest and laid a hand on her collarbone. Senri's body pulsed where they lay in contact with one another.

"Thank you," said Alina.

She nuzzled into the crook of Senri's neck. The wind had died down. The worst of the storm had moved on. As they lay there in the growing darkness, Senri heard only three things: the rain pattering outside, her own heartbeat, and Alina's breathing.

Michelle Magly

Chapter Eighteen

ALINA HATED STAIRS. THE records described steps running alongside a steep mountain cliff with a rock wall scaling the other side. These steps stood pin-like from the ground as if they were wedged placeholders for the real structure. One could not walk up them. It would require leaps over gaps, and the incline frightened her. Alina could hardly imagine climbing them without the help of Nat and Yahn. The two worked to smooth out the slope so the horses would come along. They dug their hands into the earth and pulled up, trying desperately to make the ground hold to the terraced shape it had long ago abandoned.

To make matters worse, the night's storm had left snow higher up on the mountain and a cold breeze rolled down on them. The half-frozen mud on the trail caked around their boots and softened as the day's sun rose higher and higher. Yahn and Nat worked twice as hard to keep footpaths from crumbling away underneath them. Lanan joined them in their efforts and curbed the melting snow.

Senri remained close at her side for the duration of the day's travel, though neither of them spoke much. Alina suspected Senri was as tired as her, if not more. She found it difficult to sleep while resting against Senri. As comfortable as it had been, the close contact stirred her. On top of that problem, she had also spent the night in fear that a vision would overcome her, that Senri would find her out without having a chance to explain first. That morning Alina swore she was in the midst of a vision when she woke up alongside Senri. It had felt too good to be part of reality.

Alina shook her head to clear her thoughts. The present needed her concentration. She sighed and pulled on her horse's reins. She glanced over at Senri, but the Warrior stared straight on. Alina glanced back to the road. They would be at the top of the rise soon. Hopefully, there would be enough level land for them to camp and rest. The elements had taken their toll on everyone.

"Almost there." Senri's soft tone interrupted Alina's musings. She smiled, the first one she had seen all morning. "Perhaps we'll stop and rest."

Alina nodded and looked at the pebbled ground as the incline grew steeper. The scree covering the slope grew thicker and more widely scattered toward the top. "It's been a tough climb."

Senri did not respond. Their conversation felt so restrained compared to last night. Even though they had essentially done nothing, it felt good to speak openly with Senri last night. She wanted to have that all the time. The attraction toward Senri had started out as purely physical for Alina, but had grown. *If I showed you all that I am, would you still want me?* The urge to be that open with Senri startled her more than any want to sleep with her, which seemed ridiculous in hindsight. Physical intimacy with Senri would most likely lead to her discovering the seer's marks anyways. Back in Eastwatch Keep it had been easy to discourage more clothing removal than necessary, but with Senri, she did not want to hide anything, physical or emotional.

The top of the rise revealed a saddle between two peaks. The isolated dip protected them from some of the elements and the level ground was easy to stand on. They decided to rest there.

"We have to be close," said Nat. His shoulders sagged and his hands were caked in mud.

"Seen any dragons yet?" asked Yahn.

"Well, no, but—"

"Then we're not close," said Yahn. He stood up and dug for something in his saddle pack. He pulled out a map. He pointed to a place on the map far away from any recorded dragon settlement. "It seems we are between these two peaks."

"That's a lot farther to go," said Lanan.

"Yeah, my body needs a rest," said Nat. "We have food, at least, right? I can't keep rockslides away on an empty stomach."

"We'll rest for a moment, but we need to keep going if we want to make it before winter sets in," Yahn replied.

The rest did not seem nearly long enough for Alina, but she dare not complain when everyone worked so hard for her. They kept moving well after twilight, stopping only after the last light faded. Alina wanted to make dinner for the others. She stared at the supplies on the packhorse and tried to calculate how long they would last.

What if the dragons turn us turn back? What if they offer no help at all? They would starve on the mountainside and Alina would be the one to blame.

She made a simple soup for dinner from the food stores the villagers had given them. She added in a few extra spices from her own supplies. No one really talked for the night. Alina and Senri even set up their tent and crawled into bed in silence. Alina curled against Senri's chest and sighed, feeling the warm body underneath her. She wanted to kiss Senri goodnight, to say something, but all words stuck in her throat. Senri's hand stroked her arm. It moved slowly along her skin, up and down in a comforting manner. Alina blinked against the darkness in the tent. Her nose touched Senri's neck. She could lean forward and kiss Senri.

Outside, the temperature dropped to freezing, but Senri kept her safe. The hand on her arm slowed. It stilled. Senri's breathing fell into an easy, rhythmic pattern. It lulled Alina, made her not worry about being struck with a vision in the middle of the night, made her unafraid of the things to come. Alina had known for a while that she wanted more than a simple fling with Senri. All at once, she realized she had fallen for the Warrior. She loved Senri, and before their journey came to an end, she would confess all that she had kept secret. Senri deserved it.

***

Days passed. They hiked so long and so far that the cold seeped into their bones, even Senri's. It did not matter how many layers they put on, the wind cut through all of it. Senri's legs went numb first every day, probably for the best, considering her muscles ached so much from walking. Her hands never lost feeling, however. They stayed burning hot, so much so that she kept her gloves removed and would take turns pressing the warm palms on her face and arms.

Sometimes Alina would offer her hands, but not in a romantic gesture. Alina's fingers were ice cold and she made a habit of warming Alina's hands between her own, along with anyone else who needed it. The snow accumulated on the path they took. It clung in chunks to the hems of their pants. Senri had never thought she would want it, but she desperately hoped the dragons lingered nearby.

Ever since their first night sharing a tent, Alina had not brought up the subject of them. Sometimes she would hear Alina draw in a breath as if to say something, then she would release it and settle in closer to her.

A week after the initial storm, another snow storm made them camp early. They worked hard to get a large fire going to heat the camp for the night. Alina left the camp some time after dinner. After a meaningful glance at Senri, she wandered off to a cliff side, staring out at the lower ranges they had just climbed. Senri stood from her place beside the fire and brushed off her pants. She walked up beside Alina and waited for her to acknowledge her presence. The noise from the camp had faded. They might as well be alone. Alina glanced at her and smiled. Her face reddened from the cold.

"Are you all right?" Senri asked.

"Just enjoying the view." Alina looked out over the range again and crossed her arms. "I used to spend a lot of time looking at the mountain ranges back in Eastwatch."

The wind died down a little. The snow fell in small flakes, almost picturesque if they were not stuck outside in it constantly. "Did you have snow to play in?" Senri asked. She remembered pelting snowballs at Nat and running from his counter-attacks. All the village kids would team up to build a fortress after the first snowfall. She smiled.

Alina shook her head. "They wouldn't let me."

Senri frowned and stepped closer to Alina. "Well, that's not fair of them."

"A lot of things weren't fair." Alina looped an arm through Senri's. "I plan to never let them run my life like that again."

All things considered, Senri had to agree. The mountain ranges were an extremely hostile landscape. No one in politics would have ever allowed Alina out there, yet she had made it anyways. She had not let the Council control her. Senri let out a half-laugh, a small puff of hot air against the cold. Alina had promised never to let Senri be a disposable item to the Council. If she could run away to distant land in order to rule her kingdom the way she wanted, who was to say she would let the Councilors stop them from being together? Senri looked down at the princess, suddenly aware of their physical contact on a much different level.

"Alina," she said. They turned and faced one another. "We

talked about something that night of the first storm. I think I was a bit of an idiot with my response."

Alina laughed and shook her head. "No, your concerns were genuine. I should not have pushed you, especially considering the circumstances."

"What? Being alone together in the middle of a storm was not romantic enough for you?" Senri grinned and leaned in a bit closer. She felt emboldened by Alina's easygoing manner and the gentle snowfall. The world had muted itself for them.

Alina laughed again. Senri liked making her laugh.

"It was a lovely night," Alina murmured, taking a step back and linking Senri's hands between her own. She looked down. "If we move forward, though, there is something you should know."

"Oh?" Senri tried to get Alina to meet her gaze again by raising her hands. Instead, Alina removed her grip and took another step back. Senri did not know what to expect as Alina lowered the hood to her cloak. Her fingers rose to the ties and tugged them loose.

"I haven't been honest with you, Senri," she said. The cloak fell to the snow. "I haven't been honest with anyone."

Senri looked away as Alina pulled off her leather chest plate next. The campsite fire was barely visible. No one was near to hear or see them. Still, her stomach clenched. "I don't...what are you doing?"

"Senri." Her name sounded so clear when spoken by Alina. "Look at me."

She expected to see scars. A disfigurement. Nothing prepared Senri for what was really there. Alina stood with her tunic pulled down, just above the start of her bosom. Dark lines lay etched into her skin—no, just under her skin: the seer's blood coursed through her veins. She stepped back farther. "You're a...you're a..."

"I'm a seer," Alina finished. "With no official training and no right to the throne by Osota law."

Senri's thoughts stopped in their tracks. Seer rulers had been banned ages ago. Alina was by all accounts a criminal, but had she truly done anything wrong?

"So, so you see how all this ends," said Senri. "You see that we are successful negotiating with the dragons." Even as she spoke, Alina shook her head.

"I see only fragments." Alina pulled her tunic back into place and slipped her armor on once more. "I saw war. I saw Lord Demek lead our kingdom to ruin and enslavement. What we are doing here is the work of careful thought. I believe this is the best chance we have to change course. Lord Demek offers only death. I am trying to give Osota a fighting chance."

Senri fought the urge to panic. *So she doesn't know how this turns out.* She had promised their safety before leaving the capital.

"You've seen war, then," Senri said.

"I have." Alina stooped and picked up her cloak and shook the snow off it.

"What else have you seen?"

"Not much else." She retied the cloak. "I do...know things, however, more from wit than anything else." Alina clenched her hands together and avoided eye contact with Senri. "The assassin you stopped," she said. She looked like she wanted to say more.

Senri nodded. "Yes, the assassin…"

"I may have known something." Alina's voice wavered. "I may have known he would come for me." Her eyes found Senri's.

Senri blinked. "What?"

Alina looked away again. She crossed her arms and held herself. "I knew the opposition would send someone to assassinate me after you and the other Warriors found the encampment."

"Why?"

"Because I copied the location from a Councilor's map. I knew he was planning something. I needed to find out what." Alina's voice began to strain.

"So...so you sent us into danger like that without—"

"No!" said Alina. She shook her head. "Never. I never knew what to find there. I thought if there were anything dangerous you would turn around and report it immediately. I never imagined—"

"No, I guess you didn't," said Senri. Senri's hands clenched into fists. "Well, I'll go get Lanan and the others, and you can tell them sorry too, that you didn't mean for us to be tortured or abused—"

"I didn't," cried Alina. She looked to be on the verge of tears. Senri did not care. The fear in Lanan's eyes when they found her and the scars across Yahn's back from the whip filled her mind. Alina stepped closer. "I never meant for you to go on that mission."

"Oh, so it's okay if someone else was captured?"

"Of course not. Senri, I'm sorry. I don't want people putting their lives in danger for me!"

"Well, we are," yelled Senri. She gestured to the mountains around them. "We're going to keep putting our lives in danger for you, too. But do you know what makes it acceptable? Knowing that you're honest with us about the risks involved. We're not puppets, we're people!"

Tears streamed down Alina's face. "Senri. Senri, please. It hurt me so much when you attacked that assassin. The thought that you could have been killed…"

"Maybe you should have told me then," said Senri. "What if I wasn't fast enough? You could have died." This thought hurt Senri the most, that Alina had withheld information threatening her own life. The princess cried quietly, her shoulders shaking. Senri wanted to hold her and storm away at the same time. She had always assumed Alina would not lie to her, would not use her in a game. "Is there anything else you lied about, huh? Is there an army of western troops waiting over this ridge?"

Alina shook her head. She mouthed the word 'no' through the sobs.

Senri frowned. That small part inside her still wanted to hold Alina close and whisper she was sorry for yelling, that she cared deeply for Alina, and that she had lost her temper in a stupid, childish manner. She wanted to tell her she didn't care Alina was a seer, that she wanted to be with her until whatever parted them, but anger snuffed that part out. The wind whipped her face. Cold seeped into her muscles, hunger gnawed at her stomach, dirt grimed her armor and skin. And it was all Alina's idea that they be out here, marching to their deaths most likely. Senri looked away. "I'm going back to camp." She walked away, trying to fight her own urge to break down and cry while Alina held herself and sobbed.

Michelle Magly

Chapter Nineteen

THEY SLEPT IN A collective hovel Lanan sculpted from the snow. They built up a fire in the center of the room and Lanan built thick, encompassing walls of snow with a hole in the top to let the smoke out. Alina asked her about the intelligence of this decision and Lanan explained, "It will insulate us better while giving us the opportunity to combine everyone's body heat." She winked at Alina. "Though I'm sure you and Senri have been doing a good job at that already."

Alina crossed her arms and shrugged. "Actually, we've had a...disagreement recently."

"Oh?" asked Lanan. She looked from Alina over to Senri who sulked on the other side of the ice hovel. "Oh. Well, would you like to talk about it?"

Alina nodded and the two sat down on an oiled blanket keeping the water at bay. "I told Senri about some...decisions I had to make while back in the capital and she was not very fond of them." During their travel, Alina and Lanan had exchanged a few brief conversations with one another, and before that she had often spotted Lanan speaking with Nin when they thought no one else was around, but the companionship she felt came from their shared struggles during the last week more than anything else.

Lanan nodded and leaned back. "Did she have a right to be upset?"

"I...well, at the time I thought it was the only way I could protect Osota."

"So your actions were for the good of everyone?" Lanan rested her chin in her hand and stared at Alina.

Alina had never thought Lanan to be the sensible one of the bunch, but her calm reasoning proved otherwise. "They were. Everything I've done has been in hopes of saving my people. I may have endangered myself, and though I was not aware, I endangered some Warriors…"

"But you did not know you were hurting them?" Lanan asked.

Alina shook her head. She remembered how angry she had been with Nin for sending out the young recruits. "No. Though I did knowingly put myself at risk."

Lanan smiled and pointed at her. "There's your problem."

"But we're at risk every day on this mountainside!"

Lanan nodded. "Yes, but Senri is aware of the dangers here. I'm guessing whatever you two are fighting about is some risk you took she was unaware of."

"And why aren't you mad?" Alina asked.

"Hindsight makes everything clear." Lanan shook her head. "I've also lived a little more than Senri has. Life is too short to get caught up in the should-haves. She'll see that."

Alina sighed and leaned back against a pile of equipment. Her throat felt tight. "But what if she doesn't forgive me in time?"

Lanan placed a hand on Alina's shoulder. "She will," she said. "Just give her a day or two." Lanan withdrew and Alina sighed. She glanced across the hovel again. While everyone else sat huddled near the fire, Senri leaned on the opposite wall. Even as she stared, Senri raised her gaze and caught her eye for a moment before looking down.

"You see?" said Lanan. "She's been doing that all night."

Still, it took two days for Senri to approach her. They had settled down for the evening and Alina had retired early. She lay under her layer of blankets, shivering against the cold. It had been much more difficult to sleep without Senri holding her, despite having others pressed against her in the small shelter. Not only did the loss of Senri's warmth make things difficult, but calming her thoughts proved nearly impossible. She jumped when she felt someone kneel down behind her.

"Could I join you?"

She rolled over and saw Senri sitting beside her. She appeared to have a blank expression, though her eyes held a look, regret, perhaps? Alina pulled back the blanket a little and moved to the side.

"If you wish," she said.

Senri lay on her back and Alina settled in close to her just like they had been doing before the fight. She sighed, content with the warmth.

"Better?" Senri asked.

"Yes." Alina nuzzled into Senri's neck. She inhaled the familiar scent of sweat and wood smoke. She had missed it more than she realized. They lay there quietly while everyone else muttered their goodnights. Senri wrapped an arm around her. She rested her hand on Senri's stomach. "I'm sorry."

She listened to Senri's breathing for several moments before she heard her say, "I am, too."

Alina moved into a sitting position and looked down at Senri. Alina's brow furrowed. Senri did not look tired at all. "Will you walk with me?" Alina asked.

Senri nodded and they both stood, though Alina kept the blankets wrapped around herself. Senri grabbed her sword and sheath and strapped it to her waist. She told Yahn they were heading out and they both ducked out through the small entrance. They took off around the back end of the hovel, to a small clearing where the horses stood under blankets. Alina hitched her own blanket up higher and took Senri's hand. They walked until they reached the start of the next rise. It started snowing again. Light, small flakes drifted down on them. Alina looked up, the white crystals kissing her cheeks.

"I shouldn't have yelled at you," said Senri.

"I shouldn't have deceived you." Alina eyed the Warrior, took her other hand and held them both. Senri's warm fingers felt so good intertwined with her own. She watched the small flakes land on Senri's skin and melt away. "It was the most frightening thing in the world, watching you almost kill that man," Alina said.

"You mean the assassin."

"It was still terrifying. I mean, I never once feared for my own life or yours, but watching you kill for me made me realize how much power I really have."

Senri half-smiled. "A whole kingdom's worth."

Alina nodded. Her thumbs stroked the backs of Senri's hands. "I first saw you in a vision, you know, I was struck by your gaze, I think. You seemed so serious. Then I saw you on the archery field. I knew then that our futures would cross paths more than once."

She remembered the more intense, private visions. *Were they visions or fantasies?* She just knew all of them had involved Senri and all of them had been incredibly sensual. *Please, Almighty, let them be true.*

She breathed in. "I know you were absolutely terrified at the thought of being attracted to me. At first, I thought it was merely physical attraction. But you are so much more than that. I could spend all night listing your qualities, but I think what I admire most is your desire to help, and not just because I'm the heir to the throne." Alina paused. Her heart raced like it had never done so before. She feared for a moment that a vision might overtake her. "You devoted yourself to this because you thought it was the right thing to do."

"It is the right thing," said Senri.

"I know." Alina blinked snowflakes out of her eyes. Neither met each other's gaze. Instead, they started walking again, hand-in-hand. Alina looked around the mountainside. Snow drifts lay everywhere, yet the night felt comfortable, the snowflakes more like soft touches rather than stinging needles. A faint beam of moonlight penetrated the clouds and lit the landscape. It made Alina smile. "I don't think I've been on such a lovely moonlit walk before."

Senri laughed. "The one back in the village did not count?"

Alina squeezed her hand. "That felt more like an escort, this is a proper stroll."

"You've missed out on quite a bit," said Senri.

"Oh." Alina smiled as the thought ran through her head. "I'm a little more experienced than you would think."

She refrained from laughing as she felt Senri's grip on her hand go lax for a moment. As far as her and Senri had come, she did not think she would ever tire of making Senri blush or stumble. She waited for Senri to say something in response, but the words never came. Instead, the Warrior jumped away and Alina felt a cold projectile of snow hit her in the shoulder. Alina yelped.

Senri laughed. "You said you were experienced in a number of things, yet you never played in the snow. I had to remedy it."

Alina looked around at the fresh powder before stooping and scooping up a handful. She patted it down into a compact ball, but by then Senri had darted off. She aimed and launched the snowball. It struck Senri right between the shoulder blades. The Warrior stopped and turned back toward her. Alina giggled and stooped down for more snow. When she glanced up again, she nearly cried out as Senri charged at her. She chucked the snowball, but it did nothing as Senri ran toward her and kicked through a snowdrift.

Alina raised her arms to protect herself from the barrage of snowflakes. The blankets slipped away from her shoulders. She took off after Senri, who tried to make another projectile. Alina leapt at her. Senri looked up and shrieked, raising her arms for protection. They ended up grappling, hands on arms as they pushed each other around in the snow, both weak from laughter. Finally, they stopped and came to rest. Alina panted with the effort of their play; so did Senri. They remained standing while gripping each other.

Snow still fell. Time would seem frozen if not for the snowflakes. Alina leaned closer to Senri. She wanted to be nearer to the warmth, she told herself, though she kept her mouth tilted upward. Their lips met in a soft touch at first, as if asking for permission, then more firmly. A small noise escaped the back of Alina's throat. Senri pulled her close, enveloping her in heat. She wrapped her arms around Senri's shoulder, tilted her head to the side as they kissed again, deeper this time, and again. Her hands wandered up to Senri's hair and let her fingers intertwine with the strands. Senri groaned and sucked on her bottom lip. Alina shuddered when Senri's tongue brushed against the trapped skin.

Alina lost track of the time. She did not know for how long they kissed, but she did not care, as long as she could keep kissing Senri. When they finally parted, Alina stared up at her with wide eyes. She wanted more, so much more. Her heart pounded. Her blood raced. The aching need filled her core, and she leaned forward and kissed the pulse point at Senri's neck.

Senri smiled, her eyes reflecting genuine happiness as if she had just discovered something beyond words. As they kissed again, Alina marveled how no amount of foresight showed her anything equal to that moment on the mountaintop.

***

When they returned to the hovel, they settled back in their reserved space. Senri lay on her back and held Alina close. They exchanged a few more kisses. As much as Senri wanted to kiss Alina breathlessly and make love to her, their current surroundings were not nearly ideal or private enough. Eventually, Alina's calming presence overtook her and Senri fell into a deep, dreamless sleep.

A roar shook through the night, one that reverberated through the ground and the walls around them. Senri shot up from her bed and looked around. The others had woken, too.

"What was that?" asked Alina. She still clung to her side.

No one spoke. The fire had settled down into embers, but the faint glow remained to show that nothing strange had come into their hovel.

The roar sounded again, loud, distant. Senri had never heard anything like it.

"I think we found the dragons," said Nat, pulling on his armor. The other Warriors followed.

Senri rose and armored herself. When Alina picked up her equipment, panic shot through Senri. "What do you think you're doing?"

"I'm going," said Alina. She tied off her chest piece and moved to her gauntlets.

"Wait." Senri grabbed her arm. "We don't know if they're hostile or not."

Alina pulled away from Senri's grip. "No. I refuse to sit by while you risk yourself for me."

"I can't fight them and protect you!" Senri buckled her sword. She pulled the leather notches just a little too tight.

"Isn't it the same?" Alina grabbed her bow and quiver. "And we don't even know what they want."

Another roar sounded.

"Let's move out." Yahn gestured to the entrance of their shelter. Nat and Lanan went out first. Before Senri and Alina could follow, Yahn stopped them. "Is there something I should know about?"

Senri and Alina looked at one another, and then back to Yahn. Senri took in a deep breath and said, "No, we're fine."

Yahn nodded and let them pass on. The other two waited outside for them, their heads tilted to the sky and looking for the approaching danger.

"Don't draw your weapons," said Yahn. "We don't want to appear threatening."

Even as he spoke, Senri had to resist the urge to draw her sword. She kept glancing at Alina, who stayed close to her side. Alina fumbled with the signet ring on a chain around her neck

An immense blast of energy washed over her. She nearly stumbled back, but when she looked around, no one else showed signs of feeling it. The sound of beating wings filled the air as three dragons approached, their dark figures growing in size. The wind picked up as the dragons circled overhead and landed in front of them one by one with earth-shaking thumps.

The dragons stood like humans, though with the smallest one at eight feet tall, they dwarfed the tallest person in their party; their arms hung at their sides with claws extended, black knives curving out from their fingertips. Dark red scales hung around their shoulders and over their heads like armor, layering over one another in different patterns. Their wings, attached at the shoulder blade, spread wide as they stretched the leathery appendages. When they breathed, their nostrils glowed with inner light and Senri felt the fire within them.

One growled, a low rumble released from its chest. A scar ran across its shoulder and over the soft skin of its chest. "Humans." Its eyes, two embers, locked with Senri's. "For so long you have let our people be. Why do you trespass on our lands?"

The gaze almost mesmerized her. The dragons were like giant bellows, living suns. They burned with the intensity she only experienced in momentary flashes, like in the encampment. If Senri tried to maintain such a state, she would die.

Alina spoke, "I am Alina Alexandria Mura of Osota." She stepped forward and raised her signet ring. "I am the rightful ruler of my kingdom, and I come seeking the aid of your people."

The dragons glanced at her. Two of them laughed, or seemed to. Senri could not tell what the guttural sounds meant.

"Are the humans fighting with themselves again?" the one with the scar asked.

Alina stood tall. "Another kingdom seeks to enslave ours. They are an aggressive nation, one that will not leave the dragons alone."

"Maybe we ally with them," said one, his speech a little broken. Its scales lay in a diamond pattern. "Trade good trade."

Senri glanced to the others. Besides Alina, her friends stood back with their arms crossed. No one seemed willing to accept the fact the dragons might not eat them.

"They will take all and leave nothing. They crave conquest, nothing else."

The dragons stared at her for a long while. Finally, the middle dragon with the scar spoke again. "And why should we help?"

Alina sighed, most likely releasing a held breath. Senri had been holding hers. "We can offer you goods and services. Trade the good trade, as your friend put it."

"Why would you offer this now?" asked the dragon.

Her hand rose to her signet again. "I will only speak further on the subject to your sovereign. I wish an audience with your ruler. If they will not have me, we will leave your lands."

The dragons glanced at one another. Senri hoped they were impressed, but interpreting what the strange expressions meant proved to be difficult. They muttered back and forth in their own tongue, then turned back to Alina. "We have watched you from afar for some time now. You came a long way. Our elders will listen."

Alina's shoulders lowered. "They will?"

The dragons nodded. The middle one spoke again. "We will escort you. These ones are not necessary."

"They come with me," said Alina.

The middle dragon flared its nostrils and Senri felt a blast of hot air sear her skin. "Very well. We leave now."

With one look from Alina, the Warriors moved to dismantle camp. Senri tapped Alina on the shoulder and nodded off to the side. Alina followed her to the horses. "What is it?" she asked.

Senri shrugged and tried not to look back at the dragons. "What if this is a trap?" she said. Alina raised an eyebrow. "They could be leading us anywhere, and they relented to your demand to keep us close rather quickly."

"Maybe it does not bother them," said Alina. They both pretended to fuss with the horses. "We're not used to each other's practices. Who knows when they last encountered humans."

"They know our tongue," said Senri.

"They teach it to certain dragons," said Alina. "Notice how the middle one does all the talking. The one on the left spoke a little, but it wasn't good at all, and the one on the right has not said anything that wasn't in dragon speak. The accent is old, too, as if the variety they learned was from a century ago."

"You noticed all that?" asked Senri.

Alina smirked. "Well, I am the supposed ruler of a nation." Her smile faded as she glanced back over at the dragons. "We'll see for how long, once we speak to the elders."

    Senri's chest ached at the thought, but she knew she could do nothing to ease the fear in Alina's words. From that point on, their every move would be closely watched.

Michelle Magly

Chapter Twenty

AFTER WALKING AROUND THE nearest peak, an enormous structure came into view in the distance. Of course the dragons had intervened. Their city had been around the corner. As the sun rose, she got a better view of the structure. It stood like a massive fortress set into the mountainside. Homes had been carved from the mountain while large limestone blocks built up the city walls. Alina wondered why they maintained such defenses when any dragon could fly over. The answer came to her soon enough. *They do not fight with their own kind.*

Limestone blocks had been laid as a path up to the main entrance. The path had seen little use, though they had to have some foot traffic on it to maintain it. Equally impressive, the front gate had great timber logs bound together with bands of iron. It took all three dragons to pull it open. When Alina saw the sheer girth of the logs, she understood why. A human would not be able to wrap their arms around one trunk. The wood showed scorching marks as if someone had tried to burn it down. The logs had resisted.

The scarred dragon addressed them again. "Welcome to our city. We will take you to the audience room. The elders will decide when to see you."

Alina nodded and stepped into the city. "Thank you."

Great, stone-carved manors stood on either side of the streets, cut from the very earth they stood on. They would have passed for the most austere of human homes. The large doorways and windows held no decoration. Nothing distinguished one home from another. Instead, elaborate statues of other dragons and creatures Alina had never seen decorated the center of the street. Even in the early morning light, the statues displayed a certain grandeur that the houses did not have to. "How do your stone masters carve these?" she asked, gesturing to a statue.

The middle dragon flashed her a pointed-tooth grin and displayed his claws. "By hand," it answered. She could just imagine the streets choked with artisans and other people. The city could be a center of trade, if they chose for it to be. *I'm the first ruler of Osota to set foot in here since my failed predecessor.* Pride and terror gripped her heart at the thought.

The dragons led them away from the gate. Alina had to stop herself from watching the enormous wooden doors close shut behind them. The boom echoed in the empty streets. The statues glared down upon them as they walked past hulking figures with faces chiseled into snarls. The statues became more gruesome as they walked deeper into the heart of the city. Senri stayed close behind Alina, and more than once she felt the urge to grab the Warrior's hand, but she did not want to show affection or favor toward any one person. The fewer weapons the dragons had against her, the better.

They reached the cliff face of the mountainside and entered a large, carved out hall. They moved up the stairway and into the darker recesses. The farther they went in, the more Alina noticed a strange light flickering on the cavern walls that came from within the mountain. Alina peered through a crack and saw only a deep red light. The hall grew hotter and hotter as they climbed. Sweat gathered on Alina's forehead. She turned back and glanced at the others. Everyone else appeared just as uncomfortable as her, except for Senri. They continued down the passage and into a dark, unlit room. One of the dragons exhaled flames and lit an overhanging chandelier. The metal framework held a large pile of leaves and bark shavings, which burst into flame.

"I will speak with the elders," said the dragon. "My fellows will stand guard outside."

Alina realized she did not know what proper etiquette would be when speaking with dragons. She nodded like she had seen them do. "Thank you. We appreciate your hospitality."

The scarred dragon snorted. "You may be here for hours yet. Do not think the elders will rush to hear from you." Without giving her another chance to speak, the dragons walked out of the room, the one leaving the other two standing outside the entryway.

Alina looked from face to face of her travelling companions. They had reached their destination. The Warriors stood rigid. Yahn walked the perimeter, examining the walls, the crevices, everything. Nat looked lost in thought over something and Lanan stood with her arms crossed and stared at the floor. Senri, though, stood with the same wide-eyed expression she had gained upon entering the mountain. Alina stepped forward and touched her arm. Senri did not respond.

"Are you all right?" Alina asked.

She finally blinked, the glazed look vanishing. "It's the mountain."

"What about it?"

Senri shook her head. She looked pale. "It feels...alive." When Alina raised an eyebrow at her, she rubbed her forehead. "Of course, it's not really alive. It's just really, really hot. The ground isn't ever this hot."

"Are we in any danger because of it?" Alina asked.

Senri shook her head. "No, I...I have no idea. There's just...it's like fire, liquid fire, and it's all below us."

"I believe you, don't worry," said Alina. "We'll all be fine. I don't think anything they've done is to harm us. I do think they're going a long way to intimidate, however."

Yahn walked up to them and nodded at the doorway where the two dragons still stood guard. "We can discuss this another time, I recommend we all sit down and relax until they are ready to speak with us." The way Yahn glared at them suggested that the idea was more of a strategic order. Alina nodded and grabbed Senri's arm.

"Let's go sit down," she said.

Alina guided Senri and the others to a far wall and into a sitting position. They sat with the backs against the wall. Alina watched the others find similar positions to relax in. The room held no chairs or benches. By human standards, it qualified as a holding cell. Alina sighed and rolled her neck, trying to work out the stiffness from the impromptu trek. She hoped the elders would see them early.

With a start, she realized they had also left all their horses and supplies at the front gate. She hoped the gate guards had corralled the animals. *Do dragons eat horse?* Her nerves wore thin. Alina closed her eyes. She had to clear her thoughts, to meditate or something. She drew in a deep breath and tried to still her mind like Mala had taught her. She could find calm if her thoughts calmed, first. She did not sit in a dimly lit room, imprisoned by dragons. She was home, relaxing. Or nowhere at all. In darkness. Her body fell through it, away from all the problems, away from the dragons, from Senri, from everything.

She was elsewhere, standing on a mountaintop. The ground shook. It rumbled like thunder. The dragon stood taller than any others she had seen, its scales like shields. It stared down at all of them, then collapsed onto all fours and took in a deep breath. It opened its mouth wide. Alina saw the burning at the back of the throat, and then it exhaled flames upon them consuming everything. Alina raised her arms to protect herself. The heat rolled over her in waves, and when she breathed in the ash tasted heavy on her tongue. She exhaled, pushing against the rolling heat waves. There were words in the fire-tongue, whispering to her. The ashes choked Alina's throat, or she would have talked back to the whispers.

"Hey!"

Alina's eyes flew open as she felt the hand shaking her shoulder. The ground and wall of the cavern floor came back. The feeling returned to her limbs. She gasped and blinked. Senri looked down at her, worry etched into her frown.

"Senri," Alina said.

"Don't scare me like that. I thought you were having a fit."

"I…what happened?" Alina sat up against the cavern wall. Her skin felt cold.

Senri sat down but continued to look her over. Her fingers went to Alina's hands and gripped them tightly. "You fell asleep, you slept for a long while without any problems, then you just started breathing all heavy and your eyes flew open. I thought you had woke up from a nightmare, but when I tried talking to you, you ignored me."

Alina shook her head. She thought back to what she had seen—the dragon, the flames. "Did anything happen? While I was asleep, did we hear from the dragons?"

Senri furrowed her brow. "No. It's been dead quiet. Why? Did you…" She looked around the room before leaning down close to Alina. "Did you see something?"

So she had noticed. Alina glanced around the room, hoping to find something to might divert the conversation. She did not want to tell Senri what she saw, especially since they were essentially prisoners in the heart of the dragon city anyways.

"Alina." Senri's hand cupped her cheek. "Tell me."

Alina covered Senri's hand with her own. She wanted to kiss the palm, but feared it might be a step too far. If she broke down then, she might never recover. "I saw a dragon breath fire."

Senri nodded, her eyes still locked on her. "At anyone in particular?"

Of course Senri would not settle for the short answer. "Um...us?" Alina said, unsure of how to phrase her vision. "No one died, if that makes it more confusing."

The hand left her cheek and Senri slouched onto the ground in front of her. "Right. Perfect."

"Senri." Alina leaned forward and captured her hand again. "It could mean nothing. It could have been a nightmare."

The torchlight had dimmed significantly since their arrival. Only a faint glow flickered from the overhead bonfire. When Alina asked how long she had slept, Senri shrugged and told her it had been a few hours. The answer did not bode well for their situation.

Finally, Alina heard the scraping footsteps of someone approaching the room. She stood and brushed herself off. The others did so as well. Alina could hear the dragons muttering to one another in their own guttural language. The speaker entered the room. It spotted Alina and waited for her to approach. "Has a decision been reached, then?"

"You will speak to the elders," said the dragon. "Talk with respect, and keep your...subjects in line."

Alina felt like correcting the dragon toward its treatment of her friends, but she did not want to stall any further. Instead, she looked back at the others and nodded. "Are you ready?"

The Warriors all approached her. *We'll either have what we came for or be dead.* One way or the other, the whole ordeal would be over soon. The thought comforted Alina.

Alina stayed close to their guide as they exited the corridor and returned to the dimly lit stairs. She noticed Senri's hand gripped the pommel of her sword. She knew the others would assume aggressive stances as well. She did not know how to calm them. *Too late for second guesses.*

The dragon led them to a set of guarded iron doors. It conversed with the guards. The language sounded more like rumbles and hisses, almost like a storm...or a furnace. They opened the doors. Alina flinched as sunlight flooded the hall. They were ushered out onto a large opening, a stone basin atop the mountain. *Where are the elders?* They walked out into the middle of the basin. Craggy rock formations surrounded the edges of the flat plain.

The rock formations moved. They unfurled wings, sending gusts of wind at Alina. The dragons uncoiled themselves from the stone surface and shook out their heads, chunks of rock falling away. Arms and legs appeared as they stood tall. Scales shifted and shuttered and embers glowed softly underneath, within the very creatures themselves. Alina stumbled back only to be caught by Senri. These molten, living rock formations were the dragon elders.

"Human." One of them spoke. It stepped forward, claws digging into the rocky surface. "Why do you stray so far from your kingdom?"

Alina gulped. *Do I bow? Do I challenge the dragon's authority? Do I defer to its wisdom? How am I supposed to address it?* Her political training failed her, only good for her realm of humans and ordinary squabbles. To be standing in front of a dragon elder and conversing with it felt so unreal. "I..." Somehow, she did not think the creature would like small talk or flattery. "I come to ask for help."

The dragon huffed. "A human is asking us for help." She could not be sure, but the tone sounded condescending. "It must be war, then. Or worse, annihilation."

Alina swallowed. She wanted to step back, to be able to breathe in air that would not catch in her throat and burn her lungs. Instead, she spoke again. "You do not need to lend troops. All I ask for is trade. We need the precious ores in your regions to better equip our—"

"Don't want to ally with the dragons, then?" The voice boomed as the elder took a lurching step forward. "No, why would a human anyways? We are too fearsome for you. Too..." The dragon tilted its head and stared at her through one burning eye. "Vicious."

Alina held her ground. "The fear-mongering among my people is a terrible reminder of the past. Time has skewed the record of what happened between our people. I wish to repair the damage done between our kingdoms." She waited for a response from the dragon.

It looked to its peers.

"It is true," said the dragon. "Our lands have suffered from isolation. Your ancestor would not give us the respect deserved. He came to subjugate us, the lesser folk, forged from fire and ash rather than by some deity's hand. Even our own language was too dirty for him to sully his lips with."

Alina latched onto that statement. She could apologize. Clearly, the dragons had a different idea about how things transpired between them and her predecessor.

"I'm different," she said, though the statement hardly counted as convincing. "I want to build understanding between our people again. To do otherwise will only hurt us. We cannot ignore one another with aggressors encroaching on our lands, and it was unwise of my people to ignore yours during their time of hardship."

The dragon glared down at her. It drew in a breath, as if its lungs were billows to a furnace. "And what threatens you humans? What force drives you to our homeland?"

Alina bit her lip. She did not know if she should make the armies of Shedol appear to be a mutual threat or claim ownership of the problems. The dragons could respond poorly to any situation. Even so, it appeared to be baiting her, so the dragons could already know about Shedol in the first place. "The kingdom Shedol plans to invade our shores. We lack the materials and forces to stand against them. If we fall, they will spread to our borders and to your mountains."

The dragon huffed and looked away. Alina thought she heard a deep rumbling, a growl perhaps. "And why would these humans breach our walls when others have failed?"

The gates stood in Alina's mind, the scorch marks and hacked-away chunks a glaring reminder of the city's impenetrability. The dragons would not be breached by one human army. "They will not benefit you as a neighboring kingdom." Alina crossed her arms and then uncrossed them, unsure of how to stand to appear convincing. "I am here, willing to negotiate a trade agreement, an alliance if that is what the dragons desire."

The words provoked no reaction. The dragon glanced at its fellows. They stood there unmoving for what felt like hours. Alina almost forgot the sweltering heat as a cold wind rolled off the far cliffs. The dragon turned toward her. "We have heard whispers of an honorable queen coming to the throne. I am inclined to believe you.

We will talk more of the struggles our kingdoms face. But now, you and the travelers must rest. We are not so uncivilized as to deny you that."

Alina exhaled and felt a knot of tension in her chest loosening. "I look forward to speaking with you. I trust I will prove different from the humans that came before me."

The dragon narrowed its gaze and growled. "We killed your predecessor because he was dishonest and impatient. We hope we find no cause to do the same again."

The dragon turned from her and walked away, back to the edge of the mountainside. It coiled around itself and settled down. All the elders became silent and as still as the mountains themselves.

Alina thought she might faint. The exhaustion and fatigue of their travels hit her as hard as her hammering heart. She swayed, but Senri caught and steadied her. She blinked and straightened her posture, glancing back at the Warrior. Senri smiled. She looked exhausted as well.

"Oh, Senri," she sighed, unable to help the small action. Instead of responding, Senri turned her to face the dragon escort. She tried to recover what little authority remained, but the fatigue would not leave her limbs.

"We will show you your quarters," said the dragon. "Your supplies have been moved already. Come with us." The terseness of its tone seemed to convey exhaustion as well.

Alina suspected no one had slept since their initial encounter. She hardly paid attention to where the dragons led them, though she realized it was a private complex when they arrived. Fires lit hollowed out areas of the rock walls. The dragons told them they were not to leave and food would be provided, then the dragon left. True to its word, a dragon pushed in a whole cartload of provisions, most of it meats. It was smaller than the others they had seen, perhaps the same height as a tall human, with dark scales. It cast them a wary look when it left the food.

After they settled their supplies in the main hall, everyone set out to explore the outlying rooms. The stone house had been dug out from the mountainside like many other dragon homes. The rough-cut rooms and halls were larger than most rooms in the palace, though most dragons stood much taller than humans. Still, it surprised Alina to see a home built in such a similar fashion to what any human architect might decide on. The only difference she could note was the distinct lack of decoration, though dragons did not seem keen on decorations to begin with. Alina walked into a bedroom of sorts, a small circular room carved out of the rock. She cried out. The beds were piles of thatch covered in animal skins.

Senri rushed to her side, exclaiming, "what's wrong?"

Alina frowned and let her tired frame slump against the warm body. "The beds aren't beds," she said, her voice muffled against Senri's chest.

Strong arms encircled her and Alina felt the weight of Senri's chin on her head. "Well, I was reluctant to offer at first, but seeing your distress leaves me no choice, you may snuggle atop me if you need."

Alina glared as Senri grinned. But her glare softened when she remembered their soft kisses from the previous night. Her insides ignited. She leaned up to kiss Senri, but Senri leaned back. Frowning, Alina wrapped her arms around Senri and tried again, only to be thwarted a second time. Alina whimpered and slumped against Senri once more. "Why not?"

Senri's fingers threaded through her hair and she immediately calmed again. "You are far too tired to be doing that," said Senri. Alina sighed and nuzzled deeper into Senri's chest. "See? Your emotions are all over the place."

"Aren't I supposed to be the rational one?" asked Alina.

Senri chuckled. "Yes, but right now I think sleep deprivation has switched us. Go lay down. I'll let everyone know we are turning in for the day." Senri released her and nudged her towards the crude bed. Before flopping down on it, she turned and looked back at Senri.

"You'll come back?" she asked.

Senri nodded and bowed. "Of course, my Queen."

Alina sighed and lay down on the animal skins. In truth, it was much better than sleeping on the cold ground of the mountainside. Immeasurably better, actually, and even though she desperately wanted to stay awake until Senri arrived, she found herself unable and unwilling to remain awake any longer. The day had gone on too long and had been filled with too many trials to warrant her attention anymore. Alina drifted off to sleep.

***

Senri returned later than she hoped. Yahn spent too much time discussing the arrangement of a watch and then Nat tried to corner and question her about Alina and their midnight activities. She brushed aside his comments and retrieved as many blankets as could be spared before returning to her room. Alina already slept, so Senri eased herself down next to her and covered Alina gently with a blanket. She wrapped an arm around Alina and settled down, falling asleep next to her.

Chapter Twenty-One

THEY AWOKE IN THE early afternoon. Senri blinked, feeling a weight on her and realizing Alina lay pressed against her. "Um, good morning."

"Good morning." Alina smiled and snaked her hands down Senri's arms.

"I take it you slept well?" Senri asked. A shock traveled up from her fingers as Alina laced theirs together. It started a pulse between her legs.

"I never thought sleeping with you would erase all that tension behind bad politics," she said. Alina bent down and kissed one of Senri's cheeks. "It will all come back, of course. I cannot forget about the monumental suffering of my people." Her expression fell even as she spoke the words. Senri tilted her head up and kissed Alina. When she drew away, the small smile had returned. "But at least you will keep me sane during our waiting period here in the land of improper beds."

"They're more proper than the ground," said Senri. She had slept well in comparison to the nearly freezing nights on the mountainside.

Alina kissed her again. Senri moaned against Alina's lips, her tongue reaching out and caressing Alina's. Senri shivered and arched her hips, the deepening contact not enough. She needed more. Alina's hips shifted and pressed against her own. She pulled her hands away and cupped Alina's backside, pulling her closer. Her fingers traveled up to the seam of Alina's trousers and along the smooth skin of her back. This time, Alina moaned.

"We should stop, shouldn't we?" Alina mumbled against her

lips. Their hips met again in a slow, pulsating rhythm.

Senri kissed her once more. Her insides seemed like a pool of fire and the center of the heat lay in between her legs. Never had she felt so tightly wound. Never had she explicitly imagined the thoughts trailing through her mind. Not with Alina. Senri had been too frightened to think them before. Alina's words sounded so far away. Even as Alina lifted up, Senri followed, hands still holding her close.

"What did you say?" she asked. She mumbled the question, lips pressing against Alina's.

Senri whimpered slightly as Alina pulled out of reach. To disappoint her further, Alina pried Senri's hands off her and pushed her gently down onto the mattress. "I said we should stop." A giggle followed Alina's statement as she stared down at Senri.

She frowned. "What?"

"You look so disappointed."

Senri's face grew hot. She looked up at the ceiling instead.

"Oh, don't be like that." Alina's hand cupped her cheek and brought her gaze back down. Senri took a deep breath and tried to look less wounded. Alina giggled again. "I enjoy this side of you, actually."

"The tortured side?" Senri tried shifting her weight, but Alina kept her pinned.

"The sexual side," said Alina. "You kept it under lock and key for so long."

"To be fair, thinking of you like that is a quick way to end up in the dungeon."

Alina's weight shifted. She swung off of Senri and stood by the bedroll. As she smoothed out her clothes, she muttered, "One would have to have a country to rule to fear that."

Senri sat up and took hold of Alina's hand. "They will help us. What we ask of them is a great thing." When Alina did not respond, she stood and took the other hand as well. "At least we were not engulfed in flames." Senri had been worried the entire time during their discussion with the dragons that one would get too fed up and breathe fire down upon them like Alina had envisioned. She touched Alina's cheek, a gesture that she took pleasure in performing on a whim. "Dwelling on the future does no good. You should hear what my village seer has to say about it."

Alina glanced at her and smiled. "I spoke with Mala, actually."

"Oh?" Senri glanced toward the room's doorway and offered her arm to Alina. "How was the experience?"

"Enlightening," Alina replied. "She helped me put a few things about myself in perspective." They left the room, and judging by Alina's tone, the subject about her and Mala was closed. As they stepped into the main hall, Senri could hear the voices of others coming from the main room. Lanan approached them.

"Good to see you two out and about," she said. "I was getting tired of keeping the others at bay."

"At bay, why would you have to do that?" Senri did not trust the grin on Lanan's face.

She shrugged. "Oh, I just assumed the two of you would be…preoccupied for a while longer."

Senri's face burned. She glanced down at Alina but saw nothing, no trace of emotion, except maybe an amiable demeanor. It had been like that with the dragons, too. Alina's face had been a wall.

"We'll go meet with them now," said Alina, her tone even.

Their meal for the day consisted of meats supplemented with vegetables from their packs. Nat poked at the smoked slab cooking over the fire. "I wonder if the dragons eat meat."

Lanan laughed, but Yahn glared at him. "They're right outside. Don't be rude."

Senri and Alina joined them. "So we are just as much prisoners as we are guests," Alina said.

Yahn nodded. "They were serious when they said we were not to leave."

The dragons had left guards stationed at the only entrance and exit. No one had come to contact them unless it involved bringing food or water. None had even mentioned how long they were to remain. Yahn insisted they spend most of the day talking strategy, laying out plans if things went bad. They crowded together in a tight circle, muttering their opinions and drawing in the dust on the floors.

Even with the new tactics established, Senri felt unprepared. She had not expected to wait anything out like this. She thought things would be determined faster once they found the dragons. The five of them stood. Senri stretched, her muscles cramped from not moving around. Though it felt better than the utter exhaustion she had grown accustomed to during their hike through the mountains.

"What do we do now?" asked Lanan, stretching her arms out

behind her back.

Yahn shrugged and glanced toward the entrance. "Stay out of trouble, I suppose. I don't care as long as the four of you remain in this house."

Senri caught Alina glancing at her and her face flushed. She waited for Nat to pick up on the subtle change and mock her, but Lanan dragged him away, talking about showing him the strange idols she had found in one of the rooms. Yahn followed after, leaving the two of them alone once more. Senri glanced toward a window; twilight had approached already.

"So." Alina's voice made her jump. "Can you think of anything to pass the time?"

Alina angled herself forward in just the right way to show off her cleavage, an impressive feat considering the shapeless tunic she wore. Senri's mouth felt dry and she lied. "I…uh… have no idea."

"We could always redecorate our new temporary living quarters," said Alina. She started walking toward their bedroom, her hips shifting as she moved.

"Redecorate how?" Senri stood up and followed after.

Alina stopped in the doorway and lifted a hand to the wall. She stopped. "Oh, I think it needs more fabric." She walked further into the room and moved to peel off her shirt. Senri rushed forward and stopped her.

"A door would make for fine decoration as well," Senri noted.

"They won't bother us."

Senri thought of what Nat might do if he stumbled in on them. *Probably turn around and leave.* "No, I suppose not," she said.

As they walked toward the bed, Alina grabbed her by the tunic and yanked her farther in. Their lips met before Senri realized what was happening. She recovered quickly and kissed back, pulling Alina close to her. She liked the way their bodies fit when they held each other close. It felt right. Just as she slipped her hand under Alina's tunic, a faint noise caught her attention.

Both of them stilled, foreheads pressed together as they listened. Nothing happened.

"Did you hear that?" asked Senri.

Alina nodded. "Sounded like shifting stone." They did not move for several more seconds. Finally, Senri's hand went back to exploring the soft expanse of Alina's stomach. They kissed again, and had almost lost themselves in the same fiery passion as before when Senri halted. The sound had returned. Alina cupped her cheek and directed her gaze so their eyes met. "What is it?"

Senri closed her eyes and breathed in. She could feel the warmth of Alina, the absence of warmth along the room, the cold that soaked into the stone, and then the spike of heat. "Dragons." She looked at the far corner of the room. It felt as though they came from below the surface. "I think...they're using a secret tunnel. Alina. You need to go."

Before they could speak more, a great stone section of the floor shifted in a corner of their room, and then was pushed up by a dragon. It tossed the slab aside easily and hoisted itself from the hole. Two other dragons followed it.

"What are you doing here?" asked Alina. Senri tried to pull her behind, but she resisted. "I warn you, I will fetch the guards."

The dragons leapt at them before Senri could grab her sword. Two went for Alina. Senri tried to push her out of the way, but one grabbed Senri by the shoulder and tossed her aside. Pain seared through her shoulder as she fell on her side. She watched one dragon wrestle with dragging Alina away while the other one lifted the stone slab and placed it in front of the entrance. They were trapped in the room.

Senri stood, trying to swallow down the bile that rose in her throat. The room spun. Senri could hear shouting in the hallway. The other Warriors must have heard the commotion. One dragon moved to defend the doorway. Senri ran after the dragon holding Alina, but the third one grabbed her by the throat and lifted her into the air.

"Senri!" Alina's cry rang out. "Senri, no!"

Senri tried to draw in a breath. She couldn't. Her vision faded, darkening around the edges, but she still saw the other dragon taking Alina away, kidnapping her, stealing her. She struggled against her assailant, her hands clawing at the talons around her neck, the talons pinching her flesh and crushing her windpipe. She had to stop them, had to save Alina. If she could just get free.

"Senri!"

Her fingers closed around the dragon's arm and she managed to get one breath in. The world dissolved in flame around her. A bright, blinding light stood in front her. She snuffed it out, pulling the immense heat source into her being. The claws at her throat slackened, dropped her, and the form slumped to the ground. Senri gasped. The other dragon, another blinding ball of light, pulled Alina away. Senri charged forward, weaponless. Alina screamed. The dragon puffed out its chest and the heat swelled. Senri raised a hand. The flames poured over her, but did not burn. This time she found the root of the flame, the beating sun of the dragon's heart, and she pushed out at it. The fire dwindled. She extinguished it with a thought. *Go out.*

Senri blinked the soot out of her eyes. The dragon took a swaying step toward her and released Alina, who ran to grab her bow and quiver by the bed. A few more steps, and the dragon fell forward into the ground—dead. The remaining Dragon struggled to keep the others away from the door. After seeing its comrades dead, however, it roared and charged at Alina. Senri ran to intercept the beast. She didn't move fast enough. The dragon's jaws stretched open wide, razor teeth ready to sink into Alina's flesh.

A *twang* sounded and the dragon grunted. It fell forward, writhing and trying to pull at the arrow lodged deeply in its throat, its breaths coming in ragged gasps. Alina pulled another arrow from her quiver and aimed at the heart. She shot. The dragon stilled.

The stone blocking the entrance finally cracked and crumbled as Nat and Yahn broke through. They charged in, swords drawn, but paused when they saw the assailants all dead. Before anyone could make a move, the dragon guard from outside barreled into the room. "All of them dead," it hissed, nudging a body with his foot. "My kin disgrace me." It spat on the nearest body. Senri did not know dragons could look so livid, but this one had narrowed its eyes and clenched it's clawed hands tight.

Instead of facing the guard, she ran to Alina's side. "Are you all right?" she asked. Alina's face had gone pale. Her hands shook when Senri clasped them. "Alina?" She met her gaze, but her brown eyes seemed empty.

"You will all come to the mountaintop," said the dragon guard. Senri glanced at it. The blaze seemed to burn hotter. It was definitely angry. "I will wait outside. Be quick." Without waiting for a response, the dragon left, pushing aside Nat and Lanan on its way.

"What the hell just happened?" asked Nat, coming closer.

Senri waited for Alina to say something, but her hands still trembled and she did not seem to hear Nat or anyone else. "We were attacked," said Senri.

Yahn looked around at the four dragon corpses. "Clearly, how did they get in?"

Senri nodded toward the gap in the floor. The uplifted stone tile had been smashed to bits in the skirmish. "Secret entrance." She tried to go over to examine it, but Alina clung to her tightly when she tried to move. She winced as she felt fingernails dig into her forearm. Lanan walked over instead and lowered herself into it.

"There's more than one tunnel." She ducked down and Senri heard the receding footsteps. Lanan returned shortly and pulled herself out. "The pathways lead to other entrances. This whole house is filled with them."

"Damn dragons." Yahn kicked at a chunk of rock. "They're going to murder us all in our sleep."

"I think that remains to be determined." Nat stooped and picked up a rock. He tossed it in the air and caught it. "Those guards looked very mad. I'm guessing the visit was not a planned one." One more toss, and the stone went flying into the opposite wall, embedding itself with a crack, the only sign of Nat's anger. "We might as well go out and find our escort. Let them give us a stern talking to and be done with it."

Senri shook her head and glanced at the others. "Can you go ahead? I think Alina needs a moment."

The other three glanced at her, and then to Alina. Yahn muttered something to Nat and Lanan as he left the room. They followed, but not before Nat stopped and said, "You'll let us know if you need us, right?"

Senri nodded. Nat held her gaze for a second. Any of his usual jovialness had vanished. His jaw tightened, and for a second she thought he might not leave, but he turned and walked after Lanan. She let out a sigh and drew Alina close. Even wrapped in her embrace, Alina did not show much response.

***

Concentrate on breathing. You have to keep breathing. Alina did not know what else to think. Somewhere in reality, Senri spoke to her.

"Did they hurt you?" she asked.

Alina pushed against Senri, holding her at arm's length. Some of the color had returned to her face, but red bruises already formed on the Warrior's throat. "They were going to kill you," she said.

"They were going to abduct you."

"Senri." Alina pulled away and leaned against the wall. She sank to her knees. "It had you by the throat."

"I'm alive, though." Senri crouched in front of her. "We both are."

Alina shook her head. Her lips trembled and she buried her face in her hands for a moment. Once she had her composure regained, she looked up. "I never wanted you to give your life for me. I wanted to keep you as far away from harm as possible. I even saw this happen before and was powerless. You know I ordered a detachment sent as soon as Nin told me who they sent to investigate that camp? I was so scared." The words tumbled forth. "Any time you were in danger, I nearly lost it. Some ruler I am. I can't keep my composure with you, and yet I'm expected to treat you like all the other soldiers, just send you off to die."

"You would never order me to my death." Senri gripped her shoulders. "You make hard decisions. I follow them because I am a Warrior."

Alina stared at her Warrior. Senri's gaze had haunted her since the moment she set foot in the city. "You…Senri, you are everything to me. I can't make you give your life in service to the crown." She knew it in her heart. The recurring visions of Senri had been mingled with her own desires. Desperately, more than anything, she wanted her future entwined with Senri's and she knew she would do anything to keep it that way for as long as possible. She closed her eyes and tears pressed against her eyelids.

She felt Senri's warm hand on her cheek. A thumb stroked her skin. "Alina, I have chosen to dedicate my life to this. I chose to give my life for you." She paused and gave Alina a kiss on the forehead. "You are everything in my eyes, you know?"

The tears spilled over. Alina could not hold them back any longer. She had never meant to get this entangled with anyone. The ache in her heart reminded her why. "You could have died," she sobbed. She pulled her knees to her chest and crossed her arms. "Senri, I don't know what I would do if you died." Senri's warm arms encircle her, pulling her away from the wall. Senri stroked her hair and she buried her face against the Warrior's chest. Words paled against whatever warred inside her, so she sobbed instead. When she had calmed down enough, the Warrior tilted her chin up to look at her.

"I won't throw my life away, not when I just found you." Senri kissed her. When she pulled away, they both sighed. "Will you be able to face them?"

Alina blinked and remembered the orders from the dragon. "We need to, don't we?" Senri helped her to her feet and she wiped her face. She laughed softly when Senri handed her a strip of cloth. "Is it that bad?" she asked, mopping the edges of her eyes.

"If we're lucky, the dragons don't know what it means to cry."

Alina laughed again and shoved the cloth back into Senri's hand. "All right, I suppose we should make ourselves presentable, first." Heat seared her cheeks as she eyed the tattered, singed clothes hanging off Senri. The holes revealed most of her chest.

Senri glanced down at her clothes. "Oh. Right." They pulled on their armor, though both looked disheveled still.

"Let's go," she said. Senri nodded and led her from the room. The others waited at the doorway. The dragon guard flicked its tail a little too much.

"Follow," it hissed.

They walked down familiar streets. Dragons roamed the roads or flew overhead. Many stopped and watched them. A small hatchling attempted to scurry toward them before being snatched up by its mother, or Alina assumed it was a mother. She still had no clue how to tell their genders apart. They returned to the hollowed-out mountain. Their guide led them directly to the top this time.

On the basin, the ancient dragons had already shed their guise of rock and shuffled around one another, speaking in their own tongue. The guard stood at attention at the edge, so the Warriors did, too, waiting. One of the dragons noticed and roared. The others hushed. Only then did the guard urge them forward. It nudged Alina in the back, indicating that they wanted to talk to her specifically. She swallowed and walked to the center of the plateau. The same elder she had spoken to before lumbered over to her. It released a deep rumble from the back of its throat.

"Human," it growled. "It seems my own kin have shamed me."

Alina dared not agree. Instead, she inclined her head. "We were attacked."

"Without provocation?" The dragon adjusted its stance so it sat lower, more at level with her.

"We haven't left the lodgings you provided for us. I don't know why they broke into my chambers, but they entered secretly."

"I am aware of what happened!" The blast of dragon's breath almost seared her skin. She took a step back. "What we need to understand is why." A deep rumble released from the dragon and it prowled around Alina. "You brought a sun-killer with you." The dragon glared at Senri.

Senri took a hesitant step forward. "I never killed one of your kind before today."

The dragon growled and walked over to Senri. "You are lucky it was self defense."

The two stared at one another for several tense seconds. Alina swallowed her fear. "The dragons targeted me," Alina said. She remembered struggling to get away from the one that dragged her toward the tunnel entrance. "I am supposedly unimportant, unless you determine to forge an alliance with the humans, then I am necessary. The way I see things, these creatures either acted on someone's orders or went against your wishes"

"You accuse them of betraying me?" The ember eyes burned brighter.

Alina took a step back. "No...well, yes, they did betray you, but I am sure they were doing what they thought was for the good of their people."

The dragon stared her down as if it waited for something. Alina did not know whether to look away or stare back. Perhaps eye contact did not matter to them at all. She knew nothing. Her people knew absolutely nothing.

The dragon looked away and roared at the others. Alina quickly covered her ears as the other dragons roared back. When the din quieted, her head rang with the sound.

"You are smart. Smart enough to speak plainly to," the dragon growled. "When your predecessor came, he lied to us, and we killed him. You are truly in need, however. Your last king was not fortunate enough to have desperation on his side. This makes you interesting, human."

"And what do you plan to do now that I'm here?" Alina asked. Her heart hammered. *This could all have been a trap. Demek could have orchestrated my entire fate, leading me away just to become a meal for the dragons. All this trouble just to have me killed in some elaborate way.*

The dragon huffed a breath of scalding air at her. "We will talk, and if you talk well, the humans and dragons may just have an alliance.."

Michelle Magly

Chapter Twenty-Two

THE DRAGONS DISMISSED THEM to their newer, safer quarters, leading them to rooms farther in town and higher up on the mountainside. The new view took Senri's breath away, and terrified her. The city below shimmered with torchlight and multicolored lanterns as the dragons celebrated the waning hours of the nighttime. *Are they for a special occasion?*

She shook her head and returned to her current task. After finally getting back her pack and supplies, she dug out the small, sun-shaped gem Valk had given her on her first day as a Warrior. She held the yellow object up in the torchlight and studied it for a moment. The center contained a neat hole to thread a chain through. It had always meant to be worn as a pendant, Senri supposed. She had just not had the desire. As she threaded the string through it, she wondered if it would make a suitable gift for Alina. The delicate gold chain around her neck certainly spoke of finer craftsmanship.

"What are you up to?"

Senri nearly dropped the necklace. She tucked it into a tunic pocket and smiled over her shoulder at Alina. "Oh, nothing much," she said. "Done being needed for the day?"

Alina smiled and walked over to Senri, sitting down next to her and touching her forearm. "For now," she said. They both looked out the large window. Stars glittered by the thousands outside. "How did we end up here?" Senri felt Alina's fingers caress hers. Their hands clasped.

"That is a good question," Senri said. The world felt different, as if for so long they had pushed against an unmovable force. Now, they dangled weightless and free on the precipice of something completely unknown. She turned and looked at Alina. The young woman stared up at the sky still, her eyes drawing invisible patterns. "What are you looking for?"

Alina blinked and glanced at her. "I'm reading the omens." Her gaze returned to the stars.

"Any good news?"

"Oh, it's not nearly reliable enough." Alina sighed and leaned against Senri. Her stomach knotted at the close contact. "If I really wanted to know details, I would cast my runes, but that spends energy, precious energy that I happen to need on this whirlwind adventure."

Senri laughed and wrapped an arm around Alina's shoulders. "So what details are you looking for?" She had never learned much of fortunes and fate.

"News of the kingdom, mostly." Alina moved her hand to rest on Senri's lower back. "The sky is not filled with an overwhelming amount of anything shocking, at the moment. Neither are the constellations aligned in a pleasing way." Senri nodded and moved her free hand to her pocket. She felt for the necklace within.

On her other side, Alina shifted closer. "What are you doing?"

"You had a birthday, recently," Senri replied, grasping the necklace. Before she withdrew it, she leaned in and kissed Alina. The small noise she made caused heat to spread over Senri's cheeks. She pulled away, not wanting to lose herself just yet.

"And I can think of an excellent gift," said Alina. Her cheeks looked flushed as well.

"True." Senri pulled the necklace from her pocket. "But I would still like you to have this." She held it up, letting the gem catch the faint traces of moonlight.

Alina caught sight of it. "Senri." She raised a hand, touching the small sun. "Senri, I..."

"This was given to me at my initiation as a Warrior," she explained. "I would be honored if you wore it." She smiled at the look of awe Alina gave her. Instead of waiting, Senri draped the necklace around her. She touched the small gem now resting against Alina's breastbone. "I know it's not much, but it's supposed to represent my dedication and honor to protecting Osota. Who better to wear it than you?"

Alina eyes shone. "I love you."

Senri smiled, for she did not know how else to respond to those words. Her chest felt like it might burst. She wanted to laugh. As unexpected as the declaration was, it really did not shock her. Somehow, she knew their fates would lead them to this conclusion. She grinned and wrapped an arm around Alina.

"I've known since the attack today." Slowly, she bent down and kissed Alina's forehead. "And I love you," she mumbled against the soft skin. Alina drew in a sharp breath. "I think I've been in love with you since you stole me away from the castle." Alina laughed. Senri dipped her head and caught Alina's lips in another kiss. This time, Senri moaned softly. Alina's hands cupped her face and drew her in closer.

They managed to find the bed without breaking contact. Senri nudged Alina onto it and settled herself on top of her. She felt Alina's hands slide under her shirt and shuddered as soft fingers trailed along her skin, nails barely digging in. She sucked Alina's bottom lip in between her teeth and bit down gently. Alina's hands pushed upward, taking the tunic with. They parted for a moment as Alina pulled the shirt over Senri's head, and then kissed her again. Senri's hands traveled down to the gap between Alina's clothes and grabbed a hem. She tugged upwards, pulling back so that Alina could lean forward. Once she pulled the tunic free, she stopped.

Alina's pale skin nearly glowed in the moonlight. The gentle curve of her breasts rose and fell with her breathing. Starting above the heart, pale blue lines marred their way along Alina's skin, following the path of her veins, barely noticeable without the aid of a vision to draw them out. She had been so terrified when she first saw them. Now, she could only think Alina looked beautiful, seer veins and all. She shivered as Alina's hand touched her side.

"Senri? Is everything all right?"

She leaned down and kissed Alina. "You're beautiful."

Alina's arms encircled her and drew their bodies close. Senri gasped as her skin came in contact with Alina's warm body.

"As are you," Alina whispered against her ear. She whimpered when Alina nipped at her neck.

Senri turned and buried her face into Alina's loose hair. She kissed Alina's neck, moving lower down to her collarbone. She wanted to kiss every part of Alina, memorize her whole body. The first time she had been with a woman, she had not thought of love, only of proving a point. With Alina, she did not know what to do first, what pace to take. All she knew was that she wanted Alina, all of her. And her heart ached with the knowledge that Alina wanted her, too.

Senri kissed along Alina's neck again. The pale skin felt warm under her lips. She closed her lips around a pulse point and sucked in, causing Alina to moan softly and shift her hips upward. One of Alina's legs slipped between her thighs. She groaned and pressed back. They kissed again, more hurried than before, their hands wandering. Senri reached down and tugged her own trousers off, kicking them aside before grabbing Alina's. She stopped and pulled back a bit, waiting for her to say no or show hesitation. Instead, Alina nodded and raised her hips, allowing for her to pull them off with ease.

They settled against one another. Skin-to-skin contact had never felt so blissful for Senri. She kissed Alina's jawbone, down her neck, over her collarbone. She moved down so her lips met the rise of Alina's breasts. Her lips slowed over the soft skin. Alina breathed in short gasps. Senri smiled and sealed her lips over a taut nipple. When Alina cried out, she raised a hand to the other breast, feeling along the expanse of her body, loving how Alina groaned. She was usually so practiced with her words.

She released the nipple and Alina grabbed her shoulders. "Senri, I need you."

This admission sparked a flame in Senri. She kissed Alina hard and moved her hands down Alina's sides. Anything that elicited a moan, she stopped and caressed again. She wanted to satisfy Alina as fully as possible, more than any lover before her had. Alina's body trembled before her hand even reached a thigh. Still, she let her fingers travel as slowly as possible over the unexplored skin. Slowly she let her hand slip between Alina's legs.

Alina broke away from their kiss. "Senri, please." Her hips rose, searching for contact. Senri smiled and Alina breathed deep, her eyes shining with a need Senri had never seen before. "Please," Alina said again.

Senri pressed two fingers against Alina and dragged upward, brushing over her swollen clit. Alina cried out and Senri felt fingernails digging into her back. "You all right?" Senri asked as she paused.

Alina opened her eyes. "Senri, if you're not inside me in another second, I'll—"

Senri pushed two fingers inside her and Alina's words got lost in a moan. She paused, an increasingly difficult task as the velvety heat tightened around her fingers. Senri met Alina's gaze and watched her expression change from rapture to frustration. Her hips rocked. Senri moved with her. They picked up a slow rhythm, her fingers sliding and curling forward.

"Oh Senri," Alina gasped. She rocked harder against her hand. "More, please. I need more."

She thrust faster, putting more weight behind her hand. She rested her forehead against Alina's shoulder and kissed and sucked the salty skin. Every moan from Alina pushed her a little farther. *More.* She needed to do more.

Alina cried out and arched into her. She felt the smooth muscle spasm around her fingers and slowed her movements, stopping only when Alina did. Pulling away from Alina's shoulder caused a blush to rise on her cheeks. Red marks dotted Alina's collarbone. Alina cupped her cheek and pulled her in for another kiss. Their lips met in a tender embrace, nothing as heated or rushed like before. They broke apart and Senri saw the marks once more.

"What are you looking at?" Alina patted Senri's cheek and drew her gaze back.

"I…ah…I may have left a mark," she said.

Alina laughed and leaned up to give her a light kiss. "I thought as much." She eased back into the blankets. Senri still stared and Alina gave a slight tug at her shoulder. She looked back at her. "Stop worrying. In case you couldn't tell, I rather liked it."

Senri raised her brow in surprise. "You did?"

Alina laughed. "Of course I did. You were incredible." Senri pressed her face into the sweat-slicked skin of Alina's neck.

"I'm afraid I'm not that practiced at it." Senri breathed in her scent. Alina reminded her of rainfall.

"Well, you were excellent." Her fingers drew circles along Senri's back. "I might need to compose a new stanza for that song." The comment made Senri chuckle. "Something about you being a heat reader and her Highness's most accomplished bed-warmer."

Senri pulled away, smiling. "Glad to know I'm not all talk."

"Of course not." They kissed again, slowly. Alina pressed their foreheads together. "I love you." She pressed a kiss against Senri's cheek.

"I love you, too."

Alina nipped at her neck. "Lay down," she said. Senri did as she was told and settled against the bed. Alina's gaze roamed over her body and she leaned in to kiss her neck. "You're beautiful."

Senri gasped as Alina continued to kiss downward. Alina had every intention of paying her back double for taking her time earlier. She groaned as Alina's lips lingered on her collarbone before trailing down her chest. Alina kissed her way over Senri's breasts, much like she had done for her, but Alina looked up at her with a grin that made her blood pulse. The touch of her tongue made Senri moan. She arched her back, trying to angle herself better, but Alina pushed her down.

"Stay put," she said. Senri whimpered but managed not to squirm as Alina placed a circle of kisses around her breast, avoiding the hardened peak on purpose. Her lips ghosted over it and Senri cried out.

"Alina," she groaned. She felt a wet heat envelop her and she bit her lip. Alina's tongue worked back and forth over the tip and her hips trembled in response. When she pulled away, Senri thought she would finally give her release. Instead, Alina dipped her head over the other breast and Senri released a frustrated cry. Alina's tongue felt so good, nearly too good. She needed Alina to do something, anything.

"Alina, please," she said, remembering how Alina had cried out for her. The princess released her breast.

"Please what?"

The question both excited and frustrated her to no end. Alina made it extremely difficult to answer as she kissed down Senri's chest and along her stomach. "Please touch me," Senri gasped.

"But I am." Alina kissed her hipbone. She cried out and Alina repeated the action.

"You know what I mean!"

Alina placed a hand under Senri's leg and lifted it over her shoulder. Senri glanced down. Alina kissed along her thigh, getting closer and closer to where she needed her. She bucked her hips as Alina kissed her and slid her tongue into the center of her wetness. Her tongue pressed against Senri and sucked hard.

"Alina!" She threaded a hand into the long tresses of hair, encouraging her lover to continue. Her tongue stroked faster and faster, tightening the knot in Senri's core. Alina moaned against her, and the knot came undone. Her body shook, and for a moment nothing else existed beyond her and Alina.

The contractions faded and her body went limp. Alina placed gentle kisses on her thighs before pulling herself up to lay next to Senri. Alina grinned and kissed her, settling against Senri.

"Why didn't we do this sooner?" Alina pulled a blanket over them.

Senri shrugged. "Fear of dismemberment?" She wrapped an arm around Alina and pulled her close. She yawned. "You're incredible too, by the way. Maybe the song needs a stanza about you."

Alina laughed and kissed her cheek. "I don't think so. *Savior of the Queen* would have a completely different connotation."

"If you say so." Senri stroked Alina's shoulder. She yawned again. Usually it took longer for her to drift off to sleep, but she felt so drained that night. "I love you, Alina," she said once more.

Alina sighed. "I love you too, Senri."

Senri fell asleep with an arm wrapped around Alina's waist.

Michelle Magly

Chapter Twenty-Three

THE FOLLOWING DAY, AN escort came to fetch them to go to the negotiations. They climbed to the top of the mountain where the other dragons waited. The one who had spoken with them before, the large, terrifying one, paced back and forth. When Alina and the others arrived, it stopped and glared down at them. "You are ready, human?"

Ready for what? The dragon had only spoken briefly of an oath the previous day. From what Alina had observed, the dragons seemed to stand on very little ceremony. "I suppose I must be ready," she answered.

"I have spoken with my fellows," the dragon said. It took two great steps toward her. "We all agree we cannot ignore this threat. We will accompany you to your kingdom and survey it ourselves. If what you say is true, we will arrange a more formal agreement. I give you my name, Grythumak, in binding. Take it as an offer of allegiance."

"Grythumak. I offer my name, Alina Alexandria Mura of Osota. May our two kingdoms fight as one." She could be mistaken, but it looked as though the dragon grinned at her. The razor-sharp fangs made for an unsettling sight.

"Your predecessors were too craven to offer names, Alina. You are honorable. The dragonfolk will remember that."

Alina bowed. "Thank you, Grythumak. You honor my people with your kindness and wisdom."

"I would save any praise," said the dragon. Alina looked up again. "There is still this threat to tend to."

***

Senri stood on the balcony while the others talked strategy. She had tried sitting in with them when the dragons had first called the meeting, but she did not like the way their new allies eyed her, so she excused herself. She was glad they planned on returning to the heartlands soon, though still felt a little off about having to ride back on dragons. Currently they discussed routes to take, not anything Senri was an expert on, so it shocked her when another dragon joined her on the balcony.

She waited for the dragon to speak, but it only stood there, talon-like hands clasped behind its back much like how Senri stood. It was a smaller dragon, perhaps only seven feet tall. Its midnight-blue scales showed no sign of wear. "Uh, do they need me inside for anything?" she asked. The dragon shook its head. "All right then." The two stood there, staring down at the city. Senri liked watching the families and small clutches of children scurry about. They moved differently compared to humans. The children scampered on all fours, occasionally leaping into the air and gaining a few feet before flopping back to earth, their leathery wings not large enough to support their scrawny bodies yet.

"You confuse me, human." The dragon's words came out like slow hisses.

Senri glanced at the dragon. It still watched the city. "Why is that?"

"Your heart. It is a dragon's, as if Sholok gave it to you instead of giving it to one of our own."

"And Sholok is..."

"The all-seeing. Shaper of dragons. Wind beneath wings. Fire of breath. Beat of heart." The dragon raised a clawed hand to cover a spot on its chest.

"Almighty," said Senri.

The dragon growled. "Sholok is not your...creator."

"So there are two all-powerful, other-worldly beings." Senri had never been one to closely follow the doctrines, but a temple priest would probably denounce this as blasphemous.

"And so many more." The dragon looked over at her. "Do you know what lies beyond your kingdom?"

Senri shrugged. "More kingdoms?"

"Hundreds," said the dragon. "I learned so many tongues, saw creatures I have no words for. Humans that become beasts. Trees that talk. So many creatures..." The dragon looked back toward the city. "Humans see small. They see only within borders. Dragons see the world."

Senri smiled. "Well, you certainly have that advantage over us, being able to fly."

The dragon made an odd chortling sound. The dragon nodded. "Indeed, human."

***

The dragons flew them back into the kingdom. They stayed high in the sky, above any clouds they could find. Seven dragons flying overhead would send anyone into a panic. The wind stung Alina's cheeks, and by their second day of travel, they seemed to be a permanent red. She gripped the dragon around its shoulders as they flew, her legs anchored firmly in place by the wing joints. Her arms hurt from clinging on. Nothing could be worse than flying by dragons, but it was the fastest way home. Within two days, their group touched down in the trees just at the base of the mountain range and farther east from Senri's village. Grythumak had to lay flat on the ground in order for Alina to dismount safely. She blushed when Senri came over and offered her hand. Alina took it and eased herself into Senri's embrace.

After the camp had been set up, the dragons left to hunt. They promised to return by sunrise. The Warriors and Alina ate in silence. The only comfort she took was resting at Senri's side while the fire burned down. She did not want to speak of plans, or what they would do upon returning to the capital. They had exhausted the conversation so much in the past few days. She merely wanted a few moments of peace, just her and Senri, with no one else around.

The others turned in early that night. Alina looked up at Senri with a small smile and nudged her. Without needing further prompting, she helped Alina up and led her back into the tent. They sat down, careful to avoid hitting one another in the dark space. Senri's hand found hers and squeezed. Their lips met gently at first, giving hesitant kisses. Where kissing Senri usually aroused her, that night it stirred up coals, a slow, burning heat covering the visions of ash. Her lips tasted like wood smoke, probably from the campfire. The air between them seemed so dry it could have crackled. Or was that the hitch in Senri's gasp? She pushed Senri down and straddled her. They said nothing, just kissed in the dark. There, blinded to the countless hardships awaiting her, Alina could escape.

Senri's lips glided past hers. She kissed them again, harder. She wanted to stay infused like this, trapped in the moment. When Senri's hand lowered to the hem of her shirt, she grabbed her wrist. "Not yet," she whispered into the dark. They kissed again. "Just...let me have this."

A warning murmured inside her, something she desperately wanted to ignore. The sickening feeling grew, an approaching vision. She slung her arms around Senri's shoulders, gripping at the broad, strong muscles as if they were her only connection to the world. Perhaps they were. Perhaps her grip would falter and the ground would open up and swallow them whole.

She pressed her face into the warmth of Senri's neck and kissed the heated skin. Every touch brought her a little farther from reality. Every sigh helped erase just a little more of the tension. Still, it was not enough to banish the tightness she felt in her stomach. She bit down on Senri's neck just to hear her cry out and sucked hard to draw out the moans. Alina did not care if she left a mark. If anything, it would serve to remind her of them, that no matter how many burdens the Almighty piled on her, she had one person to herself.

Alina leaned forward to kiss Senri once more, but found only emptiness. Her hands sought for a perch, but she could no longer feel Senri. The material of Senri's shirt dissolved in her fingers and the warmth from their shared body heat disappeared.

Alina blinked against the darkness, and the world flooded with light. Senri really had disappeared. Alina stood on scorched earth, a wall of flames consuming the grasslands. Ash stuck in her throat when she breathed. Heat seared her skin. The fire spread everywhere, cinders popping and the flames roaring. The scene dissolved in a blur of colors, and she stood in the palace dungeons. Lord Demek smiled wickedly as he tossed someone against a wall. The slumping figure cried out. Blood smeared the floors. The stink of copper filled her nostrils. Another blink and she stood overlooking a wall. Senri lay at the bottom, broken and beaten. She cried out to her, *"Alina! Alina!"*

She tried to breathe, but couldn't.

"Alina!"

Hands gripped her shoulders. She lay on the floor, back in the darkness, back in the embrace of Senri.

"Alina, come back." Senri's hand cupped her cheek. She breathed the cool night air. Her heart beat against her chest. "By the Almighty." Senri pulled her into a tight hug. "Don't do that to me."

Alina coughed and pushed Senri away. "It wasn't on purpose." They were still in the tent. But when she closed her eyes, Senri's broken body filled her mind. She grabbed hold of Senri and felt her arms. Her hands traveled upward, fingers tracing over the unharmed features of her lover. "Thank the Almighty."

Senri covered Alina's hands with her own and pulled them away. "What did you see? Did a dragon kill us?"

"No. Of course not." *It was a vision, just an obscure vision. It probably means anything.*

"Alina." Senri had to direct her gaze back to her. "What did you see?"

She blinked. There lay Senri again, helpless and weak. "I saw fire," she said. "I saw us fighting to reclaim the kingdom."

"Something happens to me," said Senri. Alina tried to get up, but she held her in place. "Alina, you can't keep something like this from me."

"What does it matter, anyways?" Alina forced Senri off her and got up. "If I told you to stay away, would it make a difference? Would you stay in your village if I asked?" She smoothed out her clothes, looking anywhere but at her.

"Of course I'm not going to leave you." Senri tried grabbing her arm again. "I swore to keep you safe, and that's what I'm going to do."

Alina blinked back tears. Her throat felt tight as she remembered the vision, the blood, the ruin. "Even if it means dying?"

"Yes, even that!" Alina winced at the volume of Senri's voice and turned away, pulling a tent flap aside. "Where do you think you're going?"

"To sit by the fire. I need a moment alone." Before Senri could counter, she stepped outside and let the flap fall back into place. Yahn sat by the fire, keeping a watchful eye on the surrounding forest. He glanced at Alina and nodded. She crossed her arms and walked over, seating herself beside him.

She stared into the fire for a long while, probably not wise, considering it only brought back the sensation of ash caught in her throat. She tried looking elsewhere, but the dark forest only whispered at her as the wind rustled its leaves. The camp remained quiet and motionless. After a while, Yahn cleared his throat and shifted his posture. "Onera and I have similar fights."

Alina drew her knees up to her chest. "You heard that?"

He shrugged. "It was hard not to." Alina thought he had nothing more to say for a moment, but he continued, "She doesn't like when I take the dangerous assignments voluntarily."

"Like this one?" Alina asked. Her chest tightened at the thought of causing a fight.

Yahn nodded. He took a charred branch and prodded the embers with the tip. "She was not happy about staying behind, but the farmers need her to grow crops more than we needed her to protect you."

"You made her stay?"

"No." Yahn smiled. "I couldn't make her do anything. She chose to stay because she agreed she could do the most good there."

The wind rustled the trees again. Alina thought about what Yahn had said. Onera was a very giving woman to stay behind. She did not know if she would do the same in Onera's position. Senri certainly wouldn't. "Is there a lecture in this?"

He laughed. "Perhaps a little one, considering the two of you made your disagreement so vocal." Yahn picked up a spare branch and broke it in half. He tossed both pieces into the fire. The dry peeling bark caught quickly in the flame. After tossing one more branch onto the fire, Yahn leaned back and studied his handiwork. "Is your bow nearby?"

The question came so unexpectedly Alina's reply caught in her throat. She waited for Yahn to say something, to explain further, but he remained silent and stared at the flames. "I'm sorry," she said. "I don't have it. I saw no need."

"It's a shame." Yahn rested his weight on his palms, hands touching the earth. "We are surrounded," he said, his tone much lower. "Get a weapon when I say."

Alina fought the urge to run and grab Senri, or to do something stupid like look around for the intruders. The seconds thumped by in time with her heart. Yahn took a deep breath and she heard the shifting of stone. Someone cried out and an arrow flew loose into the clearing, thudding into the dirt near Yahn's feet.

"Now!"

The two of them dove for cover. Alina rolled to the left and sprang to her feet. Her bow and quiver lay against her shared tent with Senri. She sprinted for it even as she heard the twang of arrows flying and the shifting of rock. The bow was so close, just a few steps away. She had it in her hands. Senri emerged from the tent looking bewildered. Alina had an arrow set against the string. She turned, took a breath to steady herself.

And then there was no air. She breathed again, still nothing, just her lungs tightening in her chest. Someone stood by her side, a woman in red armor. Armor made from dragon scales and belonging to none other than the Scaled Vanguard. Alina fell to her knees.

"No!" Senri ran to her, but as soon as she got close enough, a strangled gasp escaped her mouth. She still reached forward, hand outstretched and clawing at the vanguard. No breath came to Alina, just the heavy beating of her heart. The world faded. Spots gathered in her vision.

"Stop this madness!" Yahn yelled. His voice sounded muffled.

The ground shifted underneath them, and the woman went flying away. Air returned to Alina's lungs and she coughed, her whole body shuddering as she drew in all she could. As her vision returned, she saw the clearing had filled with warriors from the Scaled Vanguard. Some had arrows pointed at them. Nat and Lanan had crawled out of their tents and kept two of the vanguards at sword point.

Yahn slowly lowered his sword and turned to the nearest vanguard. "By the Almighty, what are you doing?"

The woman who had been knocked back stood up and brushed herself off. She pulled her helmet off and shook out her auburn hair. "We found a horde of dragons in the forests. They claimed they traveled with Princess Alina. If the true heir to Osota is among your ranks, have her step forward, and no one will be harmed."

"And why do you search for the princess?" Senri asked. She got up and stepped forward. "You going to kill her like that snake Demek wants?"

"Senri!" Yahn glared at her.

"That snake you so aptly speak of has let the enemy overrun the heartland," said the vanguard.

"He what?" Alina got to her feet as well. "Is it too late, then? Is the kingdom lost?"

The vanguards exchanged glances. Most still kept their weapons at the ready.

"All of you, lower your weapons," Alina said. She fumbled with the ring hidden in her tunic before pulling it out and showing it to the nearest woman. "I am Alina Alexandria Mura of Osota, the dragons are my allies, and we travel north so I may claim the throne and drive out our invaders." The vanguards stared at the ring. The embedded gems glittered in the firelight.

One by one, they lowered their weapons. A tall man pulled off his dragon scale helm and tucked it under his arm. A scraggly beard covered his face. Deep shadows sunk under his eyes. "It would seem we have retreated far enough south, then, my queen." He knelt down. "This cohort of vanguards pledges its resources to you. Our arms are yours." Alina's heart thudded. *Queen?*

"So, now you're working for us?" asked Nat. "A second ago your wind reader would have suffocated Alina without a thought."

"The enemy works in deceptive ways," said the vanguard. "We learned days ago it is better to act first."

"Does the capital no longer stand?" Alina asked. *The fires. The death. It's going to happen.*

"There are soldiers and warriors still within the walls putting up resistance. They work in secret, however." The man stood. He took a deep breath. "Presently, the kingdom of Shedol holds the capital, though loosely at best. We made a tactical retreat with the promise of finding reinforcements to the south." He glanced around the camp. "I suppose this is what the agent meant."

"Agent?" Lanan stepped forward. "Which agent?"

"A woman," he said. "She was injured during the withdrawal. We have her back at our encampment, if you wish to join us there."

Alina looked at the others. Senri still stood by her with a wary look on her face. Yahn nodded at her. Lanan...Alina had never seen such a pained look on her face. "We break camp," she said. "Our first objective is to find our allies, and I expect them to be unharmed." Alina glared at the dragon scale helm tucked under the vanguard's arm. He smiled.

"We would never act so rashly against a dragon that willfully surrenders, let alone seven that do so."

"For your sake, you should hope so," said Senri. Alina noted the definite tone of disapproval in her voice. Senri had spoken briefly of her mentor's wish for her to one day join the Scaled Vanguard. Her lover had most likely just reformed her opinion on the matter. Alina's mind reeled too much to think of anything else while they packed. The capital had fallen. More than ever, she felt her visions enclosing her, offering no escape.

***

The dragons roared at the sight of Alina, probably to mock their captors. "Here comes your queen!" Grythumak cried out. "Now let us hunt in peace before we decide you make a fine meal, little soldier."

Unmoved by the threat, the vanguard who guarded them nodded.

Alina called out to Grythumak. The great dragon marched over to her with booming footsteps, another attempt to unsettle the vanguards. "Yes, Queen?" Grythumak lowered himself to eye level with her.

"The situation has grown more serious. Make your hunt short, We have much to plan if we have any hope of victory."

"You have my word," said the dragon. He inclined his head slightly. "If there is nothing else, we will take our leave."

One of the vanguards described the location of their encampment to Grythumak. The dragons took off and the party of fighters led them eastward into the forest. Nine vanguards stood with their current party. *How many others retreated successfully? Is it enough to drive out the armies of Shedol?* She took Senri's hand and squeezed it, needing comfort.

More vanguards packed the encampment than Alina thought. They usually moved in small patrols around the kingdom, but a hundred easily filled the large clearing. Tents had been pitched by the score. Groups sat around fires and talked to one another in low voices. Several of them sported minor wounds, while a few lingered with more severe injuries. A bordering encampment had also been established for routing soldiers and Warriors as well. It was less than half of the military might resting behind the capital walls, but it was better than nothing.

"Where is the agent you spoke of?" Alina asked. She already had a fair guess of who the agent was, but she wanted to see for herself.

"We keep the infirm in the center of the camp," said the man who had guided them to camp. "I can take you to her now."

An eerie feeling stayed with Alina as he led them through camp. Many of the soldiers and vanguards paused in their conversation and muttered to one another when they passed. *How many fled in hopes of finding me with an army?* Alina feared they might be disappointed.

The guide stopped and pointed at one of the many medical tents. "She's in there. I ask that you keep the visits limited. I don't know how much excitement she could handle."

Alina nodded. Still, she held onto Senri's hand all the way up to the tent flap. They paused outside and she turned to the others. "Don't stray far," she said to Senri. She looked to Yahn and he nodded. She let go of Senri's hand.

"Alina." Lanan stepped forward.

"What is it?"

Her brow furrowed and Alina noted how much her hands shook as they fidgeted with the ties on her gauntlets. "I...please, if it's not any trouble, I'd like to go in with you. I just...I need to see..." Lanan had never appeared so meek before. Concern filled Alina.

"You may enter with me," she said.

The tension eased from Lanan's face. "Thank you."

Alina nodded and pulled the fabric aside, stepping into the tent. Lanan followed. She had to crouch to avoid the low-hanging tent cloth. Candlelight flickered from a lantern resting on a wooden block. A woman lay asleep on a pallet, her left shoulder bound and wrapped in gauze. Bruises covered her face, but Alina still recognized Nin, her loyal maid. She rushed to the woman's side, kneeling down.

"Nin!" She wanted to hold her, but paused when she saw the wounds. A gash ran along Nin's neck and down over her collarbone. Any deeper, and it could have severed a major artery. Nin would have died. "Nin, what happened to you?" She did not move. Alina reached out and gently touched the undamaged shoulder. To her relief, the woman shifted against the touch. "Did you see that?" Alina asked. She glanced up at Lanan, but the Warrior stared down at Nin with wide eyes, the blood nearly drained from her face. "Lanan?"

Nin shifted again. Her eyes cracked open and she looked up, past Alina toward the back of the tent. Another small noise escaped her throat. She raised a shaking hand, her skin pale and bruised. Lanan's eyes widened and she quickly stumbled from the tent. Nin sighed and lay back down. "Your Highness, water, please." Alina searched through the travel supplies piled in one corner for a water skin. She heard Nin groan and shift into a sitting position.

"What are you doing? You should be laying down."

Nin laughed. She took the water skin and swallowed a mouthful from it. A loose tunic hung off her gaunt form. Whatever had transpired in Alina's absence had left Nin extremely weak. "Those vanguards would have everyone believe I am nearly dead, but I'm fine, I promise."

Alina smiled. "Well, that's a relief." She settled down by Nin, suddenly aware of how important the woman was to her, more than an ally. A friend, perhaps. "Why did you take the armies south?"

Nin took another sip of water and set the skin aside. "Well, I was hoping to find you at the head of an army of dragons."

Alina grimaced. "Seven does not make an army."

"So you did find them? You were successful?"

She shifted into a more comfortable position. "We have an alliance. It's new, and formed from the threat of a mutual enemy rather than mutual benefit, but I think it will do. It has to if we have any hope of reclaiming the capital."

Nin shook her head. "So they told you about that?"

"I don't blame you for losing the heartland," said Alina. "I didn't leave you in charge of defense, after all."

Something darkened in Nin's look. "We might have held if the enemy had not taken the gate."

"What do you mean?"

"Someone from the inside opened the gates to our outer walls. They had us taken before dawn the next day."

Alina clenched her fists. She closed her eyes and took a deep breath. When she opened them, some of the rising anger stifled. "And what of those trapped in the palace walls?"

"Taken prisoner. I think they intend to use them for bargaining with you."

"They don't know I am alive."

"They are prepared, either way." Nin eased back down onto her cot. "As we should be as well. We can discuss strategy in the morning."

The thought of waiting any longer to take action maddened Alina, but she understood the necessity for rest. She let her friend drift back to sleep. It had been too long a day, now that she had taken a moment of pause.

***

Yahn gripped Senri by the shoulder when she tried to take after Lanan. "Let her be," he said.

"But she's obviously upset about something," said Senri, watching Lanan's retreating form. "Shouldn't we, you know, comfort her?"

"Lanan needs some time alone. She's been through much since the start of this whole mess. We all have."

In the months after their capture, Senri had constantly been worried about Lanan, but everyone else had assured her that Lanan was fine, that Lanan had received help. Senri looked back at Yahn. He gestured to a nearby fallen tree and they strode over and sat down on it. "What do you want?"

Yahn looked across the camp. Lanan sat under a tree, far away from anyone else, arms crossed and head slung back. "We all left some things unsaid when we left the kingdom." He looked down at his clasped hands. Senri glanced over at Lanan one more time. She had spoken about spending time with Nin, but she had never imagined the two were that close. "You were fortunate enough to have the person along you needed to say those things to."

"You mean Alina."

"You two have grown very close." Yahn laid a hand on her shoulder. "War is here, Senri. And I need to know if you are capable of doing your duty."

"I'd die defending her." She shrugged off the hand.

"The kingdom you swore your skill to? Or just Alina?"

Senri looked at the older Warrior. He had a dark look in his eyes. "Aren't they the same? Alina is the rightful queen."

"She is also your lover." Yahn leaned closer to her and lowered his voice. "If a time should come where her commands or desires put her in harm's way because of you, I trust you will do the right thing and keep her Highness alive." He paused, looking her in the eye. "Her life is valued above all others, including yours."

Yahn's eyes glinted, sending a chill through her. "I would not let harm come to her, even if she chose to face it instead of me."

"The fate of this approaching war depends on it." Yahn stood up and gave her shoulder one last squeeze. "Do not discuss this with her Highness." He glanced down at her. "Enough weighs on her mind."

Michelle Magly

Chapter Twenty-Four

COMMANDER ELKYSS, LEADER OF a strong squadron of vanguards and the same man who had led their group to the encampment, stood over a tattered map tacked down to a tree stump. "The enemy army numbers at three thousand, by our report."

Alina stood with Grythumak on one side and Nin on the other, though her former maid needed the support of makeshift crutches to stay upright.

Elkyss frowned. "Our readers number at two hundred if we combine the warriors and vanguards. We have perhaps five hundred soldiers with average combat training."

"Even with the readers, it's not enough to retake the city," said Nin. "The armies of Shedol are unpredictable, rabid men, but whoever controls them has enough sense to keep the troops within the protection of the city." She winced as she readjusted. "The archers aren't so bad with their aim, either."

From what Alina gathered, Nin had only recently escaped the palace and rallied the troops, but not before she lay imprisoned and abused by the enemy for days. "You have the dragonfolk," said Alina, gesturing to Grythumak.

Elkyss shook his head. "Though seven are an immense number compared to foot soldiers, it is still not enough to gain the advantage. If you were to pledge more soldiers, perhaps—"

Grythumak snorted. "We have discussed this, little human. I want an oath in binding that promises your vanguards to our aid."

"We cannot make such promises with an aggressive nation at our doorstep," he said. "After we have quelled the threat from Shedol, you are free to negotiate with her Highness on the stipulations of our alliance."

"Your demands mean nothing, butcher," growled Grythumak. "How dare you wear the skin of my people?"

"We dare out of the necessity to keep your wild runaways from slaughtering our villagers—"

"Enough!" Alina hated that the allies fought so much with one another. Did they not already have enough to contend with? "I did not go to the dragons for help so that we could selfishly use them." She turned to Grythumak. "If your soldiers are willing to die defending our kingdom, we are willing to do the same for you so long as we do not risk our own extermination. I think these terms are agreeable for everyone, considering it is no less we ask of the dragons." Grythumak snorted, releasing a rush of hot air. "And I am sure that after the battle has concluded, we can discuss new uniforms for the vanguards. We will, after all, have the necessary ore from trade to stock an army."

Elkyss raised an eyebrow. "You did not mention that we are trade partners with the dragons."

"There is much you are unaware of, human," Grythumak said. "You are fortunate your queen is intelligent."

Nin cleared her throat and everyone glanced at her. "If we are done arguing, I believe we have a battle to plan."

The vanguard blushed. He ran a hand through his hair. "We could plan better if we knew how many dragons to expect on the battlefield."

"Would a hundred turn the tides?" Grythumak asked.

Elkyss seemed to think this over. Alina couldn't imagine a hundred dragons. That many spitting fire would easily cut through whatever horde they found waiting at the palace, or so she thought. Grythumak was a beast of a dragon, but the average-sized soldier only stood at eight feet tall and would be extremely vulnerable to any ranged attacks. A well-placed arrow could down one dragon easily.

"That number should suffice," Elkyss said slowly. "Though we still need to be careful about our approach, our strategy. I think the enemy intends to fight to the last man standing."

"They will not budge even when faced with death," said Nin. She readjusted on her crutches. "These fighters are not sound of mind. Our plan must be brutal, because I guarantee you they can think of worse things to do."

"I will send my fastest flyer for a hundred of our strongest fighters," said Grythumak. "These mindless beasts will quake with fear yet."

Despite the sureness in the dragon's voice, Nin looked unconvinced. A shadow hung over her gaunt face. Still, Alina attempted to keep a calm, stern tone when discussing the plan of attack. If Nin could still bear herself after suffering whatever horrors at the hands of the enemy, Alina could keep her composure. Her stomach still twisted into knots.

***

They mobilized the entire army in four days, and by then had managed to pick up an extra hundred soldiers escaping the heartland. Senri tried not to listen to the horror stories of what they faced, like hordes of soldiers that pushed themselves onto swords to kill an Osotan troop, but it proved difficult when the talk ran through the ranks. She marched with the rest of the Warriors, many of them more experienced than her in combat. It felt strange to stand next to others who had completed years of service. They talked about past skirmishes, about how none had been in a fight this large. How anyone could coordinate a hundred warriors in battle baffled her.

She thanked Yahn again in silence, grateful he ordered her to a smaller task force. Still, she had wanted to spend part of the march with the others. Even Senri, savior of the queen, would not be safe from the criticism of her fellows if Alina played favorites for the duration of the journey. The cold, dried out landscape of the heartlands looked so alien from between the eye slits of her borrowed helm. The nose guard did not fit right, either. It pressed slightly into her face, causing her to breath in the chilled early winter air through her mouth. The snow had not yet completed its crawl down the mountain.

"Are you managing all right?"

Senri glanced over her shoulder. Lanan approached. How she had recognized Senri even with the helm on showed just how much time they had spent in one another's company. "I might throw up," she replied. She had never been more scared in her life. This was her first real battle, and failure meant death...for everyone.

Lanan grimaced. "Better not. It would make a poor addition to the song."

"Hush." Senri slowed to let Lanan fall into place next to her. "These people all think I'm normal."

"Oh, take that thing off. People could use a hero to rally behind right now." Lanan moved to grab the helm, but Senri ducked away and clamped both hands down on it.

"Later. Later, I promise. Just let me enjoy a few hours of peace." Lanan shot her a look of mock defeat, so Senri decided to redirect. "What about you? How are you managing?"

Lanan frowned. "And what do you mean by that?"

Senri shrugged and looked around. "You have to fight these people after…you know. Getting captured." Lanan looked at her feet. "We never really talked about it."

"I talked about it," said Lanan, her voice soft.

"Not with any of us you didn't. Just with Nin."

"Senri." Lanan gave her a hard look. "Just leave it, all right? Worry yourself about whether or not it will rain, instead." Lanan pointed up at the cloudy sky and allowed herself to get lost in the marching soldiers. Senri looked around and saw no one but strangers, not even familiar young recruits stood out of the crowd. With a groan, Senri picked up her pace to move closer to the front of the line. She could not tolerate the self-imposed isolation any longer.

"Your Highness," she called out when Alina came in sight. She walked next to Nin, who rode horseback due to her sustained injuries. Alina turned and smiled at her.

"Hail, savior," she said.

Senri shook her head, cheeks burning. Other troops turned to look at her. She hurried to Alina's side and removed her helmet. "Must you call me that?"

"If you insist on calling me 'your Highness'."

"I do," said Senri. She wanted to say more to Alina, but she could not find the words.

Things felt odd now that society surrounded them again. At nights, when they were alone in their tent, their relationship seemed to be better, but Senri found it difficult to adjust her behavior to what would be appropriate in front of the other soldiers. Alina became furious when she pretended they did not know one another, but Senri felt uncomfortable being overly affectionate. They had called a truce on all petty arguments.

"Then I shall gladly continue to call you savior." Alina slung an arm around her. "Besides, the soldiers really like that song. They like the promise of forbidden romance, of the lowly soldier stealing the heart of some noblewoman."

"I did no stealing of any sort," Senri protested. Alina laughed and removed her arm. They glanced at one another and looked away.

"We will be a day's journey from the palace by nightfall." Nin smiled. "Though we will need another day to organize the troops and issue orders."

Senri nodded and looked ahead on the golden fields. Many things would be determined when they finally stopped for camp that night. The dragons would finally rejoin them along with Yahn, who had taken his horse and rode along the river in search of Warriors and soldiers hiding with the farmers. They would have the final tally of forces. No more preparations afterward. Just battle. The warmth of Alina's fingers threading through her own pulled Senri from her sullen thoughts. She shook her head and sighed. No use dwelling on the approaching fight. Or on the sudden twist of her gut at the thought of battle.

Michelle Magly

Chapter Twenty-Five

ALINA SAT ATOP A horse, barely able to see the orderly ranks in the pre-dawn light. The sun would make it over the eastern ranges in another hour or so. They would have the city surrounded by then and hopefully take the enemy forces by surprise. The dragons had already left with the Vanguard. They would have to wait for the rest of the army before descending into the city, but if all went anywhere close to how they planned, the capital would be theirs by the end of the day. Alina had never been more terrified.

"Soldiers!" Alina said. Her speech was the last thing standing between them and battle. "Warriors and heroes of Osota." Some of the ranks shouted in approval. She smiled. "A snake has managed to slither into our kingdom. Under the guise of friendship and alliance, these honorless creatures turned you out of your homes! But will we abide this?"

"No!" The air rang with the force of the reply, every soldier yelling.

"We will hunt them down," said Alina. "We will march into our homes and turn them out. We will march on the city, on our streets. We will show them the true might of Osota!" Another yell of approval rang from the troops. They raised their swords, their bows, their shields. Alina's chest swelled. Was this what it meant to lead? To stand in front of her people and unite them in a cause?

While the armies still roared, she turned and pointed toward the capital. They marched onward, and for a moment, Alina forgot the fact she led many to their deaths, that they sacrificed all to stand at her side. In that moment, they were one cause, one purpose. She never felt so empowered.

She eventually fell into ranks with the front line, right in between Nin and Yahn. Senri lingered close behind her along with Nat and Lanan. They had decided to keep their original group together, considering all they had gone through already. Besides, they had possibly the most dangerous task to accomplish, retaking the palace.

As they marched, the approaching sun lightened the skyline, turning it pink and revealing the distant outline of the capital. From so far away, Alina could not tell the difference between it and the city they had left behind. The wear and tear of battle slowly revealed itself as they drew closer. Buildings had been half-burned. The walls had crumbled in places only to be hastily rebuilt.

The army stopped just outside of the range of arrow fire. They waited several minutes at the city's edge. Slowly, Alina and her comrades backed out of the normal ranks and moved along to the edge of the formation. Grythumak would give the signal to charge the main walls with the other dragons. Hopefully, the shock of a hundred dragons flying in with the Vanguard charging in would be enough to throw the enemy off balance.

A roar rang out from behind her followed by the deafening beat of a hundred pairs of wings. The dragons took off. The army picked up the pace of their march. Alina and her five companions would have to skirt the breadth of the city and make it into the bordering tree line. From there, they would travel to the wall bordering the Warrior's training field, the weaker point of observation for the enemy, according to Nin. The soldiers had been targeted first, so no one remained to be wary of in the barracks. She glanced behind as they ran to make sure the others kept up. Nin remained at her heel with Nat and Lanan close behind. Senri and Yahn brought up the rear.

They reached the forest. The entry point would be near the large tree that grew on the training field. Already, Alina could see leaves peeking over the wall.

Nin stopped them a safe distance away. "Once we are over the wall, there will be enemy troops to fight through. I doubt we would be lucky enough to find the area completely unguarded, even with most of the enemy dealing with the army."

Yahn nodded. "Just tell us when and we can lift you over the wall."

They all exchanged quick glances. Alina held Senri's gaze first, then looked to Nin. When no one showed signs of hesitation, Nin nodded. "Let's move out, then." They ran for the wall, hoping to avoid catching the eye of a patrolling archer. It only took one soldier to ruin everything. The wall itself looked more massive and impenetrable with every step Alina took, but as soon as they reached the base, Yahn and Nat dug deep into the earth and lifted them high upon a column of stone. The earth cracked beneath them as it bent to the Warrior's will. They reached the top of the wall and tumbled over. They landed hard on another column of rock, but Alina recovered and brushed herself off. The field seemed deserted for the moment.

"Which way do we enter, then?" Yahn asked. "It appears the soldiers will be at the city gates."

"Let's try getting in through my rooms," said Alina. "It's the fastest."

Alina surged forward, leading her friends off the field. As they neared the palace walls, Alina spotted a sentry walking toward them. She pulled an arrow back, releasing the shot and embedding it within the soldier's neck.

Nat muttered, "Better stay in her favor, Senri."

Alina rolled her eyes. "Come on, we have to move the body." They ran up, but Alina hesitated when she saw the face under the helm. The man's features seemed somewhat deformed. Veins stood out clearly under the papery skin.

"There's evil magic at work with these soldiers," Lanan muttered. "Healthy people don't look half-starved and plague-ridden."

"We'll worry about it later," said Yahn. He shouldered the corpse with some difficulty and they made it to the sewer entrance. Alina had them inside the dark tunnel in a moment and Yahn dumped the body into the sludge. They entered the dark pathway.

"Where to from your room?" Yahn asked.

Alina blinked against the darkness, feeling her way along the passage. "Wherever Demek may be hiding."

They reached the entrance and Alina held her breath as she pried the door open and pushed out the false wall panel. The room beyond was dark, almost as dark as the tunnels. The curtains had been drawn. Someone touched her on the shoulder.

"I don't like this," whispered Senri.

Alina hesitated. Everything about the room suggested a trap lay in wait. Alina glanced back at the others. "Draw your weapons." They emerged into the room, but when enemies didn't attack, they gathered in the center and huddled together. "We need to decide where to go."

"Demek could be anywhere," said Nin. "We need to find him and any other leaders of the Shedol armies. As soon as the enemy leadership is crippled, the lower ranking soldiers will have no more organization. They're...not the brightest."

Alina shuddered. Of all the horror stories that other soldiers had returned with from the heartland, the hive-mind behavior of the enemy fighters had been one of the most chilling. Alina shook her head. "Let's start with the innermost chambers and spread out from there." If anyone hid in the palace, it would make sense to be located as far within as possible.

Yahn slowly opened the door leading out to the hallway. The interior lacked any of the usual lighting, so Alina turned to Senri. "Do you sense anything?"

"It's...hard to say," Senri said, wiping her brow. "The dragons make it difficult. There's so much heat everywhere, including here. I'm sure there are people down the hall, but I have no idea if they are waiting to attack us or are just within the palace for their own reasons."

"Ready your weapons anyway," said Yahn. Alina felt particularly vulnerable without the range necessary to be effective with her bow. She drew a dagger and stuck to the center of the group as they walked out into the hall.

"I don't feel anything approaching," said Senri. They walked down the corridor. Alina's heart hammered. Never before had she been so aware of her own mortality. The palace shook from an impact and they froze.

"Probably a dragon," said Lanan.

They continued down the hall, but another impact reverberated through the stone walls. "Wait!" said Senri, drawing her sword up.

Alina heard doors bang open farther down the hall and light flooded the hall as enemy soldiers came charging at them. Senri positioned herself in front of Alina and the rest readied their weapons. When the two groups clashed, Alina hardly could track what happened. She only heard the clash of metal and the grunts of soldiers fighting. She watched for any stray assailant that might slip past. One did, but before Alina could attack, Nin had slit his throat.

"Sorry," Nin said, pulling the blade away.

A loud bang from the other end of the hall drew Alina's attention. She turned. Several more soldiers rushed at them. "More coming from this end!"

Alina raised her dagger and lashed out at the first soldier to approach. She sliced through his neck. Blood pooled and the man died with a scream. She wanted to feel horror for what she had just done, but another soldier took his place and raised a fist. The fist connected with her face and stars flashed before her eyes. Hands grabbed her and tugged her away.

"Alina!" Senri's voice sounded far away, but Alina struggled against her captors. "Let her go!"

Senri came charging at them, hacking and slashing. She cut through the enemy with a fury that Alina had not seen. She would have freed her, too, but a man with a sword and shield blocked her blow with the sword. Senri snarled and tried to strike again. He parried and pushed her weapon toward the wall with his shield, pinning it there. He kicked Senri away. She charged at him with a raised fist and tried to grab hold of him, to destroy him like she had the assassin, but the man carefully moved out of Senri's range before kicking her firmly in the stomach. The fighter had to be Demek, considering he did not wear Shedol armor, but the full helm he wore concealed his face.

"Move!" the man yelled. He pointed at Alina. "I need her alive." They dragged her off. She tried to escape, but her head still pounded. Senri got to her feet with the help of Nin, but the soldiers dragged her around a corner and into a narrow hall. Her head ached with every step.

"Alina!" Senri still gave chase. Alina wanted to tell Senri that these people would kill her. Alina was safe as a political prisoner, but not Senri.

"Turn around," she said. "Forget me." But the words escaped as mumbles. The passage they dragged her through would lead to the palace library. The man stepped aside to let the grunts sweep past him.

"I'll see you soon, your Highness," he said.

Yes, it is Demek. Alina struggled again, writhing against the strength, clawing at their fingers, but they just hit her again, harder. In a burst of pain, she dropped her dagger. If it had been one man, maybe she would have succeeded, but numbers had overwhelmed her. The enemy had overwhelmed all of them. Her friends, her soldiers, and her allies would all die because of her. Senri would die and it would be her fault.

***

Senri ran after Alina and the other guards as fast as she could. The rest of the group held off the soldiers swarming into the hallway, allowing only Senri to give chase. The man in the suit of armor turned around to face her. She raced at him, ready to suck the life out of him. She reached for his neck. He ducked, slamming a fist into her side, where a gap in the plate armor left her vulnerable. Senri wheezed, but raised her fist to slam down over his head. The man caught her by the wrist. She yelled and projected as much heat as she could into her wrist. She would melt him into nothing if she had to.

The man swung her to the side, letting go and kicking her in the chest. She flew backwards, knocking a door open and stumbling into a room. She staggered to her feet. He would come at her again, and she wanted to be ready. *Too late.* The man charged at her again and shoved, head and shoulder first, pushing her farther back so that she slammed against a wall. Pain spiked in her right shoulder. She fell to the floor. The assailant grabbed her by the shoulders and hoisted her up. She heard glass shatter and felt a breeze on her cheek. He had kicked open a window. Before Senri could react, he chucked her over the side and she plummeted, landing hard on her back on the ledge below. She stared up at the broken window. She wanted to get up and save Alina, but couldn't move.

After what felt like several minutes, Senri managed to sit up. She tried to raise her arms, but her right refused to work. It had to be broken even if it did not hurt. She looked up. The palace walls, carved from stone, formed natural hand and foot holds. Breathing caused pain in her chest where her armor had pinched down against her ribs.

Slowly, Senri stood. Her armor pressed even harder into her chest. "Damn it." She undid the laces with one hand, tearing off the plate and letting it clatter to the ground. Once the chest plate was off, she could breathe normally. She gritted her teeth and looked up again. She couldn't see her comrades. If Senri did not get up there soon, Alina could be lost.

Taking a deep breath, Senri tried lifting her arms. Her left hand reached for a higher grip, and she forced her right to hold on clumsily to a lower hold. As she climbed, the wind pushed at her even harder and smoke lingered on the breeze. The fight drew close. After what felt like hours, she hauled herself over the edge of the window and collapsed on the cool floor, panting for breath.

Senri rested for a few seconds, gathering her strength. But every second counted if she wanted to find Alina. She got to her feet and staggered out of the room, turning down the hall and following the direction she had seen them take Alina. She kicked something on the floor. It went clattering down the hallway. Senri bent over and grabbed the handle of Alina's dagger.

Senri held onto it, determined to find Alina before the soldiers could get her any farther away. With the palace under siege, their enemy had to stay put until the battle ended. Senri hoped it would grant her enough time to find Alina. As she wandered down passages, her fear climbed, tightening her chest. Clutching the dagger, she jumped at every noise. The palace shook with explosions. Senri sensed fire approaching. Her legs trembled as adrenaline coursed through her veins. *Will it be dragons? Or the enemy?* She stumbled down a new hallway littered with corpses and had to swallow a scream when one of them reached out for her.

"Wait!" It was a man, severely wounded with a gash stretching from his shoulder to across his chest. His legs stuck out at odd angles, but he definitely moved, pushing himself up to rest against a wall. He coughed and beckoned Senri over. "You, wait." She ran over to him and crouched down, searching for anything that could help stop his bleeding. At the same time, she fought rising panic over Alina's absence.

"I...I know you." He looked familiar. His skin, now a pale, waxy color, had once been healthy and full. The remnants of a neatly trimmed beard sunk into scraggly facial hair. His other hand clutched at his side, thin with malnourishment. Blood poured over his fingers from the chest wound.

He coughed again. "I am Councilor Ve...Velora. You are the Warrior who saved..." He broke off to cough again.

"Yes, that's me," she said. Senri looked for something to help him, picking up a tattered scrap of a tapestry. "Move your arm. I'll help bind your wound."

"Won't do. No time." He pushed away Senri's hands and slouched farther onto the wall. "Don't waste it on me. You need to…need to save her again."

Senri dropped the tapestry. "You've seen where they took Alina?"

The Councilor nodded.

"You have to tell me."

***

They took Alina into the library, one of the inner-most chambers in the palace. By that time, Alina could smell smoke and the air had grown hot and stale, just like her vision. *Please don't let my kingdom become a ruin.* She wanted her people to have something to return to after the fighting.

After depositing her in a chair, the grunts lingered. Alina tried to get up, but the room spun when she stood, so she sat down again. Lord Demek strolled toward her. He looked gaunt, as if he had stopped eating. His hair, usually carefully swept back, was disheveled. He had a wild look in his eyes.

"You are bold, your Highness, and courageous." He stopped in front of the armchair and looked down at her. "I am afraid it must end here."

One of the guards laughed. "Want me to do it?" he asked.

Demek turned on him in a flash. Alina barely saw him draw the dagger before it sunk into the soldier's gut. Before the other one could react, Demek had slit his throat. Alina stared, wide-eyed and was too light-headed to scream. She had just been kidnapped by a madman. Any hope of political bargaining vanished with Demek's sanity. She watched him wipe the blade on a soldier's tunic before sheathing it. He grimaced. "Sorry about that."

"What are you waiting for? Kill me." She tried to stand once more, but her stomach knotted and she felt like she might throw up. *People are dying because of me and I could not even finish the fight.*

"I can't kill you." Demek walked over to a bookcase and leaned against it. "That's not how this ends. Besides, you're a smart woman.

Tell me what killing you would accomplish?"

"Nothing, but you're insane anyways." As if to prove the statement, she watched Demek glance down at the bodies of his soldiers and smirk. "What it would accomplish does not matter."

"Are you so sure about that?" Demek pushed off the bookcase. "What you think of me does not matter." He walked toward a window. It looked out to a courtyard within the palace. Alina could see flames eating away the trees.

"If you had this kingdom's best interests at heart, you would help me drive out the armies of Shedol," Alina said. She contemplated telling Demek the whole truth. It would not hurt her anymore. He had her trapped, alone, and had successfully taken care of those meant to guard her. "I…I've seen what destruction they will bring if we allow this to happen."

"And you think I haven't?" Demek asked in a soft voice. He drummed his fingers on the windowsill and glanced back at her for a moment. "We aren't so different, Alina."

Alina wanted to ask what he meant, but the door to the library creaked open and he left his spot by the window. Senri staggered forward with Alina's dagger clutched in her grasp. She ran toward Demek, but he sidestepped her and pushed her over. She fell forward, dagger falling out of her hand.

"You don't give up, do you?" he asked. Once again, Alina tried to get to her feet. This time, she remained standing. Her head pounded just from getting herself into an upright position. Demek sneered down at Senri. "I would let you live, fool, if you weren't so busy trying to stab me." Senri reached out a hand for the dagger, but Demek stepped on her fingers. She cried out. "Don't try that again."

"Stop." Alina took a step forward. "Stop hurting her."

He looked up and the grin on his face faltered. He looked down at Senri and the grin faded completely. He removed his foot and stepped away, meeting Alina's gaze. "You care for her, Alina?"

She nodded. "And everyone else in this kingdom."

Senri got to her knees, but Demek grabbed her by the shoulder and she winced. "I know you do."

"I refuse to watch while you make them suffer any longer." Another step. She felt something touch her shoe and looked down. It was the dagger. She stopped moving.

Demek nodded and breathed deep. He closed his eyes for a

moment. Alina took the chance. She kicked at the blade, sending it clattering across the floor. Senri snatched it up and rammed it into Demek's leg. His eyes flew open, the irises the color of milky crystal. He screamed and stumbled back. Dark lines etched into his neck, faint vein-like patterns Alina recognized all too well.

"By the Almighty!" she cried out.

Senri pulled the dagger from his leg and stood, her grip shaking. She approached him with the point hovering inches from his stomach. Demek backed into a wall, still clutching his leg.

"Wait. Wait, Senri," Alina said, taking a few shaky steps forward. "Don't do it, yet."

"Why not?" she asked. The dagger trembled in her grasp.

Demek looked up at her, he gasped in pain. "You should do it. You have a chance, now. Just end it."

Senri looked at her, brow furrowed in confusion. Alina shook her head, but saw Demek's hand go for the dagger.

"Senri," she yelled.

Demek grabbed Senri's hand and tugged forward, sinking the dagger into his stomach. "I told you."

Senri let go of the dagger and took a step back. "Alina I didn't mean…"

"I know," she said.

Demek fell to his knees, clutching the handle with both hands. He drew in a rattling breath of air and met Alina's gaze. The seer's marks spread over his face like a spider web. Alina expected him to yell, or curse, but he just smiled.

"I've been…been trying to do that for years." He coughed and looked over at Alina, his eyes still crystalline. "Alina, you are so headstrong, just like your mother." Blood pooled out from the wound and over his fingertips. "Perhaps if I had been more like her, things would have been different." Alina wanted to speak, to question him, but Demek shook his head. "Don't. Let me die, please." Demek pushed the dagger deeper inside, dragging upward until his grip slackened and his head fell forward. His lifeless body slumped to the floor.

Alina reached out for Senri and took her hand. "He killed himself." Alina felt numb. Even as she ran a thumb over Senri's palm, she did not register the touch. Time felt as if it had frozen. A war could not possibly be raging on beyond the library. They had just watch a man stab himself.

Senri nodded. "But the battle isn't over."

They both glanced around the library. Everything sounded so quiet. The courtyard had been enveloped with flames. Alina breathed in and tasted ash. The palace had caught fire as well. "I don't know if there's a battle for us to return to." With some effort, Alina walked over to the window. Flames climbed higher. They would die if they stayed put. "Can you stand?" she asked, turning to Senri.

Senri managed to hoist herself up, but only hobbled over to a couch before collapsing on it. "I don't know how far I can make it. Do you think we won, or do we have to fight our way out?"

Alina glanced over at Demek's slumped form and watched the blood run down, soaking his uniform. "I don't know." She walked over to Senri and gently took a hand. Her lover let out a small hiss of pain, but welcomed the contact. Alina kissed the palm of her lover's hand. "If this counts as a victory, I suppose we did."

Senri smiled and squeezed her hand. "We should probably leave, though. We might burn to death otherwise."

"We might burn to death trying to escape, too."

"True." Senri nodded. With Alina's help, Senri made it to her feet. They began walking toward the nearest exit when something shook the palace. They stood still, waiting to see if the palace would hold. A dragon roared in the distance and Senri glanced at the roof of the library. "Alina, I love you."

Alina pulled Senri closer and helped her take another step toward the door. They needed to move. "And I love you, Senri."

The room filled with smoke and the heat climbed ever higher. Convinced they would cook before escaping, Alina finally heard the pounding footsteps of someone running down the hall. Senri held onto Alina tightly. She closed her eyes, but Alina kept her gaze fixed on the entryway. She refused to meet her fate blindly.

Nin came running into the library entrance, two bloody daggers gripped in her hand. Her eyes widened when she saw Senri and Alina standing there, trembling. Alina nodded at her, but made no attempt to move forward.

"By the Almighty, you're alive!" She grinned and wiped the soot out of her eyes. Nin turned back to the corridor and shouted, "They're here!" More footsteps.

Nat, Lanan, and Yahn came running into the room. Senri

opened her eyes and a smile spread across her face. Everyone ran forward and helped them out of the room. They shouted over one another, asking questions. Nin approached more slowly, pausing by Demek's corpse and glancing over at Alina. "So, we are victorious on all fronts, then," she said.

Alina nodded. The battle had ended. Still, she could not smile like her friends. "We are."

Chapter Twenty-Six

IN THE AFTERMATH OF the battle, Alina had many things to tend to. This room had been last on her list for a reason. Even while she stood outside, hand resting on the doorknob, she wanted to walk away. Demek was dead, buried in a mass grave with all the other invaders. She did not need another excuse to be haunted with his memory. She closed her eyes and saw him, hand gripping the knife, point pressing into his own stomach, the seer lines crawling up his face. *"So headstrong, just like your mother. Perhaps if I had been more like her..."* She hated that the man offered her no peace, even in death. But she hated how conflicted she felt over his last actions more. Even after weeks of discussing it with Senri and the others, she had still found no way to explain away his behavior.

But really, what did she expect to find? Cobwebs and piles of books referencing dark magic, blood and bottles of poison like Senri had teased, or rusted weapons. She turned the knob and pushed the door open. She had not expected this. Identical to all the other bedrooms, the large four-poster bed had been neatly made, the furniture dusted. The plain room seemed mostly untouched from the fires, though char marks still climbed up the wall on the far corner. It smelled musty, dust-ridden.

Demek's jacket lay out on a nearby chair, the medals still pinned to it. She walked over and touched one of the gold medallions. It glinted. Most of the decorations related to negotiation. Her father wore similar ones. The newest related to his rank as a lord and then as Regent. Alina dropped the medals and continued to wander the room.

His dresser held clothes. His nightstand drawer had candles. The washroom kept the standard collection of perfumes. It seemed that nothing out of the ordinary remained in Demek's private bedchambers. Alina left the washroom and sat down at the vanity. She caught her reflection in the bronze mirror. It looked off, however, warped. She reached out and touched the metal. Her fingers glided over the fist-sized dents spanning the mirror.

A wooden letter box lay on the vanity. Alina tried to open it, but couldn't. Wrapping her fingers around the rough edges, she tried to force it. The mechanism did not even rattle. She examined the small, square depression on the side. It looked like he had designed something specific to open it.

She opened a vanity drawer. Various rings and necklaces lay inside. She picked through them, tossing the gold adornments back in as each one proved to be a plain trinket. As she plunked another ring back in, the contents of the drawer shifted. A silver glint caught her eye. Alina reached in and grabbed the thin strand, then pulled it free of the others, holding it up to the light. She almost dropped the necklace. *Demek should not have owned anything like this.*

The chain, extremely delicate, was expertly forged to have so many thin, silver threads interwoven, representing different strands of the future. Alina trapped the strands in between her fingers and rubbed them together. The texture reminded her of something; the silver bracelet her mother had given her.

A stab of remorse pierced her gut. She had ruined her bracelet, tossing it into the fire back at Eastwatch Keep. All for nothing, too. No one would question her right as ruler now. She had done the impossible by allying with the dragons, and then did it again when she drove out the invaders. In a matter of days, they had recaptured all of the heartland and driven the Shedol armies off to sea. She was Alina, Queen of Fire, as Senri often reminded her. Even the soldiers whispered the name.

But this necklace, a necklace the same make of her mother's seer bracelet with the interwoven strands of silver, should not have been in Demek's possession. It had belonged to her mother. She examined it, noting the small, darkened spot along the chain where Alina had stained it with ink as a child. She pulled the two metal clasps closer for a better look. Etched into the silver were two letters, one on each clasp: SD. The clasps formed a perfect square, just like the one cut into the box. Fumbling in her haste, Alina pressed the two clasps into the keyhole. The lock clicked.

Alina dropped the necklace and exhaled. She pulled the lid back, listening to it creak as she did so. The box had not been opened in a very, very long time. Inside the box lay parchment, folded letters stacked tightly against one another. Alina took the one on the top and unfolded it. She read:

My dearest brother,

I hope this letter finds you in good company. You will be pleased to know things are, as ever, safely dull back home. Your niece has reached her third turn this week. Her father is ever-doting upon her, as well as me. He speaks of perhaps taking us along on his next outing. I think the fresh air will do us both good. The city is rather confining, as you are fond of declaring. And though I am trying to honor his Majesty's wishes, I think it might do her some good to spend time with you upon your return.

There is not much to tell. I hope you find time to write back. You can tell me about the sea. I have not seen it since we were both children. Do you remember mother's house on the shore? You will also have to tell about your adventures beyond the shoreline. I know you cannot discuss most of it, but try to find an interesting story to bring back, or at least make up one.
Ever yours,
Mura

By the time Alina finished reading the letter, her hands trembled. She felt weak. Perhaps she would faint. She dropped the paper and tried to avoid looking at the letter so neatly scrawled in her mother's handwriting. Any doubts she had while reading it had been erased by the bottom line, where her mother's name written in its loopy signature stood out as a glaring marker of ownership. Sorez Demek, the man she had watched die, possibly as a direct result of her own actions, could not possibly be her uncle.

She picked up another letter, this one addressed to her mother. It used the same vague language, talking of being abroad and lamenting how they could not spend time together. She read more, but the letters were empty of anything useful, nothing but sentimental fluff. In a way, it made things worse for Alina. She threw the letters back in the box and swallowed a sob. Tears pricked the corner of her eyes. Damn him. She bowed her head and cried into her arms, stifling the sobs with a dress sleeve. A noise startled her from her tears. She turned. Nin stood in the doorway.

"You," Alina hissed, wiping her tears quickly. "Did you know about this?"

Her maid shut the door and walked in. "If it helps at all, he was very proud of you."

"It doesn't!" She slammed the lid on the box closed. "None of it helps. It just means my own kin betrayed me, not just a fellow countryman." Alina shook her head and wiped at her tears again. "He was dirt, Nin. I spent my whole life unaware of his existence, and when he did reveal himself, he tried to turn our kingdom over to a race of maniacal cannibals."

"No." Nin sat down on the bed. "He didn't."

Alina stood. "Well then why?" she yelled. "Why did he sell our people off into slavery and nearly kill Senri? Why did he kill Velora and the other Councilors?" Tears welled up in her eyes. They had found Velora in a hall. Senri led her to him after the others found them in the library. He had passed already. Many of the other Councilors had been executed days before their army arrived. Damn the Almighty, the tears would not stop.

Nin frowned. "He was not in control of his actions."

"That doesn't tell me why. I am Queen, Nin. I deserve to know!"

The maid nodded. "You do deserve to." She waited while Alina glared at her, then gestured to the chair. "Have a seat."

Never before had Alina felt so utterly powerless. She had thought she controlled the game board for the duration of their struggle. It seemed Nin aimed to prove otherwise. Reluctantly, Alina sat down.

"I only know what my predecessor has told me, for the most of it. Your uncle, like your father, was a travelling diplomat. He actually introduced your parents." Nin paused. When Alina did not interrupt, she continued, "When your mother became with child, he took on your father's assignments for leaving the country. The child of the brother to the queen made a much more alluring target for anyone wishing to harm foreign ambassadors, and Demek had no family, save your mother. A couple years after you were born, the rulers sent him west to investigate a disturbance between bordering nations. It was a troubling assignment, and your family was ordered not to discuss it or your uncle's very existence with anyone, including you.

He was away for several years, and when he returned, he had changed."

"Like the soldiers?" Alina asked, remembering the mindless creatures.

Nin shook her head. "His mental faculties remained intact, but something had unbalanced him. No one realized until very recently that he struggled against an external force. After you escaped with the Warriors, he told me about it, that he even tried to break free once."

She thought back to his final words. *I've been trying to do that for years.* He had said when he stabbed himself. She had previously dismissed the words as rambling. "What happened when he tried to break free?"

"Your parents died." Alina's throat constricted, but Nin pushed on, "He discussed it with the King and Queen and had you sent away, the location unknown to him so that he could not be any harm to you at all."

"He… he was the one responsible for sending me to that Keep?" Alina blinked back more tears.

Nin nodded. "He worked tirelessly in your absence to root out any remaining influences the Shedol kingdom had in place. He was like a manic, swinging from mindlessly assisting the Shedol armies to undermining them at every turn. I saw a glimpse of it myself after you escaped. It was more than someone exercising leverage over him, they were in his head somehow."

"That doesn't seem possible," said Alina.

"You've seen it for yourself. I suspect that the dragons who attacked you in their own kingdom were under the same influence. And the Shedol armies, they were corrupted beyond recognition, their free will so gone they could only bleat uselessly, not even speak."

Alina took a deep breath. She had come to terms with the fact she led her nation to war, but this seemed out of the realm of her control. "So, there's a reader who manipulates people," she said. Nin nodded. "An extremely powerful one, one who robbed an entire kingdom of its free will." Another nod. "Nin, I don't see how we can win this."

The maid smiled and stood from the bed. She smoothed out her skirts. "Do what you do best, your Majesty," she said. "Lead us to the ideal world. I'll make sure the appropriate destinies intertwine." She walked toward the door and opened it.

Before she stepped out, Alina said, "You never told me what it is you actually do around the palace."

Nin smiled at her. "I am your humble maid, Alina." She curtseyed. "And that is all you need to know." She pulled the door to, leaving Alina alone in her uncle's chambers once more. She drummed her fingers on the desk then reached for the box. Unlocking it once more, she grabbed a new letter.

Taking a deep breath, Alina unfolded it and read.

Chapter Twenty-Seven

SENRI FOUND IT DIFFICULT to sit in a Council meeting all day after driving the armies of Shedol from the city and chasing them to the western shores,. She flexed the stiffness from her hands for the eighth time that afternoon. Her fingers wanted to do something. Her whole body did. Working the forge had been more entertaining that politics.

She closed her eyes and could still see the Shedol ships leaving their shores. She had raised her sword in the air and cried out enthusiastically with the rest of the soldiers. They had won. They had successfully driven off an invasion. She could still hear the roar of the soldiers around her when they had achieved true victory.

But when she opened her eyes again, it was weeks later, and she was still trapped in a council meeting. She had been asked by Alina to attend. Earlier in the morning, they had conducted an award ceremony for the Warriors and soldiers who had fought bravely. Senri raised a hand to her own medal and absently traced the intricate wreath of flames carved into it. From there, Alina opened the palace for negotiations with the dragon folk. They talked mostly about trade and a mission to hunt down the Shedol ships carrying Osota prisoners. The amount of missing civilians unsettled her. What unsettled her even more though, was that somehow the Councilors had allowed this to happen, which Alina currently interrogated the remaining Council members about. She tossed a letter down on the table. "Someone explain to me how my uncle was allowed to plunge this country into ruin."

At first, no one spoke. Few of the Council members remained to speak. Out of the eleven representatives, only four sat in front of them.

"We were coerced," said Gosman. "They threatened to burn our lands to ash, and we didn't have the forces to stop them. Lord Demek told us to stall them with negotiations." He cleared his throat and when Alina nodded, he continued. "We still do not know what we stalled for."

Senri grimaced and glanced over at Alina. Her brown had furrowed in the same, troubled way it did whenever someone mentioned Demek. Alina had been reluctant to talk about him even with Senri. "We are working on some theories as to what that might be," said Alina.

The more people they talked to, the more they saw how truly erratic Lord Demek's behavior had been. Senri still had a hard time thinking of what his end goal could have been. It could have been anything. He could have been insane, as far as she was concerned. Alina was not quite as convinced.

Gosman continued, "Your Majesty, I assure you we merely followed orders. Regent Velora backed all of his decisions."

"We are not discussing this so I can accuse you of treason," Alina snapped. That was something else that had changed. Alina had little patience for Osota's politicians in the past weeks. It made Senri worry that the stress would be too much one day. "I apologize, Councilor, but I'm trying to understand exactly what happened, nothing else."

Gosman nodded. "That task might prove impossible, your Majesty."

Alina nodded and pressed a hand to her forehead. She took a deep breath. Senri wished she could help Alina more than just sit in on her meetings "As you all are aware, we have suffered casualties as a result of the conflict." She must be ready to end the discussion if she was bringing up casualties. "I will need a list of potential candidates to fill the necessary Councilor positions. I request that you all compose this in cooperation this afternoon. I will send someone to collect it later."

Without giving them a chance to protest or interject, Alina stood and Senri followed. They left the Council chamber and Alina's shoulders sagged. Senri took her arm.

"You all right?" she asked.

Alina nodded. "I don't know how much longer I can go on like this." They strolled the halls. With the help of the Warriors and local craftsmen, the palace looked almost better than before the attack. "I never realized how much work Regent Velora did."

Senri nodded and lowered her hand to Alina's, threading their fingers together. In the wake of the kingdom's recovery, very few people passed them a second glance. Senri suspected most people were just afraid of Alina, Queen of Fire. "He did it so you could save Osota."

"He did."

They left the palace and walked around the grounds outside. Senri squinted, sunlight streaming down from a cloudless sky. "Do you think everyone else knew more of what was going on? More than us, I mean."

Slowly, Alina nodded. "Possibly since I was a child. My mother was a seer." Alina looked up at her as she said this, and Senri nodded. It came as no surprise that one of Alina's parents had possessed the sight. Alina sighed and squeezed Senri's hand. They stopped at a stone bench and sat down. The rock felt hot from the sun's rays. "It was a little too easy to leave the palace, you know? That first night we rode out to find the dragons, and all the other nights, no one came after us." Alina leaned against Senri. "I think Velora wanted us to find the dragons."

"Then he was a brave man to stay behind," Senri said. He had been buried in the royal cemetery, a place of honor.

Alina tightened her hold. The worry lines stood out in her forehead. "I think Demek wanted us to find them, too."

"Why?" Senri asked. "Do you think allying with the dragons was a mistake?"

Alina shook her head. "No, but it makes everything we do from this point on much more complicated. Demek had a goal in mind. He was working with the armies of Shedol. I saw it. But he..." Her eyes shimmered with tears. "Senri, I think I was wrong."

"You can't think like that."

Alina shook her head. "Someone has to. I'm the only one left to make up for all the mistakes. There has been so much death, and the war has barely started." She stood up and pulled Senri with her. "I know we have to fight, and I know we don't have the luxury of second-guesses. But right now I just want to have this." She held their intertwined hands up for a moment, then tugged Senri forward.

"I want to have you."

Senri smiled and pulled Alina into a loose embrace. "You have me, my Queen, whatever the next day brings." She kissed Alina lightly on the lips. "I want to be by your side."

Alina smiled back at her. "Savior of the Queen, imagine what verses Nat will compose for us now."

Senri rolled her eyes and groaned. "Please don't remind him. I'd like it if the song just went away."

Alina shook her head. "Don't say that. The song is part of us. It's part of this kingdom. It gives people something to laugh about and gives them hope. It gives them something to love." The sadness disappeared from her eyes. "I'd like for it to continue. People need songs like that."

Senri gave in and leaned down for one last kiss before they went inside. "I suppose they do."

The End

About Michelle Magly

Michelle Magly is a lesbian writer living in Alaska with her loving partner. She has discovered that the frozen tundra makes excellent inspiration. Michelle currently has one short story, "Heart," featured in the 2012 Understory anthology from the University of Alaska, Anchorage. She also released her first novel, *All the Pretty Things*, in 2013 as a collaborative effort with Rae D Magdon. When not writing, Michelle hikes, snowboards, skis, and plays a lot of video games. Aside from her partner, Michelle shares her life with her loving cat.

Connect with Michelle online

Facebook: https://www.facebook.com/pages/Michelle-Magly/

Twitter: https://twitter.com/MichelleMagly

Email: mmagly@desertpalmpress.com

Goodreads: **https://www.goodreads.com/search?utf8=%E2%9C%93&query=michelle+magly**

Cover Design by Michael King

Michael King is a freelance graphic designer and illustrator based out of Anchorage, Alaska. He is the proud father of a young parakeet named Luka, and he enjoys biking as well as traveling when the time affords for it. He can usually be found either sketching or sleeping at odd hours of the day when not working.

king.mi1707@gmail.com

Other books from Desert Palm Press

The Guardian Series by Stein Willard
A Guardian's Touch – Book 1
A Guardian's Love – Book 2
A Guardian's Passion – Book 3

Scarred for Life by SL Kassidy

Please Baby by SL Kassidy

Friends Series by AJ Adaire
Sunset Island — Book 1
The Interim — a novelette
Awaiting My Assignment — Book 2
Anything Your Heart Desires — Book 3

One Day Longer Than Forever by AJ Adaire

Dark Horizons by Rae D. Magdon & Michelle Magly

Amydyr Series by Rae D. Magdon
The Second Sister — Book 1

Available now from Smashwords, Amazon, and CreateSpace

Coming in 2014

Amydyr Series by Rae D. Magdon
Wolf's Eyes — Book 2
The Witch's Daughter — Book 3

It's Complicated by AJ Adaire

Dark Horizons Series by Rae D. Magdon & Michelle Magly
Starless Night — Book 2

Printed in Great Britain
by Amazon